Girls in Pink

by

Bob Bickford

Girls in Pink by Bob Bickford
Copyright 2016
ISBN 978-1-943789-42-8

Published by Taylor and Seale Publishing, LLC
3408 South Atlantic Avenue
Unit 139
Daytona Beach Shores, FL 32118

Cover layout by WhiteRabbitgraphix.com

Cover photo by: Donnez Cardoza, used with permission.

Eight of hearts,
I want to play.

Girls in Pink

Bob Bickford

Part One

Saxophones, Razzmatazz, and a Birthday Cake

-One-

Friday, June 27, 1947
Santa Teresa, California
11:45 am

The Browning automatic on my desk made me a little bit nervous. Not because it pointed at me—it belonged to me, but because I had forgotten to put it away before my client came in, and now it lay on the blotter between us, looking unfriendly. With no graceful way to get it into the drawer without drawing attention to it, I left it where it lay.

"Are you married, Mister Crowe?"

Her legs were crossed, and the black-piped hem of a pink dress rode up over one knee. She looked delectable, and in no apparent hurry. She had nice enough legs, and I wasn't in a hurry, either. I shook my head, no, and waited for her to finish getting out her checkbook.

"I like your suit," she said. "I like a man that knows how to dress."

She picked up the straw fedora from the corner of my desk and ran her finger along the band.

"Do you ever go dancing?" she asked. "What do you do for fun?"

She had very blonde hair drawn back from her face in what must have been expensive waves, carefully arranged around a jaunty pink hat that matched her dress. Her eyes were wide and blue, and she used them in a way she probably considered disingenuous. I knew she wasn't any such thing. She also had a small gap between her front teeth. It was probably the most honest thing about her, and I liked it, but when she sensed me looking there she closed her rosebud mouth quickly.

"I do this, Mrs. Cleveland," I said. "I don't know much about fun, I guess."

The clock on the far wall said just before noon. It was made to look like Krazy Kat. A client had given me two of them, and while I didn't see the point of it, I needed a clock and it kept time just fine. I had the other one hung in my kitchen at home.

"Charlene," she smiled. "I'm not anyone's missus anymore, thanks to you. We should celebrate."

I leaned forward, and slid a single sheet of paper, my bill, an inch closer to her. She looked at it and didn't pick it up.

"You could at least buy me a drink," she said. "You're getting paid enough money for this. It didn't take you very long."

"It took more out of me than you may realize, Mrs. Cleveland."

A fresh bottle of Four Roses snoozed in the top left drawer of my desk, and I took it out and broke the seal. I got up and blew the dust out of a couple of glasses, and then poured each of us an inch of bourbon. I set hers on the desk in front of her, and tossed mine back before I sat down again. The liquor burned nicely, but I knew right away it had been a mistake. Drinking in the middle of the day made me tired.

"How did you get my husband to agree to a divorce so fast?" she asked. "I still can't believe it's really true."

"People tend to act in their best interests," I said. "Even tough people. I scrounged up some . . . well, you could call it evidence I suppose. It was good enough to make him think letting you go represented a fair deal. We made a simple trade."

"What could possibly be bad enough for that?" she asked. "Can you tell me?"

I shook my head, no.

"I could talk you into it," she smiled. "We both know that I could."

"When you're done with your drink, I'd like to settle your bill," I said. "Not even lunch time, and it's been a hell of a day already."

"No dinner?" she pouted. "No dancing?"

She uncrossed her legs. After a suggestive pause, she crossed them the other way, taking just enough time to let me see that she'd selected her undergarments to match the dress she wore. I was too worn out, and maybe too old, to snap at the bait.

"There's nothing at all I can interest you in?" she persisted.

"We've danced enough, Mrs. Cleveland. What interests me now is getting to the bank with your check before it closes. No offense, but you're leaving town. At least, I hope you are."

She sat up and stared at me. Underneath the seductive makeup, her face changed.

"You son of a bitch," she said.

She picked up her purse and pulled out her checkbook and a fountain pen.

When she had almost finished writing it out, a teardrop splashed onto the check and ruined it. I hadn't realized she was crying. She tore it off the book, crumpled it into her purse, and started on a fresh one. I felt sorry for her, but it was too late for that.

"I hate you," she said, not looking up. "I thought I was in love with you, but you're a bastard like all of them."

After she finished, she shook the check a couple of times to dry the ink and then tossed it onto the desk in front of me.

"Maybe you won't turn down the next poor girl who needs you, who wants to share her life with you," she said. "You don't know the first thing about love."

"I don't know anything about love, Mrs. Cleveland." I felt suddenly even more tired than just the liquor could account for. "You're right about that. From my experience, I'm not sure what anyone sees in it."

She stood up and arranged herself without drying her eyes, and then went out without speaking to me again. The door stayed open behind her.

"What the hell?" I asked of no one in particular, and no one answered.

I looked at her untouched drink and decided it would be a lot of trouble to pour it back into the bottle. I stared out the window and drank it slower than the first one.

4

Looking out my third floor window, I couldn't see the ocean unless I leaned out far enough to risk falling, but it wasn't very far away. Sometimes, late at night, it got quiet enough that I could hear it. The building stood on lower State Street in downtown Santa Teresa. It wasn't much, just a waiting room with a small desk for the secretary I didn't have, and my office behind a frosted glass door. A lot of traffic rolled under my window during the day and a lot of drunks rolled out from the bar downstairs at night. It suited me and made me feel like I was in the middle of things.

When I finished the drink, I went up the hall to rinse the glasses in the men's room. I capped the bourbon and put it away. The folded check went into my breast pocket. I got my hat and locked the office door behind me.

"Share her life with me," I muttered, shaking my head. "The next poor girl who needs me."

At the bank, I asked the young woman in the teller's cage for fifty dollars in cash and to deposit the rest into my account. She threw a sweet smile my way as she counted out the bills. I figured that I'd better leave in a hurry before I made her cry, too. I folded the three tens and four fives into my wallet, and went home to take a nap.

-Two-

Saturday, June 28, 1947
Santa Teresa County, California
3:00 a.m.

Charlene Cleveland felt happy for the first time in a very long time.

Two suitcases lay on the seat behind her, and another in the trunk. They weren't much, but they would do. The eyes that looked back at her from the rear-view mirror were still young enough and pretty enough, and she had the face and legs to match them. She had five hundred dollars in her purse, a friend waiting for her in Vegas, and a belief that things worked out fine if you gave them the chance.

A radio station came into range, and she turned it up just as a saxophone blew and held a long string of notes. They streamed out the window and unfurled in the red slipstream of her taillights. Tattered by the dark wind, they swirled and floated and finally settled onto the road. The music lingered on the faintly warm asphalt long after the car was gone.

The two lanes wound their way through the canyon, up and down a forty-mile stretch of hairpin curves and sheer drops. The macadam twisted and turned and dipped. It didn't lend itself to being driven easily during the day, and it got worse at night. The price for a mistake could be a drop of three hundred feet or more into a brushy gully. Some car wrecks weren't found for months after they happened. Some were never found.

There were easier ways to get from the coastal city of Santa Teresa to the highway that raced across the desert to the state line, but all the easy ways needed a detour south

6

nearly to Los Angeles. This road, straight over the old mountains, saved at least a hundred miles of travel.

The night air smelled of cooling rock and chaparral, and carried occasional perfumes of the almond and orange groves she passed, tucked into the invisible hillsides. Their sweetness exhilarated her, and she drove a little bit faster than she should have, chasing the beams of her lights around the bends, following the white line in the middle of the road.

It all smelled like freedom. Eighteen months of bad marriage now a dream, and she wondered how long it would take her to forget her married name. She would never see the wretched city behind her again. She planned to take the tan Ford convertible she drove to a dealer's lot as soon as she got where she was heading. She loved it, but it had been a wedding present, and she planned to leave behind every single thing that reminded her of the slaps, insults, threats and infidelity.

She was leaving behind the constant sickness of fear, and that was best of all.

Two years ago, she had looked out the window of the office where she worked and saw the people running out of buildings and pouring from doorways to mill around in the street. She stared at the other girls who were typing at desks across from her, and then they all jumped up together and dashed out.

Someone in the crowd shouted "VE day!" when she asked what was going on. She had no idea what that meant but she joined the spontaneous kissing and shouting, anyway. After a little while she heard Adolph Hitler was dead and the war in Europe over. The soldiers would be coming home soon, and things would go back to the way they had always been.

7

She had laughed and danced with the rest of them, but deep inside she didn't know if she wanted things to go back to the way they had been before the war. She had a job, some money, and a lot of freedoms she didn't used to have. That night she got drunk in a series of bars where there were more fistfights, more screams, and a lot more blackness than usual. She wondered if maybe other people felt the way she did about things going back to how they had always been.

A strange man took her to a hotel. In the morning, she looked at his sleeping face and didn't remember him. When he woke up he asked her to marry him. Somehow she wasn't surprised, and she said 'yes' out loud, even though she said 'no' inside. His name was Sal Cleveland. He was older than her, and he had a beautiful face. He dressed wonderfully and knew exactly what to do to her once he'd undressed her.

He was a gangster. She found out later that he was a monster, too, but by then it was too late.

Her wedding had been a white vision, not at all the way she imagined a hoodlum ceremony would be. Blossoms filled the church, and the priest beamed at her. The satin and silk, the candles and the bright solemn words were a world away from anything Charlene had known, far removed from any expectations she'd held for herself. Afterward, the great hall burst into a riot of bubbles and clinking silverware and softly colored lights that matched the floating music. She took a slightly tipsy turn around the floor with her groom, and the guests lined the edges of the dance floor, clapped enthusiastically and nodded their approval.

They watched her dance, and she forgot all about the gap between her front teeth and didn't so much mind her fanny, which spread just a little wider than those that trailed the women in elegant fashion magazines. She had a pallid, pretty face, good legs, and fine blonde hair as yet untouched

8

by chemicals. They all watched her and she felt every bit of the power of her youth and beauty. She drank wine and laughed and enjoyed the eyes as they followed her.

Fear intermingled with the admiration she felt from the crowd, and some of that was fear of her. She was now and forever tied in matrimony to the man who had walked the city of Santa Teresa on a leash for the last decade. She sensed that behind the respectful deference lay the urgent need to please, to curry favor, or to escape attention. She was settled in now, under the leathery wing of the most feared gangster between Los Angeles and San Francisco.

She wasn't Charlene Arnott anymore. She was Mrs. Sal Cleveland, and her bridegroom was splendid. Afterward, she always remembered the lily he had worn in his lapel, and how it had smelled like a funeral. She danced and danced, and as she went around and around she tried not to look too deeply into his lovely eyes. Some instinct told her not to gain the attention of whatever swam in them and peered up from beneath their surface.

She decided it was all wonderful, and that she finally had what rightfully belonged to her. If her new husband made her a little nervous, it seemed a small price to pay.

The radio station faded, and she spun the dial back and forth, past a blur of static and meaningless voices until she found the music again. Her pale profile glimmered, nearly ghostly in the tiny glow from the dashboard gauges. She bit her lower lip. Despite the constant working of the road beneath her, she remained lost in her thoughts.

The convertible passed the entrance to one of the isolated groves tucked away in the hills. Her headlights briefly illuminated the shiny black flank of a large sedan parked nose-out, facing the road. Charlene's eyes didn't register it, and she sped by. It was a Buick, one of the new ones with mean-looking swept back rear decks that had come out after the war. A few seconds after the Ford had gone, the saloon's big engine rumbled to life and the headlights came on. It paused for a moment at the edge of the highway, and then the exhaust roared and it sprayed gravel from the rear tires as it took off, following her.

Charlene remembered the long days in the big house that overlooked Santa Teresa's harbor. Marital relations began to include slaps, insults and small and occasional bedroom humiliations that grew bolder as time went by. Prostitutes from the nightclub Sal owned, the Star-lite Lounge, became occasional visitors to their home and later to their bed.

In time, it all began to seem normal, and she believed the unhappiness she felt was her own fault. Isolated and numb, any attention at all made her grateful. Her days were spent alone, by the swimming pool. She would have liked to go into the water, but she had never learned to swim and there was no one here to show her how. She sat on a chair and looked at the ocean instead.

The road began to rise more steeply as it bent and switched its way up the mountain. She outran the beams of her headlights as she entered and exited the curves, and Charlene shifted the transmission into second gear and tried to focus on her driving. She knew her drifting thoughts were dangerous, but after a few moments she got lost in her reverie again, unable to control her hateful memories.

All of it had stopped seeming normal almost two months ago. One night Charlene awakened abruptly from a numb sleep. Sal had come home drunk, furious, and nearly incoherent. He wanted to talk, and she was at first grateful to be an ear for what bothered him. He sat on a chesterfield next to her, his head on her shoulder. She had listened, at first sympathetic and then with increasing horror. She knew what happened to people who crossed Sal Cleveland.

Behind her, as yet escaping her notice, the Buick saloon swayed on its springs as it rocketed through the curves, closing the distance between the two cars. Driven expertly, its large exhaust bellowed down straight-aways. Its brake lights flashed only occasionally as it twisted down through arroyos and up the mountain.

Sal had told her that a woman had come to Santa Teresa, a woman who had betrayed him years before, and later escaped the city. He didn't have to tell Charlene that the woman had been his lover. Now she was back, and living openly in the city. Sal didn't explain why this enraged him as much as it did. He vowed to kill her. He said he would burn her to death. He said Charlene would be there when he did it, so she understood how he dealt with betrayal.

It was too much, burning someone to death. It was much worse than beating them or shooting them with a gun. The idea had frightened her badly, so badly that she knew she had to get out. She knew she needed a divorce, and she knew that Sal wouldn't give it to her. Most of all, she knew that she needed help, and a lot of it.

A mile behind her, the Buick's driver began to catch occasional glimpses of the tan convertible's taillights, appearing and disappearing in the curves ahead. Behind the wheel, he tossed his cigarette out of the open window and smiled.

Charlene remembered how she had finally found help in the form of a private detective with a nondescript office on State Street. One lucky day she had passed his building, and seen his small sign. Surprised by her own audacity, she had impulsively abandoned her shopping and gone up the stairs and into his waiting room. He was indeed a detective, she discovered. His name was Nathaniel Crowe.

Dark and almost ordinary. he stood neither particularly tall nor exceptionally short, neither fat nor thin. His voice sounded soft, both in texture and tone. Unlike most of the men she had known well, he had no swagger and no bluster. He carried himself quietly and watchfully, with the kind of resigned sorrow she associated with priests in darkened churches.

He didn't talk tough. In fact he didn't talk much at all, but had some essential toughness about him that was hard to pin down. When she spoke, he watched her, absorbed, with a totality she had never experienced before. When she paused, he waited as though he knew there was more, and there always was.

He had smiled a little at her idea that secretly-taken photographs of infidelity would get her a divorce from a man like her husband. Instead, he had asked her a lot of questions over the course of several meetings, and then he had gone to see Sal. She didn't know what had been said between them, only that Sal had come to her and insisted on a divorce as though it had been his idea. He had packed her bags himself and held the door open for her.

Over the course of that brief time, Nathaniel Crowe began to grow on her, and she found herself more and more aware of him as a man. He affected no masculine postures and gave her no signs, but she became hopeful and almost convinced that she had been sent to him by Destiny. Fate had sent him to her as a replacement. She began to fantasize that this man would take care of her, truly and forever.

When her divorce was final, she had offered him the only thing she knew how to offer, herself. He had declined her, gentle as always, but at the same time unrelenting in his

12

disinterest. She felt the sting of tears again, thinking about it. She swiped at her eyes angrily with a sleeve and tried again to focus on her driving.

In the rear view mirror, a pair of headlights suddenly appeared around the bend behind her. It blinded her, and she reached up to adjust the mirror, getting a glimpse of her own wet eyes as she did. The other car bore down quickly, and she kept an eye on it, nearly over-correcting on the next curve. Rubber chirped angrily beneath her.

The driver wanted to pass, but she didn't know how or where she could pull to the side. She glanced at her speedometer, and then nudged the accelerator pedal further with a delicate but determined toe. The convertible jumped ahead willingly enough, and the wheels began to moan in the bends.

It didn't satisfy the following car. The bright beams came on, and Charlene heard the steady sound of its horn keeping her radio company.

"What do you want me to do?" she wondered aloud, just as the car nudged her back bumper.

Her car skidded and started to drift. The tires howled as a guardrail loomed close in the lights. She cursed under her breath as she fought with the steering wheel and her own silk-covered bottom, which slid uncontrollably on the Naugahyde seat cover.

The bumpers touched again, and the Ford swung back and forth wildly. She lost all hope of directing it anymore. It skidded a final time as it caught the edge of the road, and then she went over the side. The car screamed as it slid down into a canyon, tearing its belly and losing pieces of itself on the way. Buffeted and flung around, Charlene's legs jammed painfully beneath the dashboard, and she screamed once, twice. Her head hit the window frame beside her, and everything went gray.

At the bottom, the chassis shuddered as the car stopped with a huge impact. The steering wheel thrust into her chest and abdomen with enough force to nearly stop her breathing. She heard and felt something vital inside her guts give way, and then the noise stopped and she fell back in the seat. She knew in an animal way that she was badly, fundamentally, damaged inside.

Her headlights still shone, and as the dust cleared from the beams, she saw a house in front of her. It had no roof and the windows were empty sockets. She stared at it with dull eyes, not understanding. A car pulled up beside it and stopped. The driver's door opened and a man got out and came forward into the lights, like an actor coming onstage. It was Sal.

The pain came in waves. Charlene leaned her head back on the top of the seat and watched her husband pick his way over the dark, rocky slope to the wrecked car she sat in. The Ford lay dying beneath her. She heard the hiss from the punctured radiator and the gurgle and drip of fluids from the engine. When he got close enough to her open window, he stopped.

"Help me," she murmured. "I need help."

Her voice sounded so faint in her own ears she wasn't sure if she had spoken aloud. It seemed important to her that she explain herself clearly. If Sal understood, he would take care of things, take care of her.

"I went over the cliff. Someone was chasing me. I couldn't keep the car on the road."

He didn't seem excited, and didn't come any closer.

"I can see that," he said. "All the razzmatazz. All the razzmatazz, all the jive, all the blah-blah-blah, and now here we are, the only ones left. You and me."

"I'm hurt," she said.

He stood there, lit from behind by his own Buick's headlights. His face was shadowed and dark, and she felt his lack of expression. He took something carefully from his coat pocket. She hoped it was a handkerchief, that he was going to use to wipe her face, but then she saw the dull gleam and knew he had a gun.

"I was chasing you," he said. "You didn't think it was anyone else, did you? Out here in the middle of nowhere?"

"Help me," she said. "Please."

He pointed the pistol at her. She smelled the familiar scents of him, soap and heavy cologne. He always smelled clean. It reassured her somehow, smelling him now amid the odors of the broken car and her own blood and perspiration. She began to cry.

"I love you," she said.

She knew that she was going to die, and then he pulled the trigger and she did.

-Three-

I lived that year in a bungalow on Figueroa Street, a block from the police station and down a couple from the courthouse. It was a place to eat and sleep and to keep my clothes and not much more. I didn't have any pictures on the walls inside.

The place had a lot more space than I needed. Behind the living room in front, a hallway led back past empty bedrooms, a big kitchen and a sun room that never saw the sun, because it was always shadowy inside. A wide veranda stretched across the front, and the whole property was overhung by a trio of huge old black walnut trees. Their droppings covered the lawn, winter and summer. The decomposing nuts gave off a dark, musty smell. I didn't mind. It seemed to fit in with the rest of the place.

A garage stood beside the house, connected by a narrow drive. The previous owner had left it full of junk, so I parked my Ford coupe on the street. The car was one of the few things I owned that mattered to me. A black '40 Deluxe, with the big V-8, it went like a bird. In my line of work sometimes I needed it to.

The apartment house across from us was the only lively thing on the street. The sidewalk in front of it always stayed littered with a tangle of bicycles and tricycles. Unseen mothers screamed from upstairs windows at the children below. In the evenings, somebody would lug a radio out to have beer and conversation on the front steps. There were rumors that a guy sold a little reefer from one of the back apartments, right under the noses of the cops a block away. It didn't bother me much. If you did what I did for a living, you knew the city was full of worse things and worse people than that.

16

A shedding hedge that perpetually dropped a carpet of yellow leaves on the sidewalk separated the next door neighbor on one side. The white stucco two-story had red canvas awnings over the windows. I figured it had to be at least as gloomy inside as my place. The owners were an elderly pair named Gardiner. He'd been a doctor a long time ago. I didn't know about her. They owned an enormous old pre-war Cadillac that he piloted onto the street once or twice a month, like a black ocean liner leaving harbor. He liked to polish it, out in the driveway.

Mrs. Gardiner fed me a drink once in a while, and talked about Santa Teresa the way it had been fifteen or twenty years ago. Her husband never said much of anything. I liked them well enough, and I supposed they were the only friends I really had here.

The house on the other side had been put up for sale and stood empty for almost a year. After it sold, workmen came and went, hammering and painting, planting and pruning. They had dug a small swimming pool in the back yard. The new owner was a woman, and it became obvious that she had some money. She was an artist, apparently reclusive and maybe a little bit crazy. I had never seen her.

I knew her name was Anne Kahlo, because sometimes her mail ended up in my box and I walked it next door to put it into hers. She had a snazzy bottle-green Mercury convertible parked in back. I never saw her drive it. Some nights when I couldn't sleep, I heard her leave her house. Wherever she went in the dark, she walked.

Her house was a low, brown affair with some interesting peaks and gables in the roofline. Vines and flowers covered it, winter and summer. Something always bloomed profusely, as if nature knew the owner was

17

something special and wanted to put on a show for her. The place looked clean and fresh, like it smelled good inside.

I stood on my veranda for a moment and looked out at the street. A plane went over, climbing out of the Goleta airfield in the north. When it was gone, the street got quiet again.

I had to go out that afternoon, to close up a case with clients who weren't going to like me any better than Charlene Cleveland had. It was still early though, and I had time to kill. I went back inside to find a newspaper, the sofa, and a little bit of sleep. Maybe if I dreamed, I'd have some idea of what to do with myself next.

"He did it," I said. "Your son did exactly what they've accused him of doing."

This wasn't as pleasant as looking at pink under-things, but I had filing cabinets to fill and cases to close and accounts to collect. I sat in the living room of a big house. It stood in a nice neighborhood on a shady street that ran off upper State Street. Big bay windows looked out onto trees and the other houses on the street. It all seemed greener than the rest of the city.

I faced the couple on the sofa across from me. He leaned back and tried to seem relaxed. She sat on the edge of her seat and made no bones about having a case of nerves. He owned a land agency and wore a tasteful tie and wide suspenders. She looked as though she smelled nice, but she was sitting too far away for me to know for sure.

"He did it," I repeated. "The only proof I could dig up says he's guilty."

I didn't normally make house calls, but there had been no point in dragging these people downtown for this. I wasn't that busy.

18

"What are you saying?" the man demanded.

"I'm saying he gave the girl liquor to drink and then he took advantage of her."

The man's face turned deep red. The color spread right into his scalp. His blond hair was oiled and combed back. Since I was a detective, I made it my business to notice all sorts of little things. Everything could be a clue.

"This isn't what we're paying you for," the woman offered. "This is outrageous."

I turned my attention to her, since the man seemed to be close to popping like a balloon, and probably couldn't hear me.

"Your son was charged with the corruption of a minor," I said. "A morals charge. You said it wasn't true, and you hired me to dig up the facts and find some proof that cleared him. I took your word for it, but he lied. That means you lied too, whether you knew it or not."

"He's only a seventeen-year-old boy," she said.

"Nonetheless, he drove her to a parking area on La Marina Drive and fed her gin until she didn't know what she was doing, and then he—"

I stopped and looked at the woman. She started to cry. I was making a lot of women cry lately, and I had no idea what I could do about it.

"—he helped her out of her clothes," I sighed. "She was agreeable, as far as I can tell, or this would be a lot more serious. All the same, she's sixteen years old, and that means he committed a crime."

"She's a liar," the man said. His voice rose.

A white ceramic clock with painted gold numerals stood on an end table. It began to chime, six times, with a little whirring noise between each note. We all waited until it was done.

19

"She isn't a liar," I said. "It took me less than an hour to find three of your son's school chums that had every detail. Until the cops knocked on your door, he could hardly stop boasting about it. I also talked to the girl. She's a pretty level character, in spite of her poor judgment with your son. She says there was no . . . completion. The cop knocked on the window of the car and interrupted things. The DA believes her. If she weren't so honest, your son could be facing a rape charge."

"You're supposed to do what we pay you to do," he said.

"I did what you paid me for. I can't find what isn't there just because you want me to. It's been a short job, and I don't need any more than the retainer you gave me."

I plucked my hat off the table and stood up. The man stood up, too.

"I'm not giving you a dime," he shouted. "Not a goddamned nickel. You give me my money back. This isn't how it works."

"This is exactly how it works," I said, and settled my hat on my head. "I'm not giving you your money back."

"Of course not," the woman said. "You have a gun."

I didn't have a response for that, so I shrugged. She had stopped crying long enough to look at me like I was a bug.

"Count your lucky stars," I said. "Your son is young, and the court might give him a break if he deserves one. Let him learn a lesson and move on."

They sat and stared at me. No one had anything else to say, so I went out to my car and drove away.

Later that evening I met my next-door neighbor, Annie Kahlo, for the first time. At first I thought she must be some kind of ghost. I don't know why that idea jumped out at me. Maybe it was because of the way she moved, hardly seeming to touch the ground. In hindsight, it must have taken a lot of courage to cross the grass that separated my front steps from hers.

I had one hand on my front door knob, ready to go out to nowhere in particular. It was the kind of warm twilight that makes a person want to be outside. I felt restless, and wanted crowds and noise, neon lights and the smells of good food. I patted my pockets and remembered, as I pulled the door shut, that I had left my cigarettes inside.

She was in her forties, maybe, and slender. Her light hair was long, and her arms were tanned, copper-colored against her pale green sleeveless dress. She moved gracefully, and again I had the impression that she floated as she walked toward me. She paused before she crossed onto my yard, as though she had to get over a barrier. At the bottom of my steps she looked up.

The remarkable stillness of her face is what marked her most. She gazed at me, and I wondered if she had been drinking. It wasn't booze, though. It was something else. We stood and looked at each other for a long moment before she spoke.

"I have a birthday cake," she said.

Her voice was light, a little breathy. She sounded like one of those film stars from a dozen or so years ago, when the talkies were brand new and the voices from the silver screen all seemed to be poured straight from expensive decanters.

"I can't eat it by myself, and I wondered…"

She trailed off, looking miserable. I gave her what help I could.

"That's neighborly." I smiled. "Throw in a cup of coffee and you've got a deal."

A dark-colored sedan passed behind her, cruising slowly. A little further up the street its brake lights came on, and the driver tapped the horn. She looked over her shoulder, visibly startled. If she had been carrying the cake, she would have dropped it.

"I'm sorry. I should have come over and introduced myself before," I said. "I'm Nathaniel Crowe. Nate will do fine."

She tore her attention from the car and nodded. "A birthday cake," she said. "It's on my kitchen table. I made it today."

I was intrigued. "Happy birthday, then," I said.

The dark car blipped the horn again. Its tail lights glowed bright in the gathering dusk. I supposed it was picking someone up, but nothing stirred from the houses across the street. Annie watched it, too. Her face stayed expressionless, but she twisted a bracelet on her left wrist, and I could sense her apprehension.

She turned back to me. "It isn't my birthday," she said. "Today isn't my birthday at all."

"But you baked a cake?"

She stood and watched me, turning her bracelet around and around. Her eyes were velvet, liquid and impossibly dark. They moved across my face, reading me like a story.

"Yes," she said. "It's my sister's birthday."

"Wouldn't you rather eat it with her, then?"

She shook her head. "I don't think so," she said. "She's dead. That's no reason to waste the cake, though."

"That's true," I said, as if I had any idea of what she was talking about.

I finished closing up. She stood at the foot of my front steps, one hand on the railing.

"You lock your front door?" she asked. "I didn't think anyone in this neighborhood did that."

I decided to give her the short version. "I'm a private detective," I said. "Sometimes my work makes people upset with me. I like to be careful."

I smiled a little at myself, since I had upset even more people than usual today.

Annie smiled back at me. She was beautiful in a nearly exotic way, like a different species. Her features were finely etched, and in profile her eyes and brow had an Oriental cast.

"My parents were Hawaiian," she said, as though she could read my mind. "They met in Honolulu. My father was born in the islands, and my mother was *haole*."

I had served in the military for a few months in Hawaii, and I had liked it. I liked the weather, and the way the island smelled, especially at night. I also liked the way the people looked. I hadn't found a better way of judging people than by how they looked.

I followed her to her house. After months of seeing the place every day, it was somehow strange to find myself standing on her porch, breathing in the fragrance of her honeysuckle. She turned in the front doorway and looked at me.

"You didn't ask me my name."

"I figured you'd tell me when you were ready," I said.

"Annie Kahlo," she said, and put out her hand. "What does it mean…your name, Crowe?"

"I don't think it means anything," I said.

She held the door open for me, and I followed her inside.

23

"Everything means something," she said, looking back at me. "Anyway, I have a confession to make. Someone told me that you were a detective, for hire. I'm sorry...I wasn't honest."

"It isn't exactly a secret," I said. "I'd take out more advertisements, if I could afford it."

"I want to hire you."

I waited, but she didn't elaborate. She led me inside.

The walls were dark wood and the furniture heavy, spare and elegant. It was cool and hushed, and it all looked and smelled like it had cost someone a bundle. Even the dim light shining through the colored windows said money. A vase of white flowers stood on a table, and I stopped to look at it.

"Lilacs?" I guessed.

"Orchids," she said. She seemed amused. "They remind me of ice cream. You don't know very much about flowers, do you?"

"There's a whole long list of things I know nothing about," I said. "I've gotten used to it."

She led me further into the house. I looked back over my shoulder. The flowers did look like ice cream. We went through a dining room and into a black-and-white tiled kitchen. The cake sat on the counter. It had cream frosting and thin slices of orange and lime and lemon. "Happy Birthday, June" was spelled out on it in pale green sugar. It looked like a pretty good cake.

"She was ten years old when she died," she said.

I didn't have any idea what she was talking about. I shrugged in what I hoped was a sympathetic way.

"I used to read to her every night, but then I went away. I had to, but I wrote the story so she would still have it when I was gone. I have it now. I'll show it to you."

She went out. I heard her footsteps go across the wood floors out of sight, and then disappear. I looked around while I waited. An enameled ice box hummed softly in the corner. A little yellow bird watched me from a cage hanging in the window. He didn't say anything, and neither did I. In a minute, she came back carrying a sheaf of papers bound in a cardboard folder. She held it out to me.

"I'm illustrating it now," she said. "I always meant to. I'm an artist . . . it's what I do."

The papers were yellowed at the edges. I riffled through them. The writing on them had been done with a typewriter, and the letters were faint. Either the ribbon was tired, or they had faded with age. The top sheet said 'Goodnight, June', and below it in pencil: *To Junie, Love from Annie...June 17, 1922.*

"This is from quite a few years ago," I remarked. "You're just getting around to illustrating it now?"

"It was lost," she said. "I found it again, not very long ago."

She looked at me for a long moment, considering whether or not she could trust me. Finally, she gave a tiny nod.

"I need to find out what happened to June," she said, and I looked up. "She died while I was away. I got a telegram. Something bad happened to her, and I think it was because of me."

"Because of you?"

"I think so, yes. She was always afraid the Hespers were going to get her, and I think they did."

"Maybe you'd better tell me about these Hespers," I said, because I didn't know what else to say.

"They're the footsteps behind you on a street at three o'clock in the morning. They're the sea creatures in your bed

25

that slide and wrap cold around your legs, the men with long beards standing behind the door when you go into a dark room. They're the ones that hunt in the middle of the night. The things that follow and laugh…and bite."

"Bogey men," I said. "Nightmares."

"They get called a lot of things," she said. "Children dream about them. June always called them the Hespers. I think it may have started when she was too small to say monsters, and it stuck. I think of them as Hespers now, too. Aren't you afraid of them?"

I looked at the delicately frosted cake. The manuscript in my hands started to feel haunted, so I put it on the counter. The little bird suddenly cheeped, once, startling me.

"I'm not afraid of very much anymore," I said. "Sometimes I wish I was."

"So you'll do it then?"

I started to feel uncomfortable. I kept my voice as gentle as I could.

"Your sister is dead? And you want me to find her for you? Her grave, you mean?"

She shook her head vigorously, and again I caught the fragrance of her. She smelled wonderful.

"No," she said. "I already found her. I want to know what happened to her. Do you need a retainer? When can you start?"

"How long ago did she die?" I asked. "For that matter, how did she die?"

"She died in 1922, just a month after I went away. The telegram said she had died in a fire with my father. That wasn't true. She died, but not in a fire."

"She's been dead for twenty-five years?" I asked.

26

This was crazy. I was willing to chase crazy if the money was right, but a sister that had been dead for a couple of decades sounded like a waste of time. I looked at the woman in front of me and opened my mouth to say as much, but something about her made me hesitate. She had a face that looked like it had seen a lot of rejection and somehow kept its dignity. She looked like she expected me to brush her off, and would never let me see an ounce of hurt.

"My plate's a little full right now," I said. "Let me check when I'm at the office, and we'll talk again. How would that be?"

"You won't forget?"

I promised I wouldn't. On the way out, we paused on the veranda. I searched for a way to politely say goodbye. Her eyes had changed. Something moved in the dark behind them that made me think of lightning flickering behind black clouds. She reached out and touched a vine that trailed down from the edge of the roof.

"Night-blooming cereus. Do you know it?"

I shook my head, no.

"That's right, you don't know about flowers," she said. "They bloom all at once…only once a year, and only at night. I came in the other day and saw that they had come and gone, and I missed it."

She looked inexpressibly sad. "I counted the dead blossoms. There were eleven of them. I missed it."

"There will be other nights," I said, because I couldn't think of anything else to say. "Other years."

I went down the steps, and crossed the lawn back toward my place. Her grass was soft, lush, and I realized that I had never seen anyone water or cut it. I was embarrassed by the moldering carpet of walnut shells on my side of the drive. She spoke from behind me.

"You never had any cake, Mister Crowe."

I looked back at her. She stood on her steps, looking slender and vulnerable. I wondered if she was as surrendered to being alone as I was. I knew one thing. She was crazy, and I had enough crazy on my dance card without adding to it.

"You can call me Nate," I said. "Save me a piece, would you?"

She smiled at me. "You can call me Annie."

Her smile wasn't just pretty like a swimsuit face in a magazine. It was beautiful. The full moon in warm wind that smells like rain is that kind of beautiful. It gives you the idea that it's raining on the moon, even though they say it never does. It's a spooky kind of beautiful, something you don't forget, and her smile was like that.

I had thought I was past noticing such things, and I promised myself now to stop noticing it about her. She's crazy, I told myself again. She stayed shut in her house all day and baked birthday cakes for dead people. She went for long walks in the middle of the night. She had nothing I needed. Telling myself all of that didn't help much.

She waved and turned away, and I climbed my own steps. I didn't want to go out anymore.

"I have a feeling you're going to run me right off the road, lady," I muttered. "Right off the road."

I went inside to find my cigarettes.

-Four-

Trouble found me the next morning, and in a big way, and Annie Kahlo, her crazy ideas and her dead sister went by the wayside. I was waiting for the coffee pot on the stove to begin to percolate, and studying the cigarettes and the book of paper matches on the kitchen table. I tried to postpone my first smoke of the day until after I'd finished a cup of coffee, because I'd read a magazine article that said tobacco was unhealthy on an empty stomach. Having to wait made an annoying way to start the day, and spoiled my mood.

The telephone on the wall rang, startling me. I crossed the room and snatched up the receiver on the second ring. It was Rex Raines, a cop I knew pretty well, on the other end.

"Got anything to do this morning?" he asked. "Drop it, if you do. I'm on my way to a situation out in the canyons. County boys found something in a lady's purse. I'd like you to take a look at it with me."

Raines worked homicide out of the station up the street. He had a round face and a sunny smile that made him seem cheerful for the job, but it was a front. I knew he'd seen a lot for a man not quite forty. Part of one foot was missing, and he walked with a limp. He'd stepped on something nasty while wading onto a Japanese-held coral lump in the middle of the Pacific. He never talked about it.

He gave me directions to a place inland, in the canyons south of Santa Teresa. I figured it for about thirty miles away, outside the city jurisdiction, but I knew better than to ask questions.

"Sounds like a perfect morning," I said.

"So far, so good," he said. "I'm on my way. See you there."

I knew I had time to finish my coffee. Raines' customers usually weren't in a hurry.

Coastal fog hung a gray curtain over the city. It looked like rain, but the low cloud drifted as dry as smoke. I took the ocean highway south to Summerland, a scattering of beach cottages that clung to the hills, and I turned inland, onto the canyon road.

The sky cleared into a hot blue almost as soon as the ocean left my rearview mirror, and I began a series of corkscrew climbs up and over the Loma Linda pass. The road hung onto the dusty shoulders of the hills for dear life. In places the drop-off fell better than three hundred feet. The steep grade up forced most vehicles to slow to a walking pace, which reduced the danger of overshooting a curve. Going down the other side was a different story.

By the time I crested and started the descent, the Ford was close to boiling over, and the springs complained loudly. I used the engine in low gear as much as I could to keep from overheating the brakes. The brush grew thick, and close enough to the road to hide anything approaching from the opposite direction.

Off to the side, I saw a small collection of buildings in an arroyo. Around the next bend, a black-and-white county sedan blocked the road. A deputy in tan khakis stepped out and held up a palm, but as my smoking brakes brought me noisily to a stop, he changed his mind and waved me by. He was expecting me.

I turned gingerly into the remnants of a dusty drive that snaked down sharply into the arroyo. Several vehicles stood parked at the bottom, but my brakes were too hot to trust. I stopped the Ford at the top, took off my suit coat, tossed it on the front seat, and started down the drive. The gravel was loose under my feet as I slipped and skittered my way down.

The air had a last edge of coolness, but the sun was already starting to sting, reclaiming the hot dry landscape from the chilly night before. A mourning dove sang softly, repeating the same five notes over and over. The crunch of my steps and the monotonous birdsong were all that broke the silence.

An ordered grove of smallish trees stretched away to the far side of the valley. They probably hadn't been tended to in years, but they looked healthy and uniform with gray trunks and dark green leaves. A good-sized barn and a pair of sheds stood at the bottom. None of them had ever seen a coat of paint, and they were all the same silver color. Off to one side were the remains of a house. It sat in the shadow of the hillside, with the road running above it. It had no roof, and empty window holes dotted the walls.

A car was nose down at the bottom of the embankment, in what would have passed for the front yard. I saw the path it had carved through the brush on its way down. Raines detached himself from the small group of people gathered around the wreck and made his way over to me.

"Little bit out of your jurisdiction, aren't you?" I asked. "This is county."

"Don't care about car crashes," he said, and then stopped to think. "Unless I'm in one, maybe. This isn't what it looks like."

The ruined car was a sand-colored Ford convertible, crumpled into the base of the hill. Through the driver's window I saw a spill of blonde hair. One pink sleeve with a slender wrist and hand, hung over the doorframe. I knew the dress and I knew who it belonged to.

"Why'd you call me out here?"

"This," he said, and handed me a piece of paper. The check had been crumpled and then carefully straightened. It was made out to me. The ink had run in the middle, spattered by a single teardrop.

"Charlene Cleveland," I said, and he nodded.

"Her name is on the check," he said. "Hers and yours. She didn't get around to signing it."

I looked at the ranks of trees that stretched to the other side of the canyon. On their tops, the reflected sun glittered off waxy leaves, but the rows below them were dark and quiet.

"Oranges?" I asked.

He shook his head, dropped his cigarette and stepped on it. When he was sure it was dead, he looked up at me.

"Avocados. Oranges don't do so well up here." He thought for a moment. "You have a dog?"

I shook my head, no.

"You have to watch out for dogs in these groves. There's nothing they like to eat more than a nice soft avocado that's fallen on the ground. Once a dog gets a taste for them, you can hardly stop it from running into the trees. Problem is, these groves suit snakes, too. If you're looking for a rattlesnake, avocado trees are a good place to start."

"Good way to lose a dog."

"They should know better," he said. "Dogs can scent a snake a mile away. Most of them go after the avocado anyway. They can't help themselves."

"What you love can kill you," I said. "Is that your point?"

32

He looked over at the wreck, shrugged, and started back to it. "Don't know that I have a point," he said over his shoulder. "I'm talking about dogs."

From where I stood, the dead woman's blonde hair gleamed strangely bright in the morning sunshine, and it made me feel sad.

"Got to go some way," I said. "Might as well be love."

I trailed him over to the base of the hillside. The windows of the house watched me. I could see the remnants of scorch marks around the openings. It was a wonder the long-ago fire hadn't taken the outbuildings and trees at the same time. The support posts for a good-sized veranda remained, spaced out across the front. I wondered if the tenants had sat out at night and looked at the desert stars and wondered at their prospects, out here so far away from everyone else.

Closer to the car, I caught the stink of gasoline and oil.

"Don't light a smoke," Raines said. "Gas tank busted on the way down, and the whole hillside's soaked. Too bad for them they didn't just throw a match after her. We'd have never known what happened. They probably couldn't find their way down in the dark."

"They're stupid enough to think they staged things well enough like it is," said another man, walking up to join us. "Even more likely they just didn't care."

"Coroner," Raines said. "Mel Runtz. He got here first. Called me."

"Staged things?" I asked.

The coroner was a morose man with black-framed spectacles. He indicated the car with a nod, and we followed him, picking our way over rocks. Charlene Cleveland slumped back in the driver's seat, her body turned slightly toward us. Her features were mostly obscured by a sheaf of hair that had fallen across her face. There was no one else in the car.

Runtz leaned in, took her face gently in his hands and turned it. A red dot, like a birthmark, marked one cheekbone. I looked over his shoulder at the mess that was the back of her head. What the gunshot had left of her hat was still in place. The coroner let her fall back. Her distorted face was a long way from pretty now. Her mouth was slightly parted, exposing the small gap between her front teeth.

It made me sad, all at once. I had been wise with her only a few hours before, and she had cursed me and cried. I looked at the tear stain on the check I still held, and felt a stirring of anger at whoever had done this to her. She might not have been my type, but she hadn't deserved what she got. She had been someone's little girl.

"They shot her and pushed the car over the side?" I asked.

Runtz shrugged. "Or shot her while as she drove, and she lost control. The powder on her face means the shooter was close, probably in the car with her. They jumped out, or took the ride down with her. It isn't a big enough drop that someone couldn't have gotten out and walked away from this."

We looked up the embankment to where the road ran, on top of a thirty or forty foot drop. He was right. It was survivable.

"Seems like a hell of a risk, though," I said. "Shoot a driver in the face while you're on a canyon road at night. You wouldn't know if you went off the side how far down it went. Makes more sense if they killed her and pushed the car off, trying to make it look like an accident."

"You keep saying they," Raines interrupted. "Who's they?"

"Her husband, or his people. Seems obvious to me."

He was getting angry, and his boyish face flushed.

"You know something about this," he said. "She's got a check made out to you in her purse, and it's dated yesterday. We've known each other a while now. Why not be straight?"

I felt my own heat. The situation stunk. "You know damn well who Charlene Cleveland is," I said. "You know who she married. I helped her get free of him, that's all."

"How did you manage that? Cleveland's not the type gets pushed around."

"Maybe I just showed him he'd be happier without her."

"You could get yourself in a lot of trouble," he said, "trying to show Sal Cleveland what made him happy."

"Who was she married to?" Runtz asked, pulling his head from the car's open window.

We both looked at him, irritated at the interruption.

"Sal Cleveland," Raines answered. "Local bad guy, owns the Star-lite in Montelindo."

"I know Sal Cleveland," Runtz said. His expression was mild. "You think I moved here last week? I just hadn't heard he got married. Didn't figure him for the marrying type."

"Couple of years ago," Raines said. "And not anymore." He looked at me.

"She got her divorce yesterday," I said. "I got paid. She ruined the check she wrote and made out another one. No big deal."

"It was a big deal to someone, by the looks of it."

"You're going to want my testimony?" I asked. "That the angle? Who called this in, anyway?"

Raines looked at me for a long moment. He seemed to be making his mind up about something.

"I don't know what I want from you," he finally said. "Want to know something funny? The property owner called it in a couple hours ago. Woman owns this ranch lives in town. She was apparently out here checking on her property and found the wreck."

"What's funny about that?" I asked.

"She's a neighbor of yours. Close neighbor, next door to you, matter of fact. Strange name." He checked his notebook. "Lady's name is Kahlo. Anne Kahlo. Know her?"

"Kahlo?" I asked, startled. "I just met her. I don't mix with the neighbors much. She owns this place?"

I looked around at the steep hillsides, the ranks of avocado trees, the weathered barn and the burned-out house.

"What does she do with it?" I wondered. "I thought she was some kind of an artist."

"Don't know," Raines said, not really interested. "Maybe she likes avocados. One of the locals says these trees have been a free harvest for years. No one pays attention to who comes on the land and picks them. It isn't a huge yield, because no one irrigates the trees. The Kahlo woman isn't running a bona fide operation here."

"She isn't running the place any kind of way, but she happened to be out here?"

Raines ignored the implications of my question.

"She was here this morning," he said. "You can't see the wreck from the road. Good thing. A few days in this heat would have baked the body where you couldn't recognize it."

A black station wagon picked its way slowly down the steep driveway, leaving a lazy trail of dust that lingered in the thickening heat.

"She looks like she was a dish," Raines said. "Was she?"

"She was pretty," I said. "Sort of a type."

He looked at the approaching black wagon and shook his head. "Bet she didn't imagine when she started out last night that she'd be getting a ride home like this."

I looked at the ruined tan convertible with its crumpled blonde cargo behind the steering wheel. I felt a little stab of something that might have been grief. It had been so long since I'd felt grief that I couldn't be sure.

"So you don't really know this Kahlo broad?" he asked. "Your neighbor?"

"Not really," I said. "Met her just the once."

"She acts a little crazy," he said. "Doesn't make a lot of sense. She's kind of a dish, too, isn't she? Too bad a woman looks like that talks like a dingbat. Seems like a waste."

I thought about her dark eyes, her dead sister, and birthday cakes.

"It's a shame," I agreed.

-Five-

I walked past the old courthouse. It was done in some kind of Spanish architecture, surrounded by rows of king palms. The place was beautiful, stucco and red tile, tall and white and arched, with bell towers and sweeping lawns that were brown in the summer and green in winter. I didn't know how a place so gorgeous could have seen and caused so much misery, but I guessed a lot of things were like that, different than they appeared.

It was the kind of strange, bright California evening that you only see right on the coast. Night falls almost blue, but darkness won't quite come, and the sky stays lit up by colored clouds. The sun is dead but doesn't know it yet. Down at the wharf, the roller coaster still rattled around, and lights colored the Ferris wheel pink and yellow.

Dinner had been at a Mexican joint on Cabrillo, a plate of enchiladas and a half-pitcher of cold sangria. I had never been much of a wine drinker, even on my good days, and these weren't anything close to my good days. I knew I would pay for it in the morning, but for now I enjoyed the glow. A taxicab slowed as it passed, but I waved it by.

The whole scene felt like it was just for me, a show to keep me busy and distracted while other important things happened elsewhere. I wondered if Annie Kahlo was finishing her dinner, and maybe getting ready to go for a walk, too. Maybe she thought about me, and was figuring out what strange things she would say to me the next time we met. I wondered if I thought about her too much.

"Spare a smoke, pal?"

The voice from a doorway belonged to a bum. There were a lot of them here. Some had come back from the war with the best part of themselves left buried in the French countryside or on an island in the Pacific. They stayed as day labor to pick oranges in season and to drink where the weather stayed warm. They didn't hurt anyone as far as I could tell, except maybe themselves.

I kept walking.

"Have a good night," he called after me.

I thought about Annie again, and wondered if I was falling for her. I wondered if I could fall in love at all, and if I did, if falling for someone who seemed to have a lot of loose screws could work out. I didn't know why it bothered me. I had steered clear of good looking women who seemed like trouble before and without a second thought.

Most recently, Charlene Cleveland. I felt a flash of sadness.

Maybe you won't turn down the next poor girl who needs you. You don't know the first thing about love.

I stopped and went back to give him a cigarette and the change in my pocket, a quarter and two nickels.

"Get something to eat," I said.

I knew he wouldn't. He smiled and tipped me the hat he wasn't wearing. Maybe he was smarter than me.

The clock chimed eleven. The light from the single lamp didn't quite reach into the corners of my living room. Other than the clock and me, there wasn't much in the room, just a chesterfield and a side table. I probably needed more furniture and maybe a dog to lie at my feet. I held a scotch. I didn't care much for it, but I drank it on the nights that I wanted to feel civilized and sit in my empty living room and think about things.

Charlene Cleveland stayed on my mind. She had sat across from me, sweet and flirtatious, and I made her cry. Now the pretty face was ruined and she was dead. I hadn't liked her much, but she hadn't deserved a bullet. I had a pretty good idea who had killed her and why, and all of it sat with me like an upset stomach and made me restless.

I picked up my drink and went outside onto the porch. The night air felt cool, and the houses on the street had gone dark. Only my next-door neighbor seemed to be awake. Gold light spilled from her windows onto the vines on her front porch. I sipped my scotch. It tasted the same as it had in the living room.

I've been chased by dreams of loss since I was small. It was always nighttime, and I walked through an empty place as fast as I could. I saw the stars and something big and black over my head, and then the noises around me faded to a whisper. I woke up in my bed and could never remember the rest of the dream, but I was always convinced that years and decades had passed while I slept. Everyone else had moved on and left me behind. I was all alone, and terrified.

That's why I was comfortable on wet city streets in the middle of the night. It's why I'd go to the places no one else wanted to, and why the neon and smoke and the sound of my own footsteps felt like home. Being with moving shadows was better than being alone. Those moments passed. I'd learned to live with them, and I never talked about it. Maybe everyone else was the same, and they weren't talking about it either.

Sal Cleveland had wrecked his wife long before he killed her.

She had come to me for help, another slightly tarnished damsel in a long line of them, just another case in another day in another week. The glamour of being a hoodlum's wife had long gone for her. The imagined danger and romance of it had given way under the steady pressure of neglect and abuse, and she finally tired enough of it all to want out. She was Sal's property, though. He owned her and he wouldn't let her go.

It had been easy enough to change his mind. Cleveland sold dancers and reefer and throw-away guns out the back door of the Star-lite Lounge. There were rumors that he dipped his toes in worse things. The street gossip had it he made a lot of money selling women to the strange, the exotic, and the twisted. The women became food for the kind of creatures that hid in dark rooms during the day and only slithered out onto the sidewalks at night.

They said he ran whores up from Mexico, and that the unsuspecting women in the trucks he brought up here thought they were coming to be nannies and to clean houses. They disappeared. The street also whispered that Sal Cleveland sold pictures of children, and that no one knew where the children came from or what happened to them after the photographs were taken. It was all dirty enough that if it saw daylight, his gangster friends from San Francisco to San Diego would turn their backs on him, and not even the judges he had bought or the crooked cops who owed him would spare him.

I had a single photograph given to me by a friend in the Mexican community, a man named Danny Lopez. It showed a young Cleveland standing at the rear of a large farm truck. The truck was filled with merchandise: women and girls. They looked back at the camera with expressionless faces and black eyes. They might have been farm workers, except they were tied with rope. I didn't know why the photo had been taken in the first place. I suspected it was some kind of memento. Lopez claimed that it had hung, framed and unnoticed, for years in Sal's office, and he had stolen it from the wall.

41

I had a single meeting with Sal at a table in the Starlite Lounge, and I showed him the photograph. It became clear the discomfort it might cause for him wasn't worth one blonde wife, and we made a trade. He took back the image, and Charlene had her freedom. She got divorce papers and whatever she could pack into a couple of suitcases. She thought she had another chance to chase some happiness. He had taken it all back with a gun. I hadn't seen that part coming, and that was unforgivable. It was my fault.

Like a smug fool, I had congratulated myself on another job well done. I had taken her check and given her a receipt and shooed her from my office.

My ice had almost melted, and the last of the cubes rattled softly in the glass as I finished my drink. I looked at the dark sky and wondered if Charlene Cleveland could see me.

"I'll fix this for you. I promise," I mumbled. "I'm no good, but I keep my promises. I'm good for that much."

The words slurred in my own ears. I was drunk. I wanted to see stars, but the night was overcast and there weren't any. I raised my glass in good night to her, wherever she was now.

"I won't let him get away with it," I said. "You can sleep."

A couple of gulls screamed at each other over a waxed paper wrapper on the sidewalk, and billboards on latticed scaffolds fought with palm trees for the skyline. The dawn gleamed so pretty and blue that I looked at my Ford coupe and thought about trading it for a ragtop. It would have to wait until after lunch, though, because I had things to do.

I hung a right onto State Street and drove away from the beach. I had no trouble finding a parking spot in front of my office. I got out and turned my face up for a last taste of the morning sun before I headed inside. Across the street, the early drunks congregated on the sidewalk and waited for the Schooner Inn to open at eight o'clock. They seemed sociable, and I wondered if they were happier than I was.

I pulled my key out as I climbed the stairs, and looked up to see Annie Kahlo looking down. She waited for me at the top, hidden behind dark glasses and a bright scarf. Up close, she smelled like a summer storm; citrus and rain and something earthy. I would have liked to keep her with me the rest of the day, just for her perfume. I held on to my wits and got the door unlocked.

I had a hot plate in the corner of the office, and a coffee percolator to go with it. There was the bottle of bourbon in my desk drawer for special occasions, but it seemed too close to breakfast for that. I went up the hall to the men's room to fill the coffeepot. When I got back, Annie sat quietly in one of the chairs across from my desk.

She still wore the scarf, but she had taken off her dark glasses and held them in her lap. Dingbat or not, I thought that she was the most beautiful thing I was going to see all day.

"It's still early," she said, as though she could read my mind. "You never know."

"This time I do," I answered, as though I could read hers.

I got busy making coffee.

"You don't have a secretary, Mister Crowe?"

"I had one once," I said. "I didn't have enough for her to do. She read magazines and fixed her makeup all morning, and generally got into my liquor by lunch time. She ran off to get married, and I didn't replace her."

"That's a shame."

43

I didn't ask her why she thought so. I brought her a cup, and sat on the corner of my desk. "What can I do for you, Miss Kahlo?"

"Call me Annie, please," she said. "I told you last night. I want to hire you. I want you to do something for June. I want you to work for her—and me. The job has two parts, really. I want you to find out for sure what happened to her, and then I want you to do something else. Something even more important."

I kept my voice gentle. "Annie, June was your younger sister. She died twenty-five years ago. Unless that's changed."

"It hasn't changed," she said.

She sipped at her coffee, and set the cup on the desk beside me. She didn't look like she enjoyed it. I didn't blame her. Maybe I needed to get another secretary, one who could make coffee.

"Money isn't a problem," she said. "I have money."

"It isn't that. After this long, she's just a memory. She isn't real. There are no records and no clues. How am I supposed to find out about someone who isn't real?"

I spread my hands helplessly. She gazed at me for so long I wondered if I should say something else. I didn't though, and finally she spoke.

"I'm not real, and you found me, didn't you?"

I had no answer for that. Her dark eyes were steady, nearly serene. She sat very, very still.

"I'll tell you a secret," she said. "You're not real, either, Mister Crowe. That makes you exactly the right person to find June."

I took a deep breath. I kept my eyes on my desk top. "There's another thing, Miss Kahlo…" I glanced up, caught her expression and corrected myself. "Annie. There's

44

another thing. Yesterday I had to attend a crime scene, up in the mountains. A bad kind of murder, and the person who reported it…the police mentioned your name."

She looked away, and then busied herself rooting around in her bag.

"I'm pretty upset about it," I said. "It was a woman I knew, and it wasn't a nice way for her to die."

I waited.

"Doesn't it seem like a funny coincidence?" I asked. "A woman sitting in the very same chair as you're sitting in now, just the day before yesterday, gets herself killed on a property you happen to own. And here you are."

She stood up, went to the window and looked out at whatever went by below us on State Street. I looked at her looking. Finally, I cleared my throat and spoke. "Her name was Charlene Cleveland," I said. "She was my client, and she trusted me. I feel like I should have kept her safe. I want to at least make sure that there's some justice for her. Can you understand that?"

"June was my little sister." Her voice was flat. "I feel responsible for what happened to her. I should have kept her safe. I want to know things, too. Can *you* understand *that*?"

I felt as though unseen currents were pulling me out to places I didn't want to go. I didn't feel like I had much choice.

"If I tell you what happened to the woman, will you help me?" she asked. "Is that a good trade?"

"You know what happened to her?" I asked. "You need to tell me, or tell the police. It has nothing to do with my helping you."

"I tried to talk to the police," she said. "They don't believe anything I say. I can see it in people's eyes when they think I'm crazy."

"I don't care about crazy one way or the other. I just want to get at the truth."

"Do you carry a gun?" she asked.

"In my pocket." I touched my jacket, and then touched my desk. "A second one, just in case, in the top drawer."

"Do you like it? Having guns?"

"No, I don't. I've never found anything agreeable about guns. I don't have much choice about carrying one."

She looked at the sky outside. A wildfire burned in the hills to the south of the city. It was a long way off, but I thought I caught a ghost of smoke in the air from the open window. She turned around to look at me.

"Do you smell it?" she asked. "I hate fire. I'm afraid of it. You saw the burned house out at the ranch?"

I nodded. "I saw it."

"That was my home," she said, "When I was a girl. I still own the property. It belonged to my father and I was his only heir, if you can call it that. He didn't have a penny to leave me... just the land with avocado trees. The county got ready to take it for taxes years ago, but I paid them."

"What have you been doing there? It looks abandoned."

"It isn't abandoned," she said. "June is still there."

"What do you mean? June is still there? I thought you wanted me to find her."

There was a long silence. Finally she answered, her voice so soft I almost couldn't hear her. "You don't understand. I want you to find out what happened to her, Mister Crowe. I know where she is. I don't need you to find her."

"There's a lot more you aren't telling me," I said. "That's why I don't understand."

"My family was murdered," she said. "It wasn't an accident."

"I need more than that."

She shook her head and clasped her arms in front of her. "I can't tell you more than I already have," she said. "Not yet."

"You offer me a piece of birthday cake, show me an old manuscript, and ask me to find an imaginary girl named June…"

She looked away from the street and over her shoulder at me. "She isn't imaginary," she said. "I can show her to you."

"She's been dead for twenty-five years and you'll show her to me?"

"I'll show her to you . . . any time you say."

I had heard enough.

"I don't know how to beg," she said. "I've tried to never ask anyone for anything, ever."

My hands were spread. "I wouldn't even know how to start," I said. "Everyone seems to know something about everything except me."

"What would you charge just for trying?"

"Oh, hell, I don't know. You still owe me a piece of birthday cake, I guess."

Her face started out expressionless and then her smile flickered and flared into beautiful.

"You'll work for me for a piece of cake?"

"Why not?" I asked. "I don't know how much to charge for an imaginary job. Birthday cake is no crazier than the rest of it."

"It's a deal," she said.

She reached across the desk to shake my hand. Her fingers were warm, and felt strong. She and stood up.

"You didn't ask me what the second thing is," she said. "The other thing I want you to do."

I raised my eyebrows and waited.

"I want you to kill a man named Sal Cleveland."

"Sal Cleveland?" I was stunned. "That's the husband of the woman killed on your ranch. You want me to kill Sal Cleveland?"

"Yes, I know all about it." She shook her head once, impatient. "He hurt June. I want you to find out what he did to June and then I want you to kill him."

The crazy was getting dark, and I couldn't keep up with it.

"Back in 1922?" I asked. "I don't kill people, Miss Kahlo. I'm a licensed private investigator. That isn't what we do."

"I'll tell you a secret, Mister Crowe."

Her face stayed absolutely still. She slipped on her dark glasses, like a curtain coming down. "I see things," she said. "You're going to want to kill him. When you know everything, you're going to want to kill him more than anything in the world."

"You're seeing things that aren't there," I said. "I've never wanted to kill anyone. I want to see him arrested, if I can prove he was involved with his wife's death."

"Arresting him isn't good enough," she said and stood up. "You'll see."

She didn't seem like a woman who would notice if I stood up to show her out, so I stayed in my seat as she left. I gave her a half-salute and watched her pull the door closed behind her. She looked good, doing it. Her perfume lingered, faint as imagination, and I was surprised by the little pang of regret I felt at her leaving.

48

I sat for a while afterward and thought about things. It was still too early for a drink. I looked at the glass that Charlene Cleveland hadn't drunk from, sitting on the little shelf in the corner. I wasn't sure I'd ever use it again.

I had never been superstitious, but Charlene hung around, sort of like Annie's perfume. No one knew what happened to people when they died, or if anything at all happened, but I thought sometimes dead people hung around after they were gone. I planned to leave Charlene's glass where it was.

I needed to get busy with a manila file on my desk. A man had hired me to look into his business because he thought his manager was stealing him blind. It had been easy to prove him right. The crooked manager happened to be his brother-in-law, though, so he probably wasn't going to do much with the proof I had collected. I'd get paid, whatever he decided.

Annie Kahlo had put a damper on any urgency I felt about the day's work, and I looked out the open window at State Street and thought about things. After a while, I sat up and scribbled the man out a bill, sealed up the folder and got my hat. If I planned to chase butterflies, I'd better make a living while I could.

-Six-

"I'm not an accountant," I said, "But you really don't have to be a genius to figure this out."

I sat with a man named Roger Cameron in the office of a used car lot on Chapala Street. The place flogged cars that were high-end, or once had been. The lot was filled with shiny wire-wheeled Hispano-Suizas and Stutzes. There were a couple of concrete repair bays right outside the office door, but being Saturday morning, there were no workers around.

"How much is he stealing?"

"That's where you'll need an accountant," I said. "I just find out what and how."

He lit a pipe. After he shook out the match, he looked around on the desk for an ashtray. There wasn't one. Cameron owned the place, but he didn't come here much. He had let us in to the after-hours business with his own set of keys.

"I only opened this place on account of my wife," he said, and shook his head. "Give her no-good brother something to do. Look what I get for it."

I didn't like him much, but that didn't matter. I didn't like a lot of the people who hired me. He was outraged that his wife's family stole from him, but I knew the woman waiting in his car was his mistress. I figured he had gotten what he deserved, but no one was paying me to decide fair or foul.

"So how's he doing it?" he asked.

I laid it out for him. It wasn't very smart or very complicated.

Santa Teresa hosted a large community rich from oil, the movies, or crime. They flocked up from Hollywood and Bel Air and parked their bright, expensive automobiles in front of the Montelindo Hotel and went inside to drink and carry on and be seen with each other.

They attracted stragglers, the star-struck and leeches and con men, those who had lost a fortune and those who had never had one. They wanted flashy cars valeted from the front of the hotel, too, and settled for the cast-offs from the first group.

The business catered to both groups. If you were rich and you needed room in your garage for a strange little English or Italian sports car, he would sell your pre-war Cord or Auburn for too much money to some grateful moron who wanted to be just like you. He took ten percent off the top, and everyone walked away happy.

"I don't own a single one of these cars," Cameron said. "No inventory costs...repair and reconditioning on the side. This place should be pure profit, and it's not. It's bleeding money."

"It's a nice racket," I agreed.

"So where's all the money going?"

"It's simple. He's not reporting all of his sales," I said. "Since you don't own any of these cars, there's no inventory. If he sells a car and doesn't put the sale on the books, there's nothing missing as far as you're concerned. A lot of the people who consign cars with you don't need the money. They're just making space for new toys. Some of the actual owners might not check on their property for months, if they ever remember to check at all."

I gestured at the filing cabinet in the corner.

"If you check the consignment agreements in there, you'll find that a whole lot of cars supposed to be here on the lot are gone, sold a long time ago. You owe a lot of people a hell of a lot of money."

Light dawned in his eyes, and a red flush came into his face. He set his pipe on the corner of the desk. "He's selling cars and pocketing the money?"

"Sure he is," I said. "If an owner gets persistent, he admits the sale and dates the papers for a recent transaction and pays them off. Then he reports the sale to you, too. He's playing a shell game, and until now, staying a step ahead."

He stood up and walked to the window.

"It doesn't happen with all of them," I said. "He's probably got a good sense of when a jalopy can go missing for a while and not be missed. It adds up, though."

"I can't have him arrested," he said. "Robert is family."

"It would ruin your business if this got out," I said. "These cars are unusual. Sooner or later one of the consignors is going to recognize his old car running around with a new owner, and the balloon's going to go up. If rumors start that this place is shady, you'll be finished."

I looked out at the row of gleaming sedans and convertibles. A Packard cabriolet with ivory paint and red wheels sat nearby. I was tempted to ask the price, but I didn't. My Ford suited me better.

"What should I do?" he asked.

"Whatever he siphoned off is gone. People don't steal money so they can put it away for a rainy day. I'd get him out of here and get a bookkeeper to audit things, see what it will cost to clean up the mess."

I knew he wouldn't do it. He'd get rid of the brother-in-law and carry on with the crooked game. He'd tell himself he didn't have any choice. Maybe he didn't.

"How do you know what's in the filing cabinet?" he asked. "I assume Robert didn't just show you because you asked."

I looked at him steadily, and didn't answer. He seemed startled, opened his mouth and then closed it again.

"I'll stop by your office later in the week," he said. "Settle your bill."

I pulled a folded piece of paper from my breast pocket.

"Brought it with me," I said. "Save you the trip."

"Why don't you join us?" Mrs. Gardiner asked. "We haven't seen you in a long time."

I leaned over the back fence and looked into my neighbor's yard. After a minute, I nodded and went through the gate. They were sitting at a glass-topped table under an awning. I pulled out a wicker chair, and nodded at Dr. Gardiner. He wore a white shirt and tightly-knotted tie, even to sit in the yard. He nodded back and didn't say anything.

"There's a fire in the hills, you know," Mrs. Gardiner said. "You can smell the smoke."

I nodded. She poured a drink for me from an iced pitcher. I sipped it. The gin had been over-sweetened with vermouth, but I drank some anyway. Be a shame to waste it. "They aren't evacuating anyone yet," I said. "It isn't close enough. Montelindo had a scare last night, but the wind shifted the right way."

"I imagine we'll stay put," she said. "We don't scare very easily."

"I don't scare easily, either, but if they tell you to go, you should go."

"What exciting things have you been doing lately?" she asked. "Don't leave anything out."

Whenever I visited, she talked as though her husband wasn't there. She thought my life was exciting, and I told her a little about my cases sometimes, when it didn't

53

compromise a client. In this instance, I didn't really have a client. The last one was dead and the current one was apparently going to pay me in birthday cake.

I told them that a car had been found in an arroyo in front of a burned-out ranch house. A dead woman slumped behind the wheel, a woman who had been my employer until the day before she died. The police found the car because they were directed to the property by our neighbor, Annie Kahlo, who owned the land.

Mrs. Gardiner leaned forward and served me more martini. She was still a good-looking woman at her age, and I didn't mind talking to her.

"Annie is a lovely girl," she said. "I'm glad you two have finally met."

"Do you know her well? She's originally from Santa Teresa, isn't she?"

"I've known Annie for many years," she said. "Yes, she started out here. It was a hard start. Her parents were too much like children themselves to be raising two girls."

"You know she had a sister, then."

It wasn't really a question, but I waited for an answer just the same. If Annie wanted me to find out what happened to June, then this might be a source of information. Mrs. Gardiner seemed to know all of Santa Teresa's secrets; the last fifty years' worth, anyway. I decided to be blunt. "Annie has asked me to look into her sister's death," I said. "In that sense, she's a client. Anything you can tell me might help."

She looked at me blankly.

"After all of this time has gone by?" she asked. "Whatever for? There never was any mystery about it. The girl and her father died in a house fire at the ranch you were at today. I don't know if the house is still there."

"There are walls," I said. "Not much else, but it's there."

"They found the father's body, what was left of it. The little one had been completely incinerated. A terrible thing. Of course there were rumors."

"What kind of rumors?" I felt my instincts kick in, even though I didn't think of this as a real case. Mrs. Gardiner took a long drink from her martini glass as though giving herself a reason to talk.

"They said that the father had fallen into debt to local criminals, trying to keep his little farm afloat. He owed money he had no hope of paying, and in the end they took his life as payment. There were whispers he got shot before the house burned down. I never heard if they proved that, or even tried to."

"No sign of the girl's body?"

"No. So small." She was lost in some thought. "Nothing left. At the time, I hoped she got shot to death, too, and didn't have to experience the fire. Isn't that an awful thing to think?"

The doctor half-stood and refilled my glass. I was surprised to see it empty.

"It's a kindness," I said. "So the feeling was that they were murdered?"

"Oh, yes!" she said. "Absolutely murdered. The fire was intentionally set, and a lot of people felt it was a miracle it didn't start a major fire. It did spread a little way up the canyon, and it's hard to get any equipment up there. That probably got more attention than two dead people. It all happened a long time ago. I'm trying to remember what I can."

"They never caught anyone?"

"They never arrested anyone, even though the whole city knew who had done it. We all knew who the money was owed to, a low man named Cleveland. I remember his name, because of the city. A well-connected man back then, and the last I heard he's fat and happy, still right here in Santa Teresa."

I was shocked. "Sal Cleveland?" I asked. "Guy who owns the Star-lite Lounge out in Montelindo?"

She gave me an arch look. "I'm sure I wouldn't know about what he owns, or doesn't. His name *was* Cleveland, though, yes."

I looked at the flowers and the green grass, lost in thought. Somewhere nearby I heard the sound of a water sprinkler ratcheting back and forth.

"The dead woman they found on Annie Kahlo's ranch this morning," I finally said. "Her name was Charlene Cleveland. She was Sal Cleveland's wife, and I had just helped her get a divorce. I have a pretty good idea he killed her. Now we're talking about a twenty-five-year-old murder in the same spot, and his name turns up in that one, too. What are the odds?"

"You think he killed his wife? On Annie Kahlo's property?"

"The car slid off the road and ended up in her dooryard," I said. "I don't think it could be managed on purpose. More like Fate, maybe. I'm pretty sure he killed her though. Shot her in the face."

"Then it's simple. You should arrest him at once."

"I don't arrest people, Mrs. Gardiner."

"Well, shoot him then. You carry a gun. The police won't do anything to him."

I smiled. She was the second person who thought that my killing Cleveland would be a swell idea. We sat agreeably and drank our martinis. The glasses were crystal, the small yard was manicured, and it was all very nice. The third gin martini tasted a whole lot better than first one, and it was a big enough pitcher to last a while. The sun shone, and there were little bits of ash drifting down from the fire, like snowflakes. I felt glad of the awning over our heads.

"I do plan to talk to Mister Cleveland," I said. "If he's involved, I'll do something about it."

"I should hope you would."

I had a sudden thought. "Can I ask you something? If I were going to ask a woman to step out . . . socially, what would you suggest to do? Around here?"

"Do you mean on a date?" She looked surprised. "You don't seem like a man who needs advice about that."

"I don't socialize much since I've lived here," I said. "It was different in the military, or on the cops. I sort of fell into what was expected."

I hadn't known I would ask for her advice until I did it, and now I wasn't sure what I was asking for.

"This woman's different," I said. "She doesn't seem much like the night club type, and I don't know much else. She's sort of serious, and artistic, I suppose. Should I take her to the museum, maybe?"

"No one wants to go to the museum. Certainly not on a date."

She sipped her drink. A bowl of vanilla-colored orchids stood on the table, and she arranged them absently while she thought about it. Dr. Gardiner watched me steadily while she did it. He didn't bother me any. I was used to him.

"You're talking about Annie Kahlo, aren't you?" She eyed me steadily over the rim of her glass.

"Do you think that's a mistake?" I asked. "She might not welcome it."

She set her drink down and put her hands together.

"I think it's wonderful," she said. "She's very beautiful, you know, and she doesn't socialize much. She wouldn't be right for most people. I don't think many men would understand her."

I didn't understand her either, but I didn't think I should bring it up.

"You might like to go to a movie together," she said. "Especially since you're both shy. There's a new Dick Powell film playing that's very popular now. *Johnny O'Clock* it's called. Evelyn Keyes is in it. Gangsters and so on."

I considered it.

"Movies are very impersonal," she said. "Suited for people who don't really know each other. It can be easier later, if one or both of you wants to brush the evening off as not being a real date, or if you never want to see each other again."

"I think I'll have to see her again, regardless. Since I'm working for her."

"Well, a movie isn't a good way to get to know a person, especially if you do think you want to see that person again. A dinner is better, in a quiet place."

She was struck by an idea. "Have you tried Chinese food? It's becoming quite popular. They always had it in San Francisco, of course, but now you're finding it in other places. I like it. There's a new restaurant on Garden Street, on the corner of Garden and Cota. It looks authentic, paper lanterns and so on. The owners are real Chinese."

Dr, Gardiner spoke up. "Ortega," he said, and I looked at him, surprised. I hadn't known he could talk.

"Garden and Ortega Streets," he said. "That's where it is."

"Of course, my darling," she said. "You do the driving, so you should know."

I drained my third drink. I needed to go, while I could still walk in a straight line.

"That might be just the thing," I said. "I'll think about it."

"After dinner, you could talk or go dancing," she said. "There are all sorts of possibilities. I insist that you come and tell me about it afterward. It was my idea, after all."

I promised her I would, and left them there.

-Seven-

I took a nap to let the martinis fade. When I woke up, the afternoon had mostly gone, and the telephone shrilled in the kitchen. I found my feet and went to answer it.

"Coroner's officially pronounced," Rex Raines said. "Charlene Cleveland's death is a homicide."

"No kidding," I said.

"She's still on the table. They just finished with her. She had two broken legs, both compound fractures. Her insides were all busted up from the steering wheel. Runtz said she would have died anyway, even without the bullet."

"Still murder," I said. "The bastard."

"It gets worse. Her shoes were full of blood. Doc says the bullet killed her more or less instantly, so she couldn't have been shot up on the road. She was alive and bleeding in the wreck for a while before she got it. Makes a second car more likely. Someone walked down the drive and finished her where she sat."

"No fight, no struggle," I said. I could feel the heat in my face. "She was shot in cold blood while she sat there dying. You know what that means?"

"Means I'm going to need a statement from you," he said. "That's what it means. You know why. On account of her . . . relationship to you, and the check in her purse."

He sounded wary. Since the station was just up the street from my house, I told him I'd be there the next day. We agreed on a time, and he got ready to hang up.

"I planned to call you anyway," I said. "Want to ask you something."

"Fire away."

"I need to know how to get in touch with Sal Cleveland. I want to have a talk with him, someplace other

60

than at the Star-lite Lounge. They'll be watching for me there. He knows I can't just let this go."

"Stay away from it." His voice went flat.

"Charlene Cleveland was my client," I said. "We both know she got killed because she had the nerve to get a divorce. He killed her."

"That's my job to find out if he did," he said. "You stay away from him."

"I can go where you can't. Anything I find out, I'll gift wrap it and bring it straight to you."

He got quiet. I could hear the ghosts of other voices in the buzz on the line.

"What the hell," he sighed. "Who am I kidding? I don't care if you twist him up. Just take care he doesn't twist you first. He's been doing this for a long time. He has a lot of muscle, and he knows a lot of people. You'll be getting in deep."

He told me that Cleveland spent time in another bar he owned, a place on Olive Street called the Hi-Lo Club.

"I know the place," I said, surprised. "It's a dump. Not what I would expect for a guy owns the Star-lite.

"Maybe he's more at home in places like the Hi-Lo. Does his real business there, out of sight."

I started to thank him, but he had already hung up. I washed my face and went outside. The sky was a peculiar dark orange, a false sunset stretched from one horizon to the other over the rooftops across the street. The smoke from the wildfire caused it, but that didn't make it feel any less alien.

The fire burned just to the east of the city, somewhere in the Padre Leone hills. The radio said the highway south to Los Angeles might be closed soon. The canyon roads were all blocked, and they were evacuating some of the homes and ranches in the hills. We were in for a long summer. The sage

61

and chaparral were already as dry as tinder. Brush fires would be a regular thing this year, until the December rains came and turned the low mountains green.

As near as I could tell from the news reports, the fire burned somewhere in the neighborhood of the remains of the Kahlo ranch. It made me wonder how the old barn and groves had managed to survive all these years undisturbed. When the fires came and swept through the arroyos, fueled by the hot winds, there was nothing much anyone could do but leave the area. The Kahlo ranch should have been gone by now, wiped out by fire and then overgrown by new brush. It was still there, though.

Santa Teresa huddled against the ocean, mostly safe from whatever happened in the hills. It was a Spanish mission town, made of egg-crème stucco topped with red tile. A long time ago, the old priests had set up the missions to be a day's horseback ride apart, all the way up the coast from San Diego to San Francisco. I was never clear on why they did that in the first place, but a lot of the towns on the coastline had started out as missions.

I had been here a little over two years. When the war ended for me, I got discharged in Los Angeles. I had been stationed in Hawaii, and I liked it there. Sometimes I had thought that after the war, I might stay in Honolulu. I imagined myself marrying one of the native girls and having a normal, simple life a long way away from what I'd become. As it turned out, I came back stateside on a hospital ship, so staying in Hawaii wasn't one of my options. When I left the hospital, I didn't have much desire and even less reason to go back east. Southern California wasn't Hawaii, but it was a hell of a lot closer to it than Missouri.

I took my resume to the L.A. County sheriffs, and got taken on, but I changed my mind before my first day.

62

I had been a cop in St. Louis, and then a military cop, and I was sick of being a cop. It made me tired, wondering why I had spent so many years doing something so pointless. The people I arrested went out and did the same things again, like they had no choice. The people that I protected were worse characters than the ones I protected them from, at least half the time.

I answered an ad, got the necessary permits and permissions, and went to work for a private agency. After a few months working for them, a case took me up the coast to Santa Teresa. I stood in a telephone booth, looking for someone in the book. It's surprising how much detective work gets done in telephone directories. On impulse, I looked at the listings for private detectives in the city, and found there weren't any. A month later, I had a dusty office on State Street, and a dark house on Figueroa.

It was hard going for the first year, but I still had a little money coming in from the army, so I made do until business started to trickle in, and here I was, not doing too badly, either.

An unwritten rule of detective work: You don't get too involved with clients. You don't make judgments, and you don't take the things you saw personally. Between Annie Kahlo and Charlene Cleveland, I was breaking that rule. If I planned to break it, everything pointed at Sal Cleveland, so I knew I might as well start with him.

A guy sat on the running board of a new '47 Chevrolet coupe at the curb in front of my house. He wore a sleeveless white undershirt and a porkpie hat with a bright band. The car had a radio. The door was open and he had it running off the battery. I could hear the news, and I went down to the sidewalk to talk to him.

"What's new?" I asked him.

He peered up at me, and then took the cigarette out of his mouth. I thought I recognized him. He lived in the building across the street. I wondered if he was the one who lived in back and sold Mexican marihuana out of his kitchen. Judging by the new car with its fancy radio, the reefer business wasn't half bad.

"They say it might rain," he said. "Brother, I hope so."

I looked up. The strange orange sky had darkened around the edges. Flakes of ash from the fire drifted down and swirled in eddies of air. It didn't look like rain to me, and I said so.

"You never know," he said. "This time of year, it comes in off the ocean in a hurry. Hard rain is what we need. This fire's already gotten close to Montelindo. Radio says they're getting people out of there."

I was surprised. Montelindo was a wealthy community five or six miles south of the city. I didn't think about the filthy rich being troubled by things like fire. I pictured a black, smoking landscape dotted with swimming pools.

"That close?" I said. "Last I heard, it still burned up in the canyons."

"Winds take it places fast," he shrugged. "It could go anywhere. Why we need rain, and a lot of it."

"Let's hope so, then," I said. "Out of control fire is a bad thing."

"That's the thing about these fires. They aren't out of control. Once they get going, they go where they want and do what they want. There isn't any way to stop them. They're the ones in control and they burn until they don't feel like it anymore."

A few blocks away, a siren started up, rising from a growl to a wail. It seemed to be headed in our general direction, and we both looked across the street at the darkening rooftops.

"Most trouble is like that," he said. "It stops when it wants to, and not before."

"Or when it rains," I said. "You can always hope for rain."

We nodded at each other like we each had any idea what the other was talking about, and I turned to go.

"Wait a second," he said. "I want to ask you something."

I stopped and waited.

"They say you're a private detective," he said. "That means you work with the cops?"

"No," I said. "Sometimes we're on the same side, and sometimes we're not. I don't work for them though."

"You got a card?"

I fished out my wallet and gave him one.

"I might need you sometime," he called after me.

I waved at him without turning around. I didn't think he had a clue what I did, but who knew. There weren't enough new clients out there to be stingy with my cards. I went up the steps onto Annie's veranda. She answered the door before I touched the bell.

"I had a feeling you were coming," she said.

Her braided hair hung over her shoulder. She wore something loose and cotton that looked hand-painted. I caught her fragrance, something that went well with the smell of the flowers wafting from the hallway behind her. Her face was composed, and her dark eyes stayed on mine. My breath felt a little short.

"Do you want to come in?"

65

"I'm just here for a minute," I said. "I wanted to ask you something."

Her expression lightened. "You've found out something about June?"

"Not exactly. Not yet. I wanted to ask if you'd like to have dinner with me."

She stared at me. Her expression changed to something very close to fear. She had one hand on the door, and looked ready to swing it closed in my face.

"Dinner?" she said. "I wouldn't . . . I wouldn't know what to do."

"You wouldn't have to do anything," I said. "It would just be having dinner with me."

We stood there looking at each other. Her fingers tightened on the doorframe.

"Now?" she asked. Her voice was barely a whisper.

"No," I said. "Not now. Tomorrow night. I'll come at eight o'clock."

She nodded. Then I stood back and let her close the door.

-Eight-

I sat in Rex Raine's office in the back of the Santa Teresa station. The police stenographer sat off to one side. She was a young woman with brown hair and a dark green dress that looked too hot to wear on a day like today. She looked at me through the lenses of her glasses like I was some kind of rare bug. Raines stared up at the ceiling while I gave my statement. Since she seemed more interested in what I said than he did, I talked to her.

I said that Charlene Cleveland had come into my office on May 28, a Wednesday. I knew that because I had looked it up on my desk calendar. She was married to Sal Cleveland, a man who owned a place called the Star-lite Lounge in Montelindo, and probably a lot of other things. Mrs. Cleveland told me her husband had been physically abusive throughout their year-long marriage, and that his occasional slaps had progressed into beatings and humiliations in the bedroom.

She hadn't been a babe in the woods, but she got tired of being a punch. She had talked about leaving him and he had threatened her. She wanted incontestable grounds for divorce. There was rarely such a thing, especially if you had connections. I had done some rooting around, and I got lucky.

I stopped talking for a moment, and the stenographer looked up. I wasn't ready to tell the cops about the photograph of the Mexican prostitutes in the truck. I didn't have any reservations about selling him out. He had canceled our deal when he killed his wife. I didn't know how to explain the photo without involving Danny Lopez. I had a hunch I should hold the information in reserve anyway, so I lied a little.

I told them Sal spent a lot of his time in the company of prostitutes and dancers, and I had taken pictures of him straying. A packet of glossy photographs would give a judge enough reason to grant Charlene a divorce with minimal fuss. It made it cheaper for Sal to cave in. It made for a common enough scenario. He was willing to trade my photos of adultery for his wife's freedom.

There wasn't much else to tell. I would have told them that I liked Charlene Cleveland a little bit, even if I had turned her down. I would have told them she had a little bit of a spark, and that she ran around with a sleazy crowd but hung onto some dignity. I would have told them that no one should have shot her in the face for it, but it wasn't what we were here for, so I kept it to myself.

When I finished talking, Raines nodded and the steno girl shut down her machine and stood up. She smoothed her dress over her hips and turned her back to me while she packed it away. Her glasses hid an awfully good figure.

When she was gone, Raines stood up and raised the venetian blinds on the office window. He slid the glass up to let in some air. I could hear the cops beneath the window, getting into and out of their prowl cars, coming and going. He stood and looked out, and then turned away and came back to the desk.

"You're not thinking of doing something stupid, are you?" he asked.

"Stupid like what?"

He flicked my question away, irritated. "You're not going to let this pass, Crowe, and we both know it. Problem is, you don't know what you're getting yourself into here."

"Cleveland slapped her around," I said. "And worse. She had a lot more sand than he gave her credit for, and she got free of him."

"You don't know what she got into after she got her divorce papers, or who she mixed up with," he said. "It could have been a new boyfriend that killed her."

"Cleveland killed her. We both know it."

"Right now, I have as much evidence against you as I do him."

I thought about things for a minute. When a minute wasn't enough, I lit a cigarette to buy another.

"What's the deal with Cleveland, as far as you know?" I asked. "What's his racket?"

"You must know about him," he said, eyebrows raised. "Your line of work, you have to have crossed his path."

I knew plenty about him. "A little bit," I lied. "Like everyone. I've heard his name mentioned a lot of times. He's connected. East Coast?"

Raines crossed to his desk and picked up a half-cup of cold coffee. He inspected the surface of it for a moment and then poured it into a metal trash can. He pulled a bottle of scotch from a drawer and another cup. When he had poured a pair of short drinks, he pushed mine over and tasted his.

"He isn't really connected," he said. "Not like you think. He has his thing here, a couple of clubs, a string of hookers, some dope. He has an off-track operation going over a dentist's office on upper State. He doesn't aim for anything too big, doesn't try to expand, and the LA boys leave him alone."

I tasted my drink. I wasn't sure how clean the cup was, but the scotch was swell stuff for a cop's budget. Raines sat on the corner of the desk, deep in thought, looking out the window again. "I don't think he does the whole gangster thing for the money, exactly," he said. "He does it for kicks. I think it's a cover for what he really likes to do."

"You don't say." My ears pricked up. "What does he really like?"

"Hurting people, I think," Raines mused. "He likes to hurt people. Beat them up, scare them once in a while, kill them."

"What I've heard, too," I nodded.

"He lives the life, but it's like all the criminal stuff just gives him a good reason to be a psychopath."

"Psychopath," I said. "Big word for a cop."

He looked at me and smiled. He held the neck of the bottle out, and I put up my cup for another taste.

"I went to college for a year before the war," he said. "Must have stuck, some of it. Anyway, Cleveland's bent, and being a gangster gives him a way to be bent."

"What about scaring people?"

"That's the thing," he said. "He doesn't just like to scare with brass knuckles and guns. He also says he does magic."

"Magic? Like tricks?" I smiled.

"It isn't a joke," he said. "He makes his people believe he can control things. Supernatural stuff. The talk about magic makes people nervous."

"I don't believe in magic," I said.

"Lot of other people do. It isn't like a magician, with a rabbit and a hat. More like voodoo, reading cards, seeing the future."

"Funny life path," I said. "Major crime boss becomes sideshow card reader?"

"I've seen stranger things," he said. "Maybe he thinks it's fun. Anyway, he's been doing his thing out here for more than twenty years, I guess."

He swirled a finger in the air, indicating the building around us. "A lot of people here think he keeps a status quo in this city," he said. "Keeps the really bad stuff from L.A. or Frisco from moving in. As long as he doesn't go overboard, Cleveland gets a pass on a lot of little things."

"Little things like killing people?"

"I'm not saying that," he said. "But he gets the benefit of the doubt when the evidence is a bit flimsy, that's for sure."

"How about a little thing like shooting his wife? Will he get a pass on that?"

"If I get a solid case, I'll put the cuffs on him, same as anyone would. What do you think the odds are I'll ever get any kind of case on him?"

We stared at each other.

"I think I may go talk to him," I said. "Introduce myself again."

I drained my scotch and set my cup on the edge of the desk. I stood up and settled my hat. "I'll let you know how it turns out."

"Do that," he said. "And Crowe, I know you think you're a tough nut, and maybe you are, a little bit. This guy's crazy, though . . . dangerous crazy. Keep it in mind."

Rain fell, cold and heavy. It came in quickly, spattered the sidewalk to get my ankles wet, and then tapered off again. I could sense the huge, slow clouds over my head, invisible in the black sky. The fires in the hills above the city were probably already dead or dying from the wet air.

The storefronts I passed were all dark. I didn't need to look both ways before I crossed the streets, since there was no traffic, but I did anyway. I was in no particular hurry. An occasional light flickered in an upstairs window;

someone who couldn't sleep, or was afraid of the dark. I didn't blame them. I was going to see Sal Cleveland and I was a little afraid, too.

Light from a pair of headlights splashed across the puddles, and then a white police car with black fenders followed them around the corner. It slowed to a crawl as it passed, so the two cops inside could look me over. They decided I wasn't worth getting wet for, and the driver ground the gears and the car moved off. I walked alone again.

An aqua-colored neon sign on the next corner said Club and nothing else. I went up three steps and tried the door. It was unlocked, so I pulled it open and went inside. The place was mostly dark. Chairs were turned upside down on tables. It smelled like the usual mix of rye whiskey and smoke, but the stink of something nasty lay underneath, something that I really didn't want to identify.

I shook the rain off my hat and walked over to the staring woman behind the bar. Her eyes bulged, and she needed to wash her hair. She turned slightly sideways, like she was ready to take a punch, or give one.

"Your boss in?" I asked.

She glared at me, her mouth slightly agape. When it became clear she wasn't going to answer me, I shrugged and moved to the back of the room. I went up a short hallway and found a man sitting in an office across from the restrooms. His desk was covered in green felt, and he had a pack of playing cards spread out in a pool of light on its surface. He was playing solitaire.

"Sal?" I asked. "Remember me?"

He looked up at me and nodded. His green eyes looked flat, painted-on, as though whatever lived inside of his head didn't want to be seen. His skin was smooth and tanned. He was a good-looking guy, almost pretty, the kind that could afford to throw a woman away. He didn't look much like a hoodlum, but I had been around long enough to know that no one really looks much like what they are.

"It's only been a little while, snooper," he sneered. "I remember a bum like you who crosses me a lot longer than a few days. Practically forever, I remember that."

His voice sounded hard, but had an undertone, a vaguely effeminate whine that didn't match the tough talk very well.

"You practice your lines in a mirror?" I asked.

The air changed behind me, and I looked over my shoulder. The strange woman had slipped in behind me. She stood against the wall, cradling a shotgun under her arm. She looked comfortable with it. It didn't quite point at me.

"Tell you what I don't appreciate," he said. "Three in the morning is my favorite time. It's when I do my best work. I don't appreciate being barged in on."

"I'm looking for some information about what happened to your wife."

He looked up at me without expression.

"You and a lot of other people," he said. "You think I'll tell you anything about that bitch?"

"No, not really."

"Then what the hell are you doing here?"

"I came to tell you something," I said. "I came to tell you that she was my client, and she still is."

"You work for dead people?" He laughed.

"This time I do. I have a pretty good idea how she ended up at the bottom of a cliff with part of her head blown off. I'm not going to just let it go."

"I heard you were about the only guy in the city who wasn't taking off her skirt," he said. "Funny you'd go all romantic about her. What do you plan to do about it?"

"I haven't decided," I said. "Except I'm not going to let it go."

"Maybe . . ," he said, and then found something interesting in the game spread in front of him. After a minute, he tore his attention away from it and looked back at me. "Maybe you don't know the half of what you're getting into," he said. "Maybe what happened to my wife offended you, and you feel like you have a duty to be a hero. I can forgive you for that."

He spread his hands expansively. "I even admire you a little bit for that. I don't meet a lot of heroes. But maybe now you've fallen into something else, and you don't even know it yet. You're stepping on my toes and you have no idea. You're smack dab in the middle of something that's going to get you killed.

He turned a card over and looked at it, mouth pursed. He cupped his hand so I couldn't see. After a minute, he put it face down, and his eyes slid up to meet mine. I saw something dark and old in them; something I didn't much like.

"I know a lot about magic," he said.

"I heard something about that."

"You might want to keep it in mind," he said. "I want to make you disappear, you'll disappear."

"I think you know a lot about doing tricks. That isn't the same thing as magic."

He picked up the card and flicked it at me. It hit the front of my raincoat and fell on the floor face-up. It was the three of spades.

"Tough guy," he mused. "We'll see."

I bent down and picked up the card. I looked at it for a moment, and then I put it away in my pocket. Cleveland stared at me.

"You're missing a card now," I said. "Guess you'll have to get a new deck."

Something moved, deep in his eyes, and gave me another glimpse of what lived in there. I looked at the woman.

"I know the way out," I said.

She answered by jabbing the shotgun into my ribs. It hurt. I pushed the barrels away.

"We'll see about you later, sister."

I went up the hall, crossed the empty bar, and let myself out into the rain. The bartender followed me out.

"Stay the hell away from here," she said. "Creeper."

"Your boss keeps you chained beneath the bar when he sleeps?"

She bared her teeth at me. The rain plastered her hair to her cheek. "He doesn't sleep," she said. "Ever."

She pushed at me again with the business end of the shotgun. I was wet and my ribs still hurt, so I was in a bad mood. I had half a mind to take the gun away and shoot her with it. I didn't, though. I turned to go.

A woman stood on the sidewalk across the street, holding an umbrella over her head. She was a dim silhouette, watching us. I wondered what she was doing out at that time of the morning, but in that neighborhood all sorts of things went on that didn't add up. I walked away. My suit soaked right through to my shirt, and the cold fabric rubbed my skin and stung like hell.

I didn't look back until I got to the next corner. The bartender had gone back inside, and the woman with the umbrella was nowhere to be seen. As near as I could tell, no one else had followed me, so there was nothing else to do but go home.

-Nine-

My ribs still hurt from the night before. The shotgun had left two raw red tracks on my chest. The ugly woman had jabbed me harder than I'd thought. A shot of whiskey helped, and a couple of aspirin tablets and a sticking plaster helped a little more. I went to the office and did my day. When a decent amount of it was gone, I went home to get ready for my dinner date.

I knocked on Annie Kahlo's door exactly at eight. She opened it and stepped onto the porch without saying anything. She wore a white cotton shift, cinched at the waist with an embroidered belt. There were copper-colored stripes on the neckline, and hints of gold at her throat and wrists. I had the absurd idea Nefertiti would look like this if she stepped from her ancient tomb to have dinner with me.

She paused at the top of the steps and looked at the street, as though she needed to decide something, and then she slipped on a pair of dark glasses. At the curb, I opened the car door for her and we made the ride to the Garden Street restaurant in near silence.

The room was red and orange and green. The lights inside were soft, and the neon sign outside of the window blinked Chinese Food, over and over. There didn't seem to be any pattern to the on-and-off, and after a minute I gave up trying to find one. We waited for our food, and I looked at Annie, across the table. She still had her dark glasses on and the electric letters reflected in her lenses blinked at me.

"Chop suey," she said. "I never had it before. I don't go out very much."

"It's like a lot of things," I said. "You don't know until you try it. I like it okay."

She picked up her water glass and drank. Her throat was elegant. When she put it back down, the ice cubes chimed gently.

"I lived in England for a while," she said. "By myself. It took me a long time to get used to the food there. Maybe I never really did."

She didn't say anything else for a little while. She rested her forearms on the tabletop and slowly turned the bracelet on her left wrist, around and around. Her hands were long and lithe, with the nails cut short. They were strong—an artist's hands. She saw me looking, and put them beneath the table, onto her lap.

"I lived in Mexico after that," she said. "I liked the food better there."

"Sounds exotic," I said. "Why did you come back to Santa Teresa?"

She didn't answer.

A young woman brought small white cups and a pot of green tea. Her nylon uniform had a high, Oriental collar. Its fabric made scratching noises as she unloaded the tray. She poured and left.

"What places have you been to?" she asked.

"I'm from St. Louis," I said. "I went to Hawaii during the war. I was stationed there. I had been a cop in St. Louis, so they made me a military cop. I enlisted, but I was too old to do anything else. I landed on a couple of islands, but mostly I did base patrol in Pearl Harbor. It wasn't much of a war, for me."

I felt the old, familiar humiliation come creeping in. I had gotten an easy ticket out. I waded into a bar fight in Honolulu, and a sailor had hit me over the head with a bottle. I woke in a naval hospital in San Diego. When I got well enough, Uncle Sam said I had done my share and gave me a discharge.

"My mother lived in Hawaii," she said. "She's from there, and she went back when my sister and I were small. I'd like to go there. If I ever make it, I won't come back."

"I liked it there," I said. "More than any place I've ever been."

"So why did you come back?"

I came back for this. I came back for you. The words formed themselves in my mind, surprising me. I hoped I hadn't said them out loud. "I didn't have much choice," I said. "I came back on a hospital ship. Some drunk broke a bottle over my head, and his buddies kicked the hell out of me while I was out of it. I woke up in a military hospital in San Diego."

"Why did they do that?"

"No reason, really." I shrugged. "I broke up a bar fight. Enlisted men don't like cops any more than people in the real world do."

She sipped her tea. Her dark glasses watched me over the rim. Hawaiian parents explained the slightly exotic cast to her features; the delicate nose and brow.

"I'm glad you came back," she said.

I was glad, too. I wondered if I had fallen in love with her. It hadn't happened to me in such a long time that I wasn't sure I remembered what it felt like. I reached for one of the two fortune cookies that sat on a plate between us. Annie's hand gripped my wrist, hard.

"What is it?" I asked. "What's wrong?"

"You shouldn't open those…not ever. They aren't a good idea, for you."

After a few seconds, she took her hand away. My skin stayed warm where she had touched it.

"If you say so," I said.

She looked down at her tea, and I looked around the room. Painted dragons crawled over the walls. I counted ten of them, moving over the tops of the booths, ignoring the diners below them.

There were paper lanterns, too, with small bulbs inside bright colored veils. I liked them. There was no music except for the faint sounds of conversation around us, and the occasional clink of crockery. The restaurant felt warm, and I wanted it all to last longer than the time it would to take us to finish our meal.

"What's the worst thing you ever did?" she asked.

"That would be a long list of things," I smiled.

"The worst thing," she insisted. "Tell me."

I thought about the war, and my marriage. I thought about the ugliness I had seen as a private eye. Another memory came up, unbidden.

"I grew up in St. Louis," I said. "My parents never let me have a dog. I always wanted one."

"Why don't you have a dog now?" she interrupted. "You live alone."

"I couldn't take care of one," I said. "I'm away a lot. Anyway, there was a house I passed by on my way home from school. I was about fifteen years old, I think. I usually walked by myself. A young dog stayed tied up in the side yard, not much older than a puppy."

"What kind of a dog?" she asked.

"Just a mongrel," I said. "A medium-sized dog, brown, with a white patch on his face. After a while, it started to seem like he watched, waiting for me to pass in the afternoons. I started to save a little of my lunch for him, and I'd throw him some bread over the fence."

79

The woman brought covered bowls to the table and set them down. She took the lids off. They held steamed rice and some kind of vegetables. It smelled good.

"Like I had a dog, even though I didn't," I said.

Annie nodded. She didn't look at the food; her attention focused on me.

"One day when I went by, a big man with a red face stood in the yard. He was holding the dog's rope and beating it with a cane. He was drunk. I remember the sound of it, like a mallet on a steak, and the dog screaming. It sounded like a child. I knew the man meant to kill the dog, and he had nearly finished."

"What did you do?"

"I went over the fence. It was white and made of pickets." I showed her my right palm. She took it and looked at the white scar running across it from wrist to the base of my fingers. She kept my hand in hers when I started to speak again.

"I took the cane away from him," I said. "I surprised him, I guess, and he hardly resisted. He told me to mind my business and get out of his yard. Then I stopped him talking."

Neither of us said anything for a little while. I looked at the untouched food and Annie looked at me.

"I beat him badly, Annie, almost to death. His face was covered in blood. Even after he fell unconscious, I still kept hitting him with his cane. When it broke, I threw it away and started kicking him. People came and pulled me away. There was yelling and shouting, but I didn't hear anything but the dog whimpering and crying."

There seemed to be no air in the room. I felt like I was gasping, but my voice sounded normal.

"I untied the rope from the dog's neck and picked it up. I carried it out of the yard and took it home. My parents

80

didn't say a word. The next day, I could hardly get out of bed. I think I sprained every muscle in my body, between beating him and carrying the dog so far. When I limped downstairs, my mother was nursing the dog. They always said we couldn't have a dog, but he lived with us and they never said a word about it."

"The dog lived happily ever after," she said. "It's a good story."

I looked at her. Her smile was beautiful and so focused on me that it lightened the air just enough.

"He did, I suppose." I felt my own smile begin, despite myself. "He stayed with my parents after I grew up and moved out. Lived until 1940, if you can believe it, he was almost nineteen years old when he died. He took a drink of water, looked at my mother and fell over, gone. She called me on the telephone at work, crying. I worked on the St. Louis police by that time, and they had a job finding me to tell me there was an emergency with my folks."

I reached for Annie's plate, I took a spoon and served us both from the bowls of food, before it got cold. She picked up her chopsticks and looked at them.

"You can use a fork," I said. "It's okay. It's why they give you one."

"As long as no one minds."

"I buried him in the back yard," I said. "Then I went back to my apartment across town and got drunk. I woke up sitting out on the fire escape . . . miracle I didn't fall off and end up splashed on the sidewalk."

I tasted the food. I was suddenly starving.

"No one ever came after me about the man," I said. "His neighbors didn't tell the police who beat him, if they knew. I heard later he stayed in the hospital for a month. I learned something about myself that scared me. There's a side of me that isn't good. Whatever I let loose that day was just as bad as he was, and I couldn't control it. I learned I wasn't what I thought I was. Maybe no one is."

"You should have killed him, and you didn't," she said. "That's the worst thing you ever did."

I put my fork down and stared at her. She met my look.

"If you saw him for what he was, you should have killed him," she repeated. "You didn't finish it, you let him go, so he could get better and cause more hurt. Maybe he did worse things later. You should have killed him."

I didn't know what to say, and she became absorbed with her food, so I let it go. For a little while we ate, and didn't talk. The waitress cleared plates and brought ceramic bowls filled with clear broth.

"What is this?" Annie asked. "What's floating in it?"

"I think it's an egg."

"I'll leave it alone, if you don't mind."

"I don't mind," I said. "I think I'll join you."

An old Chinese woman sat quietly on a high stool beside the kitchen doors. Rubber bands trapped her gray hair, but it wanted to fly away from her face anyway. She watched Annie intently. When she caught my glance, her eyes disappeared in a brief toothless smile. Her mouth moved, forming words I couldn't possibly hear from across the room. When she finished speaking, she went back to watching Annie.

"Do you know her?" I gestured with a small movement of my chin.

"I think I do…from somewhere. Maybe a dream."

She looked over at the woman. Something passed between them, though I couldn't say what it was. Annie turned back to me.

"When you were very small, what were you afraid of?" she asked. "What is it that scares you, even now?"

I couldn't tell if she was serious. Her eyes gave away nothing behind the dark glasses, so I looked at her mouth and the tilt of her head. I decided she was.

"Who hid under your bed and who walked around in your dreams? When you looked out your bedroom window at night, what stood under the streetlight and looked back at you?"

I thought about it.

"I was afraid of the stars," I said. "If I looked at them for too long, I realized that I was in space. It's too big, black and empty, just too far from place to place."

She nodded. "I know. And if you make it to the next place safely, sometimes…"

"…it's too bright," I finished. "The light is white, and empty."

"Sometimes, though, it isn't empty at all," Annie said. "Sometimes it's wonderful."

She hesitated, looked around the restaurant, and then made a decision. She took off her dark glasses and put them into her purse on the seat beside her. When she looked up, her eyes were bottomless. I was astonished at my own words. They hurt my throat.

"You're going to break my heart. Maybe more than once."

Her smile was beautiful.

"Good," she said.

After dinner, we left the car at the curb and walked the downtown streets. We found an open place that sold an Italian ice cream called gelato. I'd never tried it before, and I liked it. Of course, I'd yet to try any kind of ice cream I didn't like just fine. We both chose lemon, and we found a low wall to sit on while we ate.

"You said you were afraid of the stars when you were little," she said. "How about monsters? Did you have any?"

I thought about it carefully. "Yes. My monster lived under my bed, like they usually do."

The night was warm, laden with the smells of the summer city, which was cooling down after the hot day. There was a fragrance of earth and flowers, sweetness beneath the exhausted odors of the street. Annie sat quietly beside me in the darkness. Her profile was improbably lovely, barely caught by the streetlights.

"He lay on his back beneath me, looking up. My bed was a black pool, a drowning pool, and he looked up from the bottom. I floated on the top."

Annie shifted in her seat. Her voice was soft. "What did he look like? Your monster?"

"I don't know. I never saw him."

A breeze drifted across, rustling leaves. The soft air carried a dusting of music, a lonely soprano voice in a sad, perfumed opera. A siren, blocks away, played in the background.

"He liked things to stay that way," I said. "Black and quiet. If anything went past the edge of the mattress, like my hand or arm, or even the corner of my blanket, it showed up as red on the edge of the pool. It upset him. He didn't like it, and I heard him shifting around beneath me. He swam up quickly to chop it off."

Annie turned her head to look at me. Even in the dark, I could sense her eyes, liquid and still.

"Sometimes if I drifted off, nearly asleep, I'd hear him, on his back directly beneath me, starting to move

84

around. I'd need to pull my hand or the edge of the covers in quickly, before he chopped it off."

The soprano voice floated by again. This time it brought some strings with it, some cellos and violins that told me how lonely I was. I thought about the cigar in my pocket, but left it where it was.

"I had to be still so his pool would stay black, the way he liked it," I finished. "All black and soothing. Do you see?"

She didn't answer, and turned her head to look out at the street. After a while, she reached over and touched my mouth. Her fingertips were warm.

"All black and soothing," she said. "I see your world. I recognize it."

We sat together and watched the city, and for a long time we didn't say anything else.

"How about you?" I said. "Did you have a monster when you were small?"

She was silent, and I didn't think she would answer. I was searching for something to say when she spoke.

"I have monsters now," she said. "There are monsters everywhere I go, everywhere I look. They follow me. I'm never safe from them . . . ever."

I was startled by her vehemence.

"Only my pictures help," she said. "When I can capture them, keep them on paper in pencil and paint, then I feel safe for a little while. I am safe for a little while."

"I'm sorry," I said, and wondered why I said it.

"Don't be sorry. I've made a lot of money from my monsters. It's why I'm in so many picture books for children. Children know about monsters. They understand my pictures. I guess the money keeps me safe, too. It means I don't have to go outside."

85

Headlights flooded the dark street. An automobile rolled slowly by us. It was a big car, and I had a sense that the driver looked over at us when he passed. I didn't think he could see us in the shadows.

"It isn't all monsters," she said. "It's wonderful and magic, too. It's all so beautiful that it makes me cry sometimes."

"Do you think so?" I asked. I was interested.

"Yes," she nodded. "I try to remember the colors, and numbers can be so beautiful that it's overwhelming . . ."

She trailed off, and she seemed to be deciding whether or not to tell me something else. I waited.

"I'm not just in children's' books," she said. "I have two paintings that are in museums. I've never seen them, not hung in the museums, I mean. I'd like to go someday, but I probably never will."

"Someday, I'll take you to see them. Deal?"

She stared at me. I could see the gleam of her eyes in the low light. Finally, she made a decision and nodded. "Deal."

I leaned over and kissed her. I kept my hands in my lap, and the kiss was nearly chaste. It was more than enough for the moment, though. When we broke it, I felt cool air on my cheek. Her tears were drying on my skin.

-Ten-

"I had a swell time," I said.

We stood at the top of her steps. There were yellow bulbs in glass shades on either side of the front door with a cloud of moths trying to get to them.

"Tomorrow is Saturday," I said. "I'm not doing anything, if you'd like to go for a ride or something."

She was looking at the street, and didn't seem to hear my question.

"I wanted to tell you something else," she said. "About my sister. And I want to show you something."

I felt a flash of hurt. "Sure."

I heard the clink and clatter of brass as Annie fumbled with her keys and got the lock open, and then we were inside the coolness of her hallway. I smelled orchids and clean water and old wood. She didn't turn on the lamps, but enough illumination came through the windows that I could see to follow her.

At the far end of the hall, a door showed a crack of gold at the bottom. When we got there, she hesitated for a moment and then pushed it open. We went in.

We were in a long, narrow room that ran along the back of the house. I had no idea what the space might have originally been used for. Floor lamps and table lamps were lit on every surface, a mismatched collection of bulbs joined in yellow force to keep the room's natural darkness checked. The effect was radiant, soft, like firelight. The high ceiling was a lattice of exposed wooden beams and joists, rising and disappearing upwards into shadows the golden light couldn't reach.

The walls were wood, too, although I could see very little of them. Every inch of space was hung with art, ranging

87

from enormous painted canvases to colored sketches not much larger than postage stamps. Drawings lay stacked in corners, and tacked to the doorframes. Watercolor washed every surface. A red-checkered jester looked down at me with enormous black eyes, a little girl with a yellow balloon chased her dog, and lush volcanic slopes wrapped themselves in mist. The moon was everywhere.

"What do you think?" Annie asked.

She stood with her back to me, looking at an easel that held a blank sheet, suspended and waiting. Crayons and tubes of color covered the surface of her table. There were brushes and pens, bottles of ink, tins of oil and turpentine.

I looked around me, turning my hat in my hands. "Did you do all this?" I asked.

She looked back at me, surprised. "Of course," she said. "No one comes in here but me. You're the first to see it."

I wanted to look at a painting hanging behind the work table, directly in my line of sight. It was very dark, and amid all the gold-washed color it drew my eye.

"May I?"

"I knew you'd go right to that one," she said. "I painted it for you, I think."

I saw a small island in the middle of a vast winter lake. A full moon caught the snow-covered branches of the pines on shore. Yellow lights filtered through the trees, perhaps the lit windows of a cabin.

"Do you remember?" she asked. "You've been there. We've both dreamed it."

I had no idea what she was talking about. I peered more closely at the image. The lights I thought I had seen on shore were gone now, and the island was dark. The surface of the lake had been so beautifully rendered that the water seemed to sparkle.

"I'd like to go there," I said.

"It's all still there," Annie said. "It hasn't gone anywhere."

She had come up beside me and watched raptly, as though she expected something to happen. In repose, her face was beautiful, clean, and elegant. Her profile belonged on ancient money. Her voice was hardly more than a breath.

"It's all still there," she said, again. "Waiting."

I didn't have a clue as to what she talked about. I saw the old manuscript on the corner of her table. I touched the top page.

"One sister's name is Secret . . ." I read.

Annie's hand slid up my shoulder and then around the back of my neck. Her palm felt warm. She turned me to her. I saw dark eyes, and then we were kissing. She was like cinnamon, the taste of her…her lips on my mouth, my hands in her hair, kissing her cinnamon neck…we were together, entangled until there was no more air between us and none in the room…all the oxygen had turned to cinnamon.

At some point, there in the lights and colors, I realized she was crying again. I wiped at a tear with the pad of my thumb and tried to ask her what was wrong, but she shushed me and led me up the long hall to her bedroom.

I didn't understand her, and I didn't understand what was happening to me. I wondered if I was getting myself lost. I decided that if I was, I couldn't get there fast enough.

Sometime in the night, I woke up. Sleep didn't seem much different than being awake right then. I looked over at Annie. Even in the darkness I could tell she was awake and looking at me.

"You said you had something you wanted to tell me about your sister," I said. "And show me. Then we were busy, and I forgot."

My voice hurt my throat. She slid over in the dark and reached up to turn on a table lamp beside the bed. When she turned back, she was smiling.

"We were busy, weren't we?" she mused.

Her long hair fell wild around her face. I wanted to touch it, so I did. She pulled me to her and we didn't speak again for a little while. I might have slept again, because I smelled the ocean and felt the rocking of a boat beneath me in the dark. I felt the beginnings of some kind of deep peace.

When I opened my eyes Annie's face hovered over mine and she spoke to me.

"I know something about the woman in the car," she said. "The one at the ranch."

I came awake.

"The woman that got killed?" I asked. "What do you know about that?"

"I saw her."

I sat up and propped myself on an elbow. Annie's face registered fear, and I reached out and touched her while we talked.

"How do you mean, you saw her?"

"I was there."

"You were . . . *there*?"

I had an image of Annie wandering an unlighted twist of canyon road with nothing nearby but an unlighted property; only a burned out house and not another soul for miles.

"What in the world were you doing out there?"

She looked at me, eyebrows raised.

"Why wouldn't I? The ranch is mine. I'll always keep it, because it's all I have. My mother left us when I was very small, and June was a baby. It was always my job to look out for my sister. I used to pretend that she was my baby."

She propped her chin on a bare knee, and remembered. "I was the only mother she ever had," she said. "When I turned seventeen, there was trouble, and my father sent me away to keep me safe."

"What kind of trouble?"

She shook her head.

"I can't tell you, not now. Later, maybe. Anyway, I left. I lived with my aunt in New York. That's where I first started taking art classes. I liked New York, even though I missed June. I got a telegram that my father and sister were both dead. There wasn't even a funeral to come to. They found the remains of my father in the kitchen of the burned house. They never found June. They said the fire burned hot, and there was nothing left."

I watched Annie's face as she spoke. Her eyes were dry. This wasn't a fresh grief.

"The property is mine," she said. "I paid the back taxes on it a long time ago. I moved here to be close, but I never wanted to do anything with it. My father's ashes are mixed in with the ashes of the house. It's a tomb, right?"

I understood, and nodded.

"I go out there once in a while, and talk to them, mostly to June. I never went in the barn, though. Why would I? Then one night, June's ghost came and—"

"Her ghost?" I interrupted.

She looked at me and nodded.

"Could you get me a glass of water?" she asked.

I got up, and took my bare feet back up the hall. It wasn't hard to find the kitchen, since the floor plan was a lot like my own house. I snapped on the light and looked. A big white combination range and a matching lacquered sink looked back at me. The floor was black and shiny. Like the rest of the house, everything showed apple-pie order, but it had the air of a kitchen that got used, often and well.

I found a nest of glasses behind a cabinet door, and filled one of them with cold water at the sink. I took it in to her. She held the glass in both hands, like a child, and her throat worked as she finished the whole thing. I went back and filled it up again. She sipped at it, and then didn't want more, so I set the glass on the bedside table.

"Her ghost came, in a dream, I think. She wanted to play, and said she was hiding in the barn. I don't know why I never thought of it before."

"Why was she hiding in the barn?" I asked.

"My father always needed money," she said. "Always. He had a kind of business partner, a man who used the ranch to do things and hide things when he needed a quiet, secret place. We had a lot of liquor there sometimes, barrels and barrels of it. Sometimes there was trouble. He brought people there to hurt them. My father denied it, but June and I heard things at night."

Her eyes were glossy, haunted.

"We had an understanding, the three of us. If serious trouble started, I would take Junie out to the barn and hide there, behind a kind of false wall. We wouldn't come out until my father called us that it was safe. We weren't to come out for anyone but him."

"Did you ever have to do that?" I asked.

"Once or twice," she nodded. "After I dreamed June's ghost, I started to think. If my father had serious trouble, he would have sent June to the barn, and she

92

wouldn't have come out, no matter what. If my father died, what happened to her?"

I felt a creeping horror. "You think she stayed hidden in the barn, waiting for him to come and get her?"

She nodded, definite. "If he was dead, he couldn't come tell her when it was safe," she said. "She would have stayed there waiting, no matter what. I drove out and looked, and there she was. She waited twenty-five years for me to come."

"They never found her, Annie. They declared her dead in the fire."

"No. She's in the barn."

I couldn't find my voice.

"After her ghost came, I looked. She was sitting right where she said. Now I can take care of her again. I go out to the ranch all the time. Sometimes I spend the night."

"Are you saying you see your sister's ghost in the barn? Or are you saying that her body is in the barn?"

"Both," she said.

My throat was parched. I picked up the unfinished glass of water from the bedside table and drained it. The water was still cold, and tasted metallic. I wished it was something stronger.

"You aren't afraid?"

"I walk in the cemetery at night. I'm not afraid of ghosts . . . and I'm not alone. June is with me. I was in the barn talking to her when the cars came."

"The car that the woman drove," I suggested, and she nodded.

"They came down the canyon," she said. "Two cars. It's so dark out there at night that headlights up the road change everything a long time before you can actually see

93

them. Black gets gray, and you can see shadows where there weren't any before."

"Two cars?" I asked.

"Two cars," she nodded. "One chased the other one. After a little while you could hear them coming. They were going really fast . . . too fast. Sometimes you hear drunks driving the road like that at night. Often as not they end up at the bottom of a canyon. The engines were racing, and the tires were making noise. It all echoed, and got louder."

She got quiet for a moment, remembering. I sat close and watched her. Her skin was smooth and even, painted a tarnished gold by the glow from the lamp. Her eyes were dark liquid that reflected the light back.

"They got closer and closer, and I knew they were almost to where the road curves hard, where it runs up above the ranch. Tires squealed . . . loud. I knew the first car wasn't ready for the turn, and the brakes were locked up. It didn't make it."

I hadn't thought about this scenario at all, and Raines hadn't thought about it either, at least not out loud to me. There hadn't been anyone in the tan Ford with Charlene. She had been chased by another car.

"The lights of the first car came over the edge, and at first I thought it stopped, but then it went over the side and slid down and crashed at the bottom. It got very quiet for a minute, and then I heard a woman crying. She was hurt."

"What did you do?" I asked.

"I left the barn and ran toward the car. It had landed almost in the dooryard of the house. I could smell gasoline, and I was afraid there would be a fire. I got about halfway there when the second car came down the driveway and stopped. A man got out, but then I think he smelled the gas, because he got back in and moved the car further away. It was a Buick . . . almost new."

"A Buick? You're sure?"

"I know cars," she said. "The new Buicks have a face. The grille is a mouthful of teeth. Big teeth."

"Did he see you?"

"Not at first. I just stood there in the middle of the dooryard, but the only lights were headlights, and there was a lot of dust. The woman cried and cried. He went to her car and I thought he would help her. The woman yelped once. It sounded like a puppy, and then there was a bang. He shot her, and she stopped crying."

I thought about Charlene Cleveland sitting across from me in her pink hat and dress, safe and secure in her prettiness and her lipstick and perfume. I thought about her untouched drink, and the teardrop that had splashed the check she wrote. I felt the beginnings of familiar red-and-black anger begin to bloom in my chest. My voice sounded harsh.

"Then what?"

"Then he got back in the Buick. I just stood there. I couldn't move. He saw me, though. He looked at me for a minute and then he got in, backed up and turned around. It was a man I knew a long time ago."

"You knew the man?" I asked, and she nodded.

"A long time ago," she said again. "He's older now, but I recognized him. It was Sal Cleveland."

"Have you told anyone about this, Annie?"

She shook her head. "Only you. I don't talk to people. No one ever believes me."

"Are you sure that it was him? It was dark."

95

Chin propped on raised knee, she considered it. I watched her, and thought I had never seen a face as beautiful as hers.

"I used to be in love with him," she said. "I know it was him. I sensed him. He was my first . . . lover. A long time ago. He was exciting at first, but after a while, I knew I had to get away from him. My father was horrified, and he sent me away to my aunt. When I left, Sal told me he would kill anyone that I loved."

Her eyes flicked up and held mine. I felt enveloped by her warm scent, tousled hair and sadness.

"That's what he did. He killed my father, and he killed June. It was my fault."

"It wasn't your fault, Annie. Sal Cleveland is evil. Hurting people is what he does. It's what he likes best. How can you blame yourself for that?"

"It was my fault," she repeated. "He keeps his promises."

"Would you tell the police?"

She shifted on the bed to face me. "I can try, but I don't think they can do anything to Sal. He has . . . spells. He hurts people, and no one can hurt him. Will you let anything happen to me?"

"I won't let anything or anyone hurt you, Annie," I said, and meant it. "Are you sure he saw you? Recognized you?"

"Oh, yes." Her nod was definite. "He saw me. He can see in the dark."

"We'll take this to the police," I said. "I know a guy who will do something about it."

She reached out to touch my face, and then took her hand back as though it was hot. "If I love you, he'll hurt you too," she said. "So I can't love you. He keeps his promises."

"Let him," I said. "Let him do whatever he can to me. He will have come to the right place."

"Maybe I'm going to have to give him what he wants," she said. "Maybe I'll have to love him again."

In the morning, I walked onto Annie's front porch, headed for my place next door. Rain had washed the air, and it was sunny and yellow and cool outside. It was such a pretty day and I was in such a good mood that I almost didn't spot the old hump-backed Nash parked across the street. It had been blue, once upon a time. Now it was the color of mud.

I could see two men in the front seat. From where I stood they weren't dressed like they belonged in a heap like that. They looked like a couple of fancy tough guys. I stood on the steps, undecided. One of them flicked a cigarette butt out the open window. It sat in the middle of the street and smoldered. I made up my mind, and started across to say hello.

The driver slouched back in his seat. He watched me coming.

"Help you, fella?" I asked. "You look like you might be lost."

He sat up, straightened his hat and put an elbow on the window jamb. His friend in the passenger seat leaned forward to look at me, a thin man with a striped tie and a pronounced Adam's apple.

"We're not lost, pal," he said. "Go on inside."

I paused to light a cigarette of my own.

"You're a couple of Sal Cleveland's boys, aren't you?" I asked. "Seems like I've seen you around."

"Got no business with you right now, shamus," the driver said. "Here to dance with a lady. We'll get to you later, don't worry."

97

"Give your boss a message from me," I said. "Tell him I said he doesn't have to come looking for me, or send anyone else. I'll be seeing him plenty. He'll be sick of me."

He stared at me, disbelieving. He had a beefy face and close-set eyes that probably always looked a little puzzled, anyway.

"Are you goddamn stupid?" he asked.

I heard the click as his door unlatched and started to come open. I slammed it shut, knocked off his fedora and had my gun pressed hard into his neck. It went reasonably smoothly. I even impressed myself a little, and I almost smiled. I leaned into the open window and spoke to the passenger.

"Don't move. I'll pull the trigger if you do. Then I'll shoot you, too."

He probably thought that he had been drawing out his gun, but in truth he hadn't moved. His hands were still on his lap. He stared at me, a little shocked. I turned my attention back to the driver. His face turned red and he started swelling up. I could smell his sweat. I jammed the pistol into him harder.

"Very slowly," I said, "Put your left hand on top of the steering wheel. I want you to start the car and then put your right hand on the wheel, too. When I say so, drive away. Don't even look at me . . . understand?"

He sketched a nod, his face furious. He thumbed the starter button and the engine wheezed to life.

"Here's a message from me," I said. "This goes for both of you. This is one lady you don't want to dance with. If you try to, I'll kill you."

I looked at the two of them and thought about it. "Let's make it even simpler. If I see either one of you again, on this street or anywhere else, I'll kill you. Seem clear?"

I straightened up and pulled the gun out of the driver's collar. "Get going," I said.

He let the clutch out. The Nash left black marks and a cloud of smoke as it accelerated away. I looked over my shoulder at Annie's house. A curtain in the living room window twitched and then was still.

I was out on the pier. I had to collect an overdue account from the owner of the Sea-Aire Grill, a seafood place that was one of the handful of businesses built on the wharf. The place did well, since the amusement park crowd drifted over for dinner every night of the week.

The guy suspected his wife of having an affair and hired me to get the goods. She wasn't. As far as I could tell she was more interested in shopping for clothes, listening to the radio at home, and talking to her mother on the telephone than she was in finding romance. She got my clean bill as far as hanky-panky was concerned. The restaurant owner seemed entirely disappointed and dissatisfied with this result, and he was slow to pay my bill.

I had listened to little bit of his grumbling this afternoon, but I had his check in my pocket. It felt good, since I seemed to be doing a lot of running around without getting paid lately. I stopped at the rail to take in the view before I headed back. Across the water, the carny music and roller coaster rattle were occasionally audible over the sound of the surf.

I smelled creosote, clean salt water and fish. The odors were as old as time and reminded me of birth. The wood of the railing beneath my elbows gave up the heat of the disappearing afternoon. I squinted against the glare of the setting sun as it slowly fell into the ocean. I'd read in a magazine once that there was a green flash on the horizon when it slipped under, but I'd never seen it for myself.

"Do you want to play?" a little girl asked.

I looked down at her and raised an eyebrow. She was blonde, about eight years old. She wore a pink sundress, and her skin was tan satin.

"Do I have to win?" I asked.

"This isn't a game you can win," she said. "It's just fun to play."

She reached into the pocket of her dress and carefully pulled out three playing cards. She fanned them out with small fingers and extended them to me. I supposed she had found the leftovers of a discarded deck.

"I can see why it's not a game you can win," I said. "Especially if it's played with three cards."

My car was parked in the lot at the end of the wharf. My coat and tie were left behind on the front seat, and the coming evening kicked up a breeze that felt good. It played with the little girl's light hair. She brushed it back from her eyes.

"You have to pick one," she said.

I obliged, and turned it over. It looked very old, and the inked symbols on the other side had faded from red to a dusty pink. It was the seven of hearts.

"That's you!" she said. "Seven!"

"That's me?"

She smiled at me, excited, and handed the other two cards to me, face-down, to hold while she clambered to sit on the railing.

"Don't look at the other cards," she cautioned.

When she was settled, she took them back and looked at the water's surface far below her. The waves rolled in beneath us, making it seem like we were on a moving ship.

100

If you wanted to, you could follow them in with your eyes, all the way back to the beach at the entrance to the pier, where they crashed into white foam.

"Don't fall," I said.

"Don't worry, I can fly," she said absently, and held the cards out. "Now...take the others and show me."

I did, and turned them over so she could see. They were faded hearts as well, the five and the eight. She held her hair away from her face as she leaned over them, looking intent. She touched the five with a fingertip.

"That's me," she said, and then touched the eight. "That's her."

"I'm sorry," I said. "That's her—who?"

"That's what the game is," she said. "You have to guess."

She took the three cards back, tucked them away, and held her arms out. I lifted her from the rail. She was cold to the touch, and when I lifted her down the sky darkened and a cool wind blew against my face. Once she was standing on the rough wooden planks, the glinting southern California sun was back in my eyes again. My hands were still cold.

"Where's your mother?" I asked. "She's probably worried where you've gotten to by now."

"She's in there," the girl said, and pointed to the ice cream place across the wharf from the Sea-Aire Grill.

"I'd bet she wonders where you are," I said. "It was nice to meet you."

The little girl seemed to hesitate, and then she handed me one of the cards.

"You can keep yours," she said.

She turned and walked away without saying goodbye. I watched her go, just a small girl by herself. When she reached the door of the ice cream parlor, she turned and

101

waved to me once and then vanished inside. I looked down at what I held. It was just an ordinary playing card, badly worn, with seven pink hearts printed on it.

I was lost in thought. Someone had called my name twice before I reacted and looked up. Mrs. Gardiner stood in the entrance to the ice cream parlor, waving to me. The doctor stood slightly behind her, his hand on her elbow. I went to them.

"This is my treat, once a month," she said. "Maybe more often than that. It seems like a lot of trouble, for plain vanilla. It's just so good here."

She showed me. "One scoop, in a cup . . . never in a cone."

I looked at the doctor. He didn't seem to be having anything. Without a lot of vermouth, it probably wasn't sweet enough.

"Who could blame you?" I said. "I'll walk you out."

There were a few parking spots right on the wharf, and the doctor had managed to put the enormous black Cadillac into one of them. I got the passenger door open for Mrs. Gardiner, knowing the gesture would please her. I liked the fact that she saw me as a gentleman, in spite of my profession. She was a nice lady, and she made me feel like I was still a part of the civilized world, even if I didn't get to enter it too often.

I waved at the car as it rumbled slowly away over the huge timbers, back toward the beach and Cabrillo Boulevard. I watched it until they were out of view.

An ice cream cone suddenly seemed like a grand idea, and I walked back toward the doorway of the shop. I fished in my front pocket for change, and came up with the badly worn playing card. The little girl had said it was me, and it was my card. I looked at the seven hearts and smiled, figuring I had been called worse things.

I went into the ice cream parlor, thinking that I'd like to thank her again, and perhaps thank her mother for raising such a sweet child. The place was dim, cool, and just about empty. No little girl moved among the scattering of customers, nor did I see anyone that looked like she might be her mother. I had seen the girl go inside to find her, though, just about the time Mrs. Gardiner had come out.

It all felt like it might be a symptom of too many late nights and maybe too much bourbon, except I still held the playing card. Slightly dog-eared, the hearts faded almost to pink, it was warm in my hand. It must be a lucky card, I decided.

When I got home I would to put it in a safe place, if I could find one.

-Eleven-

The barn was a lot bigger than it seemed from the road. The desert sun had bleached it into a charcoal sketch, gray and black and white. Up close, the old boards ticked in the heat. I touched the rough wood and felt tiny vibrations under my fingertips, as though music played inside. A large door on rollers hung open an inch or two. Annie squeezed through the gap without hesitating, and looked back at me from the other side. Half her face was sun-bright and the other half dark.

I hesitated, and then turned my head sideways and went after her. The edge of the door caught and scraped painfully against my chest. I strained against it, but it wouldn't budge. I felt Annie's fingers on my mine, light and warm, and suddenly I was through.

The space inside was huge and dim and hushed, like an empty cathedral in the middle of the week. Tiny cracks in the black walls were stripes of the bright sun we had left outside. Dust motes drifted, and as my eyes adjusted to the strange illumination, lavender and aqua-colored spots swam in the shadows. I looked up to where the rafters rose and disappeared in the darkness.

Something hovered over us, ancient and breathless.

"She's over here," Annie said.

An old truck sat on flat tires in the middle of the space, giving off ghosts of motor oil and gasoline. She led me past it to the back, where a jumble of machinery rusted under an overhang. In the gloom, it was impossible to tell what the angles had once been. I figured none of it was worth saving, or it would have long since been removed or stolen.

A small figure sat by itself in a dim corner, back against the wall. A little girl. Her arms hung at her sides, with one knee raised. I took a step closer, straining to see. When I got near enough, the form resolved itself into a skeleton.

"Isn't she beautiful?" Annie said from just behind me. I jumped.

The child sat with her head tilted slightly upward and to the side, as though she had a question to ask us. Her eyes were empty sockets. There was darkened skin on her face, and long hair caked her head. Her dress was dark with dust. A single tiny strip of sun lay across her, catching the dulled fabric, showing a hint of pink.

"She's a mummy," I breathed. "My God, she really is. How long have you known about this, Annie?"

I realized I was whispering. Annie had gone to her knees next to the girl. Her face was rapt. She reached out and caressed one of the delicate hands. The years and the dry heat had changed it to something that looked like a paw.

"How long have you known about this?" I repeated.

She said something, so softly I couldn't hear it. I leaned in closer and realized that she was talking to her sister, and not to me.

"I'm here, June," she murmured. "I've brought someone to meet you."

An odor of dried spices hung around the small body, a miasma of coriander or cardamom or sage. I didn't know much about spices, but I thought an Egyptian burial might smell like this. I fought down a sneeze.

"Cloves," Annie said, as though she could read my mind. "She smells like cloves."

"She's been here all of these years?" I asked.

"She must have been hiding here when they killed my father," she said, without looking up. "She hid and never came out."

"Why hasn't anyone found her?" I asked. "It seems impossible."

"I own this place, and I never knew she was here until a little while ago," she said. "It's an empty barn in the middle of nowhere. If you stick your head inside the door, you can see there's nothing of any value here. Why go all the way to the back?"

"People have come here to harvest the avocados."

"Steal them, you mean. No one ever asked my permission, or paid me for what they took."

"My point is, people have been here over the years. Surely some of the picking crews would have chosen this barn as a good place to stay overnight. They don't get to be choosy, and any roof is better than none."

"There are places that people don't go," she said. Her expression got very serious. "There are places that raise your hackles as soon as you're close. I'm sure no one but me ever went further than the doorway."

"You might be right," I said.

The little mummified girl looked up at me. The empty eye sockets seemed to spark with life, asking me to pick her up.

"You can't leave her here," I said.

"I know," she said. "I knew when I found her that I would only have her for a little while."

"What are you going to do with her?"

"I don't know what to do." Her eyes were pleading. "Will you help me?"

I nodded. "She's been here long enough."

We stood quietly, looking down at June. I heard the wind outside, moving against the sides of the barn. Annie spoke, reluctant to break the hush.

106

"She'll still be here." Her voice was eerily confident. "I'll miss her, but she'll still come around sometimes."

"I have to call in the police, Annie." I tried to make my voice as gentle as I could. "They're going to treat this as suspicious, no matter how long ago it happened. Are you absolutely, positively sure this is your sister? This could be anyone."

"It's her," she said. "Of course it's her. I know her hair and her dress, and anyway we talk."

The inside of the barn suddenly seemed unbearably, oppressively hot. I wanted to leave. I touched her shoulder, ready to guide her to the door.

"I'm crazy, I know that," she said.

I had no answer for her, and after a moment she nodded. "As long as you know that, too," she said.

"I'm going to have to call the police," I said again, to be sure she understood. "If you want me to take care of this, it's all too unusual. You can't just carry her out of here. There will be an investigation, even if it's a long time ago. They will ask you all kinds of questions. I know a guy who can handle this without a lot of fuss."

"Will he be gentle with her?" she asked.

I saw the start of her tears. "He'll be gentle with her, Annie, I promise. And with you. I'll stick around to make sure of it."

Her tears increased, and I pulled her close. I wondered if she had cried for her sister before today, or if the tears had never really stopped. We stood there in the hot barn until the light outside started to fade, and then I took her home.

I stood with Rex Raines in the circular driveway of Casita Hospital. The building was almost new, and several miles north of downtown. I didn't know why they had built it so far away from where it was needed most often; probably because the land had belonged to someone with pull. It made for a long ambulance ride if you got shot in a downtown bar.

The day before, the coroner's office had removed the child's mummy from the barn, loading it into a black panel wagon before bringing it here. One of the stretcher bearers had commented that the girl's remains weighed hardly anything at all.

The county morgue was attached to the back of the building. Raines was here to get the autopsy results, and I was here to look over his shoulder at them. The place had been backed up with more anxious customers, so it had taken them a little while to get to her.

He took a long time to finish a pipe full of bad-smelling tobacco. I didn't have the patience to smoke a pipe, but I felt no particular hurry to get inside the morgue, so I didn't mind waiting for him.

"I might have something that will make you happy," I said. "Been waiting to drop it in your lap."

"Hard to imagine," he said. "Tell me."

He inspected his pipe with obvious pleasure. The expression on his round face was mild and absent, but I knew his ears were pricked up. He didn't miss much.

"I have an eyewitness to Charlene Cleveland's murder," I said. "Guaranteed positive on the shooter."

His voice got instantly sharp. "What the hell are you talking about, Nate?"

"Annie Kahlo saw the whole thing. She was there that night. She saw Sal Cleveland walk down the drive and shoot his wife in the wrecked car."

"She didn't call it in until the next morning. Why did she wait so long?"

I thought it might be better if I didn't mention that she had probably sat in a pitch-black barn and visited all night with the little mummy whose remains lay just a short distance from where we stood; remains we would soon be viewing.

"She was scared. She hid out, and drove into the city when the sun came up. She didn't just happen upon the crashed car. She was there the whole time."

He thought about it. I could tell it bothered him that the scenario had escaped him.

"She says Sal Cleveland did it, huh?" He looked at me quizzically. "What's in this for you?"

"She says Charlene was crying in pain when he walked up to the car. Begging for help. He shot her in cold blood, and I want him taken down. That's what's in it for me."

I felt the anger stretch itself awake in my gut again.

"You said hundred-percent positive?" he asked. "Your witness knows the shooter personally?"

I nodded. "It was Sal Cleveland. Hundred-percent positive."

He stared at me. It pleased me in a perverse way that I had wiped the usual sunny expression off of his face.

"How does an artist happen to know Cleveland personally?" he said. "She run with that kind of crowd when the sun goes down?"

I shook my head, and his expression changed.

"And since when does Sal Cleveland do his own shooting?" he asked. "He has a whole crew to do his dirty work for him."

"Maybe when it's a blonde wife with a couple of crushed legs who can't shoot back," I said. "Maybe then he doesn't mind doing his own killing."

"So how does she happen to know Sal Cleveland well enough to recognize him in the dark?"

"She knew him a long time ago," I said. "He might have something to do with the dead little girl in there, too. She broke off a romance with him, and he might have killed her family as revenge."

I gestured toward the morgue. He stared at me without saying anything, and then shook his head slowly. He walked a few feet up the cement walk and tapped his pipe into the gutter. When he had satisfied himself it was out, he stuck it into a pocket and came back. "There's one big problem with that," he said. "The Kahlo woman is ditzy. She's ready for a butterfly net. Even if she really saw what she says, she'd never survive a cross-examination."

"She might be different, but she saw what she saw."

"I don't know how you come up with this stuff," he said. "I couldn't write it for a magazine. As it happens, I had her here an hour ago. She's as wacky as it gets. She didn't say a word about being a witness to any murder, but she doesn't act like she knows where she even is, half the time. I asked her to give me a formal identification of her sister, and she about flipped her wig."

"Doesn't mean she didn't see what she saw," I said again. If I said it enough, he might listen.

"Let me tell you how crazy your witness is. She claims to have found the mummy inside the morgue there, says she knows it was her sister. Okay, I say, I'll buy it. No one else is claiming the bones, and it's been a long time. The facts fit. If you want to take what's left and bury it, I say, we'll do what we have to and when it's legal you can take her."

An ambulance cruised into the entrance. Its lights and siren were off. At the top of the drive it stopped, and the attendants got out and moved to the rear of the car. They didn't seem to be in any kind of hurry.

"Part of what she has to do is identify her," he said. "No one expects her to look at a mummy and say it's her sister. It's a formality. You look at the height and hair color and say there's nothing that definitely says it isn't her, you know? It looks like her clothes. If the deceased had blonde hair, and the mummy has blonde hair, that's probably the best you can do. If you want the body, you just nod your damn head and say it's her, am I right?"

"If you say so."

"I do say so, and I told her that. So what does she do? She looks at the bones and comes unglued. She gets more and more upset, and asks me how is she supposed to say anything for sure? How is she supposed to recognize her? Why am I asking her to do what she can't? She's screaming at me, the dizzy bitch."

"It can't have been easy," I said. "It was probably a shock."

"She found her!" he barked. "She found her in the barn in the first place! That should have been all the shock there was. Why get crazy now?"

I shook my head. I didn't know. The ambulance attendants had the doors open, and they pulled out a chromium gurney with legs that folded down and locked. A sheet covered the reclining passenger. They wheeled it inside.

"Anyway," Raines said. "She's not someone who I want to put on a stand to testify against Sal Cleveland. I wouldn't know what she was going to say to a judge until she opened her mouth and said it. Nothing would surprise me. How did she see all this in the first place?"

111

"She was out at the ranch. She found her sister and it was getting dark. She decided to hold a . . . vigil, I guess, and go for help in the morning. Sometime in the night she heard the car chase and saw the Ford crash, and then the rest of it. She had left the barn and was maybe a hundred feet away when Cleveland fired the shot. She saw him in the headlights of his own car."

"She spent the night in a dark barn with a skeleton in a dress, and you think she's not crazy?"

"I imagine she had her reasons," I said.

"You know what she reminds me of, with all respect? Shell shock. She looks and acts like the guys who came back from the Pacific . . . ruined. You know the ones I mean."

"We both almost came back like that. Who says we didn't?"

"She's crazy, anyway, as far as I'm concerned. Not a reliable witness. I need more than this."

I didn't want to give up any more than I already had. "You're going to at least get a statement from her, aren't you?"

He waved a hand at me, like clearing smoke, and started walking away. "I need to think about all this," he said. "Let's go see what you came to see."

"There's maybe another problem here, Rex," I said. "If Annie Kahlo saw Sal Cleveland clear enough to identify him, there's at least a good chance he saw her, too. I chased off a couple of thugs who were watching her house already. Someone better do something fast."

"All right. I'll talk to her at some point," he said. "Maybe later today or tomorrow."

"I want her to tell you why she thinks Cleveland killed her family twenty-five years ago, too," I said. "Let me

112

work on her a bit. Get her prepared. She's been through a lot."

He started to walk away, and I followed his back.

"Unbelievable," he muttered over his shoulder. "Couldn't write it for a magazine."

He was still shaking his head as we went into the morgue.

The little girl looked up at us from the steel table. Her eye sockets were empty, and her mouth stretched away from her teeth in an expression difficult to read. She rested on her side, with legs slightly akimbo. In some places, her remains were skeletal, but in others the skin was entirely present, cured like delicate leather.

When I had first seen her in the dark barn, the shafts of sunlight had made it look as though she wore a pink dress. Under the harsh lights of the morgue, her bones were swaddled in a filthy brown rag, and I didn't know why I had seen anything pink in it. One hand was beneath her head, and the other curled on her chest. She looked like a tired little girl waking up from a nap. A corona of what looked like the stuffing from a mattress scattered the table in clumps around her head. I wasn't sure what it was.

"Her hair," Doctor Runtz said, as though he read my mind. "She was a dark blonde. A sort of honey-blonde."

"You moved her hands," I said. "When I saw her in the barn, she had her hands down at her sides."

"You remember wrong, Mister Crowe. This girl hasn't moved since she died. The body is mummified. Does she look flexible to you? You were in grade school the last time she moved any part of her body."

He gave me a queer look, and I shrugged. I knew what I had seen. Her hands and arms were in a different position, now.

"What else can you tell us?" I asked.

"There's a lot I can't tell you," he said. "I can't tell you what caused her to die. If she was murdered, I can't tell you if she was drugged or poisoned or drowned. This is more a post-mortem examination than any kind of autopsy. I'm not going to cut into her."

He reached out and touched the corpse with a forefinger, tracing down from forehead to cheek to chin. His touch was surprisingly tender.

"My own daughter was this girl's age once," he said, mostly to himself. "She isn't a horror. She's just a little girl."

"Can you guess how she died?" Lieutenant Raines asked. "Anything you know for sure?"

Runtz nodded, and bent over the table.

"I can tell you that she probably didn't die violently," he said. "There are no broken bones and no evidence of injury on what tissue is left. Her face is nearly intact, and unmarked."

"What is she wearing?' I asked. "Can you tell?"

He peered up at me, and nodded again.

"It's satin," he said. "Probably a party dress, as odd as it seems. It was pink, back when she put it on. A pink party dress."

The door to the hall opened, and an orderly in a white tunic stuck his head in and seemed surprised to see us there. He left without saying anything. Doctor Runtz straightened up and faced us.

"I'm not going to examine this child any further," he said. "She's been dead for twenty-five years, and dissecting a mummy won't give up any more answers than we have now. Her sister has made some sort of identification, enough of one, anyway."

He pushed up his glasses and glanced at Raines, who said nothing.

"I don't have any good reason to inflict more insult on this girl," he repeated. "She fits the facts as we know them. What's left here matches her physical description, and the circumstances she was found in also match what is known of her. I won't disturb her further."

"You'll sign off on this, doc?" Raines asked. "This is officially June Kahlo?"

"This is June Kahlo," Runtz nodded. "I'll make it formal, and release her to her sister, Anne Kahlo, for burial."

The three of us stood there, looking down at the little girl.

"After all this time," Raines mused. "Found, and nobody even knew she was lost."

"Annie knew she was lost," I said. "She never forgot, or stopped looking. She said she would find her someday, and she did."

"She says a lot of things," Raines said. "Most of them crazy as hell. Never met a broad so dizzy in my life."

I gave him a hard look, and decided not to chase it. I settled my hat on my head and turned to go. At the door, I turned for a last look at the girl.

"That's it, then," I murmured. "It's over, now. Goodbye, June."

Part Two

Baby Elephants and Playing Cards

-Twelve-

Friday, August 4, 1922
Santa Teresa County, California
2:30 p.m.

Outside of the barn, the desert went about its business. The sun was bright, hot, merciless and alien. Inside, the interior was dark, but the temperature had hovered at a hundred degrees since morning, and Junie Kahlo's body temperature had risen to match. The small girl had last had a drink of water twenty hours before, and she couldn't get up any more, though she didn't know it. She drifted in and out of a hot, fevered sleep that moved quickly toward coma.

A sound came from outside, and her eyes opened slowly.

The barn door slid back, noisy on its rollers, and the interior flooded with silver light. The desert was gone. A fresh wind blew, and it gusted in with a mist of rain. Junie saw a jungle outside, green and gray and dripping. She saw hills rising behind the tree line. They weren't like the dry, rocky arroyos she was used to. They were soft and alive and full of secrets.

Another small noise came from the doorway. Junie looked toward it from behind her swollen lids and struggled to focus.

A baby elephant looked back at her from around the corner of the doorframe. Shy at first, it only showed one eye. The very top of its head was sparsely covered with the dark hair that it would lose as it grew up. The trunk switched back and forth; it hadn't quite mastered the use of it. It watched her, curious. After a moment it took a step into the barn, and then another. It was pale and about the size of a small pony.

Junie smiled with cracked lips. "Are you a boy or a girl?"

Her voice croaked. The elephant didn't answer. She could hear the sound of its feet as it crossed the barn and came toward her. It made a sound like bedroom slippers shuffling on a wood floor. There was movement in the doorway behind it. Another baby elephant followed the first, and then another. Junie counted five of them, and then seven, and finally eight. They moved close and formed a half-circle around where she sat slumped.

"You've all been playing in the water, haven't you?" she whispered. "You're all wet."

Eight baby elephants stood quietly. Eight sets of dark eyes watched her. They had enormous ears that were strangely beautiful, rippling like sea fans moved by unseen currents. The water dripped from their hides and pooled in the dust beneath them. Junie wondered how old they were; not more than a few days or weeks, she thought. Just babies. They smelled of the river, green and rich and muddy.

More noise floated in from outside. Junie couldn't quite make it out. It was some kind of music, but nothing she had ever heard before. Not loud, not soft, it seemed be everywhere. Warm and sweet, it slid from the jungle and echoed in the hills. Cymbals and strings and drums mixed with the sound of thunder and of rain on wet leaves. The beat of a waterfall thrummed under all of it, torrent rushing over an edge and falling down, down, down to a river pool far below.

The music had colors mixed up in it, too. They swirled, danced, and told a story. The little girl could see it all just as well as she could hear it, and it made perfect sense to her.

She felt very tired, and she rested her head back against the wall behind her and closed her eyes. All at once she became frightened, and she opened them again. The baby elephants were still there, though, and the barn door still framed the dripping jungle behind them. The rain still fell, and the colored music still played. She shut her eyes again, reassured.

The elephants waited patiently while she slept. Eventually, she woke up and smiled at them.

"I had the strangest dream," she said. "Is it time to go?"

The girl got to her feet and smoothed the pink dress over her knees, brushing the dust and grit from the fabric as best she could. She rested a small hand on the back of the first elephant as it began to move off. She felt she belonged to it, and it belonged to her. They somehow belonged to each other. When they left the barn, the other babies fell in behind them. One of them nudged June playfully with its trunk, and she looked over her shoulder and laughed.

She didn't notice the small body crumpled in the corner, a rag doll in a pink dress just like hers. It would have meant nothing at all to her if she had seen it.

The procession moved slowly toward the jungle. After only a few moments they were lost to sight, gone into the rain and the green and the music, leaving behind only the echoes of a small girl in a parade of baby elephants. When they were gone, the door rolled closed again, and the barn lapsed back into dry heat and silence. No one else would come inside it for another twenty-five years, but it didn't matter.

Junie was ended, and June had begun.

Just like so, and just like that.

-Thirteen-

We stood quietly, far out on the pier. A sea breeze came in; it flapped and rattled the small colored flags on top of the ice cream place. It cooled the sweat on my skin and blew away the oily odors of fish and hot creosote. I slouched against the splintered gray railing and watched the waves. The sun was so bright that the Channel Islands were gone in the glare.

I took off my necktie and put it in my pocket. I wanted to take off my coat, too, but I didn't know if Cleveland's clowns had followed us here. I might need the gun in the pocket in a hurry, so I left it on.

"Did you see that?" Annie asked.

She stared at the water beneath us. I followed her look down to where the sun turned the translucence green and warm. I tried to see the bottom and I couldn't; I only saw moving shadows in the deep wash.

"What is it?"

She didn't answer. The air played with her hair, but she didn't seem to feel it.

"They made me look at her," Annie said. "My sister."

I looked at her. I decided not to let on I already knew that.

"Look at her? What for?"

"They said I had to identify her. How can anyone identify a skeleton? She was some bones in a dirty old pink dress. How could I identify that?"

She tilted her face to me and started to laugh. It was musical, lovely, a silver screen cascade that chilled me. The lenses of her dark glasses caught at the sun and the sky.

"I told them what they wanted to hear," she said. "I told them it was my little sister, dressed for a party."

She laughed harder. She leaned against the railing, hugged herself, and began to rock back and forth. "She was ten years old," she gasped. "A baby."

Her shoulders were shaking. I reached out and gently turned her away from the rail. She took off the glasses and looked at me defiantly. "It was different, do you understand?"

Her tone was harsh, gassy, and I started to worry.

"In the barn, she was still there," she said. "It was different. I could see her and talk to her. It wasn't like this. This was a pile of bones on a metal table and they said they want me to identify her. How could I identify bones?"

"You weren't, Annie," I soothed. "No one expected you to. It's a formality, that's all. They know who it is. They just had to ask you the question."

"When I got home, I looked in the bathroom mirror and I thought about taking out my own eyes," she said. "I'd rather be blind than see anything else like that. I'd rather be blind."

"It will fade, Annie. Give it time."

"Everything gets erased?" She glared at me. "Is that what you're saying? If I just wait long enough, everything gets erased?"

I brought her close. Even in the sun, I could feel the heat of her through my clothes. She felt as hot and light as an injured bird.

"Not everything," I said. "Not the good things."

A man and a woman came toward us, walking a dog. They had ice cream. I had a feeling I knew them, but I didn't know from where. The woman looked at Annie crying, and I thought she might say something, but she didn't. They walked on past.

"Fifty years from now, a hundred…" I said, "All of this will still be here, and even if it seems like we're gone, we won't be. It will all be the same. Someone will stand here and they'll look at the same water, the same sun, and they'll feel us, still here. The good things don't get erased."

She looked at my face, and then my eyes. She tried a smile. "We're good?"

"We're something good." I nodded. "We won't ever get erased."

"The ice cream will be different in fifty years," she said.

I thought about it. "The ice cream might be different," I allowed. "We'll see."

We stood still for a long time. The wind picked up, just a little, and the ocean sparkled more, but nothing else changed. When she spoke again, her voice was very soft.

"We're something good," she echoed. "So I guess we'll see."

I lounged behind my desk, with nothing much to do. The Krazy Kat clock said it was too early for lunch. I decided to look out the window for a little while. When the telephone on the desk rang, it surprised me.

"Crowe Investigations," I answered.

"When you see your girlfriend," Rex Raines said, "tell her that the coroner's office has released her sister's bones. She can call a funeral parlor to pick them up."

"What was the coroner's verdict?"

I could almost hear his shrug over the wire. "What else could it be?" he asked. "Death by misadventure. Cause unknown. June Kahlo was declared dead in a house fire in 1922. Her body wasn't found, and they figured she had been burned up. Now her body is found, and they know she didn't

122

die in the fire. She's still dead, and her bones aren't saying anything else."

I was playing with a yellow pencil. I put it down and lit a cigarette.

"She got into that barn some way," I said. "Someone put her body there, or else she went in there herself and died."

"No one's ever going to know. It was all too long ago to matter."

"Annie Kahlo says Sal Cleveland killed her father in the fire," I reminded him. "She says he was responsible for her sister's death, too. Charlene Cleveland makes three of his victims all in the same place. Seems to me someone ought to do something."

"Just tell Annie Kahlo to claim her sister's body," he said. "Tell her to give the girl a proper burial. Tell her to leave Sal Cleveland to us. Maybe if the amateurs stay out of this, it will all work out, and nobody else has to end up dead."

"Amateurs?" I asked.

"Civilians. You like that better?"

He hung up, and I decided to have a short drink before lunch. I toasted Krazy Kat.

"To amateurs," I said.

We put June Kahlo in the ground on a Saturday morning in the middle of 1947, more than twenty years after she had died. She wore a new pink dress that her sister had picked out and bought for her.

I liked the idea of it; the holding of an early morning funeral. It seemed like a starting out, not an ending. The sky gleamed an impossible crystal blue, the air so mild I couldn't feel it on my skin until it moved.

It was an applejack day, an ice cream day, exactly the right kind to send a little girl on her way.

Annie Kahlo stood beside me, wearing something light and floral. I had left the house dressed for a funeral, in the one black suit that I owned. She had shaken her head and sent me back inside to change. I was resplendent in pale seersucker, ready for a garden party if one started.

The Gardiners attended, and stood with Annie and me. The doctor looked somber and slightly bewildered. Behind her black veil, tears ran down Mrs. Gardiner's face. At one point she sobbed, and Annie took her into her arms for several minutes. It struck me odd she was so emotional. June Kahlo had been dead for twenty-five years, and there was only Annie here to even remember her. I figured maybe some people just didn't do well at funerals, and sometimes strong personalities like Mrs. Gardiner's hid a naturally soft center.

There was no one else there, really. A cemetery worker leaned on his shovel, not quite out of sight. The rented minister said a few words and the funeral home people waited at a discreet distance for the check in my breast pocket. A couple of homicide dicks were there. They looked at me over the small coffin, big men in suits that were a little too small. They'd passed the hat at the station for flowers, and I appreciated it.

"She's here, you know," Annie said. "She knows you. She told me what you are. Do you believe me?"

I looked across the cemetery. A couple of automatic sprinklers started ratcheting and sending up long sprays of water. The sun glinted off marble angels and caught at the white wings of a couple of squabbling gulls. I didn't see any small girls in dressed in pink.

"She never met me."

Annie shook her head and didn't say anything else. She looked straight ahead, invisible behind her dark glasses.

I didn't know. Maybe the little girl moved invisibly among the long morning shadows that fell off the headstones, dancing between the granite monuments. Maybe she saw me, even if I didn't see her. I didn't know a lot of things, if it came right down to it.

"I believe you," I finally said. "I believe in you, is more like it. Don't ask me that anymore."

I touched the brim of my hat and hoped Junie Kahlo saw it.

"That was a lovely service," Mrs. Gardiner said, looking like she might cry again.

A large cat appeared on the lowest branch of a jacaranda tree in the corner of the yard. One minute it wasn't there and the next, it was. It crouched in the shade, lashing its tail and watching us.

"Here we are, dear," Mrs. Gardiner said. "Put it right here."

She tapped the glass tabletop, and Annie set down a large tray with a crystal pitcher and four glasses. When the two women were seated, Mrs. Gardiner nodded to her husband. He had a cane resting across his lap, and he leaned it carefully against the wall and got slowly to his feet. He poured out four glasses of something pink and fizzy and handed them around. I leaned back against the padded bench and tasted mine. It had gin in it, but I didn't want to guess what made it so sweet.

The wind was warm and nearly constant, even in the enclosed yard, and the striped awning over our heads rattled softly. The grass was very green and littered with flower petals.

"I love it this time of year," Mrs. Gardiner said. "The breeze off the water makes all the difference. I can sit out here all day. Which way is the ocean from here, my darling?"

Dr. Gardiner considered things for a moment, and then pointed a finger. Since he was pointing more or less straight up, I didn't know what he meant.

"That way," he said. "South is always to the left."

I nodded agreeably, and tried some more of my drink.

"I leave those things to him," Mrs. Gardiner explained. "He does all the driving, so he knows where things are, usually."

There was motion across the yard. The cat had jumped down from the tree. It watched us for a moment and then moved smoothly into the bright sunlight. It was gold-colored, and covered in dark spots that undulated when it moved. It crossed the grass to the table where we sat, and Mrs. Gardiner trailed her fingertips across its back as it passed her and jumped up to share Annie's chair. She had to move a little bit to give it room; it looked as though it might weigh twenty pounds.

It lifted a front paw and began to wash with its tongue, never taking its yellow eyes from mine. Annie held her drink with one hand, and scratched its head gently with the other.

"That's the biggest cat I've ever seen," I remarked.

Annie gave me a sidelong look over the rim of her glass, and then put it back down. I didn't think she had tasted it.

"It isn't a cat," she said. "Not in the way you mean, anyway. It's an ocelot."

She stroked it gently.

"A real ocelot?" I asked. "I didn't know you could keep them as pets."

"Of course you can," Annie said. "If they're real, you can."

"It isn't a pet," Dr. Gardiner said.

"Of course it is," Mrs. Gardiner said. "It's my pet . . . and Annie's, when she's here."

The wind stirred again, and the leaves overhead dappled my arms and legs with moving shadows. I closed my eyes, felt the warm air moving across my face, and heard the rustle of fabric above me. I listened to the murmur of voices and drifted.

"I don't think it's tangible," Annie was saying to the Gardiners. "It's more like an experience. I've been there before."

I wondered idly if the spots of shade made me look like an ocelot, but I didn't want to open my eyes to look. I decided that they probably did.

"It's such a beautiful day," Mrs. Gardiner sighed. "Can you stay?"

"We're staying right here," Annie said. "There is no other place. It's all play. There's no place we'd rather be."

On Chapala Street, a block up from the beach, a drive-in restaurant served a pretty good hot dog and an even better bowl of Mexican chili beans, if you knew enough to ask for them. Danny Lopez had been serving lunches out of the same cement-and-stucco building since before any of his employees were born. He had seen a lot of Santa Teresa come and go.

He had a gardening business that catered to the wealthy in Santa Teresa and Montelindo, and he employed a lot of the people who were newly arrived in the country. He had men to run it for him, so he was here most days, making lunches and watching Chapala Street. There were other legitimate businesses under his control, but I didn't know what they were, and didn't care.

I knew enough to understand that not all of his business was in the open. Danny Lopez knew and worked the dark arteries that ran beneath the city. That's why I was here.

I backed the car into a spot where it wouldn't get blocked in and patted the gun in my pocket. I didn't know what Cleveland's goons were up to, and old survival habits were kicking in; better to act as though they were always close by.

The counter was open to the street, but shaded from the elements by a wide metal overhang of roof. Danny turned hot dogs on the grill, his back to me. The young woman at the cash register took my order with the particular kind of frost that pretty Latinas save for the middle-aged men who wander into their neighborhoods. I took my change from her and turned to watch the street.

"Taking a break, Nina," he said from behind me. "Be in the back."

She nodded and looked out the corner of her eye, speculating. Danny handed my food to me and jerked his chin at a group of picnic tables set under a fig tree at the rear of the building. I followed him over to sit.

The hot dog tasted good, with plenty of mustard and chili. The soda came in a large paper cup.

"I like my drink better from a bottle," I said.

"You'd like to sweep up glass every day, too?" he asked. "Wrong neighborhood, *amigo*."

I nodded agreement and kept eating.

"Plenty of ice in it, though," I said. "That counts for something."

"What's on your mind, Crowe?"

He sat across from me, small and brown, like an attentive cricket. He looked old and harmless, and I knew a lot of the people who had underestimated him that way weren't around anymore.

Lopez was from a small town, and had come north to Santa Teresa by way of Chihuahua a lot of years ago and joined the huge, invisible troop of workers picking avocados and oranges. Some of them stuck around to wash cars and clean swimming pools. A lot of them had children who seemed to be going places.

He had seen opportunity in need. Here in Santa Teresa lived a large group of people ignored by most of the local services and businesses. He organized liquor and prostitutes and games, but he also brought doctors and dentists from Mexico to work out of makeshift offices in kitchens and back rooms. He arranged trucks and cars and places to live. He sold all the things that the people who were already here saw no reason to sell to Mexicans.

There were rumors of dead bodies sunk to the bottom of the Santa Teresa Channel, dropped off by small fishing boats in the pre-dawn; those who had opposed his success for various reasons and those who wanted to steal the market for themselves. I didn't doubt the stories, but I didn't think any of it had happened for a long time.

Lopez was the man to turn to when there was no one else. The locals called him *el Mayor*, and in fact he had more real power than the *de facto* mayor of Santa Teresa. Through all of it, he had worked from this corner, serving hot dogs.

I thought he was my friend. He had seen a lot and done a lot, and unlike a lot of the people who I met, he never

129

got very impressed with himself. I didn't mind if some of him rubbed off on me.

I cleaned my mouth with a paper napkin and set the dregs of my meal aside.

"Wanted to talk to you about something," I said.

"Figured you did."

"You know a guy named Sal Cleveland?" I asked.

"Sure." He shrugged. "I know everyone."

He kept his eyes on my face. His attention was always complete. It was something I liked about him.

"There's a problem between him and me," I said. "I think it's going to get bigger."

I told him about Charlene Cleveland. He knew some of it already, from the newspaper and talk on the street, but not that she had hired me to help her. The help had gotten her killed. I knew who had done the killing, but there didn't seem to be much I could do about it.

"You take things too personally," he said, when I finished. "You did what the lady hired you to do. She asked you to get her free. She didn't hire you to protect her. If she needed protection, she should have known it and done something about it."

I looked at the entrance of the drive-in. It was nearly two o'clock, and it would be closing soon, since it only opened for lunch. I watched the girl behind the counter. She didn't have much to do now, except bus a rag around and watch me back.

"Did you have feelings for this woman?" he asked.

I shook my head. I was surprised at the emotion I felt, something beneath the anger.

"It's complicated," I said. "I think she spent a lot of her life not being wanted. There was no reason for it. She was pretty enough."

130

"Some people need to not be wanted," he shrugged. "They look for it."

"She asked me to have a drink with her afterward," I said. "I said 'no'. I don't make friends with my clients. I was harsher than I needed to be. She cried when she left my office, and a few hours later she was dead."

He shrugged and shook his head.

"Capone, Moran—all those guys," he said. "Cleveland's cut from the same cloth. He made his first money the same way as them, twenty or so years ago. Bathtub hooch, Mexican girls and some marijuana . . . his clubs, some property. The difference is, he was never poor. He came here from a rich family in Ohio. Santa Teresa was always big enough for him, you know? He didn't want more, or need more."

"If this is his town, it's funny I haven't crossed paths with him before now."

"You've only been here a couple of years, and that's exactly what I'm talking about. The other guys get into trouble because they want to rule entire big cities, states, buy off the cops, own local governments. Sal never did that, and doesn't now. He just has his thing and is happy with it. There isn't enough action here that anybody wants to come up from L.A. and take it away from him."

He looked at me sharply. "Not that one or two haven't tried. It didn't end well for them. He and I reached an agreement a long, long time ago. We are very polite and careful to stay out of each other's way. I stay away from his business, and he leaves the Mexicans alone. He's . . ."

Lopez searched for words in English, and couldn't find them

"*A él se le cruzaron los cables,*" he said. "*El está mal de la cabeza.*"

131

"Crazy," I said. "Dangerously crazy."

"*Si, el es psiscopáta,*" he nodded. "He isn't after money. He just thinks it's all a lot of fun, and he doesn't want attention that would spoil it for him."

"I heard he likes to hurt people. Can't say I like that."

He looked away from me, at the passing cars. His wrinkled face was almost sad, and I figured he saw things that had to do with him, and nothing to do with me. When he spoke again, I had to lean forward to hear him.

"I think, *amigo*, you put yourself too much in harm's way when you shouldn't. It's a kind of. . ." He wobbled his hand in the air. "*Orgullo*. Cockiness. . . to think you have the answers for the problems of others. I think it's why you do what you do."

"I make a living," I said. "I lost my romantic notions about it a long time ago."

"Wrong." He smiled slowly. "Romantic is exactly what you are. And a little guilty, I think, like all of us. You were supposed to save this unhappy woman, and you didn't. That makes you very angry. There's more, though, am I right?"

I nodded. "There's more. There was a witness to the killing. A woman. I think Cleveland saw her at the scene, and worse, I think he knows who she is."

"She saw the murder first hand? Why didn't Cleveland kill her, too?"

"I don't know," I said. "There's a lot I don't know. Cleveland's mixed up with her, too. She says he killed her father and her younger sister years ago, when she jilted him."

He put his hands flat on the picnic table, got himself up and walked over to the counter. He came back with two more cups filled with ice and soda. He set mine carefully in front of me and sat back down.

132

"I thought so, another woman," he said. "And this one you can save? To make up for the first one, who you lost?"

I thought about it and shrugged.

"This. . . witness . . . is maybe a little bit crazy," I said. "She's going to be hard to keep tabs on. I don't know if I can protect her."

"Most people don't want to be saved, in my experience," he said. "Everyone has their own reasons for what they do, including you. Someday you're going to rescue someone who didn't ask you to and it's going to kill you. I tell you that very seriously."

He took a drink, and looked down at the ice in his cup. "And I think you are in love with this second woman, no?"

"I'm too old and tired to believe much in love," I snorted. "I just don't want to see her get killed, too."

My friend looked at me steadily, measuring the lie. He shook his head.

"Sal Cleveland might kill you, you understand? Think about that before you get involved where no one asked you to or wants you to."

He gave me a crooked smile, and I smiled back. He made some sense.

"Or at least be in love with the woman who gets you killed," he said.

"What else can you tell me about Cleveland?" I lit a cigarette and pushed the package across the table to him.

He picked it up and lit one for himself. He held the smoke like someone who didn't do it often. "He's a *tarambana*," he said. "A good-for-nothing shit. He doesn't do any of his own work . . . he never has. That isn't even his real name, you know."

133

"I've heard that Cleveland isn't the name he was born with. He came here from Ohio."

"Who cares where he came from?" he said. "Unless you're Mexican, everyone here came from someplace else. He's so good looking he's almost beautiful. He does what he does because he has to, you understand? He has his clubs and his whores and his deals, and he plays with it like a child plays. He doesn't grow his business, he isn't interested in power and control because it makes him money."

He puffed at his smoke and spat a shred of tobacco off the end of his tongue.

"He just likes to hurt people."

"The money and power are a means to do that," I said. "A bonus."

"Are the people from Ohio so bad?" he asked. "I have never been there. Is he a typical person from Ohio?"

"People there are the same as people everywhere. I grew up in St. Louis, not so far from there. People are people, mostly."

"I thought as much," he said. "He mentions Ohio frequently, like it matters. Anyway, he likes the gangster life, he likes his clubs, because it gives a reason to be bad. He likes to be bad. He likes to hurt people."

"I understand," I said.

"Some people say he's *brujo*," he said. "A kind of witch. Does that scare you?"

I thought about it, and shook my head. Lopez watched me intently.

"Not a whole lot scares me," I said.

He nodded approvingly. "So, you have two problems with him. He killed the woman you were looking after, or thought you should look after, and there's a witness to it who you're afraid he'll come for, a woman you say you're not in love with. You want to bring him to justice?"

"I don't think it can happen that way," I said. "He's already sent some boys after the woman."

I told him about the pair parked in front of Annie's house.

"You're going to have a hard time getting to the head of this monster," he said. "He'll send his guys after you, one by one and two by two, and there are a lot of them. He never does his own dirty work. I'm surprised he shot the woman himself, if your witness friend is right."

"She's right," I said. "She says she saw him fire the shot, and I don't think she knows how to lie."

He looked strangely at me, but didn't comment.

"It will be hard to touch him in one of his clubs," he said. "You'd be cut to ribbons if you tried. You'll have to lure him out. If you interest him more than you already have, you might be sorry. Once he smells weakness, he is persistent. He enjoys it. He doesn't mind trouble."

"Neither do I."

"I know." He nodded. "Let me think on this for a little while, *si*? I'll talk to some people who I trust and get hold of you."

"There may not be much time," I said. "I think things are going to start happening fast, don't you?"

He didn't answer. He was looking at the traffic.

"I was a fisherman, did you know?" he asked. "In Corazón Rosa, my town. So very beautiful . . . on the ocean. I still have a house there, with a balcony that looks at the ocean. I'll go back one day, and leave all this to the *chacales,* the jackals."

"Corazón Rosa," I said. "Pink . . . heart?"

135

"Pink heart," he nodded. "The local mud has a certain color, something to do with minerals. All of the adobe looks pink, depending on the light. Some people think it makes the place look very beautiful."

"Sounds like something I'd like to see."

"If you get tired enough of this, let me know. Maybe I'll buy another boat and put you to work fishing. You might like it."

I touched his shoulder and went back to the Ford.

-Fourteen-

Some people think three o'clock in the morning is the worst time, the time we come closest to the sense of our own ending. The gray face that looks back from the bathroom mirror tells us what we'll look like when we're very old. It's when we know for sure that all clocks stop, sooner or later. It's the hour when investigations dead-end, when smoke tastes stale and strange things crawl out of doorways to lie down and sun themselves in the streetlights.

There's something worse, though. What's worse is looking at your watch, a little before five on a Friday afternoon, with another Friday night on the horizon. There's an anticipation of sounds—laughter, ice chiming in the evening's first drink, the whisper of silk, a ringing phone. There's the promise of lipstick and colored lights. And then you realize you have no place to go to, and no one to go there with.

I had been keeping my own company for a while, and this wasn't the first Friday night that I sat by the radio with the sports page in my lap. Tonight, the box scores all added up to numbers I didn't want to hear, and my living room was even gloomier than usual, so after a while I shrugged off the mood and put a tie on. I got my hat off its hook and locked the front door behind me. A cup of coffee and a piece of pie were going to be better than being alone. In fact, they would probably be swell company.

As I went down the steps, I glanced at the dark windows on Annie Kahlo's house. I felt a stab of loneliness and thought about knocking on her door, but in the end I didn't. Instead, I walked a few blocks up Ortega, past the cemetery to an all-night joint. Everyone called it Camel Diner, probably because there was a faded dromedary painted on the old cigarette advertisement beside the entrance. If the place had ever had another name, it was long forgotten.

I pulled open the door and went into the smells of coffee and fried onions. I didn't much like sitting at the counter, so I headed for a booth in the back.

"Hello, Nate. You're awful early tonight. You want the same as always, or you looking for adventure tonight?"

Roxanne was a redhead in her forties. She had a tired, pretty face and a husband who drove a bus. They were saving to move back to New York. They had been saving for more than ten years, and I had my doubts they were ever going to make it. You can learn a lot talking to the people in a diner, and maybe I knew more about Roxanne than I did about myself.

"I better not risk it," I said. "Same as always."

"Pie and coffee it is, then." She reached into her apron pocket and pulled out a small envelope. "Someone came in and left you something about an hour ago."

"I must be coming in here too regular," I said. "Who it was it, you know?"

I took it from her and slit the flap with a thumbnail. I shook a playing card onto the table and held the envelope up to make sure there was nothing else.

"Tall guy, thin . . . smelled kinda funny."

The card had the usual stylized bicycle printed on the back. This one seemed different to me, though, because the bicycle carried a rider, the line drawing of a man, unremarkable except that he carried a coil of rope over one shoulder.

"He smelled funny?" I said, still looking at the card. "How do you mean?"

"I'm not quite sure," she said. "Sort of sweet, like he'd been sick or something. Do sick people smell sweet? I don't know why I thought that."

I turned the card over. It was a six of spades. There was nothing written or marked on either side. I looked at the envelope again; it had no handwriting or marks on it either. Roxanne leaned over my shoulder to look, bringing in an aura of Beechnut chewing gum.

"What does it mean?" she asked.

"Beats me."

We both looked up at the tan suit that had joined us. Rex Raines smiled at Roxanne, and asked for coffee. She left to get the order. I pointed at the seat across from me, and he sat down.

"Saw you come in," he said. "I planned to get in touch tomorrow, anyway. You like this place?"

"I guess so. I've been coming to Camel's as long as I've lived here. You get to be a regular somewhere, you stop thinking about whether you like it or not."

"Like being married," he said.

"I was just thinking about that." I didn't elaborate, and after a moment he shifted in his seat, as though he was bracing himself.

"I have some news," he said. "Hopefully you see it as good news."

"Might as well just give it to me."

"He's in the clear," he said. "Cleveland didn't kill his wife."

I was instantly irate. "Says who?"

He put a hand on my arm. "Alibi's rock solid, Nate. He closed the Hi-lo Club that night. Didn't leave until after three. Bartender swears it."

"What . . . the ugly hag keeps a shotgun under the bar?" I demanded. "That's who's giving you their word?"

"There's a dozen or more folks who will back it up. He was nowhere near Highway 12 the night his wife got killed."

"Annie Kahlo saw him!"

I could feel the heat in my face. My voice raised, and several people turned on their stools to look.

"Annie Kahlo's a looney," he hissed. "Give it up, would you? You hate Sal Cleveland so bad you don't see straight any more. It's a dead end. If he did it, I'd arrest him. He didn't do it. Wouldn't you like to see the mug who shot her put away?"

I stood up. "That's exactly what I want, Rex. I guess your orders say different."

"Sal Cleveland's off-limits, and that's final. Leave him alone, or you're going to be in the kind of trouble I can't get you out of."

I slapped three dimes on the table and got my hat. I headed for the street. On my way, I brushed by Roxanne, who carried my pie and two coffee cups on a tray.

"Give it to him." I said. "On me."

I made it all the way to the door before the fury completely washed over me. I turned and marched back to the booth. Raines looked up at me, trying not to show his alarm.

"He shot her in the face!" I yelled. "She sat there with two goddamned broken legs and he shot her in the face! You have a witness to it and you won't do a good goddamned thing about it. To hell with it. If you can't do your job, I'll take care of the creep myself."

"You don't want to do that, Nate. You don't want to say it or even think it."

"The hell I don't," I snarled. "Watch me. I'll take care of this myself."

Something woke me up. I was stretched out uncomfortably on the living room sofa. I looked at the clock and wondered if it was ten past seven in the evening or the morning. The light outside the windows said it might be either. Whatever I had been dreaming about had left me with a sense of guilt as bad as the taste in my mouth. I wondered if I was drinking too much lately, and my parents or my ex-wife or the war had grown legs on a quarter-bottle of bourbon and come creeping back for a visit.

I sat up and rubbed my face. There was a knock on the front door. It was soft, tiny, and I almost didn't hear it at all. I crossed the room in my stocking feet.

Annie Kahlo stood waiting on the step, her head turned to watch the street. She wore something red-patterned and gauzy. Her hair was pulled back and covered by a scarf. Her profile was nearly severe, beautiful in the same way the old Egyptians had been beautiful. Nefertiti.

I had the absurd thought that I wouldn't much like to cross her if it came down to it.

She turned to look at me. Her eyes were dark, and said everything and nothing. I felt a stir of nerves.

"You were sleeping," she said.

"A little bit," I said, and didn't know how to take back the foolishness of it.

She looked behind her, back at the street.

"They're here now," she said. "They've come back."

"Who's come back, Annie?"

"Remember I told you that June was afraid of the Hespers? Now she's gone, and they've come for me. She can't protect me from them anymore."

141

She extended an arm straight out and pointed up the street, without turning her head or taking her eyes from mine. The gesture was odd, but I leaned out past her to look. I saw the humped trunk of the old pre-war Nash parked against the curb about halfway up the block. It had rusted wheels and faded blue paint. I knew the car.

"Son of a bitch," I breathed.

I turned inside to get my shoes, and then as quickly turned back to pull Annie inside. She resisted, and I let her go. I was down the steps and striding across the lawn in my socks when I realized that my coat with the gun in the pocket was inside. I kept going. It seemed like a long walk to the Nash. I felt the scrape of cement under my soles and my own breathing, but not much else. I slowed and stopped in the middle of the street when I came abreast of the driver's window.

The red-faced driver looked at me without expression, his eyes slitted. His partner leaned forward and smiled at me. He looked like a rat. I took a deep breath. "I told you that I didn't want to see you two again," I said. "I didn't want to see you anywhere at all, but the number one place I didn't want to see you was on this street."

"So go look somewhere else, peeper," the driver said. "Go find a place where you don't see us." He stared out of the windshield and drummed his fingers on the steering wheel, affecting boredom. The passenger door snicked open and the thin man got out and faced me over the top of the car. He held a revolver, and he rested it on the metal roof, aimed in my general direction. He kept smiling.

"You been around this town long enough you still ought not to need certain things explained," he said. "But if you do, you're in luck. We're the guys they send out to do the explaining."

The metal mechanism made a wet scrape as the thin man cocked the revolver. I had never much liked the sound of it. The gun still casually rested on the roof.

"You like to go places you ain't been invited to," he went on. "You poke your nose in where it shouldn't be. You take up for broads have nothing to do with you."

"Like Charlene Cleveland?" I asked. "Like her?"

The driver looked at me from the corner of his eye. I saw through the open window that he had also made a gun appear in his right hand. Everyone had one now, but me. I had come to this party under-dressed, and it was embarrassing.

"Like her," he nodded. "More important, like the gash across the street over there."

"The splat," the thin man laughed. "Boss calls her 'the splat'. I like it."

His shoulders shook, thinking about it. He didn't look at me. If I'd had a gun, I might have shot them both right then, but I didn't, so I couldn't.

"Sometimes you give a guy a message and he gets it," the driver said. "Sometimes he don't. Sometimes, it's like a dog. You can beat it as many times as you like, but if the message don't get through you have to take it out back and shoot it."

"That your plan?" I asked. I figured it must be.

A horn tapped once from across the street, somewhere behind me. All three of us looked over. Down the line of parked cars, the door of a plain black Hudson opened and a man got out. He adjusted his hat deliberately before he walked over to stand beside me.

"Get back in the car," he said pleasantly.

The thin guy swallowed and nodded. I saw that the guns had disappeared.

143

"Why don't you go back and sit on your porch and wait?" the man asked me, without taking his eyes from the Nash. It didn't sound like a suggestion. "I'll have a word here and then come to join you."

I didn't see that I had better options, so I walked across the street. When I went up the porch steps, I saw Annie sitting on a glider at the end of the veranda. It had come with the house, and I had never sat in it. She had put her dark glasses on, and sat with her knees drawn up, hugging herself. She didn't say a word.

I parked a haunch on the railing and looked down the street at the old sedan. The third man bent over and looked into the driver's window.

"Cop," I said to myself, since Annie wasn't talking. "Cop for sure."

The man stepped back, away from the car, and its engine started up. He watched as it coughed blue smoke and rolled down the hill. It turned the corner at the bottom and disappeared. He slapped his palms together as though they were dusty, and started toward where we sat. He wore a brown suit with a vest. His yellow tie went well with the cocoa straw hat that shaded his eyes.

When he reached us, he put a foot on the bottom step and stood staring at me. His look wasn't challenging; it seemed more like he was memorizing my face. He gave a tiny nod, like a tic, and then looked over to where Annie sat on the glider. She hadn't moved. Behind her dark glasses, she stared straight ahead and didn't shift her head to look at him.

"Those men won't bother you anymore," he said. "They were off the reservation, so to speak."

His clothing was vivid, but the man himself looked curiously bleached. He had pale red hair, going gray, and faded blue eyes that bulged.

"They weren't bothering me," I said. "I looked forward to talking to them some more."

"Suit yourself," he said.

I lit a cigarette to buy myself a minute. My mouth still tasted like metal, and the smoke was comforting.

"You going to show me your badge?" I asked.

"I don't think so," he said.

"Got a name?"

"Name's Earnswood," he said. "And you're Nathaniel Crowe. I already know so."

"And you happened to be parked on our street at the same time as those guys? Just coincidence, or do you have an interest in a guy named Sal Cleveland? Those are his guys."

He pursed his lips and thought about it. "I don't know anyone named Cleveland," he said. "Whether or not we have the same interests, we'll see."

He glanced at Annie again. She didn't return the look, and he shrugged and stepped off the porch. Halfway across the lawn, he turned back. "You said I was parked on your street. It isn't your street. All the streets in this town are my streets. You might want to remember that."

I didn't answer him. As soon as he settled in his Hudson, he pulled it from the curb and gunned it. He didn't look over at us when he went by.

"He's a liar," Annie said. "He's a policeman, and he's lying."

She hadn't moved. I couldn't read her eyes behind the dark lenses. I went over to where she sat on one end of the glider and parked myself on the other. I wanted to touch her, but I didn't.

"You know him, Annie? What is it he's lying about?"

"He knew my father."

145

Her voice was flat. She held herself very still. It worried me a little. "He was friends with Sal," she said. "He used to come to the ranch. He was younger then, but I recognize him. He's the policeman."

"He was at the ranch, together with Sal Cleveland?" I asked.

"He's one of the ones who killed my father. He's part of it."

I lowered myself to sit on the porch floor in front of her. I took off her glasses as gently as I could, and set them on the seat beside her. I took both of her hands in both of mine and looked up at her face. "Annie, the police aren't even going to arrest Sal for killing his wife. They aren't interested in justice for something happened twenty-five years ago."

Her almond-shaped eyes went wide. "I saw him do it," she protested. "I was right there."

"Even so."

It relieved me that she didn't press for details. I didn't want to have to explain why the cops didn't want her testimony, or why they didn't trust her as a witness. I looked to shift the subject.

"I don't know," she said slowly, "if you should get involved in all this. Maybe I'm asking for too much."

"This is my battle, too," I said. "I am involved. He shot my client. I forced him to give her a divorce. I showed him up, and he took it out on her. That's the truth of it."

"It wasn't your fault," she said. "She hired you to help her, and that's what you did. You helped her."

"I think it's time you told me about the rest of it," I said. "About Sal Cleveland, about this Earnswood fellow, about June and your father—all of it. About you."

Her eyes looked raw. I saw the beginnings of tears.

146

"Tell me what happened to you," I said. "Tell me, Annie."

I pulled her down to me and held her while she cried. After a while, the shaking subsided, and when she spoke again her voice sounded different.

"My parents are from Hawaii," she said. "They never should have come here. They didn't belong in this place. If they weren't from here, then neither am I."

"Both of them were Hawaiian?" I said, surprised. "I knew that your mother was."

"She was *haole.* Blonde hair and green eyes. She wasn't born there. She came from New York, and her family had money. She brought my father here, and she abandoned him here and went back. Left him . . . and us."

A man and a woman passed by, walking some kind of a Boxer dog. The man glanced over and saw us. He gave a small nod. The dog nosed at the fallen walnuts on my lawn and decided against them. They went on by and out of sight.

"Our last name was Kahala," she said. "He changed it to Kahlo because he thought it sounded American. It doesn't though, does it? Sound American?"

"I suppose not," I said. "I thought your mother was the native islander. I suppose because she went back and your father stayed."

"She was Hawaiian . . . here." She touched her chest. "He was just lost. He bought the ranch with her money."

"What was she like, your mother?"

"She was elegant. Even living on the ranch, she was perfect. She told Junie and me that nothing was ever an excuse for looking and acting like we'd fallen off a banana boat."

She smiled a little at the memory.

"One morning, we woke up and she was gone. She left a note that said she would send for us. She never did, or if she did it came too late."

"How old were you?" I asked.

"I was sixteen," she said. "June, only eight."

"Too young," I murmured, and her expression changed.

"How old is old enough to lose your mother?" she asked.

I nodded, conceding the point.

"My father wouldn't give up on raising his avocados, even if he had two girls to raise," she said. "He was in debt, and he never got out. He borrowed money from Sal Cleveland, and when he couldn't pay it back, Sal started using the ranch. He kept barrels of liquor in the barn, and used the property to sell it. He used it for other things, too, whatever he wanted to hide."

I thought about the photograph.

"Cleveland got the run of a secluded place, complete with outbuildings and a built-in night watchman in lieu of payment."

"Yes," she nodded. "When Sal got interested in something else on the ranch, and started spending most of his free time hanging around, there was nothing my dad could do about it."

"What else was he interested in?"

She looked at me steadily. A wing of light hair hung across her eyes. Her skin was gold, and I wanted badly to kiss her, but I didn't.

"Me," she said. "Sal Cleveland was interested in me. I was interested in him, too."

I hadn't expected this.

"You were awfully young," I said. "Fifteen?"

"I was seventeen when I started to be with him."

She looked at me steadily, and it struck me again how dark her eyes were.

"He was young, too," she said. "Older than me, but still young. My mother liked him."

"And your father?"

"He didn't like it. Of course he didn't like it. Sal was a bad man, even as a boy."

"So a creep, a bad guy starts to make time with his daughter, but he owes him money and has to put up with it," I said. "That about it?"

"It wasn't just the money," she said. "My father had his weaknesses, but he was never a coward. It was more than that. Sal had powers. He had spells. He's probably more powerful now."

"Not the first time I've heard that. I still don't know what it means."

"He can make people destroy themselves. If you cross him, he'll hurt you, or worse, make you hurt yourself. He knows some kind of black magic. He uses a deck of cards."

"I don't much believe in black magic, Annie. So your father put up with it for a while, and then one day he changed his mind and sent you away?"

"Yes, exactly," she said. "My father knew it would be dangerous, but he sent me away anyway. He sent me to live in New York with my mother's relatives. Sal became furious. He gave my dad a deadline to have me back at the ranch."

A half-dozen crows fluttered in and wandered the deep shadows of my small front yard. They seemed to be looking for something. Every once in a while, one of them gave a small hop, as though startled.

149

"And your dad didn't do it," I said. "He left you in New York."

She nodded. She watched the crows intently.

"What made him finally decide to get you away from Cleveland? What made him stop accepting things as they were?"

She turned her head slowly and looked at me. Her eyes were strange, blank.

"Sal told my dad he planned to marry me," she said. "He said I belonged to him. He said he loved me."

I was a little bit surprised. I didn't think about guys like Sal Cleveland being in love. Maybe he had been different when he was younger; maybe he had still been a little bit human.

"How did you feel?" I asked. "How did you feel about him?"

She got quiet for so long I was sure she wouldn't answer, but she did. Her voice was hoarse. "I don't remember," she said. "I know how I feel now."

It was a little while before I realized she was crying again. Nothing made me as useless as a woman's tears, and I'd had my fill of them lately. "What's wrong, Annie?"

"I lied," she said. "I don't lie, but I suppose I did. I don't know why they had to make me lie."

"Lied about what?" I asked. "Who made you lie?"

At some point, I had gotten up from the porch floor and sat myself on the glider beside her. I put one arm across her shoulders, and after a minute I gathered her in to me. She spoke against my chest.

"I don't lie," she repeated. "Ever."

"I know you don't, Annie. Tell me what it is that you want to clear up."

"I didn't find June's body recently."

150

"What was the lie?"

"I found her years ago, not long after she was killed. I snuck back here from time to time over the years. I was keeping her for myself. I always worried that someone else would find her, so I finally bought my house and moved back here, even though I knew it was dangerous and Sal would find out I came back to Santa Teresa."

"You were keeping your sister's body?" I asked. "Keeping it for what?"

"She was so little. I had to take care of her. I held her hand and talked to her."

I thought about the mummified little girl in the dark barn. She had been bones, skin and dried hair, held together by the rotted remains of a pink party dress. The woman I held had kept her company.

Annie was insane. I realized it now. I had met a lot of crazy people, and as a rule I didn't much mind them. Most had a natural honesty that so-called sane people didn't. I had never fallen in love with one, though, and I didn't know what the rules were.

"She was all I had," Annie said. "Now they've taken her away."

I wondered if loving a crazy person could make me crazy, too. I figured there were worse things.

"You didn't lie," I said. "You're allowed to have secrets. Protecting a secret isn't the same as lying. Don't let anyone tell you it is."

"So nothing will happen to Sal? He just gets away with it?"

"Not if I can help it, Annie."

"She should have had her life."

"I know."

We didn't say anything else. We sat there for a long time and looked at the clean California twilight. Annie fell asleep. After a while, the strollers and the playing children and the dog-walkers all went inside and left us the empty sidewalk. The streetlights came on and then I fell asleep, too.

When I woke up a little while later, Annie was gone. I went inside to bed.

-Fifteen-

The next morning, I went to my office bright and early. I wasn't always sure why I kept an office. Some guys in the business didn't; they relied on word-of-mouth, printed business cards, and the telephone. I liked having one. It was a place to go. It was a reason to brush my hair and put on a necktie in the morning.

I slid open the window behind my desk. Three floors above the street, the air felt cool, nearly cold. The sun had just come up, but it was already losing its battle with coastal smudge and the smoke from the fires outside the city. It couldn't chase away the shadows from the street below. The traffic was just getting started, and in between the occasional hiss of brakes and bursts of exhaust the neighborhood was quiet.

Somewhere out of sight, a truck backfired a couple of times with a sound like gunshots. It startled me for just a moment, and then instinct subsided and I relaxed again. State Street was somewhere between the drunken craziness of the night before and the hum of normal daylight business that was coming. It was a pause in the city that you had to get up early to see, and I liked it fine.

If I sat on the sill and leaned out far enough, I could see a sliver of the Pacific, five blocks down. No matter how many times I looked, it was never the same color. This morning the clouds were low and gray, but the ocean was a blue-green that almost glowed. Someone told me once that the water reflected the sky, but I've never found it to be particularly true. The ocean doesn't follow anyone's rules but its own.

"It's going to rain tonight."

The voice called up from the sidewalk, thirty feet below the window. Annie Kahlo looked up at me. I was happy to see her.

"It might rain any minute," I called back.

She shook her head, definite. "Tonight," she said. "The fires will all be out soon."

"Going to take a lot of rain to put this fire out," I said. "Come on up. I have coffee and a clean cup."

"The life of a private detective," she laughed up at me. "Cream and sugar, maybe read a little. Cream and sugar, look out the window."

"It's a dangerous racket," I agreed.

She wore a white dress printed with a pattern that looked like handwriting, and her hair was tied up in a scarf. It set off the gold tones in her skin. She looked like about a million dollars even, with less than a nickel's change back.

"I have a better idea," she said. "You come down. I'll buy you a cup of coffee in some strange place you've never been to."

A big truck was trying to get into the alley behind the Schooner Inn. It said "Schlitz" on the side in maroon-and-white script. The driver had some trouble with the corner, and the cars began to back up behind him. From up the line, the first horn blew. Encouraged by the bravery, others joined in. A man in a blue coupe gunned his engine and swung around. A car coming from the other direction locked its brakes and shrieked.

"Come down now?" I asked, and pantomimed looking at my watch. "Leave my office during business hours? That has to be against some kind of rules."

"Rules?" She smiled up at me. "I hate rules and so do you. Sitting in your window and yelling down into the street at strange women is against the rules, too."

154

"You aren't strange," I said.

"Oh, yes I am," she laughed. "Count on it."

"You might be right," I smiled. "I'm on my way."

I was still smiling as I slid the window back down and picked up my keys off the desk. My steps echoed down the steps around and around and out to the front door and the street where Annie waited. She was radiant.

"You look good," I said. "I worried about you last night."

"Never worry about me," she said.

She took my arm and we walked south. The sidewalks on State Street were wide and made up of colored concrete poured in geometric patterns. It looked like dusty tile. Bars ran down the block, most of them closed for whatever morning cleaning they got before another tired day of drinking got started. There were other businesses in between, but the open ones didn't have any trade yet.

"You feeling better about things?" I asked.

"A little," she said. "I read a *National Geographic* this morning. It had to do with baby elephants."

We walked a little further in silence. A man in a white shirt and tie swept the cement in front of a jewelry store. He eyed Annie appreciatively as we passed. I thought about asking him who bought jewelry at eight o'clock in the morning, but I kept my mouth shut.

"Baby elephants?" I prompted.

She looked at me, faintly surprised. "What about them?" she asked.

"Is there more?" I asked. "To the magazine article?"

"They reminded me of something. The baby elephants. Something sweet and wonderful, but I don't know what. There was so much more . . . "

"More?" I prompted.

155

"There's always more," she said. "Sometimes all at once. Aside from spelling, punctuation and grammar errors, there's always more."

Her free hand gestured around us, expansive and graceful. We were only a block from the beach, and the color of the water was still a luminous turquoise under the dirty sky. I wouldn't have minded a closer look, but she steered me into the coffee shop.

Noises echoed off the high ceilings and plastered walls of the nearly empty place. Obviously a dark watering hole until recently, the bright lights and low counter inside looked unnatural. Pale shadows on the walls revealed where pictures and menu boards used to hang.

It all looked like someone else's dream.

Hand-lettered signs pushed New York Style doughnuts for a nickel. I didn't know why anyone would want them on the west coast, but I'd never run into a really bad doughnut anywhere. We got coffee from a woman who was still half asleep and took it to sit at a wooden table where we did the cream and sugar ritual.

"Why did you ask me about the baby elephants?" Annie asked.

Her mouth was faintly amused. She always had a complete stillness about her features, but more expression moving beneath the quiet than anyone I had ever met. I struggled to find the right words. "I was interested. Just for a second, I thought they reminded me of something, too. I see things differently when you tell me about them. When you talk, I always want to hear more. I want to see what you see. Does that make any sense?"

She looked at me for a long time, and finally gave a very slight nod. "Even if it didn't," she said. "It could."

I nodded back, relieved. She understood, or close enough. I tasted my coffee. It wasn't bad at all.

"Are you feeling better about last night?" I asked.

"I'm fine," she said. "Much better now. I changed my mind."

"Changed your mind? About what?"

"I don't want you to kill anyone. You can still help me find out what happened to June, but I don't need you to kill Sal."

I stirred another spoonful of sugar into my coffee to cover up the relief I felt. "I wanted to ask you something," I said. "You were gone from Santa Teresa for what, twenty years, or more?"

She looked at me over the rim over her cup. I paused to give her a chance to answer, but she didn't.

"You lived in New York and England and Mexico. You can't have many good memories here. Why did you come back?"

Her half-smile didn't budge. I took the plunge.

"Because of Sal Cleveland? Did you come back because of him?"

Her expression changed. Her eyes moved away; she looked a little bit trapped. "I told you, I came back to watch over June."

"Do you still have feelings for him?" I persisted.

She picked up her bag and slung it over her shoulder. She slid her knees from under the table, and I realized she was leaving. My face grew hot.

"You do, don't you?" I asked. "Is that what this is all about? Asking me to kill him?"

She stood beside the table, staring at me. I realized how slender she was, and how all-at-once vulnerable she looked. I was caught right between the tides of jealousy and pity. She slipped on the dark glasses.

"Go to hell, Nathaniel," she said, and walked out.

I stayed and finished my coffee. There was no point in wasting it.

A crowd gathered in front of my building. I saw the red light blinking on the back of a prowl car pulled onto the sidewalk. Another black-and-white blocked the middle of the street, and still another sat in the intersection of State and Ortega. I crossed the road and pushed through the gathered people like I had some business doing it. Most of them moved aside willingly.

A uniformed cop who I knew from around was setting up a flimsy wooden barricade across the mouth of the alley.

"What's the excitement?" I asked him.

"We're kind of busy here, Crowe," he said, without looking up.

He fitted the end of a board into a metal brace, and then straightened to look at me.

"How you doing, Sullivan?" I asked. "This is my building."

"Yeah? You see anything last night or this morning?"

"Anything to do with what?"

He jerked a thumb over his shoulder, into the alley.

"Got two guys not moving," he said. "In the blue car back there. Someone called it in a half hour ago."

I peered over his shoulder. The gap ran between two structures; my office building in front and a repair garage in the rear. Garbage cans lined the laneway. Most of them belonged to the restaurant on the ground floor of my building. At the far end, just before the alley turned to the

158

right and out of sight, I saw the tail end of a car surrounded by official-types, milling around. The humped shape identified it as a Nash; an old one, faded and rusty.

"Son of a bitch," I murmured. "Can I get back there?"

"Let him through, Sullivan."

The voice belonged to Rex Raines. He stood fifteen or twenty feet up the alley in the shade. His normally sunny expression was closed-up and grim. The beat cop shrugged and moved aside.

"Mind you don't tear your skirt, Crowe," he said.

I stepped over the barrier and walked over to join Raines. We didn't shake hands.

"Figured I'd see you here," he said. "Said to myself 'Where's Crowe?', and here you are."

"Why? What's that supposed to mean?"

"The last time I saw you we were looking at a mummified little girl on the coroner's table," he said. "You were bent out of shape at Sal Cleveland, you said you had a witness who saw him kill your client."

"My client, his wife."

He looked over his shoulder at the blue car.

"Now I got a couple of Cleveland's gunsels sitting there with holes in their heads," he said. "Right outside your office. What're the odds, you think?"

I gave him a look, and he spread his hands.

"Not saying you did this," he said. "I just expected to see you around, that's all. This happened about an hour ago. Kitchen worker in the restaurant heard the shots."

"As it happens, I think I know the car," I said.

He raised an eyebrow and waited for me to say more.

"It looks like a car been hanging around my neighborhood," I said. "Cleveland's guys, trying to intimidate Annie Kahlo, the witness you don't want to believe."

"Never said I don't believe her," he said. "I said she's too crazy to go in front of a judge. You think it's the same guys?"

"I'd have to see them."

"Let's take a look."

The blue Nash sat and waited for us. It looked tired and sad and haunted. I don't think I'm an especially superstitious man, although I don't know if many of us came back from the war without at least a few charms laid away against the constant fear. There was always something about a scene with dead people in it that seemed to echo, as though the people who had left weren't all the way gone.

The group of official uniforms that stood around the car paused and watched us approach. They were waiting, too. Everyone waited and the walk down the alley to the car seemed to take a long time.

"You identify these guys?" I asked Raines, just to be saying something.

"Sure we did," he said. "We know these two. They've been players for a long time. We know everyone in the game. Names are Raw and Lowen."

A patrolman stood at the door of the car. Raines nodded to him, and he stepped back. He used a handkerchief to pull on the Nash's door handle. The hinges squealed loudly, like they didn't want the door to be opened.

The driver's hand fell off the steering wheel and dangled limp by his side. Blood smeared the sleeve of his light blue suit. It looked like a pretty nice outfit got ruined. I knew the guy didn't imagine when he was putting it on that it would be the coroner who took it off him.

"Guy behind the wheel is Raw," Raines said. "Goes by 'Dog'. The skinny one over there is Virgil Lowen."

The light blue suit belonged to the red-faced guy who had been sitting on my street, all right. The last time I had seen him, I'd had a pistol stuck into his collar. I held my breath against the smell of blood and leaned into the car. The skinny guy who had pulled his heater on me slumped against the far door, like a sleeping child. Both of them had been shot in the head.

"Raw and Lowen, huh?" I mused. "I told them I'd kill them if I saw them again. Someone beat me to it."

"Some mother's child," Raines said. "Somebody's broken heart, now."

He stared at the dead men.

"Bad guys, though," I said. "They broke a lot of other hearts."

"They were bad guys, yes," he agreed.

He shook his head. "I seen a lot of stiffs," he mused. "In the war, and now on the job. It gets so I don't care so much. They aren't people I know, and mostly they signed up for whatever got them. Every once in a while, it crosses my mind."

I nodded when he looked at me. I knew what he was going to say.

"Every once in a while I remember that it was a kid once. Somebody who passed out paper valentines in a classroom and watched a certain girl or boy to see how they'd look when they read it. A person who got held when they were a baby. Some woman looked down at their face and thought they were the most perfect thing she ever saw in her whole life. It hurts a little when you think about it like that."

He looked at me and shrugged. "So then I remember it's just a job, and I don't think about it anymore. One thing's a little strange here. See the rope?"

I looked where he pointed. The end of a hemp cord dangled over the seat back, between the two men. It trailed onto the floor of the back seat. It didn't look like a new rope.

"There's been a rumor for a long time that when Raw and Lowen did a job, they tied up their marks and took them someplace private for some . . . games, before they killed them."

"Women?" I asked.

"Men and women," he said. "They had a taste for sex with doomed people. That's the story, anyway. Who knows where it started, might not be true."

Suddenly, I felt a lot less sorry for them. "Cleveland kills enough people that he kept a couple of monsters on the payroll?" I asked. "He have enough work for them?"

"Nah, not really," he answered. "This isn't Tijuana or L.A. These guys may have indulged their tastes from time to time with a missing person or two. Lot of desert around this city... a missing hooker or tosspot bum vanishes, who's the wiser?"

He paused to light a cigarette. "Rope makes it look like something to me," he said. "Looks like someone might have been tied up and got free, someone who got their hand on a gun. They missed once. See the hole in the windshield? Lowen's shot in the side of the head. He was turning around. This wasn't any calm execution, I don't think."

"So . . . two guys I was having a problem with tie someone up in back of my office, someone who gets free and turns the tables," I said. "Why outside my office, first thing in the morning? Doesn't add up."

162

"Everything adds up some way, pal," he said. "We'll find out what it adds up to, sooner or later."

"Last time these guys were parked on my street, a cop named Earnswood came along and shooed them off. He had been watching them."

"Earnswood?" he asked. "Which Earnswood?"

"Brass is what I hear," I said. "Upstairs guy. You must know him. Why was he interested in these two?"

His face became suddenly guarded. "Of course I know Earnswood. I don't know why he'd be interested in these two."

"Might be a good thing to find out," I said.

He stared thoughtfully at the blue Nash. The smell of blood seemed stronger. I had seen enough. "Maybe not," he said. "That might be a good thing to not know anything about. There's one more thing."

He led me over to the open driver's door. "You'll have to lean in." He sounded apologetic. "Look at what's on the front seat. Don't touch anything. Once we get them out, the print boys still have work to do."

I did as he said, with my breath held. On the seat beside Raw's fat, slack knee, a playing card rested. It had been torn in half, and both pieces faced up. The atmosphere inside the car was unbearable, and I backed out quickly.

"Three of spades," Raines said. "Mean anything to you?"

I felt as though I couldn't get enough air.

"Not a thing," I managed.

He nodded and waved the morgue boys in. We walked back toward the light at the end of the alley.

-Sixteen-

I spent the rest of the day at the office, waiting for something to happen. Nothing did. I tried to reach Annie Kahlo on the telephone, but she didn't answer. At four o'clock, I pulled the bottle from my desk drawer. I looked at it for a while and put it back. I went home early instead.

When I got there, I left the Ford on the street in front of the house for no particular reason, except I wanted to be able to reach it in a hurry if I needed to. I stood at the curb and looked over at Annie's house. The dusk was too early for anyone to have lights on so I couldn't tell if she was home. My own windows were dark as pitch.

Halfway up the walk I fumbled with my keys. A movement caught at the corner of my eye. A woman came out of the Gardiner's house. She wore a blue dress and a blue hat that looked as though it had been run over in the road. She looked over at me as she headed for the street. She was squat and walked with an odd shambling gait that seemed familiar. She reached the passenger door of a gray Dodge before I recognized her.

The last time I had seen her, she'd been using a shotgun to poke me in the ribs outside the Hi-Lo Club.

"Hey, wait!" I called, and started toward the car.

I was too late. The Dodge blew a smoke ring at me and rolled down the hill to the stop sign at the bottom. I was suddenly very worried about the Gardiners. Cleveland's people didn't often visit to socialize. I took their porch steps two at a time. The front door stood open behind the screen. I rapped on the wooden frame and peered in. I didn't see anyone. I pressed the doorbell and heard the chime somewhere inside.

The faint sound of a phonograph recording came from deeper in the house. I looked back at the street, deciding what to do. I rang the bell again. I wasn't really alarmed. Not yet. I tried to identify the music. I'd heard it before.

"Mahler," the doctor said, appearing suddenly on the other side of the screen. "Symphony Number Five."

"You read minds, too?" I asked, relieved. "That's a pretty good trick. Is your wife at home?"

"Do you know Mahler's Fifth?" he asked.

I shook my head, no, and we stood and looked at each other for a while. Then he turned and disappeared into the house. After a minute, Mrs. Gardiner appeared in his place.

"Did you just have a visitor?" I asked her.

"Annie Kahlo came here earlier," she said. "For lunch . . . hours ago."

"Just now," I said. "Not Annie, someone else. A woman just came out of your house . . . in a blue dress."

She looked concerned. "There was no woman here just now, Mister Crowe," she said. "A blue dress? What's this about?"

"She just came out of your house. I saw her. Was your door locked?"

"We never lock during the day. Whatever for? We were in the back yard. We didn't hear anyone until you rang the bell."

"Over and over," the doctor said. She shushed him, and he turned and went up the hall.

"Why ever would someone come into our home without an invitation?" she wondered. "I don't much like the idea."

"She's connected with a case I'm working, and she isn't a friendly party," I said. "She may have been meaning to snoop around my place, and just found the wrong house. I came home early. It's just luck I was here to see her."

"Can you tell me about it?" she asked. "It sounds terribly fascinating."

I was unsure if I wanted to involve the couple. The woman had been inside their home, though, so maybe they deserved to know a little. "It's a long story," I said.

"Then come in," she said. "We were just sitting down to cocktails, and I could never tolerate a long story without a martini in my hand."

I started to decline, but decided that a drink was probably a good idea. She held the door for me, and I followed her down the hallway that led to the back of the house.

"Don't be offended, but I'm skeptical about long stories," she said from in front of me. "I mean, look at the Bible. Now there's a book with lots of words that run on. It certainly needs a drink if you're going to read much of the early part."

She stopped suddenly, and I nearly ran into the back of her. She had turned around to admonish me. "Just when one is trying to read it aloud to a young person, it goes into all the generations, this one begat that one begat another one, the sons of sons of sons. It goes on almost forever."

She looked fiercely at me, and I nodded politely.

"If anything ever wanted editing, it's that," she said. "Boy, oh boy, I'd love to have the job, too. Just hand me the nearest machete. It wouldn't take me long."

She was off again. The walls were warm wood, hung at intervals with water-colored paintings that were luminous, even in the half-light. They all looked to me like they had been done with the same hand, but I didn't know any more about art than I did about Mahler.

166

The doors at the end led into a glass-roofed conservatory and then outside from there. The air in the greenhouse was damp enough I wanted to wipe my face. Vines and plants with fat leaves covered everything, elbowing and reaching for the light. The room was hung with blossoms, and the fragrances were so heavy and alive that they were nearly oppressive.

"Pink," Mrs. Gardiner said. "This is my husband's space. Pink is the only color he grows."

I recognized lilies and orchids, but I didn't know the names of most of what I was looking at. All the foliage burst with blooms in various shades of pink.

"I like pink as much as the next person," she said. "The roses outside are mine, and I grow every color I can think of, not just pink. I like a lot of color. We keep most of our paintings in the basement. I can go down there and lose complete track of time in all that color. Sometimes I'm gone for days."

"You have a basement?" I asked. "I don't see many basements here. We had basements back in St. Louis."

"We had it dug during the war. The expense was terrible. The construction people told us that usually a basement is dug first, and then the house built on top of it, not the other way round. I couldn't see why it made a difference, and I told them so."

She motioned me toward the jewel-paned doors which led to the terrace outside. I saw the doctor already at the glass table, readying the drink tray.

"Close the door quickly behind you," she said. "He'll be fussy for hours if you let his damned humidity out. He's very scientific about it."

We crossed the stone tiles to sit down.

167

"We had a Japanese gardener," she said. "Things were chaotic when the war started, and they were going to send Mister Tsukimoto and his family to a government camp. I had the basement made for them to live in. It was a very comfortable place to hide."

"Nice of you," I commented.

"It was, wasn't it? He was an exceptional gardener, and I wasn't going to find another one like him if he got locked up. I believe in being honest about things. There's nothing wrong with being selfish if you're doing good at the same time."

I heard the peacocks rustling and settling for the night somewhere in the borders, but I didn't see them. The roses were as promised, pastel in the failing light. They trailed over trellises and climbed the walls behind the jacaranda trees. I hadn't paid them much attention the last time I had been here. Annie had been sitting across from me, and she tended to eclipse everything else.

"Are they still here?" I asked. "The Japanese family?"

"Oh, no. He found out I came from Hawaii, and got the idea that because of Pearl Harbor I would to try to capture him and his family and lock them up in the basement. As a sort of revenge, I expect. I tried to explain that I didn't hold him responsible, but he wouldn't listen. He gave notice and the very next day, mind you, took himself and his family away to live in Arizona, or maybe it was New Mexico. Anyway, some strange place, can you imagine?"

"You lived in Hawaii?" I asked. "I know Annie Kahlo had family connections there. Her parents came here from the islands, but I suppose you knew that, since you've known her for a long time. I was stationed at Pearl during the war. Strange coincidence we all know the place. Did you live there for very long?"

"How interesting," she said, and sat up to watch what the peacocks were doing.

"Bourbon," I said, when the doctor asked.

Mrs. Gardiner knocked back her drink. She usually sipped.

"Bitters, naturally," Mrs. Gardiner said. "And tell him how many lumps of sugar you take, or he'll put too many. He always does."

"No sugar," I said. "No bitters. Just a glass, if you have one handy. Sometimes that passes for civilized where I come from."

They both paused to look at me strangely. The doctor looked like he might refuse me.

"Where's the ocelot?" I asked, just to change the subject.

"I'm sure I haven't any idea," she said. "We don't keep him prisoner, you know. He often goes over the wall to Annie's house and spends time with her when she's at home."

It startled me. My own back yard lay between this one and Annie Kahlo's property. "He does?" I asked. "He goes through my yard?"

"You don't mind, do you? You don't seem to use it for anything, except to collect fallen walnuts."

"How about the peacocks?" I asked. "Doesn't he bother them?"

"Ocelots don't bother anybody as a rule," she said. "As long as they're kept fed, and this one is. Tell me about the woman in the blue dress."

I tasted my drink.

"She's someone I'm worried about," I said. "I think I'd better tell you all of it, starting with some things you already know."

The Gardiners liked to hear edited versions of my old cases, but I didn't usually spill my guts about current ones. In this instance, I was being paid in birthday cake and didn't know if it was even a real case. Besides, my business with Sal Cleveland was personal, so I didn't mind telling them a little.

I told them about the avocado ranch. I told them it was Annie's strange inheritance, the place where her family had died, and where she had recently witnessed a cold-blooded murder. All of it centered on Sal Cleveland.

Annie Kahlo was in grave danger, I believed. I didn't know if it was only because she had seen the Charlene Cleveland shooting, or if there were other reasons. Things were building, and I didn't think she would survive them if I didn't step in. I didn't mention that I had my own agenda for wanting Sal Cleveland brought down.

Dr. Gardiner sat across the table from me and watched his wife's face. His own was nearly expressionless. He reached across to pour more liquid from the pitcher into her martini glass when she needed it, and tonight she seemed to need it a lot.

"She knew Mister Cleveland when she was quite young," Mrs. Gardiner said, and looked at me almost apologetically. "I don't think she's completely gotten over him, even after all these years."

I was surprised. I had known Annie was friendly with the Gardiners, but I didn't imagine it as a very old friendship. Annie had only lived on the street for a little while.

170

"I've known Annie for her whole life," she said, as though I'd asked. She concentrated on her martini glass and didn't elaborate. I waited for a moment and moved on.

"Two men were sent after Annie," I said. "I don't know if they were supposed to kill her or to scare her. They can't do it anymore, because they were found in a State Street alley shot to death. Those men had instructions for me when they finished with Annie."

"We don't need to know about this," the doctor interrupted.

"Yes, you do. I don't know who killed them. I'm the obvious suspect, but I didn't do it. Sal Cleveland isn't going to take this sitting down."

"This still has nothing to do with us."

"The woman in the blue dress who came out of your house is named Raw. She's the widow of one of the two men. She's a nasty, dangerous piece of work, and she's going to be trouble. She ran off when I came along. You left your door unlocked, and you can't do that anymore."

"Why ever would these people want to hurt us?" Mrs. Gardiner asked. "We haven't done a thing."

"You have a connection with Annie, and that may be enough if they find out. I think you should steer clear of both me and Annie for a little while."

"Because of some woman in a blue dress?" she asked. "You have no idea of the things I haven't steered clear of in my lifetime, young man. It's quite late for me to learn to steer clear of people and situations now. If she or her friends come back into my house uninvited again, they'll be in for a shock. You can be quite sure of it."

The doctor filled her glass yet again. Her color was good, but otherwise she showed no signs of any martini effect. I thought to myself again that she must have been a hell of a good-looking woman in her day. Maybe she still was.

"Anyway, the ocelot is here," she said. "Those people wouldn't like to run into him."

"I thought you said he wasn't dangerous."

She looked at me archly. "Anything and anyone can be dangerous if the situation dictates it," she said. "The sweetest thing in the world can be deadly if it's wronged in just the right way."

I finished my bourbon and watched the jacaranda trees for any sign of the ocelot, but if he was around he didn't show himself.

"What do they call those shoes?" I asked.

Danny Lopez stretched a foot out so we could both admire his sandal.

"*Huaraches*," he said. "Hand-made, very comfortable."

"Little bit hard to be a Latin gangster in those, isn't it? They don't make you look very tough."

He leaned back against the picnic table and lit the end of a cigar stub. When he had it going, he puffed on it a few times and looked over at me. "You be tough, *mi amigo*," he said. "I prefer comfortable."

The odors of frying food drifted from the drive-in. I wasn't hungry. It was pleasant in the seating area under the trees; the sun felt soft and I could smell the beach a few blocks away. Traffic on Chapala was light. Lopez watched the cars go by.

"So there's been trouble," he said.

"There's been trouble," I agreed.

"What do you know about the people got killed?"

"It was the same two guys who I chased off my street. Twice."

"Twice?" he raised an eyebrow. "I didn't know about twice."

"First time, I told them I'd kill them if I saw them again. It didn't scare them enough, I guess, and they came back. Cop named Earnswood was parked on the street watching, and he stepped in and shooed them off."

"Earnswood's dirty," he said, shaking his head. "He doesn't work the street. He's been in an office on the top floor of the police station for many years now."

"He struck me as . . . wrong," I said. "I still don't know why he was parked watching those guys."

"Maybe he was watching you."

A carload of young Mexicans pulled in, with a girl in sunglasses and scarf behind the wheel. They piled out and headed for the counter, chattering voices and animated laughter.

"There's something we don't see yet, *amigo*," he said. "You represented the Cleveland woman."

"Charlene," I said. "Her name was Charlene."

"She gets the divorce from Cleveland, and so he kills her himself, which is unusual. You weren't a witness to it, and there's nothing you can do about it. So why does he go after you at all? If it were a different man, maybe it would be to set you as example, but Sal Cleveland never rocks more boats than he has to. He does what he does quietly, from behind. Not like this."

I stayed quiet and let him think it through.

"He preys on the weak," he mused. "And you aren't weak. Far from it, so why stir all this up?"

"Their names were Raw and Lowen," I said. "Virgil Lowen and Douglas 'Dog' Raw. Know them?"

"We know of them," he nodded. "I heard it was them. They were sick men, like Cleveland is sick. They rode around in an old car, one that would gain no attention in the poorer neighborhoods. People went missing from time to time. *Putas y borrachos.*"

His face had darkened. He waved a hand at the neighborhood around us. "They called the one 'Dog' because it is said he told people he was looking for his dog, and that's why he rode around hunting. The story made people who should know better relax. Some of his victims would help him look for his dog is what I hear. Even the mothers here tell their children to watch for that old blue car, and run from it if it appears."

"They won't have to anymore."

The group of teenagers carried a tray of hotdogs and drinks to a nearby table. They eyed Lopez as they passed. They knew who he was and kept their conversation at a respectful level while they ate.

"If you who killed those two, *amigo*, then I owe you a personal *obligacion.*"

I shook my head, no.

"If we find out one day, I will shake the man's hand," he said.

I told him about the rope found in the back of the Nash, and the police theory that someone may have been tied up in the back seat, gotten loose and shot Raw and Lowen from behind. The bodies of the two gangsters still had their own guns pocketed. Whoever had done it hadn't taken any weapon away from them.

"I don't see how they could have kidnapped someone without frisking them," I said. "Doesn't make sense that someone was tied up with a gun in their pocket."

174

"Perhaps it was someone they weren't afraid of," he said. "Someone they didn't imagine would be armed. They picked the wrong victim, simple as that."

It was almost noon, and several people drifted to the drive-in counter. The lunch rush was starting. Lopez stirred. I knew he needed to get back.

"There's another possibility," he said. "You saw the police captain, Earnswood, talk to the two men. The rope, all of it, could have been staged by the police."

"Could be. Too many missing pieces to say . . . yet."

"Yet," he smiled, and clapped me on the shoulder. "Yet. You're sure you'll find out. I like that."

He stood up and stretched. It looked like the stretching troubled him, and I was reminded of his age. His personality was strong enough to make me forget he was an old man. He looked at me, somber. "If Cleveland thinks you killed his men, he is going to send more, you know," he said. "He won't like losing those two, Raw especially. They were together for a long time."

"I think it's already started," I said.

I told him about the woman in the blue hat I had seen lurking around the Gardiners' house next door to mine. I said it was a woman who tended bar at the Olive Street dive that Cleveland owned.

"Ugly woman?" Lopez asked. "Short woman? Looks more like a man, if the man a *sapo*?"

"That's her," I nodded.

"I forgot all about her. You have bigger problems than you thought, *amigo*. That's Dog Raw's wife."

"I heard that. Think she'll want some revenge?"

"Mrs. Raw," he nodded. "She's worse than her husband ever was. A terrible, terrible woman. Cleveland keeps her very close. Some say they are lovers. They were lovers with her husband's knowledge and permission. Sal trusts her with everything. If you see her again, don't even say hello. Just shoot her."

He started stiffly away, and sketched me a wave over his shoulder.

"Watch yourself, *amigo*," he called back. "You have big problems. Remember I told you, if you see her again, shoot her. She's a danger, a killer, a woman of violent appetite. I will tell my people to watch, but . . . "

He stopped and turned around, spread his hands helplessly. "She is a *psicopata*. Just shoot her."

"Psychopath," I said.

He nodded, started away, and then turned back.

"You think any more about Corazón Rosa?"

"Move to Mexico to run a fishing boat?" I laughed a little. "Nice dream."

"Dreams are good sometimes," he said, and tossed me a wave.

I sat on the bench, soaking up the day and thinking. The kids at the next table finished their food and left. They didn't look at me as they passed. The lunch crowd was filling the place, and I needed to give up the table.

"Shoot her," I murmured to myself. "Or I can run to Corazón Rosa. Some choices."

I brushed myself off and headed for the Ford.

-Seventeen-

After dinner, I crossed my front lawn and went to knock on Annie Kahlo's front door. I was a little bit surprised when she answered it. She stood with one hand on the screen and looked at me with the closest thing she could come to having no expression on her face.

"You still mad at me?" I asked.

She didn't answer.

"There was a car in the alley behind my office this morning," I said. "Two guys were in the front seat, shot to death. It was the old blue Nash that's been hanging around here."

She didn't move, and didn't say anything.

"You know those two guys were from Sal Cleveland, Annie. It isn't coincidence that they were killed behind my office. It isn't coincidence they've been parking right out there in front of our houses. They were going to try to hurt you, or hurt me. Probably both."

She shifted her hand on the door frame, almost imperceptibly. Her bare arm was slender and tanned. She looked vulnerable. I wanted to touch her, but it would have been the wrong thing to do. "None of it's a coincidence," I said. "I worked for a woman who got killed on your ranch, a place you've kept because your family died there, and the same guy seems responsible for all it. None of it's a coincidence, it all comes back to Sal Cleveland, but I'll be damned if I see how it all ties together."

I took a breath. "The cops are going to be all over me soon. They've talked to you about your sister, and they know you may have seen the murder on your ranch. They don't think you're reliable, but sooner or later they're going to want to grill you. They're going to want to put you in a room and talk until they see where you fit into all of this, and it gets worse."

Other than my own voice in my ears, there didn't seem to be any other sound on the street. "Sal Cleveland is coming, Annie. He's coming after you, and he's coming after me. I think he's a lot more dangerous than we're giving him credit for. People don't scare me much, but he's starting to scare me."

She shifted then, and spoke. Her voice was hoarse, and it didn't have much of its usual silver screen breathlessness. "He scares me, too. I'm scared."

"I have to stop this, before it goes any further. I need you to do something for me."

"What?"

She seemed nearly worn out, and I wondered what all of this was costing her. "You saw a man shoot into a car that night at the avocado ranch," I said. "He shot Charlene Cleveland in the head. It was dark, and you saw him in the headlights of his car. You said you *sensed* it was Sal."

"You don't believe me?"

"Let me finish," I said. "This is a man you knew a lot of years ago. Have you had any other contact with him since you moved back to Santa Teresa?"

She shook her head, no.

"It makes sense that it was him." I said. "He got offended that his wife dumped him, and he punished her for it. He knows I'm trying to nail him for it, and he might know you're a witness. Now his people have been coming around, making threats. Now he's lost a couple of guys right behind my office, I think he'll stop threatening and start doing."

"I asked you to kill him, and you said *no*."

"It doesn't work like that, Annie."

"Looks like it's going to work that way for him," she cried. "Killing me is going to work fine. You're too good to kill anyone. I'm crazy, right? The idea offends you, but we'll both get killed while you do nothing!"

"Make sense, Annie."

She went silent, and I thought she would slam the door in my face. She didn't. When she spoke again her voice sounded calm. "I've said it was him. He shot the woman sitting in the car, in the face. There's nothing else I can say to you."

"Still, you're identifying someone who you haven't laid eyes on in more than twenty years. People change. They get older and look different. I want to be positive the guy you saw shooting is Sal Cleveland."

"I'm positive," she said. "How do you want me to prove it?"

"You don't have to prove anything. I just want you to eyeball Cleveland now, and tell me that he's the guy you saw at the ranch that night. I want you to look at him now, in person twenty years older, not at a memory from when you were a girl."

"Won't it be dangerous?" Her tone had changed. Her voice still rasped, but had an undercurrent of anticipation to it, almost playfulness.

"He closes the Hi-Lo Club on Olive Street every night, but in the early evenings he's usually at his other place, the Star-lite Lounge in Montelindo. It's a better crowd there. We should be able to get a look at him without anyone bothering us."

"When?" she asked.

"Now . . . tonight, if you're up to it. My car's in front."

"Let's take mine," she said. "I bought new tires and a tune up, and I haven't had a chance to take it for a ride."

179

I waited outside while she got her keys. When she came out, she had tied her hair up in a silk scarf.

She led me around the side of the house and up the narrow drive to the back. I could see the roof of my own house, just over the vines that covered the high fence between our yards. The bottle-green Mercury was already out of the garage, sitting with the top down. I got into the passenger side.

I checked my watch. Eight o'clock exactly, and the neon signs on State Street flickered and buzzed as night came down. The bars and restaurants were just starting to really get going, and the people I saw on the sidewalks and sitting at tables looked like they were having some fun. I wished that we were stopping, but we weren't. We had a date at the Star-lite Lounge.

The highway to Los Angeles ran fast in the dark along the shore. The breeze caught at the scarf on Annie's head. She glanced into the rear view mirror frequently, and from time to time she brushed a loose tendril of hair from her face. I thought I saw the beginnings of a smile at the corner of her mouth when she caught me looking at her.

She worked the shifter expertly through the gears and pushed the convertible up to about seventy. The air on my face felt warm, and I took off my hat and put it on the seat between us. She stayed in the left lane. I leaned back in the seat and watched the taillights of the cars we overtook and passed.

After a few miles, she steered the Mercury off an exit. We went a short distance along the unlit frontage road and rolled into the entrance of the Montelindo Hotel. She put the car into a corner of the lot, avoiding the valets without my suggesting it. We got out and stood together, looking.

The circular drive in front of the hotel flooded with golden light. A long, low car slid up to the door and stopped. The couple inside eased out. They made their way into the rich light and the car was whisked away. The ocean spread out darkly behind the hotel, looking as though it had been put there just for the guests. It was an ocean for looking at, not an ocean for fishing or swimming in.

We walked across a shadowed stretch of dry lawn and then through a screen of shrubbery. The Star-lite Lounge appeared in front of us, like a blue neon mirage. The letters of its name shone in blue script over the door. Electric bulbs set in the plantings around its foundation lit up the walls and the parking lot in the same cobalt shade. There were less than a dozen cars in front of the building.

"It isn't very busy," Annie said.

"It will be later," I said. "The brave ones who want to think they're living dangerously will drift over from the hotel. They'll order a drink and pretend that they belong here."

"They don't belong here?"

I shook my head, no. I pulled open a heavy door and we found ourselves in an entry hall. The floor was patterned in black and white, the walls were dull silver, and more of the blue light washed everything. The sounds of horns and a piano came from behind the closed door at the other end. A very large fellow sat on a stool with his arms crossed. He was near enough to the door to be useful if needed, but well out of harm's way. He looked at us with no expression.

"Closed," he said. "Come back in an hour."

I spoke to Annie very softly.

"Let's walk around the back," I said. "Take a look."

181

She took my hand, and I shrugged. "Sorry," I said to the big man. "We'll go for a walk, kill some time. See what we see."

The big man didn't say goodbye, or anything else, as we turned around and left. Annie's hand felt good in mine. I was glad when she didn't take it back.

We went to the left of the front entrance and circled the building. It got abruptly dark when we went around the corner, and it took a little while for my eyes to adjust to the absence of blue light. My feet crunched softly on the gravel, but Annie's steps were completely silent. Bins lined the rear of the building, pale gray in the low light. I smelled garbage and the rancid stink of cooking. I didn't know which of the two was worse.

Trash littered the weedy lot. A big Buick stood by itself. The long front hood reflected the bulb over the back door of the building. The car looked black and ridiculously shiny. I made sure it was empty.

"This is his car," Annie said. "I can feel it. I can feel him . . . close."

There wasn't much I could say to that, so I took her hand a little more tightly and went to the door.

The kitchen was a long room with a low ceiling. Three Mexican-looking cooks in white stood at a counter making sandwiches. They stopped and stared at us, but didn't seem inclined to ask us what we were doing there. I didn't blame them. A sequined and feathered woman stood by a swinging door at the far end. She had it cracked open and was looking out while she finished a cigarette. Before I could decide what to do about her, she tossed the butt into an ashtray and went out.

I led Annie past the cooks. They went back to what they were doing and didn't look at us again. I put a shoulder to the swinging door, opening it just far enough so that Annie could see into the room beyond, too.

Just to our left was the corner of a small stage. The musicians were having at it. They were out of my sight but it sounded like a smallish group. The piano, a couple of horns and a bass in the back, with a nearly inaudible brush of drums. They played a blues number that I didn't recognize. The woman who had been smoking stood at the foot of the stage, looking up at them.

There were ranks of tables, mostly empty, stretching away into the smoky indigo light. The farthest parts of the room were dark. A bar ran down the length of the right hand wall. The shelves of bottles behind it were back-lit, and glistened green and brown and amber. They looked nice after the steady diet of blue. A man sat at the end of the bar, on the stool closest to the doorway where we stood.

I had seen him before, at the Hi-Lo Club. I still had his card, the three of spades, in my pocket.

Tonight, he wore a pale hat with a matching band and a freshly pressed dark suit. His highly polished black shoes rested on the brass bar-rail. He lifted his glass and drank from it. The ring on his finger gleamed in the light from the bottles. He looked into the glass and swirled the ice around a little. Then he slowly set it on the bar and turned himself on the stool to look at us.

Annie's fingers dug into my arm. His face looked younger than it probably was. It was a face he took good care of. The eyes beneath the brim of his hat looked as pale as to be almost colorless in the dim light, but I knew they were a strange green. We watched each other being motionless for what seemed like a long time, and then the spell broke and he looked away. He raised an index finger and signaled to someone hidden in a far corner of the room.

I reached into my coat pocket and pulled out the automatic. Keeping it behind my back, I turned my head and checked the safety. Annie was still staring at the man, and I didn't much like her expression.

"It's him," she said. "That's Sal."

I couldn't really hear her over the music, but I didn't need to. I touched her shoulder.

"We've seen what we came to see," I said. "Let's get out of here."

Annie didn't listen to me. She stared, transfixed, at Sal Cleveland. He got off his bar stool more gracefully than anyone had a right to and walked over to one of the small tables. He slid one of the chairs back and held it, head inclined toward Annie. She started forward.

"Wait," I hissed, but too late.

I tucked my pistol away as I followed her to the table. I didn't try to hide it anymore. It wasn't a bad thing if Cleveland and whoever watched from the shadows saw the gun. Annie sat gracefully in the chair he held, and he adjusted it carefully for her before he sat down himself. I was left to get my own chair. The oily waiter who had appeared beside Sal took the drink order.

"Champagne cocktail for the lady," Sal told him.

Annie's face was utterly expressionless.

"Did I remember right, my love?" Sal asked her. "I never forget the important things."

"Bourbon," I said, when the waiter glanced at me. "One ice cube."

"It's been a long time, Anne," Cleveland said. "Time doesn't mean anything to me, though. I float on my own time. You should have known that."

Annie didn't say a word. Her eyes were fixed on him; luminous, unreadable and black. He kept talking. His voice was soft, his words meant only for her. "You were always going to come back here. Does it surprise you that I knew you were here even before you landed in Santa Teresa? Why did you buy a house in your own name if you wanted to hide?"

The drinks came. I tasted my bourbon; it was a lot better than what I was used to. Annie didn't look at the fluted glass in front of her.

"I've waited a long time for this," Sal said to Annie. "A long time for you."

Her eyes didn't leave his face. Beads of perspiration had formed at her hairline. They glinted like tiny jewels. She was scared, but she radiated a strange kind of determination.

"And now here you are," Cleveland said.

A pack of playing cards had appeared in his left hand. He stuck the cigar into a corner of his mouth and deftly, almost idly, shuffled them and fanned them out across the table, face down. He tapped them three times and looked at me. "We'll get to this in a minute," he said. "I have a question for this shamus. I'll just feel around the edges of things. I hope you're comfortable with that."

I had nothing to say, so I waited for him to go on. His eyes were unsettling, and I had to force myself to sit still.

"First you annoy me with questions about my dead wife, as if your blustering could bring her back to life. If it could, you'd be welcome to her, except that no one is ever welcome to what's mine. Once mine, always mine."

"Maybe you don't get to decide that," I offered. "Maybe the people you think you own have something to say about it."

His face contorted and he slammed the cigar onto the table. The broken end sparked and smoldered on the tablecloth. The cords in his neck stretched his collar. A man stepped from the shadows, and Cleveland composed his face and waved him back.

"Then you shoot a couple of my errand boys. Is that supposed to scare me?"

I sipped some more of my drink and thought about it. "I didn't shoot them," I said. "Maybe you ought to be scared of whoever did."

"Want to play with me?" he asked. "Pick a card. In fact, pick three cards."

"No," Annie said. Her hand clutched my wrist. "Don't touch them."

Sal put his head back and laughed. The sound of it was warm and genuine and delighted. "Are you afraid of the future, shamus?" he asked. "Sooner or later the future comes, you know. It's why you came here. The cards don't lie, and they tell what they tell whether you pick them or not. Go ahead."

"I'll do it," she whispered. Sal beamed.

Annie reached toward the spread of cards. I glanced over at her just as she closed her eyes. I heard her breath, and I imagined her heartbeat in my ears. There was no other sound in the bar. Everything had stopped dead, except for the cigarette smoke that drifted slowly in the blue light.

One of her slender fingers hovered. It trembled like a divining rod, then steadied and lowered. When she touched a card, her eyes opened and she slid it across the table top with a fingertip until it rested in front of her. Like an audience of phantoms, the smoke swirled and settled again. Sal Cleveland didn't look away from her face. He tapped the fan of cards three times. "That's one," he said. "Two more."

She picked a second card, and then a third. All of them rested in front of her, face down. I looked at the red bicycles on their backs, and I remembered a dark road and a man riding along with a rope slung over his shoulder. I picked up my drink and felt the tremble in my hand.

"That's three," Sal said. "Good. You know what to do now."

I tasted my bourbon and felt the cold burn in my throat. When I set my glass down, the ice cubes chimed once. Annie glanced at me, and I saw the ghost of a smile before she turned her attention back to Sal. Her eyes shone darkly. I looked at her cheek and brow, and I was reminded again of Nefertiti. I wondered if I protected her, or if her strange magic protected me.

"Three, six, nine," Sal smiled. "Of spades. No one takes what's mine, and the deal never changes. Never."

Annie passed a hand over the three cards and turned one face up. The hearts on it looked at us.

"Eight." she said. "Hearts."

"Liar," Sal breathed, his smile gone. "You lie."

She turned the second card, and there were more hearts, seven of them this time. Sal leaned forward, his face drained. I shifted slightly and moved one hand toward the Browning in my pocket. The dark room was breathless.

Annie turned the third card, and her smile was radiant, nearly angelic.

"Five of hearts," she smiled. "Five, seven and eight . . . how about that?"

Sal's face transformed. He glared at her, and then his eyes shifted to me. I flinched and looked away from what was in them, looking out at me.

"You lie," he growled. "You lie."

The music started again, and the bar was all at once noisy. The smoke moved and shapes began to form in the blue air. Sal turned in his seat and signaled wildly to someone in the shadows. I pushed myself back and heard the chair fall and clatter on the floor behind me. I yanked out my gun and caught Annie's elbow.

Cleveland raised both of his hands and snapped his fingers. I could see it, even if I couldn't hear it over the music. Whoever he signaled was still hidden in the shadows at the back of the room.

"Time to go," I told Annie. "Quickly."

-Eighteen-

I pulled her through the swinging doors into the kitchen. On our through this time, the cooks were suddenly a lot busier than they had been earlier, and the sound of our hurried steps on the tile floor got lost in the clatter of pots and pans. No one looked up.

"It might be too late," Annie called from behind me. "He threw a spell."

"I don't care about spells," I called back. "I care about bullets."

We burst outside into the parking lot. The night air was warm and dry after the air-conditioned chill inside the lounge. I glanced at the big Buick as we passed, as black and empty as it had been. I caught Annie's hand with mine. "I figure we've got about thirty seconds before they come through that door," I said. "Can you run?"

"Faster than you."

She was as good as her word. And gone. I went after her. She ran, fleet as a deer. She kicked out a delicate spray of gravel as she flew around the back corner of the lounge and made for the parking lot in front with me following about fifty feet behind.

We made it into the blue neon glow. We were headed across the parking area to the dark line of scrub and grass that separated the Star-lite from the hotel next door when the headlights caught us from behind.

"Don't look!" I yelled as Annie slowed and turned.

I heard the eight cylinders wind up into a howl. We sprinted for the trees and bushes at the parking area's edge. I felt dry grass under my feet and followed Annie's slender whiteness into the brief shelter of darkness and then tires shrieked as the Buick slid to a stop.

There was a pause, and then a gun discharged. I recognized the sound as a shotgun. The air pressure changed as pellets flew over us. Branches shredded over our heads, and then we were through into the hotel parking lot and running for the Mercury.

"Who's driving?" I yelled at Annie.

"Are you kidding me?" she answered without slowing down.

I could hear the laughter in her voice, and wondered if she was hysterical. The Mercury sat by itself, a bare outline against faint yellow lights from the hotel. We ran faster and it seemed to stay just as far away. Out of sight, somewhere behind us, I heard the Buick's big voice, raised angrily.

Finally, we reached Annie's car and I yanked at the passenger door. She was already in the driver's seat, calmly working out the ignition key. I had the absurd wish that there was time to raise the convertible roof, as if the canvas would offer some protection from what was coming.

The Flathead engine cranked and ground and didn't want to start. I watched the distant hotel entrance. Cleveland's men couldn't bring the Buick through the trees. They would have to come through on foot the way we had, and I didn't think they'd leave the car. We were going to meet them on the frontage road.

Annie got the Mercury's engine going. It was choppy and loud. She raced it a couple of times and it smoothed out. She glanced over at me, her face lit by the glow from the gauges. "Flooded it," she said. "Always happens when you're in a hurry, doesn't it? It's like a rule."

Her smile was radiant. She held it for as long as it took her to find first gear, and then the clutch went out and we were flying across the gravel lot toward the entrance. We passed the golden-lit hotel portico and came to a sliding stop at the road. It was completely dark in both directions.

"Are they gone?" she asked.

"They're here," I said. "Waiting to see which way we go."

"Which way should we go?" she asked. "Right or left?"

Before I could speak, headlights came on to our left, flooding the road and pinning us in the glare. Annie didn't hesitate. She put the accelerator pedal against the floor. The Mercury screamed, and she wrenched the steering wheel to the right. I grabbed the windshield frame to steady myself and looked back.

The Buick's high beams rocked, swayed and then steadied as it accelerated behind us. I leaned toward Annie and cupped a hand.

"Fast as you can!" I shouted.

I didn't know if she could hear me over the engine's wailing and the rush of wind, but it didn't matter. She was doing better than seventy anyway. We were going to reach the highway entrance soon. I didn't want to get on the long stretch of blacktop where the Buick's big engine would give it an advantage, but I didn't know where the frontage road went. We couldn't risk getting trapped.

"Take the highway and get back off as soon as you can!"

A different noise started, as though we had run through rocks and the undercarriage of the car was being pummeled. I looked back and saw the star-shaped bloom of flame just as the noise came again and bullets punched through the Mercury's trunk lid. They had a machine gun.

"You have to move!" I shouted. "Don't let them have a target!"

"Let me drive!" she screamed back, but began to swerve back and forth, from gravel shoulder to shoulder.

A second pulsing light flower joined the first, but there were no strikes. Annie's evasion was throwing off their aim for now. A Thompson is hard to control at the best of times, and hitting a target from a moving car takes time and a lot of ammunition.

Still, I had the sudden, sure knowledge we weren't going to survive this. There were at least two sub-machine guns taking turns with us, and shooters who seemed to be comfortable with them. The Buick was bigger than Annie's Mercury, and while the convertible might be more nimble, we were losing ground. I had spent my life thinking my way out of dicey situations, but there are times when the options have all been used up.

Annie flew us up the entrance to the highway and then pushed the Mercury as hard as it would go. I steadied my arm as best I could on the back seat. The Browning kicked against me, the noise of the shots lost in the general cacophony. I emptied it in the direction of the other car, but I might as well have been throwing pebbles. It gained steadily.

The machine guns had stopped firing, and as the Buick came abreast I saw why. Mary Raw leaned far out of the passenger window. Her eyes were slitted against the wind, and her features were stretched into a grin. She cradled a shotgun, and as I watched she brought it to bear. I struggled to reload the Browning, and knew I was going to be too slow.

There was another face in the back window, a very pale man. He watched us without expression from behind the glass.

"Creep!" Annie screamed.

Mary Raw fired, and the night lit up like a photographer's flash. Our windshield exploded into a hurricane of glass just as Annie locked the emergency brake. I grabbed onto what I could as the Mercury began a wild uncontrolled spin. There was a crunching thud as we caught a corner of the Buick, and as we slewed around I saw that it was spinning, too.

The world became incomprehensible with light and sound. I saw Annie's slender arms wrestling with the steering wheel as the cars did an insane ballet down the highway, both somehow staying on the road.

We spun, and the Buick spun in time with us, round and round, tires screaming protest against the torture of tearing metal and breaking glass. Over and over, our headlights caught the faces in the other car as they twirled close and then away again. I saw Mary Raw's lipsticked mouth opened in a long scream, and the white skin and emotionless features of the man in the back seat.

The Mercury finally shuddered to a stop. It rocked once on its springs and then came to rest. The air grew thick with the odor of boiling motor oil and scorched rubber. I looked over my shoulder at the big Buick, stopped diagonally across the road a hundred yards behind us. One tail light was out. Its headlights pointed into the brush. Nothing inside the car moved. I looked over into Annie's eyes.

"Will this thing still run?" I asked. "Can you get it started?"

She pressed the button, the starter ground and caught, and we were away again. Air buffeted the broken edges of the windshield frame. I brushed the worst of the glass pebbles from her hair as she drove.

"There's blood on your face," I said. "You'd better stop somewhere."

Annie laughed and twisted up the volume dial on the dash-mounted radio. I reached out to turn it off and she slapped my hand away. Horns and saxophones sang over the wind, about love and loss and the sick kind of lonely that can't be cured.

Five miles later, she slowed the Mercury and steered it across the gravel shoulder and then down into a shallow, grassy ditch. The wounded car struggled up the other side, and the single working headlight beam picked out trunks of trees as lined and orderly as soldiers standing at attention.

The exhaust burbled as we drove into the rows. We bumped gently over the soft dirt, and branches trailed fingers down the sides of the car when we passed. When we were well out of the highway's view, Annie set the brake and shut the engine off. After all the noise and light, the quiet darkness was a balm.

"Well, now," she said, breathless. "Wasn't that something?"

"What was that with the cards?" I asked. "Some kind of Tarot?"

She slid down and rested her head on the back of the seat. Through the exhaustion and the blood, her face was the most beautiful thing I had ever seen.

"Sort of," she said. "Hearts. Seven, eight, and five. You and me . . . and June."

"How did you do it?"

"I didn't do anything," she said. "The cards are what they are. They move by themselves."

Far off, the buzzing whine of a small engine broke the silence. It sounded like a small motorcycle. Annie was listening, too.

"That sounds like one of those Italian scooters," she said. "I love them. What do you imagine it's doing, riding around out here?"

I tensed, listening to the noise, and then I heard the spray of water that went with it.

"It's an irrigation pump," I said. "Thirsty trees."

I sensed her nod in the dark.

"Almonds," she said. "Can you smell them?"

She folded her arms around my neck and pressed her face to me. I was enveloped by her perfume; it mixed with the night fragrance of almonds, earth, and water. I tasted her blood and her tears, and I never wanted to be anywhere else, ever again.

"Where should we go?"

"Just drive," I said.

We took an unlit canyon road, climbing until the road ran out. Then we climbed the rest of the way on foot, until the city spread beneath us, a carpet of lights with the vast blackness of the ocean beyond it.

The night wind rolled in off the desert, and the surface of the reservoir sparkled. We stood above it, looking. I hoped that we'd be able to find our way back down the hill without slipping and breaking something. The loose rock and brush, easier to navigate going up than down. I knew we'd been a little bit crazy to climb up here without flashlights.

"Did we accomplish anything tonight?" she asked me.

"I know that the older Sal Cleveland is the same man you knew when you were young," I said. "You hadn't seen his face for a lot of years, and I had to be sure. It isn't just a logical conclusion now, it's a fact. I'm sorry I put you through it, though."

195

The reservoir was a column of blackness rising straight up from the city's electric glow, and to the west another rising pillar of darkness was the cemetery. I had never seen darkness contained that way. It shone straight up like twin gray searchlights in all of the yellow light.

"I used to walk there every night," Annie said, pointing at the cemetery. "It was my place to go. The silence is outstanding, but if you listen closely, it isn't quiet at all."

I looked over at her. She stared out at the city, her arm extended to point. Her profile caught the faint ambient light from below, an imperial ruler like one who now ruled museums.

"You can walk it in a loop, all the way around. The whole place changes, depending on whether you turn right or left on the path when you first go in. Whichever way you go, you know you'll come out different."

"I'd like to go with you, sometime."

"I don't know if you can or not. We could try." She turned slightly toward me, and I felt her smile. "Whatever happens, though, I'll always see you on the way out."

Something moved in my chest. I still didn't know what to think about her. We stood quietly for a little while, just looking. When she finally spoke, her voice was very soft. "I'm a little afraid of the dark lately," she said. "It's kind of scary, sometimes." She shook her head. "There, I said it."

"Afraid is allowed," I said. "I was afraid tonight."

"I don't go the distance in the cemetery anymore. I still go there, but it's very different and I'm trying to be okay about that."

I was beginning to think she might be the bravest person I had ever met, but I had no way to say so without sounding foolish, so I didn't say anything. I reached out and gently caught her wrist and held it. A warm wind moved against us, and I felt her shiver. The air smelled dry, like cinnamon.

"There are snakes up here," Annie said. "Rattlesnakes and king snakes. You have to be careful and watch where you're going, but there's really no way that you can in the dark."

I nodded. I knew about the snakes.

"It's just a matter of making a little noise," I said. "They mostly prefer to stay out of your way."

She didn't respond. She watched something in the shadows, and I didn't think she had heard me. Finally, she nodded, to herself. "I like that about the night time," she said. "You know you should be careful, but you can't."

I touched her face and then looked at my fingertips. "You're bleeding again, Annie," I said. "I need to get you somewhere to take care of it."

"Home," she said.

"I don't think home is safe tonight, for either of us."

"Home is what we have," she said. "It's the only place we can go."

The bleeding was a shock in the harsh light. Annie sat on the toilet and watched me. Her eyes were brighter than they should have been. Blood was nothing new to me, but this felt different. Water ran and splashed in the sink, and the bathroom smelled of carbolic.

"I think it looks worse than it is," I said. "Just flying glass . . . no bullet holes."

I gave her a couple of aspirin tablets and then wrung a cloth out, surprised my hands were steady. I was going to be a lot surer we were both still alive after a double bourbon and a few hours of sleep.

"What would it feel like?" she asked. "To get shot? Do you know?"

I didn't answer. I leaned down and cleaned her face as gently as I could.

"How close did it come?" she asked. "The bullet?"

"Annie, that wasn't a bullet." I kept my voice gentle. "It was a whole lot of bullets. She was firing a Thompson. When you see it in daylight, you're going to find your car is very badly damaged. It's going to need a lot of work."

"It got us home, didn't it?" she smiled. "Didn't it do fine? My Mercury is the best car I've ever had."

I held the cloth under the faucet and watched the red swirl into the drain.

"You're a hell of a driver," I said. "I won't ask where you learned to drive like that."

I looked through the medicine cabinet for a can of antiseptic powder and some sticking plasters. Three straight cuts ran across the skin of her temple into her wet-darkened hair. The bleeding seemed to have stopped, or at least slowed down.

"I don't think this will scar," I said. "I'm not a doctor. Maybe we should wake one up."

"It doesn't matter," she said. "I already have a scar. Look."

She turned her head, and showed me the thin line, pale against the amber brow. She laughed, the breathless silver screen laugh that always got to me.

"It's from when I was very little, only two years old. In a car, of course. My mother was driving."

"I want you to stay with me, Annie. At least until this is over. It's going to get harder now."

"I can't stay with you."

"You'll be safe here. I can't let you be by yourself."

"Things are different now."

"How can things be different?" I asked. "We've barely even started. We're still getting used to each other."

She didn't look at me anymore. A single tear started at the corner of her eye and I watched it run down her cheek. She didn't wipe it away. I wanted to kiss it, and I also wanted to gather her to me. I did neither.

"I can't let you be alone," I tried again.

"I am alone," she said. "I always will be."

She looked at me for a very long time. Neither of us moved, and there was only the sound of the running water. Finally, she collected her bag from the floor. She stood up, slung it over her shoulder and went out.

"Does it matter that I love you?" I said, to the empty space.

I heard the front door close. I listened carefully, but there were no more sounds, so I turned the faucets off and went to find my drink.

-Nineteen-

I couldn't sleep, so I went out.

Annie's windows were dark. She slept, or tried to sleep. I got my own coupe started and drove the empty, early streets. I circled the block twice, and satisfied myself that trouble wasn't going to follow us any further tonight. Cleveland's people knew where we lived. Not long ago I had seen Raw's widow skulking away from the Gardiner's front door.

I took the empty streets slowly, and stopped the car across the street from my office building. The first floor bar was closed. A lone man slept in the doorway of the Schooner Inn. I got out without waking him and crossed the street. I bypassed the front entrance and walked around to the alley as the side of the building.

The windows above me were all dark, and only a little light from the street made it this far into the alley. Further down, a single bulb burned over the back door of a bar. Everything in between lay somewhere between deep gray and pitch black.

It didn't much matter. I wasn't here to see anything. Raw and Lowen were long gone, in the ground and on their way to wherever guys like them went after they were shot to death. The blue Nash had been hauled away days before, but its ghost lingered here, and I could almost see it sitting in the dark, stinking of motor oil and blood.

There was a sudden movement, a shift of shadows, and I was still pulling the pistol from my coat pocket when the stray dog skulked out where I could see him. As slow as I was, he was never in any real danger. I took a step forward and he wheeled to run, so I stopped. He looked back at me over his shoulder. We watched each other a moment until we were both calm. I lowered myself slowly to sit on my heels.

He was big enough and rail-thin. He reminded me of the dog I had owned in St. Louis, although I could hardly see him in the dim light, so that was probably wishful thinking. I talked a little, to get him used to the sound of my voice.

"You can come with me, if you want to. You shouldn't be out here in the middle of the night."

He crept forward a few steps.

"I don't have anything at the house to give you," I said. "Maybe a sandwich."

He got as close as he planned to, and sat down about five feet away. I felt sorry for him, but I didn't know what I would do with a stray dog.

I didn't know what I was going to do about Annie Kahlo, either. I was in the middle of a situation that would either kill me or put me in jail. I didn't know why people were trying to shoot her, and I didn't know how to protect her. The best solution I'd been able to come up with was to fall in love with her and I wasn't doing much of a job with that. Talking to a strange dog was maybe the most sensible thing I'd done lately.

He sat and looked at me, as though he wondered what was next, too.

"It isn't a big deal to die for love," I told him. "Anybody can do that. The trick is to live a little for it every day."

His tail thumped on the asphalt, once, twice, so I figured that he understood. I stood up slowly. My legs hurt from crouching for so long.

"Let's go home," I said.

I walked slowly toward the mouth of the alley and the street. When I reached the car, I turned to look. The dog waited on the sidewalk about ten feet away looking sad. He imagined I was leaving him. I opened the car door and snapped my fingers. He sat down.

He let me come close and get my arms around him. I waited for a growl in his chest, but he was past that. I got him up and into the Ford. I latched the door gently behind him and went around to the other side.

He crouched awkwardly on the passenger seat. I didn't think he had ever been in a car. I drove him back to my house on Figueroa Street without the slightest idea why. He gobbled whatever I found for him in the icebox, and then fell asleep on a blanket I retrieved from the closet and laid on the floor in the sunroom.

I still couldn't sleep, so I sat and watched him until the sun shone gray in the trees. Sitting in the chair, I felt myself finally start to nod off. Before my eyes closed, I saw the shadow of the ocelot as it crossed my back yard on its way to Annie's house.

There wasn't much to do about things except wait. Annie wasn't going to stay with me, and from what I could see she mostly stayed inside, anyway. The damaged convertible stayed put behind her house. I saw her leave once, on foot, with a basket hooked on one arm. I stepped onto the porch, but she gave me a cool wave and went on.

Whenever I knocked on her door to check on her, she seemed vague and distant, or else she didn't answer the knock at all. I didn't know why things were different between us. Maybe I had gotten too close to her. There were things that mattered more than my feelings at the moment, so I tried not to think about it.

I called Raines to report that we had been chased down the highway and nearly killed. He didn't seem interested. "You went to the Star-lite to do what, exactly? Scare him? Sounds like he scared you instead."

"His people chased us and shot Annie Kahlo's car full of holes," I protested. "They only missed shooting us because she's a better driver."

"I told you to stay away from him," he said. "You want me to send a prowl car out so you can make a report? Save you a trip into the station."

"Forget it," I said and hung up on him.

Only the dog seemed settled. I gave him an awkward bath in my tub, and saw tawny brindle under the dirt. He was some kind of Boxer mix. With a bag of kibble and a scrap of blanket, he adjusted to life with me before I had even decided he could stay.

Once in a while I had to go into the office. There were bills to pay, and if I was going to hide from danger I was in the wrong line of work. As much as I could, I stayed home and as close to Annie as I could manage. I watched the street from my living room window. I walked around the block at all hours. I didn't know if I scouted for strange cars and strange people, or offered myself as bait.

I didn't see the Gardiners at all. I wanted to talk to Mrs. Gardiner about the ocelot using my yard as a way to Annie's house. I worried about the dog going after it. I stayed away from their door, in case someone was watching.

Nothing happened. No one shot at me, no one drove slowly up the street, and there were no screams from Annie's house in the middle of the night. It couldn't go on that way forever, and I had just about decided to pay Sal Cleveland a visit when he sent someone to me instead.

I got to the office one morning just after seven. The rains arrived early this year, and the sky lowered, wet and soft. Low thunder rolled down from the worn-out mountains

203

behind the city. I had the window open six inches or so, and the gray breeze that puffed in blew warm and cool at the same time.

I had picked up a small bag of sugared doughnuts from the bakery on Ortega. The brown paper was spotted with grease, and the smell of them went well with the odor of the coffee percolating on the hot plate in the corner. I sat down and debated whether or not to eat one before the coffee was ready.

A faint noise came from the hallway, and I heard the door open and close. Someone moved quietly into the outer office, and then the sounds stopped. I felt my nostrils flare. If I owned a set of hackles, they would have been raised. Something felt heavy to me, and I had learned to pay close attention to my feelings.

My holstered gun hung on a coat hook in the far corner. I kept a spare, an identical Browning, in the top drawer of my desk. I pushed my coffee cup away from the edge of the desk and slid it out.

"Be right with you," I called.

I stood up and went to the door. The frosted glass wasn't giving up any clues, so I opened it and looked out.

A man stood in the very center of the waiting room. His skin was remarkably pale. Both taller and older than me, he dressed like he knew his way around a men's department. His tie was floral, and his suit was arrogant. He stared at me for a long moment before he spoke. "Mister Crowe?" he said.

He didn't ask it like a question that needed answering, so I didn't. He smelled of almonds, and I had a strange image of him slapping cyanide on his cheeks before he went out in the morning. He had a face I had seen before, from the back window of a Buick. I wondered if Mary Raw waited somewhere nearby, keeping a shotgun company.

"What can I do for you?" I asked.

He colored a little, and then he opened up into a smile. He spread his hands to convince me of his good intentions. I thought he might be a man used to convincing people.

"It's more a matter of what I can do for you," he said. "My name is Fin."

"What can you do for me, Fin?"

He gestured toward my office, and I stepped back to let him go in first. I still had the pistol held out of sight behind my leg, and when he was past me I put it into my coat pocket. After he settled in the client's chair, I offered coffee and went over to the corner to get cups.

"Do you mind?" he asked.

I looked over my shoulder. He had gotten the bag of doughnuts off the desk and was peering inside.

"Help yourself, Mister Fin," I said. "You seem like a guy who usually does."

I set his coffee in front of him.

"Just Fin," he said. "Call me Fin."

He took a bite of doughnut, one careful hand cupped below his chin so as not to get sugar on his suit. Despite his delicacy, he radiated appetite. It probably didn't go well for anyone who stood in the way of what he wanted, and I had a feeling I was going to do exactly that.

I looked at his hat on the corner of my desk; the lavender-and-cream band matched his shirt and tie. Looking at it was better than looking at his eyes. The air in the office got suddenly close and very, very warm, and the pistol in my coat pocket weighed a ton.

"Une jeune femme," he said. "We're here to talk about a lady."

The smell of almonds and marzipan grew stronger, and I could taste sweet poison at the back of my mouth.

"Fine," I said. "Let's dance."

"Fig's a dance."

"An odd choice of words," I said.

"An odd choice of words," he agreed. "Because I've heard that you're an odd man. Let me introduce myself properly."

He reached into a coat pocket and extracted a leather case. He thumbed out a deck of playing cards and in a swift motion fanned it out across my desk.

"Take my card," he said. "Please don't hesitate. You'll choose the right one. I know you will."

I was tempted to end the charade, but I didn't want to shoot him yet. I reached out and moved a single card from the stack. I slid it across the polished yellow wood with an index finger. It lay face down in front of me. He smiled encouragement until I turned it over.

It was a six; the six of spades.

I looked up at him. His eyes seemed to be entirely pupil. They reminded me of something—a dark road and a man riding a bicycle along it so slowly that balance was a question. He carried a length of rope. It was a memory, but it wasn't my memory. I smelled hot smoke mixed in and swirling with the fragrance of almonds.

"Six of spades," I said. "You left me an envelope with the same card in the diner, didn't you?"

He nodded, pleased.

"Excellent!" he exclaimed, and rubbed his hands together. "You are indeed a detective, Mister Crowe. Somehow, I knew you wouldn't disappoint me."

206

"You've been sent by Sal Cleveland."

"Mister Cleveland is an old friend," he said. "We went to school together back in Ohio. We stay in touch, and from time to time he calls upon me when he is in . . . need. He doesn't send me. No one can do that."

"This is one of those times," I said. "He's in need."

"This is one of those times," he echoed. "And since we are both from Ohio, I help him when he needs help. You are very shrewd, a true detective, in fact. More than a name in the telephone directory, more than a cheap office and a rusty gun and an empty little life spent in shadows. You're a true detective, a seer of sorts."

His pale face gave away no hint he was anything but serious. I got all at once tired; tired of spells and tricks and all the trappings of intimidation. I was tired of seeing the fear in Annie Kahlo's eyes. I decided to send him on his way.

"I'm not interested in whatever it is you're selling," I said.

"You bear some responsibility for all of this," he said, his voice rising. "All of this . . . mess."

"I'd like to think so," I said.

We stared at each other, and then with some effort he drew his eyes back into their dark holes and subsided into his chair.

"I'm an orphan now," he said. "An orphan. Imagine it. It makes things difficult, the grief. All of the things one should have done, and never did. I'm sure you know about that, don't you? The guilt?"

I didn't answer.

"It's all just wind," he said. "Wind blowing through graveyards and convalescent hospitals and empty churches. I don't let it bother me. Fig's a dance."

"What do you want?" I asked.

207

"A deal," he said. "Just to make a deal."

"No deals," I said. "No deals, not ever."

"You've killed two of Mister Cleveland's men," he said. "You'll have to answer for it. I don't think you ought to let me leave here without hearing me out."

"I haven't killed anyone," I said. "I wish I had, and I might yet."

He looked at me for a long time.

"You might, if you aren't disposed of first."

I produced the Browning and laid it flat on the desk, my hand on it. My finger tightened inside the trigger guard when he reached toward the desk. He picked up his cup, sipped and put it back down. "Wherever you find cards, there are bound to be tricks," he said. "Before you put your cards into play, remember that. There are those who are more familiar with the deck than you are, and you might be stepping where you don't want to. Where there are cards, there are tricks. Be careful."

I took my hand off the gun and sat back.

"Here's what I propose," he said, and then paused to think. He drummed his fingertips lightly on the arm of his chair. "Here's how it will go."

He paused to get another doughnut from the bag. He made an elaborate show of sniffing it and then savoring the first big bite. "Your part of the bargain is simple," he said. "You simply leave the sisters alone."

"The sisters?" I asked. "What sisters?"

He looked at me cautiously, as if he was suddenly unsure of my sanity.

"The Kahlo sisters," he said. "Who else would we be talking about? June and Annie, the daughters great and small. Turn away from them and don't look back. Stop digging them up, so to speak. That's your end of the bargain."

"And what's in it for me?"

"Your life, of course. Mister Cleveland and I will let you go on living. You may continue with your shabby little private investigations. He might even employ you from time to time. You can go on with all the things you do, until you get too old and you die of old age and a broken heart."

He put his hands to his face and covered his eyes. Then he parted two fingers and looked out at me slyly. "Unless you drink yourself to death first," he said. "There's always that possibility, isn't there? We can't be responsible for that."

"Why is your boss so concerned with the younger sister?" I asked. "She's a mummy, a pile of bones. She can't hurt him."

Fin came halfway out of his chair, face contorted. "He isn't my boss," he snarled. "No one is my boss."

I felt the smile stretch my face. "He sent you here," I said. "That's good enough for me. Why are you people so worried about the Kahlo girls? Are they ghosts?"

"Walk away from the *jeunes femmes* right now, and we'll let you keep walking. That's the offer, and I'm very close to reconsidering it and leaving you to your ending."

"My ending?" I smiled. "You think I'm afraid of my ending?"

"Everyone is afraid of their own ending," he said. "Everyone."

I took my hand away from the gun on my desk. I thought carefully before I spoke again. "I'm not," I said. "Annie Kahlo isn't either. June Kahlo certainly isn't. We're all three of us ghosts, or close to it already. Maybe you hadn't counted on that."

He let the unfinished half-doughnut slip from his fingers. It fell onto the floor, out of sight. I didn't know if he was aware he had done it.

"So you want me to walk away from this whole thing, and you'll leave me alone? Does that deal go for Annie, too?"

"No," he shook his head. "It's too late for her. She made her bed a long time ago. She's finished."

I shook my head, thinking, and picked up the pistol again without realizing I did it. "I do know something now," I said. "I know you people are afraid of ghosts . . . and do you know something?"

My smile was full now. I hadn't smiled in quite this way for a long time. I felt the relief of it. "Annie and I are ghosts," I said. "So no deal. Go tell Sal Cleveland it's no deal."

"You'll be sorry," he said, and stood up. "And I'm sorry, too. I think I could have come to like you very much."

When he was gone, I went around the desk, and picked up his half-eaten doughnut from the floor. I put it back in the paper bag and threw the bag into the tin trash basket in the corner. I picked up the coffee cup that he had used. I looked at it for a moment and then I put it in the trash, too.

-Twenty-

The news called this the worst wildfire season ever. Nearly impossible to tell if it was one big fire or a whole lot of smaller ones, as soon as the brigades seemed to have things out and under control in one place, another canyon or arroyo would start sending up flames. There had been more rainfall than anyone could remember for a Santa Teresa summer, but it didn't seem to be doing much more than washing the coating of ashes off the city's skin every once in a while.

I called the police station to see if they were making any progress, since I wasn't.

"I left my card and a note on your crazy neighbor's door," Rex Raines said. "She hasn't been in touch."

"She's been busy," I said. "Cleveland's gang is chasing her around the city and trying to kill her."

"Sorry to hear that," he said. "Have her come in and file a complaint."

I had my feet on the desk. I shifted the telephone receiver to my other ear and lit a cigarette. "I'm surprised you people haven't been getting complaints about the noise," I said. "All the shooting. Her car's sitting behind her house with a couple dozen bullet holes in it."

"We can't get interested, no one tells us about it."

"The only one in the police department who seems very interested in all this is Earnswood," I said. "You ever find out why?"

"Do you have any idea what you're poking around in?"

There was a noise behind me. I put my feet down in a hurry and swiveled my chair around. A seagull had handed on the sill of the open window. He had one curious yellow

211

eye fixed on me. I thought about shutting the window and decided he wasn't bothering me enough to get up.

"I know that Sal Cleveland is popping up everywhere I look," I said. "I know he killed a client of mine. I know there's an eyewitness and you people aren't talking to her."

"Your eyewitness can't keep it together for five minutes," he snorted. "She couldn't give an answer that made sense if you asked her about the weather."

"She makes plenty of sense to Cleveland," I said. "She makes enough sense that he wants her dead. She makes enough sense that two guys he sent around to bother her get shot in the alley behind my office. Let me see."

"All right, all right—"

"Let me finish. She makes enough sense that a car full of Cleveland's people chases us down a highway and turns her car into Swiss cheese with us inside it. Enough sense that a dirty cop named Earnswood is hanging around, and not even you will say why. How's that for making sense?"

"Give me a chance to do my job," he said. "It will all work out."

There was a flurry at the window as the seagull left.

"I think it's too late for any of it to work out," I said. "I really do."

I started to say goodbye and thought of something else. "You know a guy named Fin?" I asked. "Runs with Cleveland?"

"Fin? That his last name?"

"I don't know," I said. "Could be either. Pale, creepy guy . . . looks sick but not weak. Sharp dresser. Seems like he has some authority."

"Don't remember hearing about him," he said. "What's he got to do with all this?"

212

"I expect we'll find out." I said. "Sooner or later."

A small chrome jukebox hung over every table. You put in a nickel and picked out a song. At a nearby booth, someone was playing "I Love You Madly," which seemed like an omen. Roxanne wasn't working tonight.

One of the fluorescent tubes over my head needed changing. It flickered, and buzzed louder than the clinking of china and silverware and the low, tired murmurs of the other patrons. The Camel Diner wasn't full, not by a long shot, but the exhausted waitresses were busy, endlessly moving behind the counter in a kind of haggard slow motion. I felt tired, watching them. I figured they went home every morning and crawled into their twisted bedclothes. They twitched and hummed, tried to avoid the sunlight that fell from the windows, and pretended to doze until night fell and they could get up and come back here.

I sat alone in a booth covered in an orange vinyl that hurt my eyes. I butted my cigarette in a glass ashtray and lit another. The black and white clock on the wall said a minute before twelve. I watched it and waited for the second hand to sweep me into the next day. I didn't know what else I was waiting for, except a sign it was time to go home. A waitress passed by and filled my coffee cup without slowing down.

The door opened, and Annie Kahlo walked in, bringing some of the night in with her. I could smell rain, even though a dry desert wind was blowing outside. She took off her dark glasses and stood looking around the place until she spotted me and came over. She was drop-dead gorgeous, but none of the customers at the counter looked up at her.

"I'm mostly invisible," she said in lieu of hello, as though she could read my mind.

"Want coffee?" I asked. "A piece of pie? Blueberry's pretty good here."

"I couldn't sleep," she said. "I knew I'd find you in here."

Until I'd walked in on impulse a little while ago, even I hadn't known I was coming here. I let it go. I caught the waitress' eye. She nodded, and brought Annie a cup. She seemed able to see her all right.

"What's on your mind?" I asked.

She didn't answer, intent on the ritual of cream and sugar. When she had finished, she set the spoon in her saucer. "Curdled," she said. "A little bit. I like it that way, sometimes."

Her dark eyes were quietly amused, and as always her glance left me a little short of breath. She watched me for a moment, and then tasted her coffee before she spoke.

"I wanted to tell you I think you're doing a good job," she said. "You get discouraged awfully easily, but everything feels perfectly in order."

"I'm glad you think so," I said. "So far, I'm finding dead bodies and I'm managing to annoy everyone I meet while I'm doing it. I spend most of my time looking over my shoulder at Sal Cleveland's thugs, or else the cops, and I don't know which bunch worries me more."

"Don't go on so much about making people angry. You're just creating space."

She touched my hand, and I smelled the rain again.

"Creating space?"

"You'll see."

"Annie…what exactly is in this for you? Your sister is buried. Nothing's going to come of any of this that resolves what happened to her. We're never going to know for sure. It was just too long ago. What is it you're hoping for?"

214

She thought about it for a minute, staring into her coffee. When she looked up at me, her slow smile was just about perfect.

"We'll find out when we get there," she said. "That's the whole point."

She tasted her coffee and stood up. I started to stand, and she held up a hand.

"I'll walk you home," I said.

"I'm not going home," she said. "I have things to do."

She started away, and turned back. "I saw your dog in the yard," she said. "I didn't know you had a dog."

"I'm not really sure he's my dog. He sort of found me, and hasn't left."

"What's his name?"

"I don't call him anything," I said, a little surprised. "He doesn't have a name."

"When June and I were little, we had a dog that looked like that. His name was Button. Will that do?"

"I think Button is a fine name," I said. "I'll tell him when I get home."

I had a sudden thought. Her green convertible was still out of commission, full of bullet holes.

"Say . . . did you walk here? Want to meet him? I brought the car. I'll give you a ride home, if you like."

She threw me another of her brilliant smiles. "I have a secret," she said. "Button and I have already met, in your yard, and we're friends. He knows his name. I told him. I'll take the ride, though."

When we pulled away from the curb, a set of headlights pulled out a half-block back and followed. It didn't feel like coincidence, and I made a random left turn and then a right to be sure.

"I thought we were going home," Annie said.

215

"We've picked up a tail. Probably Cleveland's people."

"I wonder why," she said. "They already know where we live."

I had done this before. I picked an intersection I liked, went around a corner and turned off my lights. I was parked in the dark, neatly in front of a delivery panel truck, when a gray Dodge sped past. I thought I recognized the car. I pulled out to follow it.

"They're watching us, and we're watching them," I said. "No one is absolutely sure what anyone else is up to, so everyone is watching everyone else. It's how the game is played. Cleveland's lost a couple of his guys, and he thinks I killed them. He's probably going to try to have me killed, but for now he's watching."

"Did you kill them?"

"Of course not," I said, startled by the question. "I have a beef with Cleveland. He killed his wife. I wouldn't waste any time or energy on a couple of his low-lifes. What for?"

"Maybe to make him suffer," she said. "Maybe to make him afraid, to make him wonder when you're coming for him."

I kept an eye on the red tail lights in front of me. There wasn't much traffic, so I was able to stay well back. The driver probably knew he had lost me, and would hopefully head for home.

"Cleveland is bringing up prostitutes from south of the border," I said. "They aren't prostitutes until they get here. They get lured with promises of jobs as domestics, told they can bring their families up later, and then they disappear."

"Why hasn't anyone stopped him?"

"He's careful, and I imagine he has friends in the right places. He's been working this city for a long time. I had evidence of some of it, enough that it couldn't get swept under the carpet easily. He could have gone to jail."

"What was the evidence?" she asked. "Can you tell me?"

"It was a photograph. It showed Sal Cleveland standing at the back of a truck full of Mexican women. Two of them were outside the truck, one on either side. He had an arm around each of them. None of the women looked happy, but he smiled for the camera. They could have been farm workers, but they weren't. An affidavit was written on the back and signed by someone who was there and knew what was going on."

"Why don't you use it?" she asked. "Bring it to the police?"

"I did use it," I said. "I traded it to Cleveland for his wife's divorce. I bought her freedom with one photograph. Fat lot of good it did her."

I was quiet for a moment, thinking. "I think prostitutition made probably the best case for those women," I said. "Some of them just disappeared. There are bad people hiding under rocks, with strange tastes. That's what Cleveland caters to. I think about the faces in that photograph, and try not to think about what happened to them."

The car we were following stopped for a red light, and I took my foot off the gas and slowed to a walking pace. I didn't want to get too close.

"It's worse than that, Annie," I said. "Some of the people in the truck were young. They looked like children, just girls."

Her voice turned suddenly bitter.

"That's the man I asked you to kill," she said. "That kind of a man. A man like that, and you were horrified at the idea of killing him. You're too good for that. You looked at me like I was crazy."

My own anger bubbled up, and I spoke before I could stop myself. "That's the man you were in love with," I blurted. "The man you're probably still in love with. The man who killed your sister. Is that the same man we're talking about?"

The slap came so hard I nearly drove into a line of parked cars. My cheek felt wet with the sting and my right ear rang like a bell. I forced my hands on the wheel and struggled to keep my eyes on the road.

"I'm sorry," I said, and I was.

Annie was crying, but there was nothing I could do about it.

I followed the gray coupe into a dead end off Olive Street. Its brake lights flickered red, and I swung over to the curb and waited. My headlights caught the white face in the driver's window as the car backed up and turned around. I was caught. There was no point any more in pretending I wasn't following it, so I turned around too. I picked up the car again at the end of the next block.

"Is that the woman who shot my car?" Annie asked.

Her voice was ragged. I looked over at her and nodded. She had curled up against the far door, and her face went gold and then dark as we passed under the streetlights.

"The bitch," she said.

"She's a bitch," I agreed. "Her name is Mary Raw."

"The same as . . . ?"

"She's Dog Raw's widow, yes. She's more important to Cleveland than her husband was. She tends the bar at the Hi-lo, but I've heard she's high up in the organization. I've

218

also heard that she and Cleveland are intimate, which is passing strange. She's as ugly as sin."

Annie started to hum to herself. The sound of it was unsettling in the dark car. The tune seemed familiar, but I couldn't put a finger on it.

The Dodge hung a right onto Cabrillo and sped up. We followed the ocean for a mile or two over to the west side of town, and then we turned off into a series of cul-de-sacs I didn't know the names of. I knew where we were, though.

The darkest, dirtiest neighborhood in town, it was a place I did my best to stay out of, one of those places where even the stray dogs stay out of sight after dark. Apartment houses crowded up close to the street; broken records played from broken windows and the air smelled like reefer smoke and cheap whiskey. The red lights ahead of us flared again and the gray coupe coasted to the curb.

I pulled over well behind it and set the brake. We sat quietly for a few minutes, soaking up the poisoned air. Nothing moved. I could see the back of Mary Raw's head in the small rear window. The engine of my car ticked softly as it cooled down, and I sighed and got the Browning from the map compartment. I checked the load and then looked over at Annie as I reached for the door handle.

"Stay in the car," I said. "I may have to break a few rules here. She's spotted us and she's stalling. She's just going to sit there until we go away. I might just have a word with her, see if I can rattle her a bit. The last time she saw me, she jammed a shotgun into me. I'd like to return the favor."

She reached for her own door handle and laughed, a sound like bells. Her eyes were strange.

"You don't know the first thing about breaking rules," she said. "You make rules for yourself."

"Those are the ones I don't break."

Just then, Mary Raw got out of the coupe. She looked back at where we were parked, made an exaggerated pistol with her thumb and forefinger and fired. Two shots, one for each of us. Then her ugly face lit and twisted into a jack-o-lantern grin. She waved and went into the apartment building without looking back.

"What are you going to do now?" Annie asked.

"Nothing," I said. "She tailed us, so we tailed her. The game hasn't started yet. For now, everyone's trying to look at each other's cards."

"Let's go home," she said.

Home turned out to be my place. Annie fussed over Button for a little while, and then went up the hall to the bedroom. She was undressing when I came in.

Our lovemaking was desperate and hurried. At the end, I tasted her tears. I woke up later and saw her silhouette against the window, getting dressed again. She left without turning on a light or saying a word. I lay in the dark and hoped it hadn't been for the last time.

I had passed the door, set into a stucco building on Ortega, a thousand times and never known there was a *cantina* behind it. There was no sign. If you didn't know it was there, they didn't want you to find out.

I sat at a tiny table across from Danny Lopez. We drank Mexican beer from bottles. The cement walls were painted a dark green, gray-white in places where they had been chipped. A string of red lights hung over the bar, an effort at festivity. It was authentic, though, I felt as though I were in a strange city a thousand miles to the south.

The strangeness made me feel safer than I'd felt in a long time.

"Sooner or later," I said, "they'll just kick her front door down and shoot her." I thought for a minute. "Hell, I don't even know if she locks it."

Lopez took a long pull from his beer and nodded to the heavy-set woman behind the bar. She brought two bottles to the table and set them in front of us.

"Why haven't they done that?" he asked.

"I'm guessing they don't know what to do," I said. "Sal Cleveland's bad business, but killing people isn't how he solves things unless he has to. I guess he thought he had to kill Charlene, and he knows Annie saw him do it. He probably guesses by now that the cops don't have her testimony. I doubt if he knows they think she's too crazy to go on the stand."

"So why chase you down a highway shooting at you?"

"I think we surprised them by walking into the Starlite," I said. "I think it was just instinct."

"Then this guy comes to try to talk you into walking away and forgetting it."

"Fin," I nodded. "And you've never heard of him?"

He shrugged elaborately. "*Amigo*, I've heard of everybody, and this guy's a ghost. No one I talk to has ever heard of him."

"He said he went to school with Sal back in Ohio. Maybe he's just come west recently."

"Then the connection is very old," he said. "Cleveland has lived here for many years."

A man in a western shirt and a straw rancher's hat sat with his elbows on the bar glaring at me. He made it clear I was unknown and unwelcome. I did my best to ignore him.

"Now Cleveland's lost two men, and thinks I killed them," I said. "I didn't, and don't know who did.

221

Earnswood's floating around the edges of this, and the cops I know don't seem to even want to say his name out loud."

"I told you, he's dirty."

Danny Lopez half-stood, looking almost apologetic, and let the man at the bar get a look at him. Recognition dawned, and the man touched his hat brim and turned around to face the bar. Lopez sat back down and returned his attention to me.

"I might need help with this," I said.

"You have my help," he said. "I've existed in the same city as Sal Cleveland for twenty years and not gone to war with him. I don't want to now, but you'll have the help you need."

"Thank you," I said. "I'll do my best to sort this out myself."

"I am personally available to you at any time, *amigo*," he said. "You are my friend. I will bring men in if I have to, but I would rather not ask people to involve themselves in something that is not part of their world."

"I understand."

The bar began to fill up. Lopez drained his beer and shook his head at the bartender. It was time to go.

"Let me ask you one more thing, Danny. Sal Cleveland came here from Ohio, right? He tells people that all the time."

"Yes. It has been many years since he came here. Why do you mention it?"

"Just curious. I wonder what drew him here."

He held my eyes. "Perhaps he doesn't want any part of where he came from. Perhaps he wants to spit at what he started as. Besides, everyone who lives here in California does so because they are running away from something, or else trying to run to something. That might even include you and me."

"Think that's all it is?"

"No," he said. "I don't think that's all. I also think this—when a man such as that looks in the mirror, he doesn't know who is looking back at him. He makes himself something foolish, because he doesn't know who he is."

We were standing on the sidewalk outside before he spoke again. "Can I make a suggestion?"

I paused in lighting a cigarette to nod.

"Stop sitting back and waiting for the bad people to do something," he said. "That isn't your strength. Do what you do. Find out what the truth of this is. You're reacting to the murder of your lady . . . your client. I think the truth of this goes back further, to that little girl's bones."

The simplicity of what he said startled me.

"Be a detective, Nate," he said. "Be what you are, and what they're not. Be a detective. Find out what the little girl's secret is. Follow the bones."

"Might be the best idea I've heard in a while."

"And remember . . ." He was smiling at me.

"I know," I said. "Corazón Rosa."

"It's always there," he said. "If you need to get out of here. That goes for the woman, too. It's a safe and beautiful place. It's better than getting killed."

I sat at my kitchen table and nursed the last of a cigar. The window over the sink was open, and air moved the curtains gently and brought the warm night inside. There was baseball on the radio. It was an East Coast game that had been over for hours, but it was better than nothing.

I thought over what I knew so far about Junie Kahlo. It wasn't much, so after a few minutes I gave up on it and thought about coffee instead. I didn't want it enough to get up and make it. I had a clock on the wall that matched the one in my office. It also rolled its eyes and moved its tail on the hour, but since it was still a little way off, there was nothing to see there.

My eyes must have closed, because when I looked up, Annie Kahlo sat across from me.

"You shouldn't fall asleep when you're smoking," she said. "It's dangerous."

"I'm not sleeping," I said. "I just had my eyes closed."

"Oh, my...you're asleep, all right. I want to show you something."

She smiled at me, and her eyes held mine as her hands went to her throat and undid the brooch pinned there. She reached across the table and gently caught my hand and turned it over. Her skin was warm. I looked at what she pressed into my palm. It was a small green-and-blue turtle, filigreed with gold.

I heard water splashing, and when I looked up, Annie was gone. The kitchen had gone with her.

It was hot daylight. The sun was bright, and it caught at the sparkles of water that jetted and hissed and poured from the enormous fountain in front of me. I was very small, and it all seemed very huge and very blue. My dead parents stood on either side of me. My father's hand rested on my shoulder.

Stone dolphins laughed and showered the gray bears playing beneath them. Granite children held hands and explored beneath small waterfalls. Mermaids rested on cement, languid and wet in the spattering, falling water. I touched the railing in front of me. It felt warm from the sun, but the mist from the fountain was cool on my face.

A large pool lay beneath the cascade, in the shadow of the fountain above it. I leaned over the rail to look into the water. My father's hand tightened on my shoulder, just a little.

The water was very clean, and I saw small spots all across the bottom. They were coins, scattered as far as I could see beneath the surface.

I looked up at my mother's face. She was very young.

"Can I swim in the pool?" I asked her.

"Not now," she said. "You will later."

"Why are there pennies in the water? Who picks them up?"

She touched my hair, and I remembered her. "Those aren't pennies, and no one picks them up," she said. "Those are wishes."

"They stay down there?"

"Forever," she nodded. "They stay down there forever. That's what forever is."

One of the mermaids lay very close to the railing where we stood. She lounged on the wet cement, chin resting on elbow, watching me. Her skin was marble, but her eyes were liquid and dark. It was Annie.

I looked at my hand. I wasn't little anymore, and my parents were gone. The day had clouded over, and the pool and fountain were in deep shade. The spray felt suddenly cold, and I shivered.

"It's a circle," Annie said. "Remember the beginning, and you'll see the end. When you understand where you came from, you'll know where you're going."

"What is this place?" I asked her. "Is this where I'm going?"

"It's a circle," she repeated.

She sat up and wiped the water from her face. I leaned over the rail to take what she held up to me. It was green-and-yellow box, small and flat. I opened the top to look at the crayons inside.

"When you were little, you were closer to the beginning," she said. "You remembered where you came from. That's why the colors were brighter. It's why you understood what they meant. You got older, and you forgot."

"I forgot," I said, looking at the crayons. "I forgot everything...all of it."

"You can remember again if you want to."

Krazy Kat sounded the hour, and I lifted my head and looked around the kitchen. The chair across from me remained empty. The refrigerator's motor buzzed and clicked off. The night outside the window was perfectly quiet. I smelled the dead cigar in the ashtray, but I also caught a trace of Annie's perfume. I looked at the pin I held in my hand. I rubbed its tiny shell with my thumb while I sat and thought.

Annie Kahlo affected me too much. She took up too much of my time, and now she had taken over my dreams, too. She wasn't a paying client, and I didn't make enough to support dragon-slaying as a hobby. I was in love with a woman who led me deeper and deeper into things I didn't understand, things that might get me killed. I wondered if the chance of death was a part of her that I was in love with.

After a while I pushed my chair back, put the turtle into my pocket, and went up to bed.

-Twenty One-

Just after five o'clock, and I was locking up the office when the telephone began to ring on the other side of the door. I hesitated for a moment, and then unlocked the door again and hurried back in to answer it.

"Are you on the run?" Mrs. Gardiner asked. "You sound put out."

I couldn't help a smile.

"Not exactly on the run," I said. "Not yet."

"We're going out to get some air," she said. "Would you like to join us?"

I had no plans for the evening, so I agreed and got directions. I knew the place she was talking about, and I went down to the street to get my car.

A lookout on Marina Drive had a small public park, with a couple of benches and a set of swings. Trees and grass were bordered by rocky bluffs that dropped straight down to the ocean. This late in the day, it was empty of people and it carried the sad, abandoned feel that bandstands, amusements and merry-go-rounds have when everyone has gone home. The lawns sloped down to the ocean view and a set of stairs to an observation platform about twenty feet above the surface. I supposed they had built it as a tourist attraction, but it was too far away from the beaches, and too hidden. I didn't think anyone ever came here except maybe for occasional kids with filched cigarettes.

I went down the cement steps. A metal railing was bolted to the side to keep people from falling down the cliff, but it didn't look like the kind of thing you'd want to trust. When I got to the landing I looked over the edge at the water beneath me. Half in sun, half in shadow, it was green and black and deep. The surface swayed and washed like gelatin, hiding the power of the currents that moved against the rock face.

Sea lions rested on rocks, and swam back and forth between the sun and shadow. They were enjoying themselves. None of them looked up at me, standing by myself and watching them. I got caught by a slash of loneliness, so real it hurt my chest.

There was a noise behind me, and I looked back over my shoulder. Annie Kahlo was coming down the steps. Her steps were light, and she reminded me of dancing, like she always did. She wasn't by herself. Mrs. Gardiner had her arm, and descended a little more cautiously. They both looked happy to see me. Annie brushed my cheek with her mouth and went to the rail.

"Look at that sky," Mrs. Gardiner said. "It's going to rain soon. I knew it would."

Pleased, she showed me the umbrella she carried under one arm. She was right. There was a massive cloud bank blowing in from sea, making it look like early night over the Channel Islands. I had a feeling that with one umbrella between us, we were all going to get soaked.

"Sooner or later, it has to put out these damn fires," she said. "They can't hold out against the rain forever."

I agreed, just because nothing lasted forever. The fires outside of the city didn't seem to be abating, though, rain or no rain.

"I come here every day in the afternoon," Annie said, indicating the sea lions on the rocky shelf underneath us. "I love them, and I almost never miss a visit. I feel like I have to keep an eye on them. They know how to play."

It surprised me to hear it, just because I seldom ever saw her leave her house during the day. Logically, she did.

Everyone had to go out for one reason or another, but I only rarely saw her on the sidewalk.

"They're all different," she said. "You recognize some of them after a while. Sometimes one of them is just gone, and you know something must have happened. They run into sharks once in a while. I always feel like I should warn them, and I can't, so I try to see them every day in case one of them isn't going to be around anymore. If I were better . . . " She turned her head to look at me. The vulnerability in her eyes pulled at me. "That's crazy, isn't it?"

"I think it's kind of wonderful," I said. "Not crazy at all."

The three of us made companionable conversation until the first drops of rain spattered the cement. The cloud bank had rolled over us, taking the last sun. Late afternoon transformed all at once into early evening. There were no electric lights on the platform. We'd have to leave soon.

"I've had enough," Mrs. Gardiner announced, opening her umbrella. "My vertigo begins to act up if I stay in a high place for too long, and it's getting dark. I'll see you in the car, my dear. Take your time. I'll sit comfortably dry and watch the rain."

She waved off Annie's offer of help, and made her way up the stairs, keeping one hand on the railing. We watched her until she had disappeared at the top.

"She's a nice lady," I said. "I like her. You've known her for a long time?"

"She's my friend," Annie said, not really answering my question. "She's my best friend. Sometimes I think she's my only friend."

I watched her face in the gloom. I was struck again by her remarkable stillness, the containment that seemed to cover so much emotion. I thought I would be happy just to watch her face for hours, and I wondered if I had ever thought that about anyone else. She opened her mouth to speak, and closed it again. There was something on her mind, and I waited quietly for her.

"They're going to kill you," she finally said. "If you don't give this up. One day, you'll be gone."

The rain came harder now, but it was so warm I hardly felt it. "Game goes nine innings," I said. "We aren't there yet."

I leaned on the railing and looked down. It was getting harder to see in the dusk. The tide was coming in, and every so often a surge washed over the empty rocks below us and spread white foam. The sea lions had all left, gone to wherever sea lions go when night is coming and it's blowing rain.

"So you're sticking around," she said. "No matter what."

"Is it up to me?" I asked.

She held my eyes for a long moment, and nodded. The rain ran down her face, but she didn't blink. I looked away, out at the water, and then I nodded, too.

"I'm in," I said. "The whole nine."

The falling water didn't make any difference to the swells and troughs. They came and went just the way they always had, and they looked exactly the same. The ocean doesn't care how hard it rains.

There was an Italian grocery a block up State Street. It was dim and smelled spicy inside. The shelves were full of cans and boxes with unfamiliar labels, and there was a white-and-glass cold counter down one side. The people who worked behind it made a pretty good sandwich to order that you could take with you. It had different kinds of meats,

230

cheeses, and marinated peppers, and they handed it across the counter wrapped up in brown paper already darkening wet with olive oil. I paid for mine and went out to the street.

An old fig tree grew beside the public library steps. I liked to sit and have lunch in the shade beneath it. Women walked by, in groups and alone, let out of their offices for an hour. None of them had ever stopped and asked to share my sandwich, but I stayed optimistic. I made it a point to pay attention to details, and it seemed like the skirts were hemmed a little higher this year. There was less pleasure in it now Annie was around. I thought about it while I ate. Maybe after looking at her, everything else had lost its color for me.

Today, there were pigeons gathered around to pick up my crumbs. They were there most days; I had no idea where they went when they weren't at the library. I liked the pigeons because they seemed to mostly mind their own business and peck at the things people dropped. They got a bad rap.

Since I was my own boss, I could go back early if I wanted to, and so I returned to my office in less than an hour. I stopped on the stairs between the second and third floors. Something seemed different in the cool, dim echoes; something I couldn't put a finger on. The smell of perfume lingered in the stairwell, but it could have been from anyone. I went down the third floor hallway cautiously.

My office door stood ajar, just a crack. I looked at the window pane lettered Crowe Investigations in black and gold. Nothing moved in the light behind the pebbled glass, so I eased the door open with one finger. I took in the wooden chairs and old magazines of the waiting room and then saw that the inner door to my office also stood open. Someone sat in the client chair across from my desk.

231

It looked like a woman. She was absolutely motionless, and appeared to be looking up at the corner of the ceiling.

"Hello?" I tried. "Can I help you?"

I went in and looked down at her face. Mary Raw didn't say anything to me, because she couldn't. Her filmy eyes stared, and her dark blue dress was a bloody bib. Her chin pointed up, and I saw the bullet wound in her throat. Her eyes bulged, and she looked even uglier than she did alive. She had jabbed my ribs with a shotgun in the Hi-lo, and shot Annie's car to pieces with a Tommy gun. I hadn't liked her, but it had probably been a hard way to die.

Nothing else in the office was disturbed. I picked up the telephone and asked the operator for the Santa Teresa police. Raines was in the station, and they found him for me. He hung up after I had said just a few words. I looked around for a place to wait, since I didn't want to sit across the desk from the corpse. I went out to the waiting room.

On impulse, I went back in and sat down in my chair. The room smelled of burned powder, and it got stronger when I opened the top desk drawer. I took a handkerchief from my pocket. My spare pistol still felt slightly warm. I sniffed the barrel before I laid the gun on the far corner of the desk.

"This might be a problem," I told Mary.

The dead woman sat in the same chair Charlene Cleveland had the last time she was here. Maybe there was some kind of justice in it since Mary had been Sal Cleveland's right hand and his strange lover. I remembered Charlene's pink dress, her pretty legs, and what she had said to me. I felt a flash of sadness.

"Maybe you won't turn down the next poor girl who needs you," I murmured. "You don't know the first thing about love."

I had seen a purse on the floor next to the woman's chair. I went around the desk and unsnapped the clasp without picking it up. The handle of a large revolver rested inside, at the ready. I was sure that Mary walked around ready to use it. Whoever had killed her had completely taken her by surprise. I had a hard time imagining who she had let her guard down for.

I noticed the blue corner of something, held in her dead fingers. It was a playing card. I got a pencil and teased the corner of the card with it to be sure. I saw the three of spades.

"Who killed you?" I asked her. "Sal Cleveland? What were you doing in my office? Waiting to ambush me, maybe . . . and he decided a frame might work better? Did he get tired of you?"

She stared at the ceiling. If she had any answers, she wasn't giving them to me. I went back to my chair and sat down.

"I bet you don't know the first thing about love, either," I told her.

Heavy footsteps thumped in the hall. I put my hands flat on the desk top and called out to the cops to come in.

"We can't just let this go," Raines said. "Even you have to understand that."

"I don't have to understand anything," I said. "If this is a frame-up, it's about the clumsiest one I've ever heard of."

The table top was brick-colored, some kind of Bakelite covered with random scratches. They looked like letters, but they didn't spell anything.

233

They had finally taken the handcuffs off. We were inside the Santa Teresa County lockup, about five miles outside of the city. It troubled me that I had been taken here instead of the police station downtown. Rex Raines' demeanor alarmed me. Every trace of the man I considered a friend, or at least a friendly party, was gone. His usually amiable face set itself in an expression that was nearly hostile. There were two other suits in the room, and the district attorney would be along shortly.

"You've had it in for Sal Cleveland since his wife died," he said. "You've told anyone who would listen to you that he killed her and got away with it."

"He did kill her," I said. "And she wasn't his wife, not anymore. He absolutely killed her."

"Says who? A crazy woman?" he yelled. "He had an alibi. We checked it . . . *I* checked it. He didn't do it. He had a million opportunities if that's what he wanted to do. He didn't just happen to be on the same highway at three in the morning, run her off the road and shoot her."

"That's exactly what he did."

"We all know what he is!" he shouted. "We all know who he is! If he killed his wife, she would just have disappeared. He has people. She'd just be gone, and no one would ever have found her. She was leaving town anyway, right? You've been listening to a crazy woman, and you've lost your own senses, too."

"Annie Kahlo isn't crazy!" I shouted.

My voice echoed against the cement walls. They were painted white and rose to the high ceiling with only a grated window near the top. The echo brought home to me the possibility of confinement here.

"She isn't crazy," I said again, more softly. "Neither am I."

"Two of Cleveland's guys were found dead in the alley behind your office." Raines said. His voice lowered. He looked suddenly exhausted. "I gave you a pass on that one, Nate. I went to bat for you. No one was very sorry to see them dead, and it was maybe circumstantial it happened there. This is different."

"Do you think I'm stupid? Do you think I would shoot someone in my own office, with a gun from my desk drawer? And then call you?"

He eyed me steadily.

"Who else would shoot someone in your office?" he asked. "With your gun? A person employed by someone you've held an open grudge against?"

He scraped his chair back on the concrete floor and stood up. The suits followed him to the door. He turned back just before he went out. "I'll talk to the D.A. in a little while," he said. "I think you're going to need a lawyer, Nate. I'm sorry, believe me."

The door closed behind them and I was left alone in the concrete room. Four walls, a high ceiling, one window, two chairs, the table and a heavy steel door that I knew was locked. I supposed it served as some kind of a meeting room, but it was as close to a jail cell as I wanted to come. I felt the first stirrings of claustrophobia and panic.

I sat for twenty minutes, waiting for something to happen to me. I had been a cop. What I did now was a little grayer, in terms of the law, but I had never been so firmly on the other side of the fence. It occurred to me, not for the first time, that Annie Kahlo would be alone, a sitting duck, with me locked up. She fancied herself tough and independent, and in many respects she was. But she wasn't tough enough—not against Cleveland's crew.

235

A key rattled the lock and the door swung open. The cop named Earnswood stepped into the room and the guard started to pull it closed behind him.

"Leave it open," he said. "I'm leaving with this man."

He was a splash of color in the cement cube. He wore a light green suit with a peach colored tie, and his shoes and hat were saddle tan. His washed-out were the same faded blue I remembered, but today they were bloodshot. Their bulge seemed more prominent. He put his hands on the table and leaned down close to my face. "I'm bringing you one last chance," he said.

His breath was terrible. "You don't look like you've been getting much sleep, Earnswood," I said. "Something bothering you?"

"You're a wise guy," he answered. "They told me you were nothing but a smart mouth. You're a two-bit, washed-up gumshoe who couldn't make it as a police officer in St. Louis, and couldn't do the job you were asked to in Honolulu. You're not doing any better with a private license."

"I do pretty good at stepping on toes. Why am I stepping on yours?"

"You want out of here, or not?"

"Why?" I asked. "So Cleveland can kill me himself? Is that what he told you?"

He stood up straight. "Last chance," he said. "You playing ball, or not?"

I looked up at the barred grille on the high window. I knew I could be in rooms like this for a long, long time. Either Sal Cleveland meant to deal with me himself, or else someone was very worried about what I might say if I started talking to a judge. It didn't matter; Earnswood represented my only way out of here.

"I'm playing ball," I said.

I followed him to the door and out. We were in some kind of administrative area with no cells. Earnswood nodded curtly to the guards we passed. We reached an area with a long counter. Uniforms moved around behind it and I saw Rex Raines. He looked at me disgustedly and headed for the door. I figured I had lost a friend.

"Here's your ticket out of deep water," Earnswood said from beside me. "You're going to go home and forget about the new friends you've made the past few weeks. Go chase divorces and sit in your cheap office and try to stay alive. Understood?"

He gave me a little push toward the counter. He gave the uniform my name, signed a paper.

"Keep your mouth shut," he said. "Amuse yourself with something else. Next time, I won't throw away the key. I'll eat it. This is the last time we'll speak to each other."

He nodded curtly and left. I scribbled my signature where they told me to. The sergeant behind the counter shoved across my wallet and keys without looking at me.

"Where's my gun?" I asked.

"No gun. This is what I have, so guess what? It's what you have."

"Swell," I said. "Thanks for nothing."

I wasn't going to see the Browning again. My spare pistol was now a murder weapon, so it certainly wasn't in my desk drawer at the office any more. I would have to go naked until I could round up something else. Given Sal Cleveland's likely reaction to the death of Mary Raw, that wouldn't be a good idea for very long.

"How am I supposed to get back to town?" I asked.

"Beats me," he shrugged. "Walk. That's what most do."

237

I walked down the drive to the frontage road. The late afternoon sun was sinking fast but still hot, and the institutional plantings along the drive were dry and wilted. I wished I'd asked directions to a water fountain before I started out. I had barely started the long walk to Santa Teresa when I heard the whine of a motor approaching from behind.

The car was an old hump-backed Packard, painted a pale blue that made me think of ghosts. The sound of gravel crunching under its white-walled tires was louder than the gentle tick of its engine. It came to a stop, and the figure behind the steering wheel waited, perfectly still. I opened the passenger door, leaned in and caught the odor of poison.

"Get in, Mister Crowe. I'll drive you back to the city."

He was as lanky and pale as I remembered. I got in, closed the door, and the car moved back onto the road. He drove slowly and carefully. The fragrance of almonds and marzipan was intense and I looked for the window crank. As though he could read my mind, Fin waggled a long index finger in the negative, so I put my hand back in my lap. The clock on the dashboard was dead; the hands were stopped at three minutes past three o' clock.

"Did you keep my card, Mister Crowe?"

"The six of spades? I think I have it somewhere."

He nodded. "Wise of you. Keep it with you in case you ever want to talk to me."

There was a trace of the East Coast in his voice; Massachusetts perhaps. I tried to place it, and decided it didn't really matter. "Why should I want to talk to you, Mister Fin?"

"Just Fin, if you please. Just Fin." He glanced over at me, and then back at the road. "Sixes are nines upside down, or did you realize that already? Six is nine *dans un déguisement, à l'envers*...often as not. I would tell you to be careful, but I've already tried, and careful isn't something you know about. You blunder and persist. Am I right, Mister Crowe?"

"If you say so."

"Oh, I do say so," he sighed. "I do say so, and I like you. I've tried to warn you away from the Kahlo woman and her unfortunate young sister . . . the little mummy. There's a lot of Egypt in all of this, have you noticed? If you can read the signs."

The smell in the car and the sound of his voice were giving me a headache. They had taken my gun away at the jail, which was too bad. If I'd had it, I could have shot him and got out. He smiled as though he could read my mind, and opened the map compartment. He removed a pistol wrapped in a handkerchief and handed it to me. I turned it over to look at it.

"The cops gave you my gun?" I asked. "How'd you manage that?"

"Where there are cards, there are tricks, Mister Crowe. Don't underestimate what I can do."

We reached the city limits, and we didn't say anything else while he wheeled the car into downtown Santa Teresa. It was strangely quiet. The sun was down and lights flickered on, but the streets were almost empty. A dozen blocks later, he pulled the car to the curb in front of the Hi-lo Club and waited for me to get out.

"This is probably the last place I want to be," I said.

"The death of the unfortunate Mrs. Raw is going to upset Mister Cleveland a great deal," he said. "If you act very quickly, you might surprise him, before he surprises you."

"Whose side are you on, anyway?"

He looked delighted, and took his hands from the steering wheel to rub his palms together. "Ever the detective," he chortled. "How I enjoy my conversations with you. I shall be very sorry when Mister Cleveland succeeds in killing you."

He peered at me with a sudden solemnity that was almost comic. "He was very fond of Mrs. Raw, you know. A man like that might appear to be hardened and without feeling, but strange affections often run deep. Now that she's departed, found cold and bleeding in your office, he will very certainly kill you."

"I know he's going to take a shot at it," I said.

"He's very good at it," he said. "Killing people."

"I've heard that."

"Yet you persist, Mister Crowe. You persist. It makes me so very sad. What will make you stop, I wonder? Whatever will make you stop?"

I pulled on the door handle and got out. On the sidewalk, I slipped the gun into my pocket and leaned back into the car. The aqua-colored sign across the front of the Hi-lo Club buzzed gently. The neon light shimmered. It looked a little like it was underwater, even in the daytime.

"Annie Kahlo's in a mess," I said. "That's why I persist."

"The Kahlo woman has drawn her cards," he said. "You have nothing to say about it."

"I have plenty to say about it. As long as she's in the wind, I won't stop . . . ever. Understand that?"

"It's all just wind," he said. "Wind blowing through sanatoriums and empty bedrooms and bare trees. I don't let it bother me, Mister Crowe. Fig's a dance."

I closed the door. He waggled his fingers at me. I didn't return the wave, and the Packard pulled away. At the next corner, it turned and disappeared, taking away its strange driver and his marzipan odor of poison.

If Fin was expecting to deliver me into the lion's den, it didn't happen. Cleveland wasn't waiting for me. The sidewalk outside the Hi-lo Club was deserted. The place hadn't opened for the evening, and nobody came out to ask me if I had killed Mary Raw. Maybe the news hadn't travelled this far, yet. I figured Cleveland would blame me for her death, sooner or later, but I was going to have to wait for that trouble to find me.

I slung my jacket over my shoulder and walked home in last of the warm afternoon.

-Twenty Two-

The sun was just about gone, and the water in the canal turned lavender. The breeze from the coast smelled of lemons, and felt strange, someplace different from Santa Teresa on a Thursday night. I had never been to India, but I thought it might be something like this. I looked around for elephants and didn't see any.

I told Annie that Mary Raw was dead. I mentioned that she'd been shot, but I didn't see any point in going into a lot of detail about it. She leaned on the cement railing and listened. She looked at the water and the passers-by, and I knew she didn't see any of it. When I finished, neither of us talked for a while.

"I got a letter once," she finally said. "From a man. He wanted something that I didn't want to give him. I sent him back a note, and asked him not to write to me anymore. He didn't."

A woman came across the bridge, walking a very small dog. She glanced at Annie, pulled on the leash, and hurried her steps a little a she passed us. I started to speak, thought the better of my question, and then asked it anyway. "What did he want?"

"Me," she said. "He wanted me."

"Are we talking about Sal Cleveland?"

Without taking her elbows from the rail, she thumbed her hair behind her ear. She looked over at me. Even in the twilight, her almond eyes were impossibly dark. Her voice dropped, and I had to lean closer to hear her.

"Yes," she said. "That's who we're talking about. When I moved back here to Santa Teresa last year, he didn't find me. I found him."

I felt like I stood at the edge of something very high, and the smallest gust of air might blow me off. I stayed very still and waited for her to go on.

"All these years later I came back here. I found out where he lived and I wrote to him and told him that I thought I'd made a mistake. I told him that I'd changed my mind."

"What did he say?" My voice sounded hoarse. I didn't want to hear what she said.

"He didn't answer," she said. "Not a word. I wrote another letter, a month or two later. He didn't answer that one either. I grieved."

She straightened up, rummaged in the shoulder bag, came up with her dark glasses and put them on. She turned toward me. "Isn't that silly?" she asked. "I hadn't seen him since I was a girl. I didn't really even know him in the first place. Silly…but I grieved. How could I be so upset?"

I thought about it. "Maybe it wasn't him you grieved over." I said. "Maybe it was you. There's almost no time. It's too short. We're only here for a little bit, and then we have to leave. We grieve over the things we didn't get a chance to see, the things we never did."

"…that we should have done?"

"How are we supposed to know?" I shrugged.

"We're tourists," she said. "We don't get to stay."

I nodded.

"This whole thing is my fault," she said. "He killed my father, and he might as well have killed my sister. I still wanted him and look what it's caused. Maybe he's not the monster. Maybe I am."

"Things are usually more complicated than they seem, Annie. I can vouch for that. I can promise you're no monster."

The air shaded into purple as the water gave up its color. The light wind was turning cool. A rustling noise grew around us and over our heads, and the dusk was suddenly full of the sound of wings. A colony of bats poured out from beneath the bridge. They paused and spun and fluttered above us, a black pinwheel against the coming night. All at once, they swirled together, dipped, and then the sky was empty again.

"What do they call that?" she gestured. "What do they call that many of them at the same time?"

"A cloud," I answered. "A cloud of bats."

She took my arm.

"A cloud of bats," she said. "I like that. I like it a lot."

I walked Annie home, and waited until she had locked the front door behind her. She didn't invite me in. I was still restless, and I looked at my watch. It said just past nine o'clock, and I hadn't eaten since the sandwich at lunch. It had been a long day, and I felt famished.

I walked to the Camel Diner to get a hamburger, or the blue plate if it seemed edible. The place was nearly empty. Roxanne was at her station and she came to the table. I hadn't been in since Rex Raines had told me the cops were happy with Cleveland's alibi for the night of his wife's murder. I had stormed out, and now I felt bad about it.

"You going to eat what you order tonight?" she asked. "Or just pay for it and walk out? Save me going back and forth to the kitchen if you are."

"Sorry about that," I said. "I was rude."

Her look softened.

"You weren't rude," she said. "You don't know how to be rude. I just worried a little about you. The guy with you looked like a cop, sort of."

244

"He is a cop. He told me something I didn't want to hear. No excuse for brushing you off."

"Everyone has problems." She took out her pad and pencil. "You were always real friendly with me, and I appreciate it. Have the meatloaf tonight."

I nodded, grateful she had taken the small decision out of my hands. I felt battered by the day. I wondered what it would be like to have a wife again; someone to lean on sometimes. I had been married once, before the war. I had met her on the job in St. Louis. She was a nursing student and the dormitory she lived in got burglarized. She had walked in on the robber, who had fled, but she was badly shaken when I arrived in response to the prowler call.

She was sweet and pretty, and the courtship was done in a matter of weeks. We picked a house and a church, in that order. Within a month of her vows, she realized her mistake had been spectacular. We were two decent people with nothing in common. She was appalled by my job, and I found her presence bewildering. She was discouraged by the financial and social prospects for a cop's wife. She complained that our only friends were other police couples, and I didn't see anything wrong with that.

Within a year she was gone. I didn't realize I had probably been in love with her until she wasn't there anymore. I never had the urge to try marriage again. I figured I wasn't cut out for it.

I finished the tolerable meatloaf, said goodnight to Roxanne and headed back to the street. It had gotten dark, and I needed to sleep. It seemed like a longer walk home past the cemetery. My legs were starting to ache with fatigue, and I wished I'd driven the Ford tonight.

The wrought iron fence on my left stretched away into the nighttime ahead, disappearing and reappearing in the streetlights. My heels on the sidewalk made the only sound. I wondered if Cleveland's people were watching the street. I touched the gun in my coat pocket. I didn't think it would help me much if it came down to it, but I wanted it handy just the same.

There was motion in the darkness. A small girl had come out of nowhere on the cemetery side of the fence. She ran her fingertips soundlessly along the metal bars as she walked along with me. She wore a pink pinafore over her dress and skipped lightly around the occasional headstones in her way.

"Not a place for a kid, this time of night. You ought to head for home."

My voice sounded hoarse. The girl didn't look at me, and didn't answer. She didn't bother me any, so I shrugged and kept walking.

"June?" I asked. "Are you June?"

I felt instantly foolish. I didn't know where the question had come from. I was relieved that the girl didn't seem to have heard it. She kept pace with me on her side of the fence, never looking at me.

Up ahead, a man stepped out of the shadows. He stood under the yellow light watching us approach. His hat pulled low, hiding his face, he bent and carefully placed something in the middle of the sidewalk, and then he turned away and went between the parked cars at the curb. I watched him cross the street and vanish into the dark.

I thought about chasing him, but I couldn't think of a good enough reason. I glanced over at the girl, but she was gone, too.

When I reached the spot where the guy had been, I looked at what he had left behind. A playing card, face down. I picked it up, turned it over, and saw the three of spades. I stood and looked at it in my hand for a little while, but it didn't do anything and didn't change, so I put it into my pocket.

The cemetery fence finally gave way to houses. Most of the windows were black, but I supposed the girl had gone into one of them. Two more blocks and I reached home. The dog greeted me at the front door. I checked his food and water, and went to bed without turning on the lights.

The dog's barking woke me up in the middle of the night. He had stopped by the time my eyes were all the way open, and I wondered if I had dreamed it. It was too dark to see much, but the luminous dials on the alarm clock said six minutes to three. I put my feet on the floor and was listening to the house tick when he started barking again. It alarmed me, since I had never heard him bark. Instinct kicked in, and I had the Browning in my hand as I started up the dark hallway.

I followed the noise to the kitchen. I glanced at the darkened window as I went in. The night was bright; nothing silhouetted against the glass. The ceramic sinks and water tap caught some of the light from outside. The dog scrabbled at the back door, nearly wild.

"Button," I hissed. "Button, stop!"

If he knew his name, he didn't show it. I finally caught his collar, herded him to the bathroom off the hall, and closed him in. He tried the door as I walked away. I heard his nails on the wood. I went back through the kitchen and peered through the glass. I heard myself take a breath as I snapped the switch mounted beside the back door. The yard flooded with light, and I opened up.

The Gardiner's ocelot sat thirty feet away, staring at me. In the dim light, it looked like nothing more than a large house cat. The breath left my lungs, a long exhale.

"Troublemaker," I said. "Go on home."

In a blink, he bolted over the fence into Annie's yard.

I looked over at her house. The windows visible over the hedge were dark. I went far enough into the yard to see the Gardiner place on the other side. Their house was unlit, except for a single bulb over the back door. Everyone appeared to be sleeping, undisturbed by the ruckus. I looked at the moon for a minute; it was full enough to make the outside light pointless. I headed back inside, and stopped with my hand on the knob.

There was a bullet hole in the door glass, and a playing card stuck into the frame. I hadn't heard a shot; the dog's barking had awakened me. I looked at the spidery bicycle drawing for a moment and then pulled the card free. A three of spades, just as I'd known it would be.

I locked the door behind me and let Button out of the bathroom. There was no chance I would get back to sleep tonight. I took the bottle of bourbon from the cupboard, poured myself a knock and sat at the kitchen table to drink it. I was pretty badly rattled and got through it in a hurry. I stood up to get another as the telephone rang. The sound made me jump.

I heard silence on the line, but it wasn't dead. I could sense the person on the other end. I waited.

"I'm done playing with you, pally."

"What do you want, Cleveland?"

His breath was audible, coming almost in pants.

"This time you went too far, you son-of-a-bitch," he said. "You went too far and you're going to pay in ways you can't imagine yet. You're going to pay and pay."

248

He seemed to be having trouble with some of his consonants, and I realized he was drunk. I also realized something else. He was crying. "I'm going to get you for this, and I'm going to do it personally. If I wasn't going to do this myself, you'd be dead right now. Look over your shoulder, you bastard. I'm coming."

"I didn't kill her, Cleveland. I found her there."

"Goddamn your excuses!" he half-screamed. The sound was harsh, gassy. "To hell with your lies! You couldn't get to me, so you took her out! You're going to get your chance at me, do you understand? Do you?"

"I understand," I said.

"That bitch should have died in the fire," he said. "This is all her fault. None of it would have happened. She and her mother started the whole thing, and they deserved to be in that house. They should have died."

I had no idea what he was talking about.

"Who should have died?" I asked.

"The little girl died, and that wasn't my fault," he sobbed. "Do you hear me? It should have been them! They let the little girl face the music."

"Are you talking about Annie Kahlo?' I asked. "Make some sense."

"Now she's got you running around, killing for her," he sobbed. "I'm going to burn the bitch before I kill you, snooper. I'm going to burn her alive, and I'll make sure you know about it before you die. Do you hear me?"

I held the receiver away from my ear and looked at it. His voice got tiny, but it still buzzed in my palm. I put the handset back in the receiver like it was infected, cutting off the sound of him. After a minute, I got up to pour my second drink. After I finished it, I picked up the telephone again.

Danny Lopez answered on the second ring. He didn't sound like he had been asleep.

"I'm going to need some help," I said.

"I figured you would, *amigo*. We're not very far away."

I waited on the veranda until an old truck with a staked bed rattled up the street and parked in front of my house. A man got out of the passenger side, crossed to the far side of the street and disappeared into the darkness. Lopez came up the sidewalk and mounted the steps. He indicated the direction the other man had taken with his chin.

"My man will stay around tonight and watch the street," he said. "We'll organize this better tomorrow."

I led him through the house and showed him the broken window and the playing card. I told him about the identical card dropped on the sidewalk in front of me earlier in the evening.

"Think he'll come now?" I asked. "Or is tonight some kind of warning?"

"Cleveland isn't warning you," Lopez said. "It's too late for that. He's taunting you. He's telling you he can get to you anytime and anywhere he wants to. If he can get close enough to deliver cards, he can easily deliver bullets."

"Not much I can do about it. I'm mostly worried about Annie. He says he's going to burn her to death, and that's just sick enough to have me worried."

"It's simple, *amigo*. If we don't let him get close enough to deliver cards, the threats don't mean anything."

I told him I had seen Mary Raw on the Gardiner's veranda before she got killed, and I didn't know why. They weren't involved, but I was still a little bit worried about them, too.

"We'll watch the whole street," he said. "You and your neighbors. Like a barrio . . . no one gets in or out unless we know about it."

"I'll need to tell them what's going on," I said.

He clapped me on the shoulder.

"We'll meet up with them tomorrow," he said. "Get some sleep. Everyone's safe tonight."

Part Three

Handwriting, Green Tangerines, and a Pink Heart

-Twenty Three-

Monday, July 21, 1947
Santa Teresa, California
11:00 pm

The yellowed papers had aged terribly in just these few weeks, and Annie handled them carefully. Crayon, paint, ink…they were alive, but not quite enough. This demanded colors that were lit, that would shine out against a huge darkness and bring it all back to life. She didn't know if the same darkness, which had followed her since she was a small girl, was finally going to swallow her.

She did know the dead didn't always stay dead, not really, and that the most perfect beginnings were sometimes made out of endings.

She moved the easel to the corner of her big desk, and sat to look at the crumbling pages.

There was a noise from outside. Annie looked up and sat listening, her head slightly to the side, and then pushed her chair back and went to the window. There was nothing beyond the glass but the dark. She leaned forward and looked up, but the sky was empty. Out on the road, a figure stood beneath the yellow street light, perfectly still. She watched it for a moment and decided it had nothing to do with her. She crossed the room again, back to the colors.

A children's verse, she thought, but not just for children. With the right illustrations it could become a book, and books were alive There was no safer place, really, but she was afraid anyway. She picked up her brush and read softly. Her lips moved, but her eyes were still.

She painted until it was time to go, and then she stood up. It wasn't enough, but the unfinished nature of the piece almost seemed to demand she return to it someday. It comforted her. She spent the next hour collecting what she needed. Now it was going to end, one way or another.

At the open door, she shrugged on a raincoat. It was too warm for it, really, but she needed what was in the pockets. She checked to be sure she had the playing card. She did; she pulled it out and looked at the hearts in the dim glow from the street light. It was the last one in the deck, and she hoped its magic would be enough.

When it was safely back in her pocket, she locked the door behind her and went down the walk to her car.

-Twenty Four-

"I used to live in Mexico," Annie said. "Near Sayulita. I had a little house on the water. It was a wonderful place to paint, a wonderful place to live. I miss it. Sometimes if I close my eyes, I'm there."

"I know it well," Lopez beamed. "My town is not too far to the north. Corazón Rosa. On a clear day, you can see Las Islas Maria from the beach. They seem to be close enough to swim out to."

"Corazón Rosa . . . Pink Heart. What a lovely, curious name. Why is it called that?"

We sat at the glass table in the Gardiner's back yard. The sun was bright, and the shade under the striped canvas awning felt blessedly cool. The flowered bushes on the borders moved in the breeze, alternately dappled with light and shadow. I looked for the ocelot under the jacarandas, but he was somewhere else today. The doctor served his over-sweetened martinis from a blue pitcher, but Annie and I stayed with the lemonade she had made in the kitchen. I was going to need what few wits I had.

"I can't say for sure. Many of the buildings are in the old adobe style. The clay in the area has a lot of . . . "

Lopez sipped at his martini, and grimaced appreciatively. I felt for him.

"Delicious," he said. "Absolutely delicious."

"A lot of . . . ?" Annie prompted.

"Iron. It gives the mud a funny color, and the adobe remembers a little of that color when it is dried. In certain lights at the beginning or end of the day, the whole town looks pink. *Rosada.*"

"I love that," Annie said.

"That may not be the whole reason for its name." He spread his hands. "All I know is that Corazón Rosa is the most beautiful city in the world."

In the far corner of the yard, the peacocks squabbled briefly. They flared wonderfully, defended their dignity and then subsided and stalked away in opposite directions. I closed my eyes and listened to the sound of running water. This all seemed very far from the business we were here to arrange, and I wished it could all last longer than it was going to.

"With all respect," Mrs. Gardiner said to Lopez, "I'm glad to help, but I'm not sure what it is you're going to do here."

He leaned forward. I had thought the Mexican *jefe* might be uncomfortable with the Gardiner's eccentric hospitality, but he was relaxed, courtly and nearly magisterial.

"There's some trouble on your street," he explained. "There's a very unpleasant group of men who may cause problems for Mister Crowe, here."

"Sal Cleveland and his boys," she said. "I'm not a fool. I go to the movies like everyone else."

"Exactly," he said. "A few men that I trust will be watching over these houses—yours, the lovely lady's, and *Señor* Crowe's. We will be here and there, as invisible as possible, and we hope it is only for a short while. We might ask to come in, or possibly to set up a cot in your front room."

"I don't care about that," she said. "I like company. Are your people gangsters, too?"

Lopez sipped at his martini again, and pursed his mouth.

"We are simple gardeners," he said. "No more than that. If you have any yard work you need done while we are your guests, we will happily do it."

"There's an ocelot that lives here," she said. "I won't have you or your men bothering it."

Lopez looked at me, confused.

"It's like a small tiger," she said.

"More like a small lion, really," the doctor offered, in a rare outburst.

The look of bewilderment on Lopez' face cleared and turned to mild alarm.

"It's a big house cat," I told him. "You won't see it . . . it hides. It goes between all three backyards. If it doesn't bother the peacocks, it won't bother you. Just don't let your men shoot it, whatever you do."

"I think you are some kind of good gangster," Mrs. Gardiner told Lopez. "This Cleveland man is looking to cause grief for Annie. If Mister Crowe vouches for you, then you must be the good kind of hoodlum, a sort of Spanish Robin Hood. My husband and I will help however we can. You can stay as long as you like. When will all this start?"

"It has already started."

Lopez looked at me.

"I think he won't try anything drastic until things have cooled off," I said. "There's already been enough trouble drawing attention to him. There's no way to be sure of that, though, and that's why we need to be careful right away."

"He'll move when the numbers tell him to," Annie said. "He'll move when he sees it in the cards."

All of us looked at her and waited. Behind the dark glasses, her expression stayed unreadable. A brightly-colored scarf wrapped her hair, and she played with a corner of it while she thought. When she finally spoke, her voice was slow and nearly dreamy. "Sometimes numbers speak," she said. "Numbers and colors and symbols. They all play together, in love and war and everything else. You can see patterns. Sal understands that, and he always did. The cards tell him what he should do, and the cards confirm his power."

"Like Tarot?" I asked. "But with regular playing cards? Is this a game he made up himself?"

She shook her head, impatient. "It isn't a game at all, and the cards don't matter. It's the symbols and the numbers. He could use colored sticks, or dried leaves, and the effect would be the same. He can set a course, decide what to do, where and when. He can see, and that makes him magic."

Danny Lopez leaned across the table. He had a way of fixing his total attention on what was being said to him, and he and Annie locked gazes. "Are you a little bit magic too?" he asked. "Do you understand these . . . numbers and symbols?"

"Yes," she whispered. "Numbers and colors."

He stared at her for a long minute. No one else at the table spoke.

"I think you must decide where your loyalty is," he said. "It cannot be divided. Lives are at stake here."

"My loyalty is to my sister," she said. "Only to her."

"Your loyalty needs to be to the people who are in danger with you," he said. "And to those who are trying to protect you."

He was a little bit angry. He tasted his drink again, shuddered almost imperceptibly and put it down. He thanked the Gardiners and asked me to walk him out. On the street, we stood beside his ancient green truck.

"She wears dark glasses so her eyes cannot be seen. Do you understand that?"

"She's shy," I said. "And a little eccentric. She's an artist, Danny. All artists are a little strange."

"The woman is involved in this, more deeply than she should be. That's why she doesn't want us to see her eyes. I think she is deeply connected to Sal Cleveland in ways you don't suspect."

I got impatient. "Sal Cleveland killed her family years ago," I said. "Annie had the bad luck to see him shoot his wife. She's a witness. She's his albatross, and I think he's finally going to do something about getting rid of her. How could she not be involved?"

"She is a danger to you, *amigo,* and a danger to herself. If you have feelings for her, send her away until this is done."

"Where would I send her?"

"I have offered you a safe place, and if you care for her, the offer stands for her, too. Send her to Mexico. You heard her. She loves the country, she speaks the language. I can arrange transport for both of you to Corazón Rosa. Food and a place to stay, as long as you want. If you won't leave, at least get her out of here."

"She's tougher than you think," I said. "I don't think she'll run, whether she loves Mexico or not."

"I don't care if she's tough, *amigo.* I care that if shooting starts, I don't know if I can trust her or not. I can't identify her. I don't know what she is." He paused to light a small cigar, and stepped carefully on the match. "We don't need any more fires," he said. "It pays to be careful."

"Any news on the fires? This seems to have been going on a while. Too close to the city for comfort."

He looked at the sky, as if scanning for smoke. "We've had some rain on the coast . . . actually a lot of rain for this time of year, so I'm not too worried about the city, you know? In the mountains though, these fires play like children in an alley. The *bomberos* chase fire into a canyon and spend a couple days getting it under control, and then when they think it's out, it runs up an arroyo and now the next valley is on fire. Some of the ranches have a lot to worry about."

"The news says the firefighters are getting the upper hand."

"Let me tell you something, *amigo*. You don't beat these fires. You hope the wind changes and the fire turns back on itself. That's the only way these things end . . . when the fire gets turned around and burns itself. That's the only way they get beat, when they beat themselves."

"Then let's hope they do that."

He savored the cigar for a minute, turning it in his fingers to appreciate the burn. Then he looked at me, eyes piercing in his wrinkled face. "I'll tell you something else, *amigo*." He waggled his fingers. "You aren't as tough as you want to be. You've seen a lot, and it has made you tired, but it isn't the same as tough. You have a good *corazón,* and that can get you killed. You can't save everyone."

He left me there. I stared after him, at the place he had been.

You can't save everyone.

It was three o'clock in the morning. I stood on Olive Street, watching the front entrance of the Hi-lo Club. Smack in the middle of a pretty nice block of downtown, it stood out like an infected boil. It was a place where you could get a drink, a little reefer, put down a bet, arrange sex, or have

259

someone beaten up. You could probably do all of it at the same time, as long as you had the money. It was closed for the night, though.

I had no particular reason to be there, but in my experience doing something beat doing nothing. The Raws were dead, as was Virgil Lowen. I didn't know any of the other faces that were around Cleveland. I didn't know how many soldiers he had left, or who would be his right hand now that Mary Raw was gone. There was a lot I didn't know, and it might be better to know some of it before it came to me.

I waited in the doorway of a dentist's office that was closed, too. Across the street and down a little bit, Woolworth's was dark, and so was the art museum. In fact, nothing on the street had shifted for almost an hour. It started to rain; just a drop or two at first, and then it spattered the sidewalk. Within a minute the water sound grew to a noisy roar.

A white stone lion stood on the museum steps. I watched him carefully to see if he would make a move to stay dry, but he stayed where he was. He was probably keeping an eye on me, so I shot him with a finger.

"Just you and me," I murmured. "But somebody's going to show up, wait and see. I'm a detective and I know things."

Nothing happened for another twenty minutes, and then a long-nosed car crept out from the next corner, so quiet it was almost invisible. I dropped my cigarette and moved a little deeper into my doorway. It passed in front of me and parked in front of the bar. I recognized the sloped trunk. It was Cleveland's Buick.

A half-block further up, a second car with its headlights out pulled to the curb and stopped. I smiled at the lion. "Told you so," I whispered.

Three men got out of the first car and stood under the streetlights, looking around. When they were satisfied with that, the group of them went to the door of the Hi-lo. I heard a jingle of keys, and then they disappeared inside. After a minute, they all came back out, trailed by a fourth man. It was hard to be certain in the rainy darkness, but it looked like Cleveland. All of them piled in. The tail lights flashed red, and the car drove away.

I pulled my automatic and held it down by my side as I splashed up the sidewalk to where the other car waited in the dark. I recognized the Mercury, and when I saw Annie Kahlo behind the wheel, I put the gun away. I got into the passenger side.

"You got your car fixed," I said.

"Good as new," she said. "It cost a lot to do it. At first, the man at the garage looked at all the bullet holes and said it wasn't worth fixing. I would be better to buy a new car. I'm not interested in another car. I love this one. When I love something, I keep it, no matter what."

I cracked the window down an inch and lit a cigarette.

"What are you doing here?" I asked.

"I've got a plan to end this," she said. "I can't tell you yet."

"You've got a plan?" I asked. "Really? You're not exactly being careful, if your plan includes surviving. Lopez has men watching the street. That was the whole point—to keep you safe. How did you get off the street without them following you, anyway?"

Her smile was sweet and dark. I locked eyes with her.

"I'm mostly invisible," she said. "You know that."

A small revolver lay on the seat beside her. The lights from outside the car gave it a dull shine. I picked it up and looked at it. It was a snub-nosed .38, not something usual for a lady's purse.

"Where did you get this?" I asked.

"Someone gave it to me a long time ago," she said. "It doesn't matter. Also, I hate plans, but now I have one and I won't be careful."

She looked out at the street. The rain got harder, and it drummed on the car's canvas roof and ran down the window glasses. I didn't have anything else to say, so I pulled the door handle to get back out.

"How about you?" she asked. "You got a plan?"

"Mexico," I said. "Samoa, Argentina, Hawaii—anywhere you want to go, I'll take you. I just want to be with you."

She didn't answer. We sat quietly for a minute, watching the downpour. I kept my hand on the door handle. A dark-colored cat slinked up the sidewalk, casting left and right. It looked up at me as it passed the car. I had always thought that cats disliked being out in the rain, but this one didn't seem to mind.

"I may never get anywhere," she finally said.

"Up to you," I said, and got out.

I was wet in about three seconds. The rain dripped off my hat brim. I went around the back of the car to cross the street.

"Hey," she called.

I looked over my shoulder. Her face was a blur in the driver's open window. She had to raise her voice to be heard.

"I talk to you in my head, twenty-four hours a day, seven days a week. You're always here, and you're always with me, if that's okay."

She put the Mercury into gear and rolled away. It was far too late to bother moving to shelter. I watched her tail lights up to the next corner, where they turned right and were gone.

I stood in the middle of the street and nodded at the place where the car had disappeared.

"That's okay," I said.

The gardeners Lopez assigned to guard us worked the street diligently. I knew there were guns secreted under piles of clippings in their wheelbarrows and probably anywhere else they would be instantly at hand. They seemed to be pretty good at gardening, whatever else they did. They did some work in the Gardiner's yard, under the doctor's watchful eye. Annie's masses of flowers had always seemed to me to be tended by elves and fairies, but I saw them there, too.

On the first day, they worked in my yard. The moldering carpet of nut shells that been gathering for years was swept up and disappeared. They trimmed and cut the lower branches from the massive old black walnut trees. When the sun came up in the morning, it poured through the windows and lit up the rooms, probably for the first time in many years. The dog lay on the kitchen floor and basked. He seemed to approve.

They had changed shift at first light. An old red truck had rattled its way up Figueroa Street and brought new guys. They had conferred with the night crew, who took their old blue truck and left. They said Annie hadn't come home last night. They were certain. They hadn't seen her go; she had just slipped away, so I knocked on her door to be sure she hadn't slipped back in. I remembered Earnwood's turn of phrase.

"Bad time to be off the reservation, Annie," I muttered to myself. "Real bad time."

She had been in front of the Hi-lo Club at three o'clock, but I didn't know why, or where she had gone from there. I worried. Annie Kahlo wasn't the kind of woman who took orders, but Lopez' men were there to protect her in the main part, and it was pointless if she didn't stay around to be protected. I didn't know for sure the Gardiners were in any kind of danger, and I had been taking care of myself for a long time.

I would have to try to talk to her.

A blue-gray Packard rolled slowly to a stop against the curb in front of my house. The gardeners, three of them, were working in my yard. One them casually put down his rake and moved to a nearby wheelbarrow. The others sauntered away.

I recognized the car even before Fin waved to me from behind the wheel. I moved across the yard to the opened passenger window, and caught the sickening, cloying odor of marzipan.

"Your men are certainly alert, Mister Crowe. What exactly do you hope to prevent? I would have hoped you would use better soldiers than mere gardeners."

"Gardeners? These men have been through things that would make you faint."

I looked at the man standing at the wheelbarrow handles. The other two had melted away, out of sight. I knew they weren't far away, and had their guns trained on the Packard.

264

"Do not presume to know what would make me faint, or what I may have been through, Mister Crowe."

It was hard to tell if he was amused, or angry. His pale face stayed blank, so maybe he was neither. Maybe Fin didn't feel emotions.

"They're pretty good gardeners," I said. "I have to give them that. I never thought my place could look this good."

He glanced at my yard, disinterested.

"I want to bring you some good news," he said. "You don't have so much good news lately that you'd turn away a little more, do you? I'm here as a messenger."

"I don't want to be rude," I said. "Can you get to the point?"

Fin turned and stared straight ahead through the windscreen glass. Deliberately, delicately, he touched the button on the dashboard, and the Packard's engine went quiet. He placed his hands in his lap. After a long pause, he turned to look at me. Blotches of color had crept into his white complexion, as though he ran a high fever.

"Mister Crowe, you fancy yourself to be on a mission. A cheap, tawdry woman was killed, a rancid life no one will ever miss. You have appointed yourself as her avenging angel, wielding a wooden sword. You have killed several people, and you believe yourself to be justified and protected by your own goodness."

"I haven't killed anyone."

"Do not interrupt me. You are insignificant, a character from a children's book." He pointed at Annie's house. "Read the cards, if you can. The woman is a player in this, and Mister Cleveland is a player in this. You are an accident, just a misdealt card that has somehow found its way onto the table."

265

He took a silver pillbox from his breast pocket, snapped it open and delicately removed a white tablet. He placed it under his tongue and closed his eyes for a moment while it dissolved. He opened them again and looked at me as the sweet odor of poison filled the car.

"You gave up on yourself a long time ago," he said. "You are putting in your time, drawing one breath after another, until old age and the bottle can finally take you away. Until you can find some peace."

He put the pillbox away without taking his eyes from mine. The sounds and colors of the street faded, until the world was a study in black-and-white. I only saw Fin's face and listened to his voice. He seemed to be speaking inside my head.

"Your problem, Mister Crowe, is that you see meaning where there is none. You want to believe in love, to believe in good. You trust beauty. You are the worst kind of fool, the kind who knows he is a fool. There is however, one thing that sets you apart from other fools. Do you know what that is?"

I shook my head. The smell of marzipan got stronger, almonds and sugar. It wasn't unpleasant. I wanted to breathe the poison deeper.

"You persist, Mister Crowe. You persist and you persist, and for the life of me I don't know what it is that drives you on, even in the face of your own despair. You cannot save yourself, but you go on with the idea that you can save the secret sister."

With a long index finger, he indicated Annie's house again.

"You cannot save her, Mister Crowe, any more than you can save yourself. You long for darkness, and peace, and yet you fight your own nature on her behalf. You blaspheme your own self. You cannot save Sister Secret. She is gone to you, as gone as the small girl in pink."

"What do you want?" I whispered.

"Fig's a dance, Mister Crowe. The wind blows and the wind swings, through sanatoriums and empty bedrooms and bare trees. It blows and it swings, blows and swings. You cannot save the girls in pink, and yet you persist. What can you hope to do?"

"I can die trying," I said. "I can stay the full nine. I can hope for that."

He stared at me, startled. The spell lifted, and the day came back into focus.

"You surprise me, Mister Crowe," he said. "You do, indeed. No one stays the full nine, not even me."

His pale eyes crawled across my face. I wouldn't look away.

"Watch me," I said. "What do you want, Fin?" I asked again.

"It isn't a matter of what I want . . . this time," he said. "It's a matter of what you want. Mister Cleveland is offering a meeting. He does not want you to kill any more of his people. He is willing to discuss an accommodation."

"I wonder what my chances would be of coming out of that meeting alive."

He looked surprise, and then affected hurt. "You would have my guarantee, Mister Crowe. You would have my personal assurance, as a neutral party."

"I think I'll pass."

"Are you going to keep these men here forever? Do you think that if Mister Cleveland brought the full force of his anger to this street that these foreign laborers could stand against it?"

"I'll tell you again, they've been through tougher times than you could imagine," I said. "I'd stake my life on their competence, anytime."

"Not tougher than I could imagine, I promise you that."

He threw his chin up and laughed merrily. The feverish spots of color on his cheeks deepened. I heard him laugh for the first time, and I didn't much like the sound of it.

"And I'll tell you again, you don't want to imagine where I've been or what I've been through, Mister Crowe. It would take your imagination far past its breaking point."

His laughter vanished as quickly as it had come. He peered at me shrewdly. "This might be an alternative to more killing, which will see you yourself killed, sooner or later, by Mister Cleveland, or by the electric chair. Dead is dead, when it comes down to it . . . it's all wind and would be all the same to you."

I got suddenly impatient, and deeply tired. This was all catching up with me.

"When and where?" I asked.

"Three o'clock tomorrow morning." He smiled. "The Star-lite Lounge. The Hi-lo Club has sad associations for Mister Cleveland since the demise of unfortunate Mrs. Raw. Sadly, it is closed and likely to remain closed."

"Then some good has come out of this," I said. "I'll be bringing someone with me. I'm not stupid enough to go into that place alone."

"I will be there," he said. "You have nothing to fear. Oh, and Mister Crowe, if you're thinking about bringing your Mexican friend, Mister Lopez with you . . . "

"That's exactly what I thought. Nix that and there won't be a meeting at all. I won't come alone."

"I started to say, before you interrupted, that we insist you do. The Mexican is involved, as you well know. We insist he be there, too."

"Three in the morning. Star-lite Lounge."

"Only you and the Mexican," he said. "Don't try to deviate. Where there are cards, there are tricks, and we've been playing cards for a long time."

"No tricks."

"Fig's a dance, Mister Crowe," he said. "Good day."

He reached across and cranked up the window, closing off the intense odor of the poison he carried with him. He looked at the watch strapped to his wrist, looked pleased and nodded to himself. He pressed the starter button and drove off without looking at me again

-Twenty Five-

I couldn't think of anything else to do with myself, so I went downtown to the office.

I wheeled the car to the curb in front of my building and shut it off. I sat for a couple of minutes, looking at nothing and listening to the Ford tick as it cooled down. Then I got my gun from the map compartment. I slipped it into my pocket and got out.

State Street was hushed. The offices were shut, the stores were closed, and the sidewalks were still. The daytime cars and people were as gone as if they'd never been there. It was too early for the drinkers and the haunted women to crawl out of wherever they came from, and across the street the Schooner Inn entrance gaped dark and empty.

The light was gold, and the air felt wintery, at least as wintery as it ever got in Santa Teresa. I smelled something sweet and cold blowing from the ocean. I stood with one hand on the car door and looked up at the window of my office. All of a sudden, I didn't want to go there, so I stood and waited to see if anything was going to happen.

I saw motion on the corner, and a familiar green convertible with a tan roof nosed into the intersection. The car sat for a moment, as if it was thinking. Then it turned toward me, came slowly looking, and pulled in behind mine. I walked back to meet it.

Annie Kahlo looked up at me from the driver's window.

"Where have you been?" I asked. "There are men in front of your house watching out for you, and you're out here. Think you could stay home for a day or two?"

She didn't answer. She took off her dark glasses and tossed them onto the seat beside her. A peach and yellow scarf covered her hair. It went well with the car. A gust of air brought the faint sweetness again, and she turned her face to it.

"Do you know what Mock Orange blossom is?" she asked. "Can you smell it?"

I nodded. Across the street, a saxophone started up. Someone in the bar blew a few notes, getting ready for the evening. It was an upside down reveille, and I halfway expected the night people to suddenly appear, but the street stayed quiet.

"The fires will be out soon," she said. "The air smells different."

"I have my own fires to put out," I said. "Things start to look like they're happening too fast, and then it gets too quiet, much too quiet. I'm caught between Cleveland's people and the cops, and I don't have a printed program. I didn't stay alive this long by feeling my way in the dark."

"Maybe that's exactly how you stayed alive this long," she said. "Maybe feeling your way in the dark is what you do best."

She smiled at me, and I smiled back in spite of myself. She had that effect on me. I pulled out my package of cigarettes, looked at it, and then put it back.

"I wanted to tell you something," I said, and started to have trouble with my voice. "Or ask you. When this is done, will we . . . "

I felt foolish, and stopped. We looked at each other for a long time. Her face was motionless and absolutely serene, but her dark eyes were liquid. Like I always did, I found myself looking for color and movement in them. She startled me when she finally spoke.

"You've changed, Nathaniel Crowe. You've moved back toward how you began, before things went wrong for you. You're not the same man who came to my house for a piece of birthday cake."

The cool air smelled like perfume, and the fragrance of orange made me almost unbearably sad.

"Will we go on after this, you and I?" she murmured. "Together? I see things that aren't there, and sometimes I even see things are coming, but I can't see that. I think maybe we will if we want to."

I felt a flood of relief. Maybe she could see things, after all. Hell, maybe she could even be invisible like she said.

"I'll settle for that," I said. "That sounds like a pretty good deal."

She gave me one of her lovely, dark looks. She had a smile I would die for, I thought. I hoped I wouldn't have to.

Danny Lopez came by to check on his men, and we met in my front yard.

"A meeting. For what?" Lopez asked.

"I don't know," I said. "Cleveland is asking for a meeting. Maybe he wants to negotiate some kind of peace before anyone else gets killed."

"Negotiate," he scoffed. "When does a man like that care about people getting killed? It doesn't make sense. He could send fifty guns onto your street any time, finish both you and the woman, and your annoyances would stop. Why would he negotiate with you?"

"You're around now," I reminded him. "You and your men change the odds by a lot."

"It's a trap," he said.

"Maybe not. Maybe he just wants to find a way to make me go away."

"You said out loud you would break him for what he did to his wife. Someone has killed three of his people. As far as he's concerned, that was you. It makes little sense it could be anyone else, unless it's a wild coincidence."

He gave me a chance to respond, and when I didn't, he went on.

"You have sworn yourself as his enemy," he said. "You said you were going to avenge his wife's murder, since the police would not arrest him. Why would you even consider such a meeting?"

I went into the house for my cigarettes, and when I came out Lopez was squatted down to look at the dirt in my front yard. He rubbed the soil between his fingertips like a lady examining a dress fabric.

"Nothing will ever grow in this again," he said. "The earth is poisoned with all the years of walnut shells. It's too late."

"I don't plan to grow anything," I said. "I'm fine with it the way it is."

"Can I ask you something?"

His look sharpened, and he held my eyes. "A thing that might seem a little . . . discourteous?"

I shrugged my assent.

"Are you feeling like yourself?" he asked. "Are you well? I've known you a long time, *amigo*, and stupid is one thing you never were. I never knew a time you would walk into a death trap like this. Do you want to hurt yourself . . . and me? Is your judgment gone?"

"You don't have to go." My face got hot. "I'll go myself. Forget it."

"I won't let you do it," he said. His voice was mild. "I have my own interest in this now. I think I want you to

273

look at yourself in the mirror, because you may be a danger to yourself and everyone around you."

"How so?"

"You are distracted," he said. "You are driven by emotion now, not logic. I can see it in your face and hear it in your voice. Men like you and me do not survive very long when they allow emotion. Something has gotten under your skin and changed the way you think. What has happened to you, my friend?"

I couldn't answer. I resisted what he said, but the kindness in his voice was making my throat tight. I thought about Charlene Cleveland, dead in her pretty pink dress behind the wheel of her smashed convertible. I remembered the little girl, another pink dress, dried out and silent in the barn. I thought about the photograph of the Mexican women, caught forever in the glare of a flashbulb, all of them long gone to whatever horrors had waited for them.

Most of all I thought about Annie Kahlo, more beautiful than any woman I had ever known, haunted and frightened by things I couldn't even see. My voice choked.

"This isn't even a case," I managed. "I don't have a client and I'm not getting paid. I resolve things, maybe not always the right way, but that's what I do. I resolve things. I keep pulling on the loose thread, and it gets worse and worse. Sal Cleveland is in the middle of everything, and I can't see the end of this. I can't see a resolution."

Lopez put a hand on my shoulder. It was almost fatherly, and not the kind of gesture characteristic for him to give, nor the kind I usually accepted.

"There may be only one resolution," he said. "A bullet for Sal Cleveland might be the only thing that ends this, and it might be a thing that gets done without answers. You might not have a chance to be judge and jury in your own mind, and without more answers than you have, you might not pull the trigger."

He took his hand from my shoulder and looked at the street.

"I have no such reservations," he said. "I've seen enough, and the very existence of that photograph, twenty-five years old though it might be, is justification enough for me. I want you to know that, and be ready for it. I will go with you to this meeting, and understand that if opportunity presents itself I am going to kill him."

"At least one of us knows why he's going," I said. "One of us has a general plan."

"I think you have a plan, too, even if you do not let yourself say it out loud."

He still held a handful of dirt in one closed fist. He opened it to show me. The earth looked wet and black.

"You are a romantic," he said. "You think you are hard, but you are not any such thing."

"I'm the furthest thing from romantic," I muttered.

"Something good is growing in dirt that is poisonous. It has almost no chance of survival, but as long as it grows and is alive, you will do anything to protect what small chance it has. What is itself hopeless has given you hope."

"If you say so."

He let the black soil trail from his hand to the ground. "I will see you tonight," he said. "We will walk together into *la boca del lobo*."

His face creased into a sunny smile, and I saw what he must have looked like as a young man in Mexico. He left me and made his way slowly to the truck at the curb, and the illusion of youth vanished. One of his men waited behind the wheel. I had a flash of worry. I hoped I wasn't getting him into something that might get him killed, too.

What is itself hopeless has given you hope.

I thought about trying to take a nap. I wouldn't get much sleep tonight, and I would need any edge I could get, because Danny was right. We were doing something stupid—we had accepted an invitation to go right into the wolf's mouth.

"Something happened to me when I went for my walk last night." Annie said. "It was a wonderful vision, everything I needed. Something bad came first, though."

We were strolling along Cabrillo Boulevard, looking at the ocean. The smell of salt water was strong. The sun was edging up toward noon and was hot, even with the breeze that blew in off the water. Colored flags fluttered on the tops of the hotels, and the sound of surf and gulls washed over everything. Ranks of king palms marched down the boardwalk. We passed under one of them and the huge beard of dry fronds rattled high above us. Annie looked up.

"I love the sound of that," she said. "The wind in the palms."

I didn't think just air did the rustling. The trees were full of rats, but I didn't see any percentage in mentioning it to her.

"I went to the cemetery to feel safe," she said, "like I always do. I was surprised to see the big gates standing open. I went in and closed them behind me."

A black Cadillac passed us very slowly, headed in the same direction we were. Its windows were up. The brake lights flickered, and it nosed into the curb a half-block away and stopped. Against the bright colors of the beach it looked faintly obscene, a spill of night-time on the blue-and-gold day.

276

"There was something very mean there," she continued. "I felt it...very near, and even though I couldn't see anyone, I blamed it on Sal. I turned around to leave. It upset me."

"You think it was his people?" I asked, watching the black car. She nodded.

An ice cream truck parked across the street, on the beach side. I caught snatches of the music playing from the speaker on its roof. I remembered the tune, but not the words. I looked up the street at the Cadillac again, and gently took Annie's elbow.

"Want some ice cream?" I asked, and she nodded again.

We waited for a break in the traffic and then crossed. Up close, the melody from the loudspeaker competed with the drone of the freezer unit. The truck was spotless, as was the driver. He stood at the small window and waited for us. Dressed in white, crisp and clean, his small bow tie was black, matching the brim of his hat. The slashes of black-on-white reminded me of the hands on a clock.

Annie stood on tiptoe at the window to talk to him, and he leaned down to hear her. A gust blew off the water, and she reached up with one hand to hold her hat. All light cotton and tanned skin, it struck me again how cool and lovely she was. I turned and watched the water with one eye, and the black car with the other.

"What'll you have, pally?"

The ice cream man stared at me. Annie held a cone filled with pale green that matched her dress. She had a tiny taste and smiled. A list of flavors had been painted on the side of the truck, covering most of it from top to bottom. I saw the usual chocolate, vanilla and strawberry, familiar

Neapolitan and Tutti Frutti, but below them the menu offered cola, eggnog, orange, and black licorice.

"I didn't know Good Humor had flavors like these," I said. "I never saw them before."

"You see a Good Humor sign on my truck, pal?" he asked. "You see that anywhere at all?"

I glanced one last time at the black car. I had the sense it was getting ready to do something. I moved closer to Annie. The wind blew harder, and it was time for us to go.

"I don't know," I said. "Vanilla. Give me vanilla"

"Everywhere you go, there's gotta be some kind of wise guy," he grumbled, and turned away to get it.

"Sal Cleveland wants a meeting," I told Annie. "At the Star-lite, after it closes . . . three in the morning. I'm going to end it tonight, if I can."

She tasted her pale ice cream and nodded absently, looking up the street. I followed her gaze to the black Cadillac. As if it sensed us looking, it started with a puff of blue smoke. The brake lights flashed and it pulled into the traffic and drove away.

"The dark things are getting closer and closer," she said. "The cards say so. June told me that I'm not going to live through this."

"June is dead, Annie. She isn't real. The things she tells you aren't real."

Her eyes were vacant, lost. I felt a sharp jolt of alarm, and turned her toward me.

"Of course you're going to live through this," I said. "I'm not going to let anything bad happen to you."

"You have to," she said. "If you love me, you have to let bad things happen to me."

"I won't, though," I said. "Let me send you away, until this is over. It won't be for long."

She touched my face. Her fingers were light and dry, barely a brush, but somehow painful.

"Don't you believe in happily-ever-after?" she asked. "Don't you read the stories?"

I didn't answer, and after a moment she nodded as though I had. The ocean air caught at the ends of her hair, and she brushed them back off her face and turned her attention back to her ice cream.

"If you want happily-ever-after, play the cards as they land," she murmured. "Just play the cards."

-Twenty Six-

The Star-lite Lounge was all lit up. The blue flood lights washed the walls, and the neon script across the front of the building glowed a slightly brighter blue. It all made me feel more tired. I shut off the car. Danny and I sat quietly and studied the building for a moment. The place looked haunted.

We got out and walked across the empty parking lot to the front entrance. The place had been closed for an hour, but a large man still sat on a stool beside the door. I couldn't say for sure if he was the same one who had been there the last time I was here. If he recognized me, he didn't say hello. He hoisted himself from the stool with a grunt. I saw the gun under his arm before he straightened his coat. It looked as big as a cannon.

The lounge was as silver and blue as it had been the last time I saw it. A couple of women were sweeping up and stacking chairs on the tops of the tables. A pall of smoke still floated and drifted in the colored light. I wondered if it ever completely went away. The bartender waited at his post in front of the racks of bottles, and he watched us go by with an expression I didn't like. He looked like a guy on the inside of a big joke.

I thought about stopping to ask him for a drink.

"Bar's closed. You'll get drinks inside."

He stopped at the door of Cleveland's office and looked inside. When he was satisfied with something I couldn't see, he gestured for us to go in. The room was full of people. Sal sat directly in front of us, behind his immense green-topped desk. The lamp lit his face. Everyone else seemed to be in gloom, and I wondered if he'd arranged it that way deliberately. There were two empty chairs directly in front of him. He gestured at them and we sat. Two gunsels occupied the shadowed corners of the room on one side. They leaned against the walls, Tommy guns at the ready. The opposite corners were empty. They had obviously thought about cross-fire, which was disappointing.

Captain Earnswood had pulled a chair up to the desk, on Cleveland's left, close but outside of the lamp's circle of light. Fin sat on the other side, his face set in a sort of pleasant bemusement.

"Evening, Earnswood," I said. "Or I suppose I should say good morning. I feel a lot safer knowing that Santa Teresa's finest is on the job here."

He stared at me, face immobile, and said nothing.

There was a rustle beside my chair, and I looked up as the bartender put a glass full of bourbon and ice into my hand. He had another glass for Danny Lopez, and when he had finished serving I heard the door latch closed behind me. I tasted my drink. It didn't taste as though it had been doctored; in fact, it tasted swell.

Cleveland was as freshly combed and shaved as if it was the beginning of the evening, not the end. His collar was crisp, and his tie was knotted tight. He didn't look nervous. I was struck by his good looks, and the knowledge that Annie Kahlo had lost a part of her heart to him. He idly fingered the customary spread of playing cards in front of him. From time to time, he glanced up at me.

"So?" he asked.

"You called me here," I said. "I assumed it was because you had something to say, not so I could watch you play solitaire."

"Not in the mood for small talk?" He smirked. "You have plenty of time for cracking wise when you're on your own street."

"The last small talk I made with you, you started crying," I said. "It embarrassed me. I'd rather just get to the point."

His face flushed, and he put a hand flat on the desk. His eyes went wide, and a tic started up in his cheek. Fin leaned forward, touched his arm, and said something too quiet to hear. Cleveland settled back and visibly brought his face under control.

"I was drunk," he said. "I'm not drunk now."

"We all get that way sometimes. No shame in it. I'd still like to get down to it."

"You've managed to kill three of my people," he said. "That's a drop in the bucket. I have a lot more people."

"You say I killed them. I say I didn't."

"I've decided to put this behind us," he said, ignoring me. He tried on a smile. "You're a major pain in my keester, but I have to admire that, a little. I could keep a guy like you pretty busy. Wouldn't you like to give up your lousy office and your lousy house and your lousy car? Start enjoying some nice things?"

"That's what this is about?" I asked. "You think you can buy me off with a job? You think I'll forget what you did to your wife and come to work for you?"

"I'm a businessman," he said. "I see things in terms of business. I don't get emotional about them, and I want to keep on doing my business without looking over my shoulder all the time. You, on the other hand, get emotional about everything. You're a nuisance, and I want it to stop. I could have you killed in about ten minutes, but like I say, I sort of admire your guts. I can sweeten the deal, maybe."

"What else are you offering?"

He spread his hands expansively,

"Tell me what you want," he said. "There aren't many wishes in this town that I can't grant."

I thought about Charlene Cleveland, crumpled over the wheel of her pretty Ford convertible, with two broken legs and a bullet hole in her pretty face. I thought about a mummified little girl in a pink party dress. I thought about the endless, proud tears that Annie Kahlo hid behind dark glasses. I felt the rage bloom inside me, huge and red and hot.

"I want you dead," I said. "I want to go to your funeral and then buy myself a nice lunch. I'm not sure if I'm ever going to get that, so why don't you tell me what's the second best thing you're offering."

His eyes widened in disbelief. "You have the balls to come in here and talk to me that way?" he asked. "Here in my place? After you've been back-shooting my people?"

Beside me, Lopez had slipped out a pistol. He held it casually under the table, against the inside of his thigh. I willed my face not to reveal my shock to the men across from us. I had no idea what he would do.

"You say I killed three of your people," I said. "Trouble is, you're the killer here. You shot your wife like you were putting down a dog. Before she died, you told her that you were going to burn Annie Kahlo to death. This all seems to have started when you killed Annie's father and burned his house down on top of the body. Her sister ended up dead. People die wherever you go."

"Burn Annie Kahlo to death?" he asked. "Is that what the dizzy bitch told you?"

"You scared her," I said. "Enough to finally leave you."

He passed a hand over the cards, one way and then the other. He turned one over, looked at it and put it back.

283

"I said she would burn to death, because it's what I saw. I didn't say I would do it. She's had hot pants for me since she was a girl. She's too crazy to wake up to in the morning, but I wouldn't mind tossing her again."

"You killed her father," I said. "Are you going to deny that?"

"I had a problem with Frank Kahlo," Sal said. "Why would I lie about it? Done is done. No one cares anymore. He borrowed a lot of money to keep his pisspot ranch floating. Guess what? It didn't float. He couldn't pay me what he owed. After all this time, no one cares any more, if anyone ever really did."

He took a drink. I hadn't known his name was Frank. It seemed like an odd thing not to know.

"Back then I was a nice kid," he said. "I tried to find other ways for him to keep up. His place was private, and close enough to the city to suit me. I used it for a little bit of business, now and then."

"You used his barns to house girls and women," I said. "On their way from Mexico to wherever you had sold them."

"Pretty good, shamus. How'd you know?"

I pointed to the picture on his desk.

"The photograph I traded you for your wife's divorce. There was a truck full of women and girls, and you standing in front of it. There was a house in the background. It didn't mean anything to me, just a house. When I saw the house, it was burned down . . . just the walls and part of a veranda still standing. It took a while to make the connection, but I did. It was the Kahlo house in the picture."

"I was young," he said. "What can I say? It hung over there on my wall for so long I didn't see it any more, until it went missing, and you showed up trying to sell it to me. Sell back what you stole."

He saw the look on my face.

"It's business, shamus," he said. "Just business, which you know nothing about. That's why you work and live in a dump."

He looked over at Lopez. "When I got it back, there was a signed affidavit sworn out on the back of it, one that wasn't there before you stole it. You stated the circumstances, and that it was you took the photo, Mister Lopez."

"Maybe so," Danny shrugged.

"No sir, not so." Cleveland's voice rose. He pounded the photograph on his desk with one finger. "This photo was taken twenty-five years ago, and it wasn't you that took it. You were back in whatever Mexican shithole you crawled out of, cleaning fish and chewing on a tortilla."

"So I lied." Lopez shrugged again. "You sell Mexican women to people who rape and kill them, and I lied and said I saw you do it. Seems fair."

I tasted my bourbon. It was excellent, better than anything I could afford to buy for myself.

"I deal in whores," Cleveland said. "I don't tell people what they can do with them, any more than I'd sell a car and tell the buyer to drive careful."

"You made a deal with Frank Kahlo to use his place," I said. "You killed him, anyway. Why?"

"Ah, that's the question, isn't it?" Cleveland smiled. "That's the question. Frank Kahlo had a sentimental side. He saw his daughter had fallen for me, and he sent her away. It annoyed me, but I was willing to let it go. The girl was a looney, even when she was young. I got tired of her, to tell you the truth. She had a lot of strange ideas, gave me the creeps."

He stroked the fan of cards laid out in front of him, brushing his fingers as lightly over them as if he were remembering the feel of a woman's skin.

"When she was gone, old Frank got a little nervous and strange around me. Maybe he got some romantic ideas about the Mexican hookers coming through his ranch. I don't know. We'll never know. Maybe Frank got an attack of conscience. Maybe he just wanted to screw me. Whatever it was, he took his story to the cops."

Lopez stirred a little. He still held the pistol out of sight under the table.

"Did the Santa Teresa Police Department take his story seriously?" Cleveland smirked. "I should say they did. They took Frank right upstairs to see the brass, that's how seriously they took it.'

He indicated the man sitting to his right with a grand flourish.

"Take a bow, Captain Earnswood. And did the captain here take the story seriously? Dead seriously. Too bad for Frank."

He laughed out loud. The teeth under his mustache were very white and even. I thought he looked like a pale version of Clark Gable.

Earnswood smiled, but it was as strained as if it rubbed a canker sore.

"A five-gallon can of gasoline and a bullet, and poof! Frank Kahlo didn't have any more worries. I did him a favor, really."

"You killed his daughter," I said through gritted teeth. "You killed a ten-year-old girl."

"You read that in an old newspaper," he said. "Let me set your mind at ease. There was no girl in the house. Kahlo owed me a lot of money, and you can believe I turned the place upside down and inside out before I struck a match. There was no girl in that house. I had no clue where she got to, but I knew she wasn't in the house."

"In the barn," I said. "She hid in the barn, waiting for her daddy to tell her it was okay to come out. Her daddy never came, because you had shot him. She died in that barn, waiting."

I looked at Earnswood.

"You had to have heard we found a mummified body in the barn," I said. "That's the kind of thing cops at the station would gossip about."

"I heard about it," he said. "I assumed it was one of the Mexicans, if it was even anything to do with all that. Kid could have been anyone. I didn't pay a lot of attention, tell you the truth."

"Not important," I said. "Frank Kahlo was dead and couldn't blab to anyone else. If one of his daughters got left to die, no big deal, right?"

"I never would have left the kid behind in that barn," Cleveland said. "I didn't know. I might be cold, but I'm not like that. I met her once or twice. She was a cute girl."

"I wouldn't know," I said. "She wasn't very cute when we buried her."

"What else?" His voice got soft.

"You might as well have killed Annie Kahlo while you were at it. You broke her heart, turned her life into a nightmare. She'll never be a happy woman."

"And so, you want to kill me," he said. "I didn't kill my wife, but you think I did, and that's the cherry on the sundae as far as you're concerned. Am I forgetting anything?"

"Why don't you tell him the truth?"

The voice belonged to Fin. He sat back comfortably, as though he were watching a game of lawn tennis.

"What are you talking about?" Cleveland growled. "The truth about what?"

Fin ignored him, and held my eyes. He seemed to be enjoying himself. His voice took up the whole room.

"Young Anne Kahlo promised herself," he said. "She went back on it, she broke her promise, she reneged. She disappeared for parts unknown, and her father helped her to do it. Mister Cleveland tried to be reasonable, you have my assurance. Mister Kahlo stayed obstinate and wouldn't give up his daughter's whereabouts. It was, shall we say . . . a Mexican standoff."

He looked at Lopez, who looked back, his face impassive.

"Beg your pardon, of course," Fin said, not sounding very sorry at all. "My friend Mister Cleveland still held a substantial promissory note, with little chance of repayment. Mister Kahlo held his daughter's location, and refused to offer it up. Then he went to the police in an attempt to ruin Mister Cleveland, who had no choice but to settle the matter himself, as fairly as he could."

"He took Frank Kahlo's life, and he burned his house down on top of him," I said. "That the fair payment you're talking about?"

"Mister Kahlo had other reasons for wanting to ruin Mister Cleveland. They don't have any bearing on this story, so we'll respect the dead and let those reasons rest with Mister Kahlo's ashes. I will simply assure you that when Mister Kahlo met with no success in telling tales to the

288

police, he would have eventually resorted to violence of his own. Mister Cleveland was defending himself, as anyone has a right to do."

There was complete silence. Cleveland started to say something, and subsided. From the other side of the room, Earnswood gave me his dead-eye stare. The evil in the room increased, as if a cat got loose and climbed the curtains.

Danny Lopez broke the silence. "You were going to take the little girl," he said. "You were going to take the little girl as payment."

Only Fin seemed unperturbed. "Of course they were going to take the girl," he said. "Frank Kahlo didn't have anything else to take, did he? Not even avocados. He couldn't even make a go of that, poor soul."

He took the small silver pill-box from his pocket and opened it with a thumbnail. He selected a tablet and put the box away. "Annie Kahlo ran away," he said. "She was engaged to marry Mister Cleveland, and she ran away, much like his late departed wife ran away, with your help. Running away from debts and responsibilities is not something Mister Cleveland allows, from men or women. It's bad for business, bad for his peace of mind, and perhaps bad for his soul. The consequences are reasonably dire. They have to be."

"What would you do with her?" I asked. "She was too young to be of any use to you, unless . . . "

"There are certain private collectors who will pay very dear for a pretty young girl, the younger the better, one with no questions attached to her. A girl who can come out to play, but doesn't ever have to go back home. Some of these collectors are quite respectable, I can assure you, wealthy men in very high places. Not the sort of men who would be seen with gangsters at all."

"Which is where Earnswood comes in," I said. "A police captain, a pillar of Santa Teresa. Your ambassador to the depraved scum at the top of the food chain. You people are monsters."

"I didn't kill the girl," Cleveland said. "I turned around, and she was gone."

"We know that," I said. "I helped to bury her. When you were busy shooting her daddy, she ran away and hid from you, didn't she?"

Fin put his hands together, looking delighted. "You, sir, are truly a detective!" he exclaimed. "I can see the wheels grinding slowly in your head. The girl vanished! Poof! Looked high and low, they did, and couldn't find her! What good is a vanished girl to anyone?"

"You know what?" Cleveland said. He put the card he was examining face down. "I'll tell you the truth. Why the hell not? I shot Frank Kahlo because he had lost control. He lost control of his wife, and then he lost control of his daughters. I couldn't trust him anymore, and then he wouldn't hand over the girl, and then the little bitch gave me the slip."

"So you had nothing," I said.

"I had nothing." He smiled. "That's why I set the place on fire. I was sure she was hidden somewhere in the house, and she'd come out. Since she didn't, I figured she went up in smoke. Surprised the hell out of me when they found the body after all this time."

I felt a wave of emotion, thinking about June. I didn't know if I wanted to cry or to lunge across the desk to strangle Sal Cleveland. What he said next startled the lump right out of my throat.

"The littlest Kahlo girl would have taken to the life like a fish to water," he said. "After all, her mother was a whore."

"Her mother wasn't even around," I said. "What are you talking about?"

Cleveland gave an elaborate shrug, and didn't try to contain his spreading smile. At his side, Earnswood grinned, too.

"The sister gets around," the cop leered. "Don't let the snooty act fool you. She's a hot tamale. I can tell you that for a fact. So was her mother. It runs in the family, all right."

I felt the heat in my face. This was pointless. We had come here so that a bunch of hoodlums could mock and gloat and egg each other on.

"I ought to do the whole city a favor and just shoot you, Earnswood," I said.

"You're headed for a long rest behind bars," he sneered. "Only you won't make it. They're going to find you floating under the wharf first."

I stood up. I ignored Earnswood and looked at Sal.

"What about burning Annie Kahlo to death? You still planning on trying to do that?"

He looked at me and couldn't hold my eye.

"Nah," he muttered. "That was talk. The cards say she'll burn to death, but it won't be me. For a long time, I thought about setting her house on fire, with her in it. I would have liked to strike the match myself, but you started butting in and showing up everywhere. It wasn't safe to show myself, so I sent Mary around to do the deed."

I remembered Mary Raw scurrying from the Gardiner's house, dressed in her shapeless hat and dress. Now I understood what she had been doing there, and was relieved for the old couple.

"She went to the wrong house," I said. "I surprised her coming out the front door."

"She went to the wrong house," he echoed. "Poor Mary."

"You don't have anything against the Gardiners, then? They have nothing to do with any of this."

"Who the hell are the Gardiners?"

"The neighbors," I said. "The house Mary Raw was in."

"Wrong house, like I said." He shrugged. "She saw that right away and left. You showed up before she could figure out which house she was supposed to be at."

I had nothing else to ask. The meeting didn't seem to have resolved anything, and I wondered if we had been lured here just to get buried. I felt like a fool for coming here in the first place.

"We're done," I said. "Are you going to let us walk out of here?"

"I didn't have you frisked when you came in," Cleveland shrugged. "The Mexican has been sitting there with his gun in his lap. If I were going to shoot you, it would already be done."

Lopez stood up, too, and put his gun away.

"This was your one chance to make things right with me," Sal said. " When you leave, you're as good as dead. I'll do it someplace I don't have to clean up the mess. This was your one chance."

"Let me be clear," I said. "I know you shot your wife dead. She sat in a wrecked car, badly hurt and crying. You shot her in the face. When I started this, I wanted to see you in the electric chair for it."

I looked at Earnswood. When he didn't say anything, I went on. "I was a chump to think there could be any justice, Cleveland. The law here is as dirty as you are. You'll never even see a day in prison."

Lopez touched my elbow, and I turned to leave.

"Here's a promise, though," I said. "I'm not done. You killed your wife, and you wiped out the Kahlo family, and you're going to live just long enough to wish you hadn't. I'm going to see to it."

He threw back his head and laughed. It was a pleasant laugh, and it went well with his white teeth and green eyes. I wondered if the nice laugh had attracted all the women he had ruined. I wondered if Annie had fallen in love with his laugh.

"You're not going to see to anything, peeper," he said. "The next time I see you it will be at your funeral. Just for old time's sake, I might bring along the Kahlo broad to see you off."

"Do that," I said, and followed Danny Lopez out of the room.

We headed for the parking lot. The skin between my shoulder blades crawled, but no one spoke to us or tried to stop us on the way out.

-Twenty Seven-

I chased my headlights up Figueroa Street and parked in my driveway. I checked my watch; it was just before five. The sun still slept, and I needed some sleep of my own, pretty badly. One of Lopez' men emerged from nowhere, sketched a wave at me, and then melted back into the shadows. I was going up my front steps when I spotted Annie Kahlo coming down hers.

"I'm going for a walk," she called.

I thought about asking her again what the point was of having protection on the street if she slipped it every chance she got. She would have said something cryptic, and I was too tired to figure her out.

"I was just thinking that a walk would be fine idea," I lied. "I'll go with you, if that's all right."

"Get Button," she suggested. "He doesn't get out enough."

"At five in the morning," I muttered to myself.

I unlocked the front door and got it open. The dog bolted by me and had a joyous reunion with Annie on the sidewalk. I went in and found his leash. I tried to hand it to her when I joined them, and she shook her head.

"He doesn't need a leash," she said. "He knows what to do."

"I think this is your dog," I said. "I just feed him."

"I think so, too. We can share him, though. He loves you, too."

He loves you, too. My heart jumped a little, and I waited to see if she would elaborate on it, but she didn't.

"Are you going to tell me about the meeting?" she asked.

294

"Not much to tell. Cleveland is losing people, and he's trying to deal with it. He'd like to just kill me, and you too, but this whole thing is shining a spotlight on him, already, and the cops are watching. He's willing to settle for me just going away, and he'll even put me on his payroll and make me a little rich if I do."

"What about me?"

"He didn't mention you, one way or the other," I lied. "I guess he assumes if I go away, you will too."

"Sal doesn't care about the police," she said. "He owns the police. They're deep in his business."

"Earnswood was there at the meeting," I said. "The captain you recognized. I think they're very nervous."

She stopped walking, and turned to face me. Ahead of us, Button stopped too, and looked back. She began to laugh softly. I didn't much like the sound of it.

"They aren't nervous," she said. "No one in this whole mess is nervous, except maybe you. These people don't get nervous. They might be asking you to stop, but this is fun. Do you not see that? This is how Sal Cleveland has fun. It's the only reason he does any of what he does, and it's why I told you to kill him."

"I might still have to do that," I said. "Depends."

"What else?" she asked.

I moved to start walking again, and she caught my elbow.

"What else?" she repeated.

"I found out about June," I said, and took a breath. "Nothing really, that we didn't already guess. She ran when they shot your dad. I suppose they were busy doing that, and when they turned around she had disappeared."

"You said 'they' shot my father. Who was there?"

"Cleveland shot him," I said. "Earnswood was there and helped search for your sister. Fin told me a lot of the story, but I don't think he was there. I don't know who else. Cleveland and Earnswood for sure."

I told her the rest of what I knew. Her eyes and her face didn't let me hold anything back. Sal had tried to take June because Annie had run away, and he felt he was owed. June had run and hidden herself, and after spending most of the night hunting for her, he had set the house on fire and left her for dead. She was in the barn, not the house, but she had been too scared to come out. He had killed her just the same as if he had pulled a trigger.

When I had finished, we started walking again. Up ahead, Button had waited patiently for us. He looked like he was glad to be moving.

"What now?" she asked.

"The meeting didn't change anything." I shrugged. "If anything, it cleared some things up, but I'm not going to let this go, and Cleveland knows it. Things are bound to explode."

"Are you scared?" she asked.

"I don't bother much with being scared," I said. "Usually no point in it."

"So what will you do? You can't sit back and wait for him. He's too strong."

"I don't know yet," I admitted. "Sitting back is how I operate, usually. In my line of work, I've gotten used to poking and prodding and watching, until something gives. Something eventually happens, and then I deal with whatever it is, and hopefully things get resolved. I play the cards as they fall."

The streetlights weren't doing much good. I touched her elbow as we stepped onto the sidewalk.

"Are you afraid of anything?" she asked. "Anything at all? Everyone is afraid of something."

The rain had cleared and the sky was full of moon, brighter up there than down here on the ground. The pavement was wet and the street steamed. The vapor floated and moved slightly, for as far up the block as I could see. It hung in the dark air, a congregation of dreams, dancing to music too soft to hear.

"You've asked me that before."

"You never answer."

I thought about it. "I never saw much action in the war," I said. "Too old. I was lucky to get in as a military cop. Before I got stationed in Honolulu, I got bounced around a couple of islands, and mixed in with the troops like a real soldier."

I thought about the 'real soldiers' that had died while I broke up bar fights and wrote reports about stolen gear, and some of the old bitterness returned. I stopped talking for a minute, remembering. The sound of my heels was loud on the cement. Annie's steps were silent.

"In the Pacific, we landed different places," I said. "We never knew why, or what waited for us on them. Beautiful ocean and perfect, hot day . . . you felt like you should be wearing bathing trunks, not a helmet and pack. The water underneath the boat turned brown, churned up by the landing crafts in front of you, and you were almost on the beach. They'd always turn up then, the sharks . . . like they knew."

"They knew what? What did they know?"

Brick buildings rose high on either side of us. Here and there a dim yellow or orange light was visible from one of the windows high above us, but I didn't think there was a soul awake behind any of them. The curbs were lined with

297

empty cars that looked like they had never belonged to anyone.

"The sharks came to the surface, and it was hard to believe how big they were, and how close they were to the boat. They were a nightmare, just about the color of the water. Sometimes they splashed a little to make sure you knew they were real, or roll to let you see an eye. They were never worried, or in a hurry."

"They came after you?"

"Not really. They were just . . . there, and they might get you and they might not. They didn't care much either way. If they didn't eat today, they would tomorrow."

I took a shallow breath, remembering. "Then you were close enough to the beach, and the brown water swirled and waited and you had to go in. Your rifle weighed about five hundred pounds, and you wondered why you were worried about getting it wet, because bullets can't kill bad dreams."

The Camel Diner appeared on the next corner, a small splash of fluorescent and neon reflected in the soaking street. Annie stopped me, and turned me toward her.

"Somewhere ahead, hidden in the trees or hills or jungle behind the beach, there might be some sweating little guy behind a machine gun. There might be a lot of them, gritting their teeth and feeling triggers under their fingers, just as wound up as you were and dreading you getting close enough they'd have to fire."

Her eyes searched my face. I couldn't read her expression.

"What are you afraid of?" she persisted. "Right now?"

"It always surprised me how warm the water was, and you prayed that if today was your day the little men with machine guns had good aim, because you'd rather die by them than the sharks. Anything was better than the sharks."

"So you're afraid of being eaten?" she asked. "That's what scares you?"

Her look held me, as dark and quiet as the street behind her. Neon flickered and flashed, and the steam swayed like it was alive. "No. It's not that, Annie. We all get eaten, sooner or later."

I was almost out of words, so I took her arm and we started to walk again. The diner looked good, bright lights and the promise of coffee and a piece of pie.

"I'm afraid of the things that don't care," I said. "I'm afraid that I'll die and no one will know, or notice."

She squeezed my arm. Her smile washed over me, sweet and dark. "Don't be afraid," she said. "I'll know, and I'll always notice, so there's nothing to be afraid of."

I pulled her into a kiss. She didn't resist, and after a few seconds returned it with a lot of interest. Her mouth and her arms were warm. I hadn't realized how cold I was.

"I never told anyone else about that," I said.

"Why would you tell anyone else but me?" she asked. "Let's go home."

She whistled for Button, and we did. The sun came up just before we turned up the hill on Figueroa Street and followed the dog home.

Annie was asleep when I left her bed a couple of hours later. I stuck my tie in my pocket, since I was only going next door. I carried my shoes through the cool hush of her house. The flowers, the polished wood and the paintings were a different world than what went on outside these walls. The dog slept on a sofa in the living room. He opened one

299

eye, but made no move to follow me out. I left him where he was.

The morning was still waking up, and the street wasn't moving yet. The new sun glinted off the cars parked at the curb. I scanned them instinctively to be sure none of them were occupied, even though I knew Lopez' men weren't going to miss a trick.

Mrs. Gardiner stood outside her house, hunting through her mailbox. I wished her a good morning as I crossed my yard, and she waved me over to her.

"I'm very worried," she said.

"Things are quiet," I said. "The street is perfectly safe."

"No. Not that." She frowned. "The fire. They can't seem to get it contained. The news said it flared up in the hills east of Summerland. We'll be evacuating soon, and I shouldn't be surprised."

I remembered what Danny Lopez had said about wildfires. *There isn't any way to stop them. They're the ones in control and they burn until they don't feel like it anymore.*

"I'm sure they won't let the fires get any closer to the city than they have." I said. "Those state fire boys know what they're doing. They haven't let this one get too big. It's just been as persistent as the devil. It can't go on forever. It will burn itself out."

"Well, I hope you're right about that," she said.

She seemed distracted, and not in the mood to talk anymore, which suited me. I went inside to look for breakfast. I was starving. I looked in the icebox to see about some eggs, but there weren't any, so I poured some corn flakes into a bowl. The milk in the bottle looked slightly turned. I smelled it, and then poured it down the sink. I ate

300

the cereal dry, looking out the kitchen window, and when I finished, I got my hat and went to the office.

I picked up a tail along the way. It didn't really surprise me, and I didn't mind. I liked to know all the players in the game. This was a car I hadn't seen before, a blue Lincoln Zephyr. I watched it in my rear view mirror. It was a flashy car to follow someone with. Unless the occupants were stupid, I figured they meant to be seen.

A black-and-white radio car was parked at the curb across the street from my building. I glanced at the lettering on the door; a city car, not county. I didn't recognize the face behind the wheel, and he carefully didn't meet my eye. The powder blue Lincoln parked diagonally across from him. The side skirts and white-walled tires stood out like a hooker at Bible study. A couple of hard cases sat in the front of it. I figured them for a couple of Cleveland's boys. They didn't look my way, either.

I stood on the sidewalk, and watched everyone deliberately not watching me. After a minute, I shrugged and climbed the stairs to my office. I spent the morning moving some papers around and making telephone calls. I needed to drum up some business soon. I had been working for birthday cake for nearly a month, and unless I wanted to eat it for every meal, I'd have to pay more attention to my paying clients.

Maybe I needed to think about hiring another secretary. At least there would be someone in the office to take messages while I ran around and chased my tail. It would be someone to talk to, someone to tell me about real things that made sense, like her boyfriend and her cat. It would do me some good to spend time with a normal person, and wouldn't hurt to place an ad, so I got out a pad of lined paper and started making a list of qualifications. When I got

301

to the third item: Must like baseball, I figured I wasn't serious and tossed the pencil on the desk.

It was nearly lunchtime, anyway. At the window, I looked down at the street and saw that the police car had left. The bad guys still sat in the blue sedan. I didn't much care what I had for lunch, so I thought I might walk across and ask them if there was anywhere particular that they wanted to follow me to. I got my hat off the hook, and got ready to go out.

On impulse, I picked up the telephone and tried Annie Kahlo's number. Maybe she would join us for lunch. I was surprised when she answered. Her voice sounded clear and very quiet.

"I think maybe you shouldn't see me for a while," she said.

"What are you talking about?"

"I need to be alone for this," she said. "I can't be alone when I'm with you."

"What about everything that's going on?" I asked. "You can't be alone with that."

"I can, and I will."

I slept in your bed last night, I wanted to say but didn't. *You got me to do what you asked. We have a deal now.* We were silent for a long minute before she spoke again.

"Do I have to give you back your dog?" she asked.

"Keep the dog," I said. "It isn't my dog, anyway."

"It's your dog," she said, and there was a tiny click as she hung up.

When I got down to the street, the blue Lincoln had gone. It seemed like everyone was leaving, all at once. I went to lunch by myself.

The sky over the ocean shone such a deep blue that it hardly seemed real. It was streaked with reds and oranges that looked as though they had been painted on. They said the spectacular sunsets we were getting were on account of the wildfires inland. The smoke in the air did something to the light.

I stopped the car at a beach joint, right on the water at the foot of Salinas Street. It was in a part of Santa Teresa that I never gone, probably because it was full of respectable people. They never got into trouble, and if they did, they kept it to themselves and didn't call up private detectives to talk about it.

The outside of the building was rough gray wood, and the parking lot was mostly full. The cars scattered on the gravel were newer models, in pastel colors. The sign on the roof lit up, even though it wasn't quite dark yet. It said Rick's Seaside Grotto. I lit a cigarette and headed for the front door.

Inside, the place was crowded. The walls were covered in fish nets, and pieces of driftwood and shells were glued onto every surface that would hold still for it. I wasn't sure why they were working the maritime angle so hard when the ocean sat barely thirty yards from the front door. I got a bourbon and water from the bar and slipped into a booth just as a group left it. I probably seemed rude to take up a four-seater with the place so full, but I didn't feel like small talk. The bench was upholstered in aqua-colored Naugahyde, and it felt a little bit sticky beneath me.

I sipped at my drink and looked around the room. There was a dance floor at the far end. People drifted on and off it, with merry groups forming and dissolving around the edges. The constant babble of voices rose whenever the horns and snare drums ebbed. Cigarette smoke drifted in the coral and pink light. Everyone seemed to be having a swell time.

A woman passed close to the table and stopped. She had on a green dress, with a hat and gloves to match. She stood with her back to me, holding her drink carefully away from her body, like she didn't know what it was for. She looked lost. I leaned forward and spoke up over the hubbub. "If you're looking for a mermaid, I don't think there are any here."

She turned, a little startled, and gave me a considering look before she allowed a cautious smile. She touched fingers to her chest, right beneath the single strand of pearls, and color crept into her face. She was pretty, but not pretty enough to be sure about it.

"As a matter of fact, I wasn't," she said. "May I ask you for a favor? Could I leave my drink on your table? I need to leave, and I don't want to elbow my way back to the bar."

"By all means," I said. "It doesn't look as though you've touched it, though."

"I'm supposed to be meeting someone," she said. "They seem to be held up. I thought I'd order a drink while I waited, but I didn't expect—"

"That there would be no place to sit," I said. "And here I am, with an entire booth all to myself."

"Inconsiderate," she said. "Unfeeling." She laughed at my expression. It was a nice laugh. "I'm sorry. I shouldn't tease you when I don't even know you."

"Why not sit and have your drink?" I asked. "I won't seem so selfish if you do, and your party might show up if you give it a few minutes."

She looked at the front door and made up her mind. She put her drink down and slid into the booth across from me, staying at the very edge of the bench.

"Maybe," she said. "I may as well stay and wait for a few minutes. You never know."

"Might as well," I agreed. "You never know."

She took off her gloves and rummaged in her handbag. She came up with a single cigarette and put it in her mouth. She snapped the purse closed and set it on the seat beside her. Realizing she had forgotten about her lighter, she looked at me and got embarrassed by the awkwardness of it. She started for the purse again.

"I'm sorry," she said. "I should have offered you one. I'm not thinking very clearly."

I snapped my lighter. She leaned into it, and sucked her cheeks in. She didn't look as though she had gotten much practice smoking. Her lipstick was pink, and when she took the cigarette from her mouth it looked as though it had been kissed.

"I don't do this, usually. I mean . . . I wouldn't sit with someone I didn't know. I knew you were safe, though."

"You did?"

"Your voice didn't get higher when you spoke to me," she said. "That's how I knew it was safe to sit down with you. You're completely taken. I can tell. I hope it doesn't offend you, my saying so."

"That's all right," I said. "I didn't mind. Higher than what?"

"When a strange man speaks to a woman, and he's interested in her or has intentions, his voice gets higher. Yours didn't when you spoke to me."

"I see," I said, and didn't.

"Also, you're sad." She was definite. "You're missing someone who doesn't know that you are, and your heart feels broken. I can tell."

This was some funny kind of woman. I tried not to think about Annie Kahlo. I didn't think I had much heart to break. I had gotten drunk by myself in a lot of strange places, so this didn't mean anything.

"You have a lot of theories." I smiled. "Do you use a crystal ball?"

"I don't need one," she said. "I feel that way sometimes, too."

She stubbed out her cigarette, a little clumsily, and a tendril of smoke curled from the ashtray. She looked at the front door again.

"I'd better go," she said.

She slid out of the booth. She started to put her gloves on, changed her mind and stuck them in her purse. Then she changed it back again, and put them on.

"It was nice meeting you," she said, and turned away. "Good luck."

I felt a stab of loneliness, or something. It wasn't a familiar feeling, whatever it was.

"Just a minute," I said.

She looked back, in her careful hat and gloves, her hair and makeup. She was an awful lot more than she thought she was, but I couldn't think of a way to tell her that. She was none of my business, anyway.

"Whoever was supposed to meet you here is a damn fool," I said. "No loss."

Just for a moment, her eyes went raw, but just as quickly she collected herself.

"Do you think so?"

"I know so," I said.

"Thank you," she said. "You should tell her how you feel, whoever she is. Maybe she doesn't know."

I watched her all the way to the door, and then a waiter passed and I indicated my empty glass. When I looked back at the doorway, she was gone.

"You don't know the first thing about love," I muttered to myself.

-Twenty Eight-

I found a spot at the curb, halfway up the small hill to my house. This late at night, the street tended to fill up. One of these days. I needed to clean out my garage so I could start using it. I got out and started walking.

I reached a spot where the sidewalk buckled and heaved over the roots of a huge fig tree. There was no streetlight there, and I had to be careful in the dark—catch a toe and I'd go face-first into the cement. I was feeling the couple of bourbons in me, so I took my time. I kept an eye out for Lopez' men in the shadows, but they stayed out of sight.

Annie Kahlo was still on my mind. The woman in the bar had suggested that I tell her how I felt, that maybe she didn't know. I wasn't sure if I knew how I felt. I knew Annie seldom left my thoughts anymore. I knew I had never felt quite like this about anyone, ever before.

From behind me, headlights flooded the road. I moved sideways and blended myself into the shadows. I had no particular reason to hide, but I had stayed in one piece because I followed my instincts. A dark-colored Hudson rolled by slowly. The exhaust burbled softly and the tires crunched pebbles. When the big car reached the top, the brake lights flashed and it pulled to the curb.

I started to walk again, a little bit faster than before. A man got out of the car and stood beside it, looking up at the houses. His long coat and fedora were silhouetted in the low light. He tossed his cigarette away and it made a tiny spark when it hit the street. I kept my steps quiet and tried to stay in the shadows as I came closer.

One of Lopez' men stepped out of the dark, quiet as a ghost. One minute he wasn't there, the next he was right beside me. I felt glad that I wasn't going up against these boys.

"Lady say okay," he said, voice low. "*Ella está esperando un amigo. Su novio.*"

"She told you she's expecting someone?" I whispered. "Did you say. . .her boyfriend?"

A yellow bulb came on next door, and the man started moving. Annie's front door opened and she came outside, slender and unmistakable. He went up the steps. She came into his arms and they kissed for a long time. For me, it was the forever kind of long time.

I stood there in the dark and looked at the two of them there in the yellow light. My eyes burned, and my chest hurt like my heart had fallen out. I hoped it had.

About the time I couldn't stand any more of it, they turned and went inside. The porch light went off. I waited for lights to come on inside, but the house stayed dark. I supposed they didn't need any lights for what went on in there. I knew I should go into my own house. Annie Kahlo was none of my business, not now, not anymore, but I couldn't tear myself away.

Suddenly, the small dark glass over the front door went bright, once, like a photographer's flash. I heard the popping noise that went with the light.

"Annie," I said, in a voice that wasn't mine.

I ran toward the darkened house, hauling the pistol off my hip as I went.

I pushed her front door open with my shoulder. Inside, the familiar fragrance of flowers was overwhelmed by the red stink of burned gunpowder and blood. I felt for the light switch. Captain Earnswood lay on the floor, clutching his middle. He rocked back and forth and began to moan, a keening noise that rose and fell. It sounded like he was singing. Annie stood over him, legs spread and arms extended.

"What the hell are you doing?" I shouted at her.

She looked back over her shoulder at me. Her eyes were hot and dark and bright. I was paralyzed with shock.

"He killed my sister," she said. "Remember?"

She extended a toe underneath Earnswood's head and forced his chin upward.

"Look at me," she commanded. "Look."

Earnswood's complexion had gone nearly white except for two feverish, livid spots on his cheeks. Tears leaked from the corners of both eyes. He shook his head back and forth, back and forth, without a break in the moaning. Annie stopped the movement with her foot, took careful aim and fired again. The bark of the .38 nearly deafened me in the small vestibule. The shot took him in the face and slammed his head back against the tiles.

"Annie!" I screamed.

I caught her by the wrist and pulled her to me, trying to keep the gun in her hand pointed away from us. We struggled; she was incredibly, improbably strong. I fought her for the pistol and murmured to her as if I were trying to calm a panicked animal. She finally relinquished it and subsided against me. I held her close and rocked her, smelling the perspiration in her hair and feeling her shoulders shake with sobbing.

"What the hell, Annie," I murmured. "What the hell did you do that for?"

Her shaking increased, and I turned her face up to mine and saw with some kind of horror that she wasn't just crying. The sound bubbled up at me; she was laughing, too, long peals of lovely, silver screen laughter. Any actress in

310

the country would have sold her soul to own that delectable, sweet, Annie-laugh.

I let her go, and she stumbled backward against the wall and went down to the floor, a puddle of hilarity and weeping and blue-and-white cotton.

"He killed my sister, the son of a bitch. They all did . . . all of them."

I saw her tears and her madness, and I knew that I had never loved anyone as much.

I went to one knee and checked Earnswood. He lay on his side with his knees drawn up, like a boy taking a nap. He didn't look like he was asleep, though. Dead people always look dead. I didn't need to take his pulse or even to see the spreading mess beneath his head. The bullet had caught him square in the chin, and he was a whole lot uglier than he had been when he was alive. His eyes looked at me and at nothing. I let him fall back, and I wiped my hand on the leg of my pants without realizing I did it.

Annie sat on the tiles, her back against the wall. She had her head on her knees. The pieces were falling into place for me.

"You killed them all, didn't you?" I asked. "The men in the Nash, Mary Raw. All of them."

No answer.

"What's next? Are you planning to kill Cleveland, too?"

She lifted her face. Her eyes were swollen with tears, and she dragged them over to focus on me. Her smile was gorgeous. "Yes. If I'm really lucky."

I helped her to her feet. My mind raced. "How did you set these people up, Annie?"

She began to laugh again. I put an arm around her shaking shoulders and led her to the porch. Lowered to the

311

top step, she clutched herself and began to rock. I turned back inside. Earnswood was just as still and dead as he had been. Other than dragging his corpse out to the closest flower bed, I didn't have any good ideas. It looked pretty hopeless. Even if one of the neighbors hadn't already called it in, too many people knew.

Lopez had his men on the street, and they didn't miss anything. The fact that they were staying in the shadows meant they knew it was one of the enemy dead, and they weren't needed. I didn't want to burden Danny with the weight of a cover up. None of this was technically his fight, and he had done enough. I was going to have to bring the cops in, and figure a plausible way to keep Annie out of it.

I eased the front door closed behind me without touching the knob. There were lights on in the several of the apartment windows across the street, and in a couple of the nearby houses. The street hadn't slept through it. I started down the front porch steps just as one of the Mexicans stepped out of the shadows.

"Get off the street," I told him. "It's over, for now. We've killed a cop. The street is going to be swarming with them in just a few minutes."

"*Yo sé*," he said. "We saw the whole thing. It was Earnswood . . . *escupo sobre su cuerpo*. I spit on him."

He did something strange. He turned to where Annie sat, leaned down and took her hand very gently. He spoke softly to her in rapid Spanish. I couldn't make out any of it, but she looked up at him and nodded. When he finished, he kissed her hand and settled it back in her lap.

"*Ella es una santa,*" he said to me. "A hero." He nodded at me, and was gone.

"Maybe I need to spend time in a different place," Annie said. "My car's around the block, ready. I put some things in it this afternoon. It's better if I'm invisible until I finish this."

The engine on the Hudson still ticked once in a while as it cooled down. The guy on the floor inside the house was cooling down, too, but if he made any noises I didn't hear them. I kept my voice as gentle as I could.

"Finish this? What do you mean, finish this?"

"This isn't done yet," she said. "Not quite."

"It isn't too late, Annie. I'm going to deal with the cops. We'll say he broke in. Let me do the talking."

"He is a cop . . . was. They won't listen, and I don't want them to listen," she said. "I want them to know that I did it. I want them to know why."

"How did you set these people up?" I asked again. "These were all careful people, who had every reason to be wary of you. How did they even let you get close?"

Her face changed. She looked almost savage.

"They all wanted the same thing," she said. "Everyone wants the same thing, even you."

"That isn't true," I said, stung. "I've never given you a reason to think that."

"I have to go," she said, and turned away.

I took a plunge. "I'm going to say that I saw him break in, and I went over to protect you . . . "

"Go to hell."

"I can help you with this."

"Go to hell. Get out of my business. Oh . . . and Nate? You failed. You had a chance to make things right, and you didn't. I had to do it myself."

She spun away and headed across the grass. I watched her go.

You failed.

313

I faced the worst decision of my life. I had spent a decade as a cop in St, Louis. Earnswood was dirty, but he was still a cop. I didn't work for bad people if I could help it. Annie Kahlo was a murderer. She had killed more than once, and she wasn't done killing. If I let her go, I would be no better than Sal Cleveland.

I watched Annie disappear around the corner.

There was no way to take any of this back. There was no way to stop loving her, either, and I didn't know what to do. The man in the moon peered over the rooftops across the street from me. He wasn't offering anything. As I took a deep breath, I heard Charlene Cleveland's voice, as clearly as if she were standing right beside me.

You don't know the first thing about love.

I started to run.

The convertible sat at the curb, already idling. Annie didn't speak or look at me when I got in the passenger side. She put Mercury in gear and pulled away even before I could get the door closed. The engine sound wound up into a howl, and she pushed the car into a hard left turn and sped up Olive Street. A block away, a pair of headlights came toward us. I didn't need to see the red light on the roof to know it was a prowl car.

Annie raised her voice to be heard. "Why are you doing this?"

"I told you I would stay in for the whole nine," I said. "That hasn't changed."

Parked cars flashed by, inches from my window. The passing buildings were mostly dark. Only an occasional burst of colored neon interrupted the street lights.

"If you are, then give me back my gun," she said.

I hesitated, and then took her pistol from my pocket and laid it on the seat between us. It was the last thing I

314

wanted to do. It seemed like a point of no return, even if I had probably passed that the first time I met her. I smelled the burned gunpowder and in my imagination, the blood.

"Come to think of it," I said, "I guess this is the ninth inning,"

Over the sound of the Mercury's engine, there came the faint warble of the approaching siren. It quickly grew louder, and then the radio car flew past. The driver's face was a white blur.

"No, it isn't," she said. "Not yet."

For just a moment, in the glare of headlights, I had seen her smile, like a sweet secret, dark and serene. It made me shiver a little inside, so I looked back at the road.

This late, there was almost no traffic. Annie drove the streets of Santa Teresa, apparently with no destination and no purpose except to keep us moving. I heard faint sirens from time to time, and once I saw a prowl car paralleling us a block away. I wondered if the police knew they were hunting for a green Mercury convertible.

The ride spun by like some kind of dream. She turned the car away from State Street, and the neon-soaked sidewalks went shadowy, all at once. We spun through block after darkened block. This was the city where I lived and made my living, and I recognized none of it.

On Mission Street, deep in the Mexican *barrio*, we had to slow down to a crawl because the narrow street was full of people. The crowd poured out of a stone church and overflowed into the road. Figures milled around in the dark and stepped out into our lights. Some of them were shaking *maracas* or slapping at *tambores,* dancing to music I couldn't hear.

A flight of steps led up to the church, which was open and unlighted. The door was a black hole. I leaned out and looked up; the steeple disappeared into the night sky.

"In the middle of the night?" I asked. "Who goes to church in the middle of the night?"

"I thought almost everyone did," Annie said. "They don't?"

"Not in my experience, they don't."

She smiled again.

"That's a relief," she said. "I thought I was the only one who didn't."

A young girl in a wedding dress appeared next to the car, close to my door. The light caught at her veil and made her face radiant. A rabbit, wearing a string tie and beaded vest, had her by the hand. I saw that all of the people around her were wearing animal masks. A bird growled and held up two fists. It feathers bobbed as it moved aggressively toward us. Annie tapped the horn and moved the car forward. The crowd parted reluctantly, and then was gone. We were back into empty streets.

"This is my world," Annie said. "I wander here constantly. I think it's because I'm so afraid of everything."

The Mercury flew south on side streets, back out to Cabrillo Boulevard, and the beach. The hotel entrances burned brightly and their signs sparkled and flashed, but only an occasional pair of headlights lit the roadway. If we got caught here, we had nowhere to hide. On my right, there was a huge blackness. The ocean was dark and nearly infinite, and it seemed like a place to hide, a riddle that no one would ever solve.

A traffic light turned red, and Annie braked to a stop.

"Where are we going?" I asked.

"I don't know yet," she said. "I'll drive until I do."

316

A small, dark shape waddled in front of the car, following the crosswalk to the other side. I had to strain to see it in the dark, and I wondered if I was seeing things. It looked like a duck. An old woman hurried out of the darkness, caught up with the bird in front of our car and bent over it. After hoarse laughter and a lot of fuss, she straightened slowly and settled the duck on her shoulder.

"Sorry thing," she said, still laughing.

She sensed us watching, and turned her face in our direction.

"Mind your potatoes," she called, and started away.

We watched her as she moved from streetlight to shadow.

"Ducks make me laugh, too," Annie called after her.

When the light turned green, I looked over my shoulder as we pulled off. It was strange that I hadn't seen a single black-and-white in the last twenty minutes or so. I figured they had to be looking for us by now, and it wouldn't be long before they figured out what kind of car Annie drove and broadcast the description. I wondered if they were looking for me, too.

We drifted through a small business section on Milpas Street. A few stores had their signs turned on, even this late. Annie pulled to the curb and stopped. She looked out her window, deep in thought, and lightly drummed her fingers on the steering wheel.

A little girl pushed open the glass door of a liquor store across the street, and came out onto the sidewalk. The two men leaning against the payphone on the wall ignored her. As she left the fluorescent doorway and moved into the light from the neon sign, her dress changed from white to pink. She spotted us and started toward the car, carefully looking both ways before she crossed the street.

Annie's reaction startled me. She jammed the transmission into gear and pushed the accelerator to the floor. The tires yelped and the rear end of the car swung sideways. Her lips were drawn back from her teeth. I grabbed at the dashboard with one hand and my hat with the other. She didn't slow down for nearly a mile.

"What the hell was that about?" I asked.

Focused on her driving, she didn't answer right away, then said, "Radio Hill. We'll go to Radio Hill."

"All right," I said, and didn't ask why.

The highest point in Santa Teresa was a bluff that overlooked the entire city and had a dazzling view of the Pacific Ocean beyond it. They called it Radio Hill because of the tower that stood watch there, tall and delicate and spindly. It was the most logical place to put a tower like that. There was a house up there, too.

It was a breathtaking property to put a house on; a million-dollar view. The place was a large modern stucco affair with a lot of glass, surrounded by a low wall and lush plantings. No one had ever lived in it. The owner made his money back East in the twenties, and lost most of it in the thirties. The house had been put up for sale before he ever moved in.

It had never sold. The contradictions were too much. It was tantalizingly close to the city below it, but to actually reach it involved a narrow lane that bent and switched its way up the steep hill. The road was vulnerable to sliding mud, and running out for a bottle of milk would demand a certain commitment. In my experience, the wealthy liked the reassurance of having their own kind close, and the base of the hill hosted the poorest neighborhood in Santa Teresa. Worst of all, the big, unsightly radio antenna towered over it.

318

Annie whipped the green Mercury up the hill, around bends and twists. The headlights hardly had time to show the road before it wrenched out of sight. At the top, a low white wall crowded the road. She tucked the car in close to it, and shut the engine off. She went to the wall and hoisted herself up, ignoring my offered hand. I followed her over, and we walked across the lawn. The moon shone bright; in its light the plantings looked tended and lush. Someone was maintaining the property. It reflected off the glass walls of the house, which seemed to look blankly out across space at the dark ocean, far below us.

On the far side of the lawn, I put my elbows on the wall. The lights of the city were spread out as though they had been spilled. I saw the lights of cars crawling along the streets. Some of them were looking for us.

Sirens cried from somewhere at the bottom of the hill. They sounded close, but if they were meant for us they didn't seem to be getting any closer. Up here, I figured sounds probably carried funny. Enough faint light came from the moon to see my wristwatch; it said just after three o'clock in the morning.

I checked my pistol. It was full of bullets but empty of any promises. Unless I planned to start shooting at cops, it wouldn't do me any good. I thought about throwing it away, but I'd had it for a long time, so I put it back into my pocket. I realized that Annie wasn't beside me, and called her name softly.

She was sitting partially hidden at the base of a small tree. The low branches were full of green fruit; the citrus orbs almost glowed in the reflected light. I crossed the grass and bent to look at her.

"They're going to find me, aren't they?" she asked.

"No point in thinking different," I said. "If we plan for it, then we can try to change things."

The wind picked up. I wondered what it would be like to live up here, to build a house far above everything and everyone else. I could look down at the city, and never go there. Annie looked down at all of it. I knew she was seeing something else. Her voice was a murmur, and I had to strain to hear her.

"These are green tangerines," she said. "They're ripe, but they always go to waste because no one knows what they are. It makes me sad."

I lowered myself to sit beside her. Her shoulder against mine was warm, and the ground beneath us still held the heat of the day. I leaned back against the tree and closed my eyes. Then I opened them again, afraid that I'd fall asleep.

"What happens if one of us dies first?" she asked. "Will it be the same?"

I stared ahead of me. The city was laid out far below us, in faint lines of light that mirrored the stars overhead. I was so tired that the patterns seemed like the answer to a question I hadn't asked. Beyond it all, the black ocean spread itself from one edge of the night sky to the other. I touched the back of her hand.

"One of us was always going to die first," I said. "That's how it works."

She shook her head, impatient with me. "I mean tonight," she said. "What if one of us dies, and the other doesn't? What if it's you? What if they kill you?"

"If they do, I'll wait for you."

I surprised myself. I talked nonsense, and a lot of it, but I didn't know where my own words had come from. This was something new. I kept talking, anyway.

"If I go first, I'll be on the other side of your last breath," I said. "Waiting for you."

"Even if that doesn't come until I'm very old, you'll wait?"

She was looking at me intently, and I nodded. She stared again at the distant city lights and seemed to consider it, and for a long time we didn't say anything else. "That's good," she finally said. "It will be like walking out of a dark movie theater. Or into one, depending."

An empty swimming pool was dug into the terrace of the house. I thought I saw something move at the edge of it, and I sat up and strained my eyes. Instinctively, I touched the gun in my pocket. There was nothing else, though. Not yet. There wasn't much we could do except wait until there was.

"If I die first, I won't leave at all," she said. "You won't have to look far for me."

I leaned back and closed my eyes again. The dark was soothing, and I felt my own smile.

"That's fine, then," I said. "I'm glad you won't be far. Where should I look for you?"

"Where do you look for me now?"

"I don't. You just turn up from time to time."

"Yes, exactly."

Her head rested on my shoulder now. It felt exactly right.

"I'm glad that's settled, then," she murmured. "I wasn't worried, but I'm glad, anyway."

I must have fallen asleep then, because when I opened my eyes she was gone. I stood up in a blind panic and scraped my face on a tree branch. I called for her, but I somehow knew she couldn't hear me. I felt a flash of something like relief, and hated myself for it. Clouds covered the moon now, and it was a lot harder to see my way down the hill than it had been coming up.

When I got to the bottom, there were streetlights again. The curb where the Mercury had been parked was empty. I started the long walk back to Figueroa Street.

-Twenty Nine-

They blocked off bottom of my street. A couple of black-and-white radio cars were angled across the road. Several uniformed cops stood behind sawhorses, ignoring the reporters with pads and pencils who were trying to pester information out of them. They perked up when they saw me coming. Two of them caught me by the elbows and kept me company the rest of the way up the hill.

There were two dark sedans in Annie's driveway, and a half-dozen black-and-white radio cars on the street. People were gathered on the steps of the apartment building across the street, watching the official-types milling around, going into and out of Annie's front door. Rex Raines saw us and came down the front walk. He waved off the uniforms that had my arms, and gestured toward my house. I followed him to my veranda, and waited with my arms crossed.

He looked exhausted, and angry. "Anne Kahlo is officially a wanted woman," Raines said. "If she contacts you, turn her in, or you're going to get caught in the crossfire." He shook his head, disgusted. "A beautiful cop-killer. The press is having a field day with this, already."

"You don't know that she killed anyone," I said. "There's a body in her front hallway. That's all you know."

"How do you know that? You just got here."

I didn't answer. He walked across the veranda and leaned on the railing.

"She killed four people that we know about," he said. "And this has barely started. I don't know what else we're going to find out."

I started to speak, but he held up a hand to quiet me. "She killed Douglas Raw and Virgil Lowen in the alley off

323

of State Street. She shot Mary Raw to death in your office. Now she's killed Captain Earnswood."

"How do you think you know all this?" I asked, "What evidence is there?"

His voice got heavy. He didn't look at me. "I don't need evidence, Nate. She called me a couple of hours ago from a phone booth. She confessed to all four murders. I told her she couldn't do it on the telephone. I needed her to come in and tell me in person."

"You said yourself she's crazy. Why should you believe her?"

"She said she couldn't confess in person," he said, ignoring me. "She said she would be dead. She promised to write out a confession and leave it with her mother."

"Her mother?" I asked, startled.

"She stayed true to her word. She wrote it and signed it, and her mother witnessed it. It's been forwarded to the district attorney."

"Her mother?" I asked again, feeling stupid. "She hasn't seen her mother in years . . . ran off. Lives in Hawaii, far as I know."

"Her mother is a woman named Gardiner," he said. "Lives right on the other side of you."

"Mrs. Gardiner?" I was stunned. "That's crazy. That doesn't even make sense."

"Like all the rest of this." He shrugged. "Everyone has a mother, even killers. Someone has to be her mother."

I leaned on the railing and looked over at the Gardiner house, trying to make sense of it. Annie had told me that her mother had left her and June with their father and gone back to Hawaii. She was long gone by the time Annie's trouble with Sal had led to the father's murder, the house burning and June's death in the barn. Neither she nor Mrs.

324

Gardiner had ever given me the slightest hint that they were more than friendly neighbors.

"Why would Annie give you a confession?" I asked.

He looked at me, eyebrows up. "You really don't know?" he asked. "Who do you think has been my number one suspect in all this? Who do you think was first in line to take the rap for all this? It wasn't Anne Kahlo, I can tell you that."

I thought about it.

Raines looked at me, impatient. "Who swore he would fix this himself?" he asked. "Who yelled at me in front of a whole restaurant of people that he would take care of Sal Cleveland if the cops wouldn't, or couldn't?"

I had said it, in the Camel Diner. Raines had told me Cleveland had an alibi and was absolved of his wife's murder, and I had vowed to take care of him myself.

"Sooner or later, I was going to have to cuff you," he said. "You got cut all kinds of slack, but sooner or later the pile of dead bodies around you just got too high to ignore. Ask yourself who played prime suspect in all this."

"Me."

"You," he said. "Never would have figured the Kahlo woman for it, crazy or not. You were going to get arrested. She confessed to protect you, simple as that. She was protecting you."

"Hell," I said. "I don't know what to do about this."

"Nothing you can do," he said. "If you try, you'll get killed. No point in it."

He pushed himself off the railing, straightened and went to the steps. He looked like he had aged about ten years in the last week.

"Don't leave town, and so on," he said.

"He was dirty, Rex," I said to his back. "Earnswood was in Cleveland's pocket for a long time, before you or I ever saw this city. He was as dirty as they come. Annie doesn't deserve to go to prison for him."

On the sidewalk, he turned around to look back at me. His face was bleak. "She isn't going to prison, Nate. She isn't going to make it to prison."

"What's that supposed to mean?"

"You can't save her, Nate. She's gone too far down this road. They'd execute her for this, but she isn't going to get that far. Cop-killers don't generally make it to the gas chamber. All the law enforcement in the county is looking for her, and by tomorrow the teletypes will start landing all over the state. They're going to shoot her on sight, and maybe that's better than her suffering. She isn't going to last the week, and if you try to interfere chances are I'll go to your funeral, too."

"I'm not going to watch her get killed," I said. "If I have a chance to save her, I will. You should know that."

"Then I'll be bringing you flowers," he said. "Any particular kind you like?"

"I don't know much about flowers," I said. "I don't know what you should bring. Whatever looks good to you."

He shook his head, and went out to the street. I shook my head, and went inside. I had a feeling I'd better get some sleep while I could.

Mrs. Gardiner opened up her front door before I could knock. It was the first time we had seen each other since the trouble at Annie's house, and we watched each other carefully. Everything was different, now.

"So you're her mother," I said.

She nodded once. She looked as though she expected me to hit her. When I didn't, she visibly relaxed. Her reaction made me feel bad. I had no right to judge her, and didn't mean to.

"Annie said to tell you that she has the dog," she said. "She's taking good care of him."

"I figured she did," I said. "She told me. I'm not worried about the dog. He liked her better, anyway. I'm worried about her."

"It's strange to take a dog along when you're on the run, isn't it? Don't you think so?"

"She might have wanted some company," I said. "I don't think she worries much about whether something is strange."

"She never did. She's attracted to whatever seems strange. Perhaps that's why animals are drawn to her. She always seemed to understand my ocelot better than I did."

"Do you know where she is?"

"I'm her mother," she nodded. "Of course I know where she is."

"Will you tell me?"

"You'll see her very soon," she said. "Don't worry. Will you come in for a drink?"

I followed her into the house. It was cool and quiet after the bright sun outside. I looked again at the ranks of water-colored paintings hung on the wood-paneled walls. I recognized them now as Annie's work. We went through the conservatory. The light through the greenhouse glass was muted, and the masses of pink blossoms looked sad today. They seemed to signify something, but I didn't know what.

The drinks trolley already sat beside the glass table, and I did the honors.

"Where's the doctor?" I asked.

"He's having a rest," she said, and looked perturbed. "He's grown very fond of Annie. He never had children of his own . . . probably why he fusses so much over his flowers and that damn big car. This has been very hard for him."

"Why didn't you ever tell me that Annie was your daughter? Why didn't she tell me?"

"Because she doesn't acknowledge it, that's why. She doesn't call me Mother, or anything like it. When she came back to Santa Teresa, she bought the house two doors down, so she must know. She treats me as a friend. We *are* friends, and I've settled for that."

The ocelot put in a rare appearance. I hadn't seen him crossing my yard in some time. He padded across the grass and disappeared into the jacaranda trees.

"In some ways, I suppose it's been a blessing," she said. "We never acknowledge the past. It's been a fresh start, and we are able to be friends and confidantes, without the burden of childhood dramas."

She sipped her drink and made a small show of distaste. I didn't make them like her husband did, but I knew she'd soldier through it, and probably ask for another. She set the glass down and reached across the table to touch my sleeve.

"She loves you, you know," she said. "Even if she never said so, there are things a mother knows. I'm still her mother, and I can tell she has feelings for you."

Her look was a little bit defiant, so I nodded. I had no idea what Annie thought about me, and I couldn't keep track of what I felt for her.

"She called the police and told them what she'd done, so they wouldn't blame you for it," she said. "That's some kind of proof, I'd say."

"They told me she called in a confession, and left a written one with you."

"You can't love someone much more than that. She told me in the beginning that you were going to kill Sal Cleveland. I wish that you had. None of this would have happened."

"I don't hire out to kill people," I said. "I went after Cleveland because his wife was my client and he murdered her. I never said I would kill him for it, though. I wanted to see him arrested."

The air was warm, but the yard seemed cool. It was probably the overcast sky, and the mood. I wondered if Mrs. Gardiner would let me sit here and pour myself drinks until I got too drunk to feel gloomy, or any other way. I thought she would probably match me, drink for drink.

"Annie just turned seventeen when she brought him home," she said. "I don't know where she met him. I felt glad she had a friend. She had reached an age when it wasn't healthy for her to be so isolated."

"Brought who home? Sal?"

"He was her first beau," she nodded. "He was as handsome as the devil himself. Sea-green eyes, and his clothes always pressed. Never a hair out of place. So young, but so much older than his years. My husband despised him . . . said he'd heard that Sal was involved in criminal things. Annie adored him, right from the start. She told me that she was going to marry him."

"What happened?"

"What happened is that one afternoon, he came to the house when I was home alone. He seduced me, or I seduced him."

She stared at me, ready to be angry. "Does that surprise you? An old woman like me? I wasn't always old,

329

you know. Most men would have been happy to see me disrobed."

"You're a fine-looking woman now," I said mildly. "I'm sure you're right."

"He was unusual, for being still almost a boy," she said. "He acted both savage and curiously gentle. He knew things about women, maybe more than it's good for a man to know. It became like a drug."

"It happened more than once?"

"It became a habit," she said. "He escorted my daughter into town to buy ice cream sodas, and undressed me on alternate days. Maybe he undressed her, too. The mother one day, and the daughter the next. Does that shock you?"

"Nothing much shocks me. I'm a private detective, and a policeman before that. I lost the capacity for shock a long time ago."

"I think it's more than that," she said. "I think there's something good about you. You don't judge."

I didn't want to talk about my character, and I steered her back. "How long did the situation go on?"

"A month or two . . . until I turned up pregnant. I had thought I was too old. A possibility I had never thought of, and no chance it could be my husband's child. We hadn't . . . do you understand?"

"I understand. You told Sal about his child?"

"I had an idea that I would marry him, despite the difference in our ages. I begged him to take me away with him. I pleaded. He laughed, and asked me what he would want with a forty-five-year-old woman. He said I was . . . never mind. I was proud of how I looked, and he humiliated me. It didn't stop me from begging, though, and I got on my knees."

330

"What about Annie?" I asked.

"That was what made it unforgivable, don't you see? Not just the indiscretion. I didn't just betray my daughter, I had been willing to take Sal away from her, and to break her heart. I was ready to both abandon her and to take away somebody she loved."

"How did it end?"

She looked into her glass, into the past. Her face grew bitter. "He beat me," she murmured. "Sal beat me, and still I begged him not to go. He did leave, though, and my face was marked. I was bruised, and a baby on the way. When my husband came back, I had to tell him. I told him everything. It was another mistake."

"Did he go after Cleveland?"

"He went after me," she said. "He gave me my second beating of the day."

I felt a wave of pity, and then anger. "What did he do about Sal?" I asked. "Or was hitting you enough for him?"

"He said he would kill Sal, and that I had to leave. If I packed a suitcase right away, he wouldn't tell Annie what I had done. I had a little bit of money that I had put away. He was never any good with money, and I kept it for an emergency."

"So you left," I said. "You didn't see choices. I think I would have done the same."

"What was I going to do? I was middle-aged, alone and pregnant. I didn't know anyone here who could help me. I sat for two days in a cheap hotel in Santa Teresa, and then I booked passage back to Hawaii. At least I had family and old friends there. When I got there, someone helped me to find a doctor who could provide a . . . solution."

"You couldn't afford to have the baby."

331

"No, I couldn't," she said. "The doctor I went to was very kind to me."

"His name was Gardiner," I guessed.

She looked at me, mildly surprised. "Is being a detective something one learns to do, or is it a matter of intuition? Yes, it was Gardiner, and he eventually married me. He gave up his practice. He could afford to. He brought me back here."

"Why did you come back?" I asked. "Your husband and June were gone. Annie had left. Why did you want to be here?"

She drained her drink and put the tumbler down. Then she reflexively picked it up and sipped at the ice cubes. I got the bottle of gin and splashed some into her glass.

"Maybe I wanted to be closer to my girls," she said. "Maybe I had nowhere else to go."

"Did you know June's body was in the barn?"

"Of course I didn't know," she snapped. "I'm a fool, not a degenerate."

"By the time you came back, the trouble at the ranch was already over."

"Long since over. My husband was dead, and my youngest daughter lost in the fire. Annie ran away to God knows where. It wasn't until her art began to surface that I had any idea she was alive. She's an astonishing artist, you know. She has paintings on display in museums."

"I know. Did you ever find out what happened when the ranch burned?"

"My husband said he would kill Sal, but that isn't the way it worked out. My husband was in many ways weak, and Sal bent him to his will instead. He put all kinds of pressure on. He used the police, the county government. He had water rights revoked, and other things. He loaned him money that he couldn't possibly pay back. Then he began to use the ranch for business—illegal things that my husband got implicated in. He had violated his daughter and his wife, and in the end he violated my husband just as thoroughly."

"Sal took an enemy and turned him into an unwilling partner as a way of breaking him."

"Yes, but the point was that my husband had threatened him. Sal Cleveland doesn't allow that sort of disrespect. He could have killed him any time he wanted to. My husband was a farmer, not a gangster. He played with him first, completely humiliated him and when he was absolutely broken, he finally pulled the trigger. Sal likes to play. He knows about women, but he knows about men, too."

I had another thought. "Does Sal Cleveland know you're in Santa Teresa?"

It worried me. None of the women who crossed paths with him did very well.

"My name is different now," she said. "Besides that, even if he came face to face with me, he wouldn't recognize me. No one sees an old woman."

Mary Raw had been in the Gardiners' house. Sal had told me that she simply had the wrong address while looking for Annie. I hoped it was true. Things were exploding, and I didn't need to worry about Sal exacting some kind of revenge on Mrs. Gardiner.

"Do you love my daughter?" she asked, breaking into my thoughts.

"Your daughter is a troubled woman. I don't think love comes into it, in the usual sense."

"Do you love her?" she asked again. She leaned forward. Her eyes were watery, and that made her look even older than she was. It felt almost like she was begging me.

"I don't understand half the things she says to me," I said. "I watched her kill a man. She surprised him and disabled him with one shot. When he was helpless and begging, she finished him off. It was worse than anything I've ever seen, even in the war. It was absolutely cold-blooded."

I looked down into my glass. The melting ice made tiny swirl patterns in the brown liquor. The yard felt breathless.

"Yes," I finally said. "I love her."

She handed me a piece of paper, folded small.

"Then this is where she'll meet you," she said. "Will you take care of her? Will you keep her safe?"

"I don't know if I can," I said. "I don't even know if she'll let me. She has some pretty strange ideas about independence. I'm going to try."

"Then do try. Do what you have to do," Mrs. Gardiner said. "And for God's sake don't look down."

I liked Cabrillo Boulevard; I always had. It meandered slow and broad along the beach, taking in the sights like it had nowhere that it needed to be in a hurry. The road got separated from the sand and blue water by a wide expanse of grass. Shacks for hot dogs and rented sun umbrellas dotted the boardwalk. A mile-long row of king palms stood and watched the traffic move below them.

The slip of paper Mrs. Gardiner gave me had an address and a time of day on it, scribbled in Annie's handwriting. When I figured I was close enough to what it said, I checked the rear view mirror carefully. I saw no sign of the black Packard, so I wheeled my coupe to the curb. I got the Browning from the map compartment, stowed it in my pocket and got out. I wanted to walk the rest of the way.

334

The sky was an orange haze, flaring bright as the sun sank below the horizon, tinted by the fires burning outside the city. I could smell the smoke mixed in with the odors of salt water and sugar taffy. It didn't seem to bother the beach-goers any. Skin shiny with coconut oil, they slapped sandals along the sidewalk as they passed. Their sunglasses looked right through me. Next door to the pier, the roller coaster rattled and shrieked around its track, just like it did every other day.

Over the water, a silver biplane flew in low. It banked, belched and dropped. For a moment it looked like serious trouble, but then it straightened and roared along the surf line, trailing a long banner over the bathers' heads. I had time to read something about aftershave, and then it was gone again, circling out to sea.

I kept walking. In the next few blocks, the pedestrian traffic thinned, the hotels and restaurants faded, and I came to the sign for Ocean Lane, the street I wanted. I stopped on the corner, turned and bent to light a cigarette. Looking over the match at the sidewalk behind me, I didn't see anyone who looked like one of the Star-lite gang, so I turned the corner and walked up Ocean.

It was a dark street, even in the daytime. Narrow, not much more than an alley, it was closed to car traffic. There were stucco walls crowded close on either side of it. Something pale moved over my head, and I looked up. Six blouses were hung to dry on a metal railing over my head. They moved very slightly in unseen air currents, stirring like a group of complaining ghosts who wondered why I was there.

A phonograph played from an upstairs window. The last notes from "I Love You Madly" trailed off, and then the saxophone fell silent.

At the top of a flight of stone stairs, the lane opened up. The sun was just about gone, and the air turned sapphire. It was the rare kind of light, just at the end of the day and in just the right place that doesn't need neon to make it glow.

Ahead of me, I saw a plastered wall covered with bougainvillea vines that were flourishing, even in the low light. I headed toward it, and saw Annie in the doorway of a shop, browsing a rack of colored post cards. The sign over the door said Hush, and nothing else.

I looked over my shoulder again and went to join her.

"Hush?" I smiled, when I came close. "That's what they call it? What else do they sell here? Peace and quiet?"

"Just post cards," she said.

Her face was serious and composed. She wore something loose and white. The tiny bits of turquoise and gold at her throat and ears played with the color of her skin.

"Is that why we're here? To buy post cards?"

"I'm looking for a card for June." She thought for a moment. "If I can find the right one, I'll send it to her. Sometimes there isn't one she'd like, so I don't buy anything. I want to send her one now. I might not get a chance later."

She went back to flipping through the cards. Her fingers were lovely, strong and slender, walking and sorting and looking. Her nails were cut short.

"June is dead, Annie," I said. I kept my voice gentle. "She's been dead for a long time. How can you send her anything?"

"In the mail, of course," she said. "How else do you send things to people?"

I didn't have any kind of answer for that, so I waited quietly and watched her while she searched the racks. Her look was serene, and her fingers were deft as they moved the colored cards. I realized that I was trying to memorize her

336

eyes and her brow, the shape of her mouth and the hair that fell across her shoulder. I had no way to keep her voice, no way to save her laugh, or to remember all the improbable things she had said.

I couldn't turn back the clock and change any of what had happened, and I couldn't change what was going to happen. It was too late to stop any of the things that were in motion, and if I tried to, it would mean losing her faster than I was going to lose her anyway.

She paid for something at the cash register, and took my hand when she came back.

"Let's walk," she said.

We went back the way I had come, all the way to Cabrillo, and then we strolled and looked at the ocean and the hotels, the cars and people. I watched for prowl cars. I didn't pay a lot of attention to the traffic otherwise. I figured Cleveland would be keeping his men close and letting the cops look for Annie. I stayed conscious of the weight of the Browning in my pocket. I didn't want that kind of trouble, but I couldn't bear to watch Annie gunned down, either.

"Don't you worry about being seen?" I asked.

"I'm invisible, mostly." Her smile was an enigma. "I'll let them see me when it's the right time."

The sun had touched down into the ocean. The day was leaving fast, and the beaches were emptying. The waterfront would take on a different life in the next hour as it got dark. The smell of suntan oil would be replaced by perfume, and down the strand, the sparkle of sun on water would give way to the lights of the Ferris wheel.

Annie took my arm and stopped me. I turned to face her.

"I'm leaving," she said.

The quiet became absolute. The noise of the street went away completely. There was only the hush, and only her face.

"I know," I said. "I guess I've always known. You don't have a choice now. Where will you go?"

"Even if I know, I can't say. Not now."

The pain came then, and stretched the moment out. All of the things I finally wanted to say seemed pointless now.

"I played so long," she said. "I need to rest."

She stood on the sidewalk and looked at me. She was very, very still.

"Will you come back?" I asked.

The twilight painted us blue; signs and windows were lit softly behind her. It was how I mostly remembered it later, the other colors mixed gently into all of that blue. I suppose there were traffic noises, and perhaps drifts of music. There must have been the smells of a dry summer, bougainvillea, vanilla, hibiscus, and the ocean underneath all of it. I don't remember any of it; I only see the watercolor evening.

She pressed something into my hand. I knew without looking down that I held a playing card.

"If I can find my way, I will," she said. "It's mostly crumbs, but a pebble, just in case."

I stood there, afterward, watching the place she had been. The skin on my face stayed warm for a long time where she had kissed it. It was the end, but I didn't know that then. I didn't know yet that everything perfect begins with an ending.

-Thirty-

For the next two days and nights, nothing happened. Sometimes it felt empty, like everything had already happened. Other times, it felt like everything was about to start, and I found myself pacing from room to room and looking out the front window. The police stayed busy at the Kahlo house next door for most of the time, but eventually they couldn't find anything else to be busy about, and they packed up and left. The last of the newshounds that had been loitering at the curb packed up their pencils and went with them.

No news came about Annie. She didn't contact me, and no one spotted the Mercury. She didn't kill anyone else.

The Gardiners stayed inside. I thought a couple of times about going over for a drink, and decided I wouldn't be good company and didn't. The apartment house across the street looked deserted. Mothers kept their children inside, as though what had happened might still be hanging around. At first, there was a lot more traffic on the street than normal. A stream of cars drove slowly by to check the address from the front page news, but it died to a trickle on the second day. There were other headlines, and there wasn't much to see.

I stayed relieved that my own name hadn't made it into the papers, and I hated my own sense of relief. There was no reason it should have been, really, but I was in the thing up to my neck. It was strange to be left out of it in the lurid newspaper accounts. I told myself it would be terrible for my business to have that exposure, but I still hated my own sense of relief.

They ran Annie's picture with the stories. She looked absolutely beautiful, and I knew it added to the drama. I wondered where they had gotten the photograph. It was strange to see someone whose hair you had touched and whose jokes you had laughed at portrayed for the public to see.

I kept the radio in the living room turned on. I listened with half an ear, hoping I didn't hear news of a shootout.

My telephone rang on two occasions. I jumped at it both times, hoping it would be Annie. Rex Raines called once to ask me how I was. I thought he wanted to be sure that I hadn't left town. I also thought he cared how I did, and I was grateful. I couldn't talk to him, though. He was chasing Annie, and that made him my enemy.

He had disturbing questions for me.

"What if she's after you, now?" he asked. "What if you're next on her list? Am I going to find you dead?"

"Why should she want to kill me?"

"Did you do what she asked you to? You said she hired you to bring Sal Cleveland to some kind of justice. Did you do that? Maybe in her mind, if you had she wouldn't have had to do all this killing."

I dismissed it as nonsense, but I couldn't help glancing at my unlocked front door.

I tried not to think too much about the fact that I had fallen in love with a killer, one who would probably never change or get any better. I tried not to think about the line that I had crossed, the dirty secret I was keeping. I was desperate to see her again, and would do anything to help her get away. I was never going to be myself again.

The other call came from Sal Cleveland.

"She cried at the very end," he said. "I wanted you to know that. She wasn't afraid. She wept because she was happy to see me."

340

His voice sounded relaxed. He sounded calm and reflective. My hand tightened on the receiver. I thought that he had killed Annie.

"Who are you talking about?"

"My wife," he said. "Who else would I be talking about? Didn't she start all this? Isn't that what got you all worked up in the first place? I thought you deserved to know how it went for her, at the end. You've worked so hard."

"I already know how it went," I said. "When she was defenseless and probably dying, you screwed up enough courage to shoot her."

"At the very end, she was relieved. She thought you were going to rescue her, and you didn't. You let her down. I was the one there at the end, and she cried."

"You're a goddamned maniac," I said. "When you look in the mirror, do you see what a monster you are?"

"You let the other one down, too. She's going to die, too. Maybe the cops will get to her first and cheat me out of the chance, but it will get done and that's good enough. I wonder if she'll think about you at the very end. I wonder if she'll hate you on the way out."

"You son-of-a-bitch," I hissed.

"You know what, pal? She probably won't think about you at all. I bet she cries when the bullets catch her or the noose goes around her neck, because she loves me. She probably misses me already."

"I'm going to kill you," I said. "I'm going to put a bullet in your head."

"Do your best, pal," he said. "I planned for a long time to have you killed, but I'm starting to feel different about it. I think maybe I'll let you live. It might be worse for you . . . a whole lot worse."

My reply got wasted, because he hung up.

341

The rapping on the door insisted, and pulled me from the first good sleep that I'd had in weeks. About the time I roused myself enough to identify it, the noise stopped being polite and turned into banging. I undraped yesterday's pair of pants from a chair by the bed, pulled them on and headed downstairs.

I saw a head and shoulders silhouetted in the frosted glass.

"Leave the thing on its hinges, would you?" I called to it. "I'm coming."

My voice sounded raw, and I wished I'd stopped off for a glass of water. The racket went quiet when I flipped on the porch light. I pulled open the door, and was faced with a badge in a leather case.

"Police. Come on out here, pal."

The speaker pocketed his case, turned and went down the steps to join his companion. He tossed his cigarette onto my lawn as he went. The two of them faced me from the darkness, just beyond the reach of the yellow bulb over the door. I stood alone in the light, and figured that was on purpose.

"What do you guys want, can't wait until morning?" I asked.

"It is morning," one of them said. "It's after four. How much morning do you want?"

They both laughed.

"What do you want?' I asked, again.

"Works a lot better, we do the questions and you answer."

The two men stood, shoulder to shoulder, nearly identical in the blue gloom. They were dressed in dark coats and ties against luminous shirts, and they smelled of late nights and hair oil. A pre-war Plymouth coupe idled at the curb. The streetlight reflected off the chromed spotlight mounted on its doorpost.

"You're Crowe?" one of them asked, and I nodded. "How well do you know a woman named . . . Anne Kahlo?"

I glanced at the house next door. The windows were dark, and crickets chirped softly in the hedges. I tasted the sorrow of her leaving all over. If I ever saw her again, I figured things wouldn't be the same. They never are.

"I know her."

The cops looked at each other. I didn't need to see their faces to read them. Finally, one of them spoke up. "We were sent to pick you up," he said. "Lieutenant Raines wants to see you. Get your shoes. We'll take you to him."

"What's happened?"

They wouldn't tell me more. I dressed as quickly as I could, splashed my face with water, and followed them to the car. I sat in the backseat and looked out the window. There was no more conversation. We threaded our way through a downtown still asleep, and out to the highway. The driver pushed the sedan up to seventy all the way through Summerland and Montelindo. I didn't realize that I held my breath until we had passed the exit for the Star-lite Lounge. Apparently, that wasn't where the trouble was. Annie hadn't confronted Sal, at least not yet.

We left the highway and started climbing inland, up the same canyon road that led to the old Kahlo ranch. I remembered the previous trips here, to see Charlene Cleveland in her wrecked convertible and June in her party dress. I hoped I was done with seeing bodies out here. I started to feel apprehensive.

Several miles in, we rounded a bend and found a pale green Forest Service truck blocking the road. An exhausted-looking firefighter stood on the center stripe with one hand held up. He came to the driver's window and nodded when he saw the badge. His face was smeared with soot. The truck got started and moved enough to let us squeeze by.

"Fires have gotten this close?" I asked.

The cop in the passenger seat looked back at me and raised an eyebrow.

"Look that way to you?" he asked. "You private operatives don't miss much, do you?"

I decided it would be pointless to talk to them anymore, and looked out my window the rest of the way. The smell of smoke in the car got stronger, and became visible in places, hanging in pockets in the hillside. When we reached the stretch of road running above the Kahlo place, the hillside showed patches of black. A collection of vehicles, marked and unmarked, scattered the road. They all looked official. We pulled over and stopped at about the spot where Charlene's convertible had gone over the side.

I got out, and was surprised at the weak feeling in my legs. I acknowledged, for the first time, the sense of dread that had been building inside of me ever since we had turned up this road. I recognized Rex Raines, standing and waiting for me. He wore his hat and coat, despite the heat. My escorts left me with him.

"They say the fires are out," he said. "This is the last of it."

I didn't say anything. We stood together at the top of the hill and looked down into the arroyo. Everything was ashes. Black spikes stuck up from the ground in uniform rows as far as I could see, all that was left of the avocado trees. The outbuildings were gone. Low piles of rubble indicated where the house and barn had been. Smoke drifted across everything.

"Funny thing," he said. "It's never one fire . . . did you know that? It's always a whole series of them. The conditions were just right for it. The brush has been piling up for thirty years or better. Once it started in one place, then it just started all over the place, just took the one thing to get the ball rolling. Separate but connected. The fire boys explained it to me, but I don't really understand it. It just all seemed like one big fire to me."

"What's this about, Raines?" I asked. "Why am I here?"

My voice hurt my throat. I would have given just about anything not to hear what he was going to say next. He looked at me bleakly. His eyelids looked heavy and red. He had aged some in the last twenty-four hours. I hated to guess what I looked like.

"She's dead, Nate," he said. "Annie Kahlo's dead. I wanted to tell you myself. I'm sorry."

I felt as though I had fallen out of an airplane. I didn't know what would stop me, and then some kind of merciful numbness settled over me, like cotton around my brain and senses. I looked at the empty, smoking landscape below and waited for him to go on. Even the dirt was black.

"She made a play on Cleveland last night," he said. "We knew she would. We had him covered. We were watching."

"You protected him," I said. "Should have been the other way around. If you people had been better at protecting people from Sal Cleveland, none of this would have ever happened."

"Cut me some slack, Nate." He sounded very tired. "This isn't my mess. I'm just the slob who got detailed to clean it up."

345

I wanted to sit down, but there was nowhere to sit. I thought I might need to sit on the ground.

"So just tell me," I said. "Where is she?"

He pointed to the mound that had been the barn.

"She's in the barn," he said. "It's still too hot to get a close look, but one of the fire boys went down there, as close as he could. Part of what's there is a Mercury convertible, or used to be."

He took his hat off and fanned himself with it.

"Let me correct myself," he said. "There's the burned out shell of a car in there, a convertible. Sheriff's deputies followed her up here at high speed. They witnessed her turn into the drive here. She almost turned over leaving the highway. The place was already on fire, including the barn, although the structure was still standing. She drove right in. It was too hot to follow. By the time they radioed fire trucks in from the next ridge, the barn had collapsed. Since a car is still there, it would be crazy to think it isn't her."

"Is there a body?"

"I don't know if we'll find anything when this cools down or not. Ashes are ashes, probably nothing left that we'll recognize as a body. There's no doubt she's there, though. Don't hurt yourself with hope. They all saw her drive in. No one came back out, and the place was engulfed."

"You're telling me she drove straight into a burning building?"

"Straight in, Nate. Didn't even slow down. There were seven cars that chased her up here. They followed her all the way up from Montelindo."

"And not a one of them did a thing," I said bitterly. "They stood and watched her burn."

346

He put a hand on my shoulder. "Hell, Nate. I'm sorry. I'm as sorry as can be. I know you cared about her. It wasn't going to end well, anyway you cut it. This is how it ended."

From the corner of my eye, I saw his shrug. I started walking down the hill.

"Nate, don't go down there," he called from behind me. "It's too hot still. There's nothing to see."

The mound that had been the barn radiated its own intense heat, like a charcoal burner. There wouldn't be anything left of Annie to bury. I had an absurd catch of grief, seeing the place that had hidden June for so many years gone. A curved lump close to the center of the smoking debris might once have been a car. The longer I looked at it, the more the convertible's remains seemed recognizable.

I saw her light hair, her dark, dark eyes and the enigmatic, lovely smile she turned on and off for no apparent reason. I smelled her hair and touched her skin, heard the silver screen voice.

I played so long . . . I need to rest.

I stared until my vision blurred. It must have been the heat off the smoldering barn that made my eyes water, because my grief went a long way past tears. After a while, Raines walked up beside me, and I let him put an arm around me and lead me away.

It didn't take much to jimmy the lock. I thought in passing that I'd have to talk to Annie about getting some better locks installed, and then I realized I wouldn't be talking to her again, about anything. I opened the front door and slipped inside. I saw right away that someone had cleaned up the blood in the vestibule, leaving no trace of the violence that had happened there.

347

The dim air felt empty, as if the house had been abandoned for years, and not just hours. I left the lights off, and walked a little way down the front hall. From the living room walls, her paintings looked back at me, bright watercolors turned blue-gray and black by the dark. A vase of orchids had drifted dead petals across a table top.

The hush was perfect. There was no drip of faucet, no creak of floorboard; just the tiny sound of the clock in the living room. Underneath the scent of wood polish and oranges, I caught the palest ghost of Annie's fragrance. I strained for the faint sweetness of her, as though I could follow it to wherever she had gone.

As I looked up the stairs to the second floor landing, the sound of her voice startled me badly.

"That's where you'll find me," she whispered.

It came from everywhere, and nowhere. I heard my own pulse, and reached for the banister to steady myself.

"You're dead now," I whispered back.

No answer came, just the tick of the clock in the next room. All at once I knew. I was going to find Annie Kahlo, dead or alive. As quietly as I had come in, I let myself out and made sure the door latched behind me.

All at once, I had somewhere to be. I was going to kill Sal Cleveland.

-Thirty One-

I got off the highway in Montelindo and drove along the frontage road, past the Montelindo Hotel. Ahead of me, a big black car pulled out of the entrance to the Star-lite Lounge and drove off in the opposite direction. Instinctively, I stepped on the gas, but it didn't turn out to be Sal's Buick. I let it go and turned in. Not quite lunch time, and the parking area was deserted.

Outside the car, the morning was blue and soft. My feet crunched across the broken shells. The sound of a meadowlark came from somewhere out of sight, to keep me company. Nothing else moved. I didn't care very much, but I had to believe that Cleveland would sense me coming for him. I wondered why he assigned no welcoming party, and if an ambush waited. I shrugged off the feeling, since I didn't really expect to walk out of here.

The stool beside the big front doors sat empty, the big man who usually guarded nowhere in sight. The front doors were unlocked, and I went in.

The main lounge was empty, dim and shadowed. Ranks of tables bristled with the spindly legs of upside-down chairs. The silver walls were lit here and there by spots of sun from the tiny windows set high up, near the ceiling. It was different without the nighttime blue glow and smoke. Potted trees stood around on the black-and-white tiles, perfectly still, and watched me to see what I would do next.

A thin man in a jacket and tie stood behind the bar, polishing glasses and cutting fruit and doing whatever bartenders did when they had no customers. I crossed the room to talk to him. The sound of my heels made a muted echo.

"Sal Cleveland around?" I asked him.

349

The soothing murmur of hidden voices from the kitchen made the quiet seem quieter. He kept working with his white rag and ignored me, so I repeated the question a little louder. He stopped and gave me a deadeye look.

"It's eleven o'clock in the morning," he said. "Does this place look open to you?"

"If I order a double bourbon and you give it to me, then we'll both know it is."

"Not too early to crack wise," he said. "Never too early for that, for some people."

He went back to what he was doing. I pulled out my wallet, found a five-dollar bill and laid it flat on the bar top. He didn't look at me, but it got his attention like I thought it would. Without a word, he took an expensive bottle from the rack. He barehanded a couple of ice cubes into a tumbler and got them good and wet. He slid the glass across the bar. It was all as smooth as silk, and he made my money disappear the same way.

"Water?" he asked, and I shook my head.

I picked up the drink and tasted it. The whiskey felt cold in my mouth, then hot the rest of the way down. It was swell stuff, eleven o'clock in the morning or not.

"Boss is here . . . in the back," he said. "In his office."

"Five bucks buys a hell of a drink here," I remarked. "Considering you're closed."

"Enjoy it," he said. "Chances are, it's your last one. Drink it slow."

I raised an eyebrow. "Think so?"

I took another sip, and set the glass back onto the bar. The ice cubes chimed gently. The air that moved against my face was cool and pleasant, laden with the ghosts of last night's cigarette smoke and perfume.

"I know so," he said. "Matter of fact, make book on it. You walk into Mister Cleveland's office, you're not walking back out."

I was all at once terribly tired, and I closed my eyes. I thought about Annie Kahlo, her eyes and her voice. She seemed very close. Her sweet, dark looks and slow smiles were gone for good, and that hurt a little, even over the numbing burn of liquor. Maybe it hurt a lot. Some things just didn't go away easy.

"Suits me," I said. "There are worse things than that."

He shrugged and turned away. After a minute, he thought of something he had to do somewhere else. He flipped the towel onto his shoulder and left, his footsteps echoing on the tiles. I took a last sip of bourbon, and left the half-finished drink on the bar. I took the Browning from my pocket and went up the hall to Cleveland's office.

The door stood open six inches, and I stopped outside and listened, pistol up and ready. I waited, perfectly still. After only a few seconds, the smell on the air told me someone had fired a gun inside, very recently. A worse smell wormed under the spicy scent of gunpowder, the unmistakable odor of blood. I eased the door open a little further with a toe, and went in all at once.

I stopped still. Sal Cleveland sat in his chair, slumped forward. He wasn't looking at me, because he had his head on the desk. His left arm bent in front of him, across a careful fan of playing cards. He looked as though he were napping, except for the blood. The pool around his head had soaked into the green felt and ruined some of the cards. The gunpowder-and-blood smell was very strong, mixed with something sweet.

"Come in, Mister Crowe."

The voice came from my left. I turned to see Fin relaxed into a deep leather armchair. His suit was vanilla, set off with a lavender tie. I realized it was an intense fragrance of almonds I smelled under the odor of fireworks.

"Don't point your gun at me, please," he said. "I do so hope this little scene makes you happy, but I know you came to do this yourself. Someone has beaten you to it. If I could offer you some consolation, he would have shot you like a dog. You would have been the dead one. That might have suited you just as well. You seem to have lost much of your appetite for living."

"You think so?"

"That he would have killed you before you killed him?" He laughed gently. "I don't think it, Mister Crowe, I know it. You have strange scraps of honor, and you would have wanted to explain yourself to him before you killed him. You would have been compelled to offer justification to yourself and to him, and in your hesitation he would have killed you before you pulled the trigger."

"So you killed him, Fin. Why? I can't imagine you were doing me a favor."

He laughed again, and leaned forward to pick out one of the cards that had escaped the spreading blood on the desk. He gave it a cursory look and then tapped it thoughtfully against his chin.

"Oh, I didn't kill him," he said. "I can assure you of that. I walked in here less than a full minute before you did. People are more useful and interesting to me when they are alive."

"You want me to think this was suicide?"

"See for yourself."

He nodded at Cleveland's body. I went a little further into the room.

"Don't touch anything," he said. "You'll spoil it."

I went slowly around the desk, instinctively giving the body a wide berth. Cleveland's right foot was pulled slightly back, as though he had been preparing to get up. The pistol rested on the floor beside his chair. I got down on a knee and sniffed the barrel.

"You want me to believe he did this to himself?" I asked. "Men like Cleveland don't kill themselves. The cops won't believe it, no one will."

"Perhaps you're right," he said. "I'll have to think of something else. Perhaps he'll simply go for a walk and not ever come back. So very sad. No one will ever know why."

"The person who shot him knows."

"Interesting, but who did it? If I didn't kill him, and you didn't kill him, and he didn't kill himself, then I wonder who did?"

Fin leaned forward and put the card he had been holding face-up on the green felt. The queen of hearts lay in the pool of light. She stared up at us and said nothing at all.

"Do you believe in ghosts, Mister Crowe?"

"Even if I do," I said. "I don't believe that they can fire a .38 round into someone's head."

"Perhaps we'll never know who did this then," he said. "Perhaps that's for the best. I'll clean this unfortunate . . . mess, and I won't let it bother me. After all—"

"It's all just wind," I finished for him.

"It's all just wind," he agreed. "The wind blows and the wind swings, through sanatoriums and empty bedrooms and bare trees. It blows and it swings, blows and swings."

"You've done this before," I said. "Made corpses disappear."

"More than once, Mister Crowe. It's no different than doing a card trick. The principles are the same.

353

"What are you doing here, anyway? How is it that you happen to be here?"

"I am often here. Mister Cleveland enjoys the flash and the sparkle of ownership, while I prefer the shadows. I only come out when the water gets . . . deep."

"Like now."

"Like now." He nodded. "The ownership of this establishment, as well as many others, now reverts to me. I need a public partner, a face for the businesses. I've had my eye on you since the start. Your qualifications are immense, as would be the rewards."

It took me a minute to understand what he was offering. I was shocked.

"You want me to take over for Sal Cleveland? No thanks."

"I'm offering you a complete reversal of fortune," he said. "You can be rich and powerful, starting right now. Think about it."

I did think about it. I thought about swimming pools and big cars and marble floors. I thought about swank clothes and fancy broads and endless music. And then I thought about Charlene Cleveland with a bullet hole in her face.

"No, thanks," I said again.

"Even if this body is never seen again, there are those on both sides of the law who will believe you responsible for Mister Cleveland's disappearance. I don't think you're going to survive the streets of Santa Teresa very long. You need me as much as I need you."

"No deal," I said. "You ought to go back to Ohio, if that's where you're really from. You don't make any sense here."

"I only bother with sure things, and I'm confident we have a deal," he said. "You simply haven't acknowledged it yet. You want to play the shy bride, and talk yourself into it. Don't wait so long to accept that not even I can save you."

"I'm leaving," I said. "No deal. I assume you're going to let me walk out of here?"

He did his best to look offended. "I quite like you, Mister Crowe. I've told you that. Stop at the bar and finish your drink on the way out. I expect the ice has hardly melted, and we never know when a small pleasure might be our last, do we? I expect I'll see you again, very soon."

"Not if I can help it."

I headed for the door, and had a foot in the hall when he spoke from behind me.

"She isn't dead, you know," he said. "Fives, sevens, and eights. Where there are cards, there are tricks. She isn't dead at all."

I felt my pulse speed up. The sweet smell of poison was overpowering, and the room swam in my vision. The body sprawled across the desk, the cards and the blood all faded, leaving only Fin's face and eyes to fill my vision. I couldn't speak, but I heard my own voice.

"Are you talking about Annie Kahlo?"

He nodded. We looked at each other for a long minute, me in the doorway and him in the deep chair. I had been turning my hat in my hands, and I realized I was crushing it. I straightened the brim and settled it on my head. I wanted desperately to believe this strange man, but it was more hope than I could afford.

"All the evidence says she died in that fire," I said. "There isn't any real doubt of it."

"Evidence," he mused, and looked at Cleveland's body. "We were just talking about evidence, weren't we? Do

355

you know what I always say, Mister Crowe? Do you remember?"

"Fig's a dance," I said.

His face lit up. His features were blotched and ghastly, but for just a moment his smile was strangely beautiful. "You are exactly right, Mister Crowe," he beamed. "Fig's a dance."

I took the frontage road along the ocean, all the way back into town. I needed time to think. At the curb, I got out and stretched. The day had gotten warm. Something felt different, and it took me a minute to put my finger on it. The fires were finally out, and the smell of smoke was gone. The air was sweet, and I could smell the ocean several blocks away.

The Gardiner's enormous black Cadillac sat berthed in the driveway. When I got to the driver's window, I tapped the glass with a knuckle. After a minute, it got cranked down slowly. It made a small squeaking noise. Mrs. Gardiner looked up at me. She put both of her hands back on the steering wheel, as though she were still moving. She looked ancient. I kept my voice as gentle as I could. "You killed Sal Cleveland, didn't you?"

She stared at me and didn't answer. Her eyes were vacant, haunted.

"You were at the Star-lite Lounge." I said. "I saw you leave. A dozen bodyguards, and you just waltzed in and shot him."

"No one pays attention to an old woman. No one even sees me anymore."

I opened the car door and helped her out.

"I see you," I said.

"Are you going to arrest me?"

"I'm not a policeman, Mrs. Gardiner. I wouldn't arrest you even if I was."

Her lip trembled. I felt bad for her. She was far too old for any of this.

"Did I do a bad thing?" she asked.

She sounded like a very old child. I thought something inside of her was broken, probably for keeps.

"I don't know," I said. "I think you did the only thing you could. Sometimes that's all the good or bad there is."

"I'm tired," she said. "I'm so very tired."

I put my head in the car. The big purse lay on the seat, and I undid the clasp and looked inside. The automatic was a business-like number with a blued finish. Not a lady's gun, but it smelled strongly of burned powder, so this lady had managed to use it. I got it out and slipped it into my pocket before I turned around.

"You'll be okay," I told her. "It might take a little while, but I think you have a lot of steel."

I put an arm around her and helped her up the walk to her front steps. When she had the door open, she turned to face me.

"For the record . . . " I searched for the words I wanted. "For the record, I think your daughter had more guts than anyone I ever knew, and I think she got them honestly. I think she got them from you. It looks good on you. She'd be proud."

Her face got a little startled. "Proud. That's a funny word, don't you think, Mister Crowe?"

"I think it's the right word," I said.

The pistol weighed heavy as sin in my pocket. I needed to make it disappear, quickly. If the cops came around to talk to her, the best I could do was to make sure the gun went away.

"You don't lie, do you?" she asked.

"Sometimes I do," I said. "Not often. Mostly I don't see any point in it."

"And you don't ever leave anyone behind."

I thought about all of the lost girls, the gone girls. In my mind's eye I saw Charlene Cleveland and June, both dressed in pink. They were separated by decades, brought together by their endings. I saw the doomed Mexican women in the truck, looking out at me from the old photograph. Mostly, I remembered Annie Kahlo. Her dark eyes and sweet smile were gone for good, but would be never far away from me.

I shook my head.

"I don't leave anyone behind," I said. "Not when I can help it."

I saw her tears, and I thought that was probably a good thing. Nothing could heal any of it, but tears were a way of trying.

"In the end, neither did you," I said.

"She called me Mother when she left. She knew who I was. I have that much."

"You have that much," I agreed. "You should lie down for a while. Do you want me to help you inside?"

The tears were mostly winning, but she tried on some kind of a smile, anyway.

"I'm very tired," she said. "I'm also very old, but I'm not an invalid, at least not yet."

I smiled back at her. "Take care of the peacocks," I said. "And the ocelot."

There was nothing else I could do for her, so I left her standing in the doorway. I didn't think I would ever see her again, and it occurred to me that I had never known her first name. For some reason, it made me sadder than any of the rest of it. I stopped at the bottom of the walk and turned back.

"What's your name?" I called. "Can I ask you that?"

"Grace," she said. "My name is Grace."

I nodded. It suited her. When I looked again, she had gone and the door was closed. I headed for my own front door. I needed to pack a suitcase and get on my way.

-Thirty Two-

Plenty of neon light from the street filtered through the venetian blinds, so I left the wall switch alone. I got a glass off the shelf in the corner, blew the dust out of it, and bought myself a drink from the bottle in the desk drawer. The Browning sat on the blotter in front of me, but more because of habit than anything else. I didn't think anyone would come up the hall and try the door. I didn't know if there was anyone left who wanted to kill me, but old habits die hard.

I tilted my chair back, slipped my shoes off and sipped warm whiskey. My office was different in the dark. Whatever went on here at night when it was empty and silent had nothing to do with me and what I did during the day. It didn't make me feel particularly welcome. I wondered if Mary Raw's ghost still hung around. I wondered if anyone had ever been killed by a ghost. I figured I had been playing with house money for a while now, so I didn't mind too much, one way or the other.

I wondered if ghosts got lonely.

The phone rang once. It startled me badly. The noise it made was much louder in the middle of the night. It didn't ring a second time, but I picked it up anyway.

"Hello?" I said.

There was no answer and no sound on the line. I caught a quick ghost of fragrance, though, from nowhere. It was light and sweet and smelled like someplace that was far away from here, like flowers and wet leaves.

"Annie?" I asked.

The sign outside the window flashed, on-and-off, on-and-off, a flood of blue that came and went. I held the receiver a little bit tighter and thought I heard a single breath.

Then I heard rain and a faint, faraway sound like . . . elephants. I had only ever heard them trumpet in films, but that's what the sound reminded me of. Elephants.

"I'm coming," I said.

Epilogue

The couple sitting at the table had left, and the slowly spinning ceiling fan moved air over the now empty cantina in Corazón Rosa. One blade ticked, sounding like a persistent water drip every time it went around. It was the only sound in the room until a woman came from the kitchen area. She collected a plate and a knife, set them on a tray, and wiped quickly at the wooden table top with a rag. She saw the playing card and paused. It lay face down, beneath where the woman's plate had been. She picked it up.

It was old, the five hearts of hearts faded to pink. She stood very still, looking at it in her hand. When nothing happened, she shrugged, put it into the pocket of her apron, and carried the tray back to the kitchen.

Outside in the street, pockets of shadow were formed as the sun went out of sight beneath the rooftops. Echoes of voices, mothers calling children inside filled the air. Fishermen straggled home in ones and twos, boats left behind for another day. The street dogs were awake and watchful, collecting themselves against the coming night.

On the twilit shore at the foot of town with the black sand almost deserted, the wind gusted off the water, warm but getting cooler. It carried the smell of the ocean, salt and perfume and a little bit of rot; the ancient fragrances of blood and birth. The palm fronds turned dark against the sky as they clattered and rustled and sighed.

A small girl in a pink bathing suit played alone on the beach. She sifted sand from a metal can to a glass jar. The painted label on the can showed signs of rust, but still was legible enough to boast of a deluxe mix, fifty percent peanuts or less. The coarse sand held onto the warmth of the afternoon, the fall of it heavy and good against her small

362

hands. The pouring was an arcane ritual that only she understood. Her brow furrowed with the importance of it; the tip of her tongue showed in one corner of her mouth.

As if drawn by the magic, a man and woman approached. They walked where the shore was packed wet, just out of reach of the surf. A dog ran ahead of them, dashing in and out of the foam.

The man wore a fedora. He carried a suitcase in one hand and his jacket over his shoulder. He moved slowly and looked around him, quiet and watchful. He looked like a man who had seen things that grieved him, but when he looked over at the woman walking beside him, the shadows cleared from his face.

The dog trotted over to investigate the girl. He was a medium-sized brown dog with a white face. He sniffed at the sand she poured and sneezed. The man called him back. He didn't seem the kind who missed much, but his eyes passed over the little girl and went on without a pause, like she was invisible.

"I'm a ghost," the girl said to herself. She laughed softly, startled and pleased by the idea.

The woman was graceful and solemn. She was the kind of slender that made her look taller than she really was. She was draped in something loose and pale that covered her head. Her feet were bare. Something about her beauty evoked queens from long ago and far away, the ones in picture books. She took the man's free hand as they passed.

She looked back over her shoulder and smiled at the little girl. The girl smiled back at her, and they held it for just a moment. It was a shared secret, and it lit up everything.

"Bye, June..." the woman called softly. She had a voice like a movie star.

Fireflies began to spark, echoing the candle flames in the windows of the buildings above the beach. The little girl didn't go anywhere. She kept playing, scooping sand from can to jar and back. A dog barked, and she looked up. The moon showed pale against the lowering evening sky; its light glimmered on the waves and the empty beach. She didn't see the man and woman anymore.

They were as gone as if they had never been there at all, vanished in the distance and the dark.

#

Coming soon from Taylor & Seale Publishing:

Hau Tree Green - A Nate and Annie story

Other books by Bob Bickford:

Deadly Kiss, Black Opal Books

Caves in the Rain, Champagne Books-January 2017

A Song for Chloe, Black Opal Books-Summer 2017

All books are available through the publisher or on:

Amazon.com
B&N.com
booksamillion.com

CPSIA information can be obtained
at www.ICGtesting.com
Printed in the USA
LVOW07s1249191017
553016LV00004B/423/P